Tales of the Fae

Rogue Assassins

1

I WAITED until dusk to transport myself from the coastal Roman village I'd chosen to call home to the Faerie Queen's cottage deep in the forests in Northumbria. The sun had already dropped below the treetops, creating long shadows that stretched across the clearing, striping the wide expanse of mossy ground and the patch of garden in front of the tiny four room structure where I'd grown up. It was almost mid-summer, and ripe plums weighed down the gnarly limbs of the short trees. Stalks of lavender bowed to me on the breeze as bright red roses bobbed on the bushes and the leaves rustled their welcome. The calm in the clearing gave no hint that the new moon gathering of the Faerie Queen's Court was about to begin.

Shadows moving across the windows of the cottage caught my eye. Some of my sisters had already arrived. I hurried to join them, nearly reaching the edge of the garden when a panther prowled out of the woods, padding along on silent paws to intercept me. I paused, recognizing the creature. In a blink, the animal shifted form, replaced by a tall female with short curly hair that accentuated her delicate pointed ears.

"Sorcha! How does it feel to finally be of age?" My sister Maera pulled me into a hug, then held me at arms length to study my face.

As the youngest of seven High Fae sisters, I was always the last to do everything. Our mother walked the earth for over a thousand years before departing to rest with the Ancients. After completing only twenty-five turns around the sun, I was barely considered a full adult.

"No different," I said.

Her lighthearted laugh filled the clearing. "That's what we all said when we were in your place." She winked at me. "Just wait. You'll see tonight."

My heart sped at the thought I'd finally have a title and a responsibility that fit my status as the High Fae sister of the queen. I'd taken my Oath to serve my eldest sister at her coronation. When she inherited our mother's crown, I was still a Faeling. So, despite my Oath, I'd never been given any official position on the Court. Perhaps that would change tonight.

I followed Meara through the garden and through the already open front door. Inside, the space had been transformed. Chains of lilies hung from the ceiling. Thick candles had been set in all the windows, ready to be lit at sunset. A garland of lilac had been draped across the mantle. Every surface was covered in rose petals, and tiny glowing orbs hovered in the air.

My eldest sisters, the Faerie Queen Godda and her Commander of the Guard, Flida, shared this cottage now. They'd moved in with me to take our mother's place after Godda's coronation. Both had survived over fifty circles of the sun by the time they took responsibility for raising me. I loved them with all my heart, but that hadn't stopped me from moving out on my own soon after my tenth circle. Fae aged quickly for the first ten years, then almost imperceptibly after that. I'd been in my adult form for nearly fifteen years, waiting for the moment the others would finally stop treating me like a Faeling.

My sister Isleen welcomed Meara and I as we entered the cottage. She wrapped an arm around me and tugged me close. "Our baby's all grown. Just look at you." She smoothed my hair back from my face and placed a kiss on my forehead before releasing me. There was no way I could have changed significantly since she'd last seen me, even though she'd been around less frequently since our mother faded.

Niamh wandered into the front room next. "Indeed. Just now I almost mistook our little hawk for Godda. They could be twins."

My heart warmed with her praise. Godda was known for her beauty. Each of my sisters had a different sire because male Fae could only sire one Faeling. Our mother had chosen her pairings with an eye to building alliances between the various Fae factions, instead of choosing only one to take as a mate. Godda's sire and mine were twins, so it made sense that I resembled her more than I did my other sisters, but I didn't dare to hope I'd be half as beautiful as our queen.

"Is she here, yet?" I asked.

Niamh and Isleen exchanged a look. Isleen pursed her lips and shook her head, causing her springy coils to bounce.

Before she could answer more fully, Rionach burst in through the cottage door. "Am I late?" She twirled the stem of a garden rose between her fingers, using her magic to shed the thorns before sliding it behind the point of her ear. I admired the barely unfurled flower, now resting against her temple, noting that the color matched the red of her lips almost exactly.

"You're right on time," Meara said, crossing to the window to peek outside. "It appears we're waiting for Godda." She turned and leaned against the wall next to the window with her arms crossed. "And, it looks like Issie and Nia know something about why she's late."

"Oh good. Just in time for the gossip, then." Rionach danced through the room, planting kisses on cheeks, and saving me for last.

"Perhaps we should wait." Isleen shot another look across the room to Niamh. "Sorcha—"

I cut her off. "I'm an adult and a member of Godda's Court just like the rest of you."

"She has a point." Rionach grinned. "And I don't want to wait. I want to hear the gossip."

Flida entered through the door to the kitchen. "Oh, good. You're all here."

"Except Godda," Rionach said. "And Issie was about to tell us why that is…" She raised an eyebrow at Isleen.

"Godda will be here soon." Flida set a tray of fresh fruit on the table. "She's hunting."

Niamh snorted. "I suppose that's one way to say it." She conjured two goblets and handed one to Rionach and one to Flida. Then she conjured two more as she made her way over to Meara, who waved a hand and filled the empty vessels with wine. Her sire had been an Elemental, and she'd inherited some water and earth magic in addition to her High Fae gifts.

I searched each of my sister's faces in turn. Their eyes danced with mischief and some shared amusement as they sipped their drinks. "Has Godda chosen a mate, then?" I asked.

Meara giggled. "Hardly."

My cheeks burned and my fingers curled into fists at my sides. "Someone better tell me what's going on, or I'm leaving."

Niamh scoffed. "Oh don't pout. If you want Issie and Flee to treat you like an adult, then you'd better stop acting like a spoiled Faeling." She took a long sip and savored her wine.

I glared at her, hating that she was right, and forced my hands and face to adopt a more mature demeanor. Then I responded in a calm and careful tone. "If I'm an adult, then I want what you're having, and I want to know what Meara finds so amusing."

"Oh, me too! I'll take a drink and a laugh," said a voice from behind me. I turned and found our eldest sister framed by the doorway. The last rays of sunlight lit her golden hair as it tumbled over her shoulders and down to her waist. Tiny flowers nestled in the waves as though she'd walked through a rain of blooms.

"See?" Flida pushed a goblet into my hand. "Nothing to worry about."

"Were you worried about me, little hawk?" Godda cupped my face in her hands and kissed my cheeks. "You're so sweet."

"Flida said you were hunting, but she's Commander of the Queen's Guard. I thought that was her job." I tried to keep my voice from shifting to a whine as I explained my concern.

"Oh, I see." Godda's lips curled up into a grin. "Not that sort of hunting, pet." She wound one arm around my waist as her other hand received a goblet from Flida. The attention from Godda, the closest thing I had to a mother, reassured me and made the tingle of suspicion that something was wasn't quite right easier to ignore.

"My queen," Flida dipped her head. "Shall we begin?"

"You needn't call me that here." Godda's pink lips twisted into a brief scowl. "Here we're just sisters."

"You're always our queen." Flida's eyes fixed with Godda's conveying some additional meaning that I longed to understand.

Godda waved Flida's intensity away. "Yes, yes. All right. Just perhaps we can do without the formalities for the evening. It's Sorcha's night tonight." She smiled at me. "Are you ready little hawk?"

"I wish someone would tell me what all the fuss is about." Her question rekindled the hope that she was ready to finally give me a title and an official position on her Court.

"Then let us begin." Godda led me into the center of the group as the others formed a ring around us.

When I glanced at the faces surrounding me, I realized they'd assembled in order of age. Flida next to Isleen, then Meara, Nianh, and Rionach. They'd left a space for Godda to stand between Flida and Rionach, completing the circle.

"I call this meeting of the High Court to order." A crown of twisted golden vines appeared in Godda's hand, and she set it on her head. "Tonight we welcome our sister, Sorcha, into the ranks of the High Fae and celebrate her coming of age as she accepts new responsibilities, befitting the beloved sister of the Faerie Queen."

My heart pounded with excitement. Meara had been right. This was it.

Flida took a half step forward. "Sorcha of Maeve, are you prepared to take your place on Godda's Court?"

I calmed my excited nerves and nodded.

"Then, I will bestow you with a title suiting your nature." Godda glanced around the circle before revealing her choice. "As my only sibling who shares my Rogue blood, I have decided to make you my Master of Illusions."

My breath caught in my throat. The only thing I valued about my Rogue blood was that I shared it with Godda. Other than that, I wanted nothing to do with that faction. If I had, then I would have begun training with my sire and my kin, learning how to use my Rogue abilities. But, I'd avoided the Rogues and shunned them, and now Godda wanted me to be her Master of Illusions, responsible for maintaining the mirages that kept humans from wandering into the Fae Forest.

I reminded myself to breathe. Six pairs of eyes watched me as I dropped to one knee before my queen. I told myself the important part was that she was finally granting me an official position on her court. I bowed my head over her extended hand. "I vow to serve you loyally so long as I walk the earth."

As I kissed her knuckles, I said a silent prayer to the Ancients that she'd change her mind about my title.

"Rise, Sorcha of Maeve, Sworn Master of Illusions." Her fingers gripped mine, and she pulled me to my feet.

My sisters closed in around me, crushing me in their embrace. Meara broke away to open a window, and called to the pixies hiding in the surrounding forest. At her command, they began to play. The sweet trill of their flutes drifting in on the breeze. Meara waved a hand and our goblets splashed full of liquid once again. Then, with Godda in the lead, we pranced out into the moonlight to dance among the flowers in the garden. The tiny glowing orbs followed us out onto the lawn, dangling in the sky like low hanging stars.

I edged closer to Godda, hoping I might whisper my words of concern into her ear so the others wouldn't overhear. But, Isleen spun her out of reach, and Rionach grabbed my hand, twisting me in the opposite direction. As the gnomes joined in with their drums, the tempo increased. We drained our goblets and started to spin. Starlight swirled above my head. My braid tapped a rhythm against my back in response to the one my bare feet beat into the warm earth.

Then the music stopped suddenly, and I froze. When I regained my balance, I realized we were surrounded by men on horseback. Humans. Their mounts huffed and tossed their heads as they stomped through the delicate garden blooms. One with dark eyes and an angular jaw kicked his horse into motion, scattering Meara and Niamh who stood closest to him. He rode straight for Godda, who stared at him from the center of the garden.

Flida rushed to Godda's side, only just missing her as the human lifted our queen off her feet and up onto the saddle with him. In a flurry of hoofbeats, they were gone. All of them. My heart lurched as my world shifted. Humans in the Fae forest. Impossible.

We stared after them, until Meara broke the silence with her laughter.

"Is that him?" Niamh asked.

"Must be," Meara said before bursting into another fit of giggles.

"We need to go after her." I closed the short distance between me and Flida. I'd nearly reached her before Godda had been scooped up and carried away. I set a hand on Flida's shoulder when she didn't respond.

She shook her head. "She'll be back."

"But—"

"You'll see, little hawk. Someday, you'll meet someone and your brain will go straight to your loins like our dear sister's apparently has done." Isleen exhaled an annoyed sigh as she plopped down on the garden bench, just outside the cottage.

Niamh and Meara danced, holding hands and spinning toward the hedges, singing. "Hunter or hunted, which will it be?" They laughed and skipped as though nothing at all was the matter.

"Flida?" I asked. My fingers pressed harder, forcing her to turn and face me. "Are you sure?"

Rionach laid her arm across my shoulders. "He's just a plaything. You'll see. She'll set him in his place and be back by sunrise."

Flida scowled. "Perhaps Rio's right, and she'll be back with the dawn." She bent to retrieve a discarded goblet from the ground and used her elemental magic to fill it with water pulled from the air, but didn't drink.

If Rionach was right, why had the human come here with a band of hunters? Something wasn't right about this, and I didn't plan to wait when Godda might be in danger.

Niamh and Meara raced past us. They'd changed to their animal forms. Meara's panther chased Niamh's fox around the garden, swatting at her until Niamh doubled back, darting around Meara's legs causing the panther to tumble to the ground. Niamh scurried to grab hold of the fur on the back of Meara's neck, tugging at the scruff as though she planned to drag Meara off like a misbehaving cub.

"I can't believe you're all acting as though this is normal." I stalked off in the direction the human had ridden, but I didn't get far before a panther and a fox blocked my path, fur standing on end and teeth bared.

"If you won't go after her, at least let me," I said, staring them down.

Niamh transformed first. "You should wait until morning. Really. Have you never had a lover?" Her lips twisted into a scolding frown.

The fact that I hadn't was no business of theirs. "Why are you so sure he's her lover?"

"I've seen them," Niamh said.

"Seen them where?" Perhaps this was what she'd told the others and why she'd been exchanging those odd looks with Isleen when I arrived.

"In the forest." She plucked a broken sprig of lavender from a nearby bush and twisted it between her long fingers. "I stumbled on Godda 'hunting' one day. I've heard that Rogues need humans to feed their magic, but I'm fairly certain there was nothing magical about what those two were doing."

"Did she see you?" Meara asked after transforming back into her Fae form.

"A herd of angry gnomes could have stomped through that glade and those two wouldn't have noticed." Niamh's words set Meara on another fit of bubbly laughter.

"That's enough." Isleen's sharp voice cut off Meara's giggles. "Come help me prepare the feast."

One by one, my sisters returned to the cottage until only Flida remained. "Come, little hawk. The evening's not over, yet. You'll need to transform for this next ritual."

My desire to trust in their confidence warred with the feeling in my gut that told me Godda needed our help. I wanted to believe she'd be back in the morning, but my intuition warned me that this wasn't some lovers' quarrel. These humans were dangerous.

2

NO matter how hard I concentrated, I couldn't force my features to shift. Every time I opened my eyes to check my reflection in the gazing pool, my black eyes and hairless face stared back at me. Not even a curl crowned my head or dusted my chin. If I kept this up much longer, I'd need to feed again, and there was no time for that.

The twins' laughter escaped from the cracks between the skinny logs of the lean-to. They couldn't see me, but their mirth suggested they knew I'd failed. Again. They'd warned me what would happen if I returned with this face. I needed to master the practice of morphing before they drained the water-skin. Pressure did nothing to improve my ability.

A smallish hawk landed in the tree nearby, distracting me. It folded its speckled brown wings tight against its body and cocked its head to one side, staring back at me with an eerie intelligence. I paused to watch it, wasting valuable time. Just as I was about to return my attention to my practice, the hawk glided down from its perch and shifted. A beautiful Fae female took its place. She wore the tunic and armored vest of the Queen's Guard with her long golden hair woven into a simple braid that hung down her back. For a moment I mistook her for the Faerie Queen.

Godda visited my mentors often enough that I no longer managed more than a dip of my head before she started in, asking me about my training. I wouldn't consider her a friend. Rogues didn't have friends. But, I liked to think she might make a temporary ally, should I ever need one.

This female appeared to be a slightly altered copy of the queen, one with lighter hair and fuller lips. Since only the High Fae possessed the ability to take the form of an animal, I had a suspicion as to who she might be. One of my mentors would be thrilled to see her here. The other would not. For Godda's sake, I decided I should warn this female and stood to intervene before she could enter the hut.

"I'm here to see my sire," she said, eyeing the willow reeds hanging across the doorway behind me.

"Yes." As I suspected. She was Rowan's offspring. The last of her line. A living, breathing broken promise to the Rogues. Riagan would destroy her.

A burst of laughter followed by a howl from the twins resting within the lean-to caught her attention and she started forward, attempting to push past me.

I blocked her path. "If you'll just give me a moment to announce you first?"

"Who are you?" Her eyes scanned my body from smooth-skinned skull to booted toe.

"Bryn of the Rogues. I serve your sire and his brother." I dipped my head out of respect, and she used the gesture to step around me, ignoring my response. I caught her arm as she passed.

She glanced down at the point where my pale bony hand gripped her bicep. "Release me at once," she said.

My fingers relaxed, but hovered over her arm. "I think it would be best if you allowed me to—"

"Do I need an invitation to pay a visit to my sire?" she asked.

"No."

"Is he in there?" She pointed at the thatched roof lashed between the trees at the edge of the pond.

"Yes." My tongue stuck to the roof of my mouth, allowing me only one word answers under her fierce glare.

"Then I'll announce myself." She charged ahead, pushing back the willow curtain that hid my mentors from view.

I coughed loudly, hoping it might alert the twins. But they carried on as though they hadn't heard, until the female stepped inside. She sucked in a breath and froze when she saw them, causing me to stumble into her back. I caught myself, then pushed away. Standing clear of her to apologize.

"Sorcha, my dear, what a pleasant surprise." Rowan stood, brushing crumbs from his lap. His offspring had likely never seen him in his natural Rogue form. It was not unlike mine. Hairless. Black eyes with no pupil to mark their center of focus. Pointed teeth and thick black tongue. The differences were subtle. Identifying marks recognized by other Rogues. But most Fae could not tell us apart in our natural form. Most Fae had never seen us in our natural form.

Rowan's eyes stared past Sorcha and locked with mine. I recognized the annoyance in his manner and expected a rebuke later for allowing his estranged offspring to catch him unprepared. Riagan continued to recline, sipping from a goblet balanced on the outstretched fingers of his left hand. He turned his attention to the platter of fruit, spiking a ripe berry with his long, sharp fingernail and lifting it towards his grinning mouth.

While Rowan scrambled, torn between his duty to serve his High Rogue brother, and the unannounced arrival of his offspring, Riagan appeared merely amused at the interruption. I knew it to be a ruse. Riagan had earned the title of High Rogue, at least in part, because he'd sired the queen. He'd made it clear to his brother exactly what he thought about the last of Maeve's daughters. The one who failed to honor her mother's commitment to the Rogue Faction. Riagan's faint grin promised retribution.

To Sorcha's credit, she appeared unaffected by the twins, though I could sense her unease. She straightened her spine, met her sire's eyes. "Godda is missing."

Her declaration wiped the smile from Riagan's lips. "What's this?" He sat up, taking an immediate interest.

"Last night, a human came and captured her. My sisters swear he's just a lover, but she didn't return with the dawn. They refuse to go after her. That's why I came to you."

Rowan scoffed. "If it's a lover, perhaps she'll return by nightfall, or by the rise of the moon. I wouldn't worry." He sat, but none of the tension drained out of him.

Riagan set down his goblet with a thunk that rattled the low table between them. "Godda would never be so irresponsible as to run off with a human and you know it."

Rowan shifted. "I never claimed she was irresponsible." Tight cords of muscle flexed in his neck, revealing his tension, even as his hands rested flat on his thighs and his fingers tapped lazily against his knees.

Sorcha wisely kept her mouth shut. I tugged on the sleeve of her tunic, hoping to convince her to withdraw and allow them time to sort it out. Instead she turned her blue eyes on me, pinning me with her glare. Then she returned her attention to her sire and his twin.

"Will you help me, then?" she asked.

"What are you suggesting?" Riagan asked.

"I want to go after her, but humans are dangerous. This one arrived with a band of hunters. I know I shouldn't go alone. I'm asking for assistance."

"We should not interfere." Rowan advised. He ran a hand across his bald head and scratched behind one of his pointed ears.

"On this, I agree with you, brother," Riagan said. His eyes moved past Sorcha to land on me.

I stepped back, rustling the dried leaves on the willow branch curtain as it brushed against me, blocking my exit.

"She needs a guide," Riagan said. He touched his brother's hand, drawing his attention. They exchanged a look, then they both turned their eyes on me.

"I agree," Rowan said. "It's time."

"Past time." Riagan grinned, flashing his pointed teeth.

No. No. No. I kept my face placid even as the voice inside me screamed, anticipating what would come next.

Sorcha shifted back a half step. Any more and she'd run into me. I wondered if she knew what was coming. If she recognized that she was the focus of Riagan's plotting. This was unlikely to be what she'd expected to find on her first visit to her sire's lair.

"Yes." Rowan's smile held a tightness, as though he longed to disagree with his brother's scheme.

"You'll help me, then?" Sorcha asked, mistaking their words for agreement.

I should never have let her in. Or, if she'd insisted, I should have left her to it and stayed away. Now my future would be locked to her punishment. Any chance I had of becoming the youngest Confirmed Rogue was about to dissolve.

"We'll assign you a guide," Riagan said, confirming my suspicion.

I stood still, as though that might cause him to forget my presence.

"A guide?" Sorcha surged forward, forgetting her fear. "What good will that do?"

Rowan shifted away from his brother and took a few careful steps toward Sorcha. "You will need someone to train you in the ways of the Rogue."

Sorcha crossed her arms. "I'm not here for training. I'm here to rescue my sister. Our queen."

"Yes." Rowan laid a hand on her shoulder and her back stiffened. "But training is all we are willing to offer you. You've neglected your responsibilities. You should have been assigned a tutor at ten turns. If you want our help, you'll accept the terms of our agreement."

"How will training with this guide help me rescue my sister?"

"If you knew anything of our powers, you would already know, wouldn't you?" Riagan reclined in his chair, stretching out his legs and crossing them at the ankles. "They will help you develop the skills you'll need to succeed and will help you rescue Godda…assuming she needs rescuing."

"And who is this guide? You, sire?" she asked, returning her attention to Rowan who now stood halfway between his offspring and his brother.

At least Riagan couldn't see Rowan's stricken face. The High Rogue likely knew the effect he was having, but Rowan was making a valiant effort to hide it.

Riagan scoffed. "No. If you knew anything about your kin you wouldn't bother asking such an insulting question. Rowan has more important responsibilities than training Fledges." He reached for his goblet. His nails clicked together as his fingers twisted the stem. The facets of the gems imbedded in the metal reflected a rainbow of light across the roof of the lean-to. He announced my fate with a flick of his wrist. "Bryn will serve."

Sorcha spun to face me. "You?"

So she hadn't entirely ignored me when I'd introduced myself. The realization was only a small consolation given the circumstances.

Rowan flashed me an apologetic grin once Sorcha's back was turned. The glimpse of sharp teeth against blood red lips did nothing to ease my mind. "Bryn is our most talented young Rogue. It's past time for our Apprentice to become a Candidate and take on responsibility for a Fledge."

Just last moon cycle Riagan had been telling me I was hopeless and would never amount to anything. They both knew I still hadn't mastered morphing. Rowan couldn't be lying, but he certainly wasn't telling the whole of what he believed to be true. Even if I was overdue for being assigned a Fledge and promoted to Candidate status, training one and placing them with a mentor wouldn't bring me closer to Confirmation. Not unless I could morph.

"You honor me, Rogue Leaders." I bowed my head, buying time as I searched for the plan within the plan. The spike that would skewer me if I agreed to their bargain. Such was life among Rogues.

"Do you accept your Fledge, then?" Riagan asked.

If I refused, they might never give me another chance, and as my Masters, I climbed the ranks or descended on their word. But, I had a chance to include a term of my own.

"I accept this assignment, and look forward to advancing to Candidate once I am successful." I pressed my lips together and waited to see if my gamble would work.

Rowan nodded. "It's settled then," he said. "Teach her what she needs to know."

"And help me bring back the queen," Sorcha added.

Riagan ignored her. Anger at my forwardness and his brother's capitulation to my terms colored his voice. "If you fail—"

Rowan cut across his brother's warning, finishing his twin's sentence to ease some of the tension he'd caused by accepting my counter. "You'll be forced to wait until we decide you're worthy of another chance." He grinned at Riagan, and the two began laughing.

Sorcha tried to speak, but I knew it would be pointless. I pulled her back through the willow. She shoved at me, resisting.

"If you want their support, you should behave," I warned. My words were lost under the cackles of the twins, but she heard me and followed.

"I don't have to listen to you," she said, marching away from me as soon as we were outside.

"Ah, but you do." This was my chance. I may not have mastered morphing, but that hardly mattered now that I had a Fledge to train. All I had to do was teach her the basics of Rogue magic. So long as I could teach her the basics and place her with a mentor of her own, I would advance from Apprentice to Candidate and free myself from the torture of serving the twins. Taking Rowan's child as a Fledge seemed like an easy way to achieve that goal. The twins were two of the most powerful Rogues, so I assumed Rowan's child must have inherited some natural skill.

"I don't care what they say. I'm not interested in learning to be a Rogue. I'm Sorcha of Maeve, Sworn Master of Illusions. I don't take orders from Rogues like you."

"If your sister didn't think she was too good for training, why do you think you are? What sort of 'Master of Illusions' will you be if you leave your Rogue abilities untrained."

"Godda never trained with the Rogues." Sorcha folded her arms across her armored chest.

"Did she tell you that?"

"No."

"Then how do you know it's true?"

"She would have told me if she had." Her voice wavered as though she questioned her words even as they tumbled from her lips.

"Perhaps she was too busy being queen to bother telling you what should be obvious. I've seen your sister here. I know her mentor. She never attempted the Confirmation testing, but she could have, if she'd wanted to."

"Confirmation?" Sorcha's eyes narrowed. She really knew nothing.

"Does this mean you're ready for your first lesson?" I asked.

She cocked her head and fixed me with a look that reminded me of her hawk form. "Godda has a mentor, and I've been assigned a tutor like a Faeling."

"Because like a Faeling, you must first learn the basics. Then, once I'm sure you won't discredit me, you'll be assigned a mentor. But for now, you're my Fledge."

"I'm a Sworn member of the Queen's Court. I'm not your Fledge, and you can't speak to me that way." She set her hands on her hips.

I waved a hand. "None of that matters here. If you'd bothered to learn anything, you'd know that. Now, I'll pretend you haven't insulted the entire faction with your words, if you're ready to begin."

"This is ridiculous."

"Do you want to rescue your queen, or not?"

"I didn't agree to this. You all agreed to that plan without any input from me. I don't have to abide by your rules. I'll rescue Godda without your help."

"Suit yourself."

She shifted into her hawk form. With a few flaps of her brown wings, she soared up above the treetops and disappeared. But I knew she'd return. She'd made a bargain with the Rogues, whether she realized it, or not. Only death or completion could break those bonds.

3

BY the time I returned to the cottage, still fuming from my visit with my sire and uncle, my sisters were just beginning to stir and stretch. I found Niamh and Rionach at the table in the small kitchen, rubbing sleep from their eyes while Meara floated cups off the shelf on a current of air controlled by her magic. They paused in midair long enough for her to fill them with steaming honeyed milk that she poured from a glass jug warmed by her fire magic.

My mouth watered and my empty stomach begged me to join them, but I continued past, marching over to where Isleen and Flida sat on a couch, huddled together and talking in hushed voices. Isleen noticed me first. She sat up straighter, causing Flida to turn toward me.

"Oh. Sorcha. I thought you might be—"

"Godda?" I asked. "She hasn't returned, has she?" I'd left the cottage just after dawn, when it was clear that Godda had not returned.

"No, but I'm sure she'll be back by nightfall." Flida pressed her lips together into a worried line.

"You said that she'd be back by dawn." I crossed my arms and stared them down. She wasn't lying. Fae couldn't lie. But I found it hard to believe that she thought the humans would let Godda go so easily.

"She's never been gone this long," Isleen said, setting her hand on Flida's arm.

"She wouldn't leave us, and no human is powerful enough to hold her against her will." Flida stood. She smoothed the fabric of her loose shift dress and began braiding her long brown hair.

"Unless they have steel and bind her." If these humans knew where to find us, then they almost certainly knew how to bind us. "We should check on her. Do you know where they took her?" I asked.

"I won't let you go after her. Not yet and not alone," Flida said.

"Then send some of the Queen's Guard with me, if you must." Humans were dangerous. At best they might only want to use us for our power. At worst, they might know enough to kill us and use our stranded magic to create demon spawn. "But I'm not going to sit here and wait for her to return when she might need our help."

"When who might need our help?" asked a familiar voice.

All of us turned to find Godda, bright and glowing with life, standing in the open door.

"I hope you weren't worried about me." She smiled. "I'm sorry I missed the rest of your party, little hawk." She kissed me on the forehead, then continued on, toward the bedrooms at the back of the cottage, humming a tune and swaying to music only she could hear.

"You gave us a bit of a scare," Flida said, keeping her voice gentle.

Godda paused. "Nonsense. No need to worry about me."

"How did he find us and what did he want?" Isleen asked. She'd always been the bravest of us all.

"Who do you mean?" Godda flicked her wrist in the

direction of the kitchen and one of the mugs Meara had been filling appeared in her hand. She lifted the beverage to her lips and inhaled deeply before taking a sip.

Rionach, Meara, and Niamh hurried in from the kitchen to join us.

"The human," Isleen said, fixing Godda with her best no-nonsense stare. "The one who scooped you up and carried you away last night." She placed a hand on her hip. "And, so long as you're at it, who were the men with him and what were they doing here?"

"He is a bit more clever than I'd thought," Godda said, draining the mug of honeyed milk.

Isleen raised an eyebrow, silently inviting Godda to continue.

Godda sighed, and the mug disappeared from her hand. "His name is Edric. Lord Edric, as it turns out. I came across him in the forest one day while he was hunting. He amused me. We met a few more times." She paused, frowning. "I wasn't expecting him to enforce his invitation quite so dramatically."

"What does he want from you?" I asked. Fear prickled the hairs at the nape of my neck.

"He wants to marry me, little hawk." Her bare shoulders gave a tiny shrug, shifting the thin straps that held up her airy summer dress.

The sudden intake of breath from six pairs of lungs threatened to suck all the oxygen from the cottage.

Flida recovered first. "Oh, Godda. I told you…" Her voice trailed off at whatever she saw in Godda's eyes.

"Yes. You did. And since you appear to be so much smarter than me, I think you should be queen." Godda extended one hand and a golden crown appeared, dangling from her fingertips.

Flida stepped back and bowed her head. "I'm not smarter, my queen."

"I've agreed to marry him," Godda said, gripping the

vine-shaped metal and twisting it so the embedded jewels caught the morning light.

"No!"

"But you can't!"

"That's impossible!"

Niamh, Rionach, and Meara's voices called out all at once, joining into one jumbled response. Flida lifted her head, but didn't say a word. Isleen also remained silent.

I began to guess that this decision came as less of a surprise to them, that maybe this had been what they'd been discussing when I'd returned from my visit to the Rogues. It appeared that Godda's human was indeed dangerous, but not in the way I'd expected. The Queen of the Fae controlled the magic that returned our souls to the ether when we faded. Without that, our power would weaken and eventually disappear completely. If the humans controlled that magic, they would control us.

"You're our queen," I said. "You can't marry a human."

"Then I won't be queen." Godda lifted her eyes from the twisted metal to meet mine. "Flida can act as queen regent until the eldest of your daughters comes of age to take my place."

None of us had daughters, or any offspring for that matter. Most Fae didn't care to reproduce until they glimpsed the end of their exceptionally long lifespan on the horizon. Godda might be able to put Flida in charge of ruling over the Fae factions, but until a new queen matured into her powers, any Fae who wished to fade would risk untethering their magic and allowing it to be used by any wizard or demon for dark purposes.

"Please don't. Please reconsider, my queen…" Flida dropped to one knee and stared up at the sister she'd sworn to protect.

Godda set the crown on Flida's head. "See? It looks as though it belongs there."

Flida tore the crown off and stood. "Don't. It's yours. We need you. Please don't…" She held the metal circlet out for

Godda to take.

Godda shook her head. "It's done. I pronounce you Regent Queen of the Fae." She pushed the circlet back toward Flida. "Name your second-in-command."

"I won't."

I'd never seen them argue. Not once in all the years I'd lived with them. Not once since our mother faded. Judging from the stunned silence in the cottage, it appeared the rest of my sisters had never seen Godda and Flida at odds, either.

Godda stepped close to Flida and touched her cheek. "He makes me happy."

"He'll die." Flida's eyes narrowed.

"I know."

"What then?"

"I won't return." Godda retrieved her crown, then settled it onto Flida's head once more.

"You could insist on maintaining the current arrangement." Flida reached up, but Godda caught Flida's hands in hers and pressed them together, holding them fast between her own.

"I won't put my kin in danger. As it stands, he knows very little of the Fae. Only rumors and superstitions. He doesn't know our weakness. If I refuse him, he won't stop until he discovers our secrets. He'll use them to control me. I won't let that happen."

"Then we'll kill him," I said.

"No." Godda's eyes locked with mine over Flida's shoulder.

"You'd give up your title. Your birthright. For this barbarian human? A mortal man?" As usual, Isleen spoke the words we were all thinking.

Godda shook her head. "I can't stay long. I need to return before he realizes I've gone."

"He *is* holding you captive, then," I said. If she wasn't free to leave, then she was a prisoner, not a wife.

"I'm no captive, little hawk." Godda dropped Flida's

hands and stepped back. "Someday, you'll understand."

I'd never understand how she could walk away and leave us for a mortal. The only way this made sense was that she was sacrificing herself for the good of the Fae. Like a queen. She'd said it herself. She'd refused to let us kill him, but that wouldn't stop me from finding a way to save her.

Godda disappeared into her bedroom. Flida followed. The rest of us stared at each other in stunned silence. Niamh beckoned Isleen and me to join the others in the kitchen. She pulled the door shut behind us. Not that such a gesture would keep our sharp-eared elder sisters from hearing us, if they chose to.

"We need to do something," I said.

"We need to let her go." Rionach traced the rim of her mug with a finger.

"She made her choice." Isleen leaned back against the counter and crossed her arms.

I stared at each of them in turn. "You heard her. She's scared of him. When have you ever seen Godda scared of anyone?"

"She said she loves him." Meara sighed. "I'd give up being queen for love."

"For a mortal?" I asked. "This isn't right. How can you not see that?"

"You're not wrong, little hawk." Isleen wrapped her arms around me from behind and pulled me into a hug. "I know you love her. We all do. But she decided on her path, and it's not our place to interfere."

I tensed. "We're Sworn. It's our responsibility to protect our queen."

"It's Flida's responsibility to protect Godda. It's our responsibility to be loyal and obey her commands."

I tensed in Isleen's arms. "She never commanded us to let her go."

"She commanded that we not harm her human." Isleen rested her chin on my shoulder.

I frowned. "She commanded us not to kill him."

"Sorcha…" Rionach shook her head.

"You don't understand…" Niamh sighed.

"I wish you would all stop telling me what I do and do not understand." I pushed away from Isleen's embrace. "I've done my twenty-five turns. I've Sworn my Oath. I've accepted my place on the Queen's Court. I even ate the heart of that poor defenseless rabbit to fulfill the ritual you said would strengthen my animal form. What is it going to take for you to stop treating me like a Faeling?"

They all remained silent in the wake of my outburst. For a moment, I thought I'd convinced them. Then I realized they were staring past me, eyes fixed on the door at my back. I turned my head and found Godda grinning at me.

"Look at you," she said, cupping my chin between her hands. "My little hawk is all grown up. You're going to make an excellent Master of Illusions." She kissed the tip of my nose and released me.

I wouldn't. I didn't know the first thing about Rogue magic. I needed to find a way to tell her before she left us unprotected. I watched her make her way around the kitchen, embracing each of us in turn and saying her goodbyes. Once she'd completed her round, we followed her out into the yard.

"Will we see you again?" Meara asked.

"I would invite you to the wedding, but the less Lord Edric knows of you, the better," she said. "I'll return when I can. Maybe not every new moon, but as many as I can manage."

"And after he's gone?" Niamh asked.

"There will be a new queen. I'll likely fade, as is my right."

Flida shook her head. "Should you need us…"

"I'll send a sprite." She looked at each of us one last time, then blew us a kiss from the edge of the garden.

Flida didn't say a word. She just turned and walked back to the cottage. This was my chance to speak with her, alone. I raced after her and followed her through the garden.

"What is it, little hawk?" she asked as she continued past

the garden and into the clearing, closer to the treeline, where the magic protecting the cottage ended, allowing for transit in and out.

I hurried to catch up to her. "I have to tell you something."

Godda turned to face me. "I already know."

I paused, frozen in place. "Then why did you give me that title? If you know I haven't learned Rogue magic, if you know I can't protect the forest, then why make me Master of Illusions?"

She took my hand and squeezed it. "It's more important now than ever that you complete your training. You're the only one of us who can repair the illusions that keep our forest hidden from the humans."

"But the Rogues are—"

"Everything they say about the Rogues is true, but also not." She paused, then shook her head. "Learn from them, little hawk, but never trust them. Our mother made them a promise before you were born, but that promise faded with her. My sire may hold that against you."

"They're awful." I grimaced, remembering our sires' hairless bodies and smooth faces. Those solid black eyes and the translucent vertical lids that slid across them.

"They're our kin."

"What did our mother promise them?" I asked.

She dropped my hand and stepped back, toward the trees. "It doesn't matter, now. Do your duty, little hawk. Serve Flida as you would serve me, and keep our forest safe. And remember, never bargain with a Rogue Fae."

I opened my mouth to protest that I wasn't ready. To tell her once again that we needed her. That I needed her. That there was no way I could return to the Rogues and that humiliating tutor her sire had assigned to me. But the words stuck in my throat, and before I could find my voice, she disappeared.

4

BY the time Riagan called for wine, Sorcha hadn't returned, and I hadn't managed to morph my features to anything resembling High Fae or human. I would have to return to the twins with this face and take my punishment. I checked my reflection to ensure there weren't any lingering signs of my failed attempts. Then I ducked my head and pushed aside the willow reeds to enter the lean-to. Keeping my head down, I made my way toward my masters, hoping my deference might delay the inevitable consequences for my failure.

"How good of you to make time for us." Riagan said as I filled his goblet.

When I dared to glance at him, his face rippled and morphed to take on the chiseled contours of a High Fae. He was taunting me. Still, I admired the ease with which he adopted his chosen form, and his artistry. Long golden locks cascaded from his previously bare scalp to skim his lean shoulders. The solid black of his eyes had shrunk to small dots that floated like islands in the center clear blue lakes. He resembled Godda in this form, but with a flat chest, a square jaw, and sharper cheekbones.

"It is my duty to serve you." I finished filling his goblet, then tipped the neck of the bottle over Rowan's cup.

"I suppose we could relieve you from some of those duties if you need more time to train your Fledge," Rowan said.

"I can manage." I couldn't let them find out that Sorcha had left and refused training, and I didn't want them to ask any questions.

Before they could say anything more, I set the bottle on the table, retrieved the water skin, and transported myself deep into the forest. With luck I would have time to feed after I refilled the water skin. As I made my way to the stream, a muffled sob caught my attention. The priestesses and acolytes who maintained the nearby temple didn't usually venture this far into the forest, but perhaps the Ancients were smiling on me for once.

I filled the water skin quickly, then crept my way toward the sound and hoping for an easy meal. Unfortunately, the figure I discovered wandering the forest would be unable to satisfy my hunger. The patterned Queen's Guard vest and the golden braid belonged to none other than my runaway Fledge.

"What are you doing?" I asked, stepping out onto the path behind her and forcing her to turn around.

Sorcha's eyes narrowed as she studied my form. "Bryn?"

Of course she didn't recognize me. I sighed. "A Fledge does not address their tutor by their given name. You will call me Guide or Teacher. Since you appear to lack any sort of acquaintance with the rules of Rogues, I'll consider that to be your first lesson."

She swiped her palms across her cheeks and straightened her spine. "I told you. I don't want any lessons. I'm going to rescue my sister."

"Alone?" I admired her bravery, but her impulsiveness would get her killed. I doubted, if she died, that the twins would assign me a different Fledge to train. It would be like them to consider that a failure.

"I don't need your help. My sire may have been a Rogue, but that doesn't make me one, any more than it makes Meara and Flida Elementals."

I stepped closer. "And yet, your sisters all know how to wield the powers they were born with, don't they? Even if they claim the maternal birthright of High Fae over the one bestowed on them by their sires." I took another step forward and continued, not waiting for her response. "All except you. Why is that 'little hawk?'"

Her mouth dropped open. "How do you know that's what they call me?"

I ignored her question. I wasn't about to share my secrets with her. "What do you have against Rogues?"

Sorcha put her hands on her hips. "Rogues are tricksters. They can't be trusted."

I grinned, and she flinched at the sight of my teeth.

"You're scared of me." Rogues kept to themselves. I'd always thought it was to protect our secrets, because our magic made the other Fae uncomfortable. I never imagined that they might fear us.

"It's just…" She hesitated. "My sire never…"

Perhaps I was wrong, and she didn't fear our power, after all. Maybe it was only my form that she feared. "You never saw your sire in his natural form. Why would you?" I stood tall in front of her and gestured to my body. "This is the true form of a Rogue. And yes, we all look like this."

"I didn't know." She grimaced.

"If Queen Maeve had honored her promise, then you would have known." Without thinking I'd imitated a taunt that could have come from Riagan's lips and even delivered it with a mimic of his sneer.

I expected her to defend her mother, but instead she cocked her head to the side. Curious.

"What did my mother promise them?" she asked. "Godda wouldn't tell me."

I hesitated, turning the secret over in my mind, examining the angles, testing it to see where sharing this knowledge might lead. "She promised that, if she took Rowan's seed, their offspring would be raised a Rogue."

Sorcha swallowed. "She faded before my tenth turn."

"Yes." I wet my lips. "Before you were old enough to be assigned a tutor." I let the weight of the implications settle in the air between us. Riagan believed she'd chosen to fade at that time on purpose. Rowan, when he was feeling brave, suggested that it was only an unfortunate coincidence.

"So Godda and Flida raised me, instead." She folded her arms across her chest. "The bargain died with my mother. It's fair."

"After your mother faded, Godda offered to take your place. Even though Riagan wouldn't agree to bargain with her, she decided to train, hoping it would heal the alliance between the Rogues and the High Fae."

Sorcha opened her mouth, then closed it. The truth rippled across the smooth plains of her pale face. "Then why did Godda make me her Master of Illusions?"

"There are some threads that can't be avoided, no matter which pattern you choose."

She glared at me. "Do you always speak in nonsense and riddles?"

I pressed my fingers together under my chin and blinked at her. "You've Sworn to serve your sister, our queen. She's made her choice. Now you make yours. Do you agree to train or not?"

She studied me for a moment, then nodded.

"All right, then." I reached for her hand. "We're going to trap a human."

"What? No!" She backed away from me.

I wagged a finger at her. "Ah, ah, ah. You agreed." Before she could say another word, I grabbed her wrist and took her with me when I disappeared, transporting us to the edge of the forest, just outside the Lady of the Hunt's temple.

She twisted free and shoved me. "You can't do that."

"Do you want to be prepared to fight the humans to get your sister back?"

"Of course, but what does that have to do with trapping a human?"

"You need to feed before you attempt illusions." I watched the acolytes cross the field in small groups, searching for one who had wandered off on her own. "There." I pointed to a dark-haired woman near the edge of the temple. "First we set a trap. Then we lure her away."

I knew from experience that we were close to a circle of gnarled oaks, the perfect place to set a faerie trap. I tugged on her hand, pulling her with me toward the spot.

"What do you mean 'feed'? Are we going to hurt her?"

"No harm will come to the human." I stepped into the circle of trees. "Press your hand to each of the trunks, in turn." I indicated the ancient trees surrounding us.

"Just touch them?"

I nodded. "And whisper their name to wake them as you do." I crossed my arms and waited, trusting her High Fae tutors had at least provided her with a basic understanding of common Fae magic.

She glared at me for a moment, then proceeded.

After hesitating as she reached for the first trunk, she moved from tree to tree with confidence, waking them from their slumber. The ring hummed with magic, imperceptible to almost all humans.

"Now what?" she asked.

"Now we lure her to our trap."

"How?"

"That's too much to explain now. I'll do it this time. Luring will be part of your next lesson." I sniffed the air, then snapped my fingers in the direction of the temple. Flickering faerie lights floated through the forest, marking a trail to our location.

Sorcha scoffed. "I know how to cast faerie lights. I could

have done that."

"You didn't know that was the lure that would draw this human. It's not always faerie lights. I'll teach you how to know. But now we hide and wait."

It wasn't long before the dark-haired human appeared. Once she'd crossed the threshold of the trap, I signaled Sorcha to emerge. She hesitated, then stepped out, in front of the human, who immediately dropped to her knees.

"How may I serve you?" the woman asked. Humans weren't always this compliant. This one was making Sorcha's lesson easy.

I cast my voice into the circle, making it appear that the sound was coming from Sorcha. "Close your eyes, human."

Once the woman's eyes shut, I motioned for Sorcha to join me at the woman's side.

"Can she hear us?" Sorcha whispered.

"Only if I wish her to."

Sorcha tilted her head to one side. "Is that what you plan to teach me?"

"No. I plan to teach you lies."

"Lies," she repeated.

I nodded. "Humans lie. Fae cannot. Rogues feed off human lies. It replenishes our magic."

"You said you wouldn't harm her." She took a step back, away from the human.

"This won't hurt her." I reached for Sorcha's hand and tugged her closer. "Place your fingers on her temples."

Sorcha lifted her hands to touch the woman's face, and I adjusted them until they were in position. "Good. There. Now, do you feel the lies?"

Sorcha shook her head.

I pressed myself against her back, placing my hands over hers so I could help her search. "Sometimes they are slippery. Elusive. Other times they're scabbed over by gnarled layers of thought." I tugged the lies toward the surface of the woman's mind.

Sorcha's body tensed. Her hands recoiled from the woman's head, and I caught them in mine.

"It's all right." I guided her fingers back to the woman's temples.

"That's pain. You want me to absorb that? Are you trying to kill me?" She kept her voice low, but she needn't have bothered. The acolyte had gone into a trance and couldn't hear us.

One of the reasons I'd chosen to start here was that these women served the Fae. Even though Sorcha didn't look like her sister Flida, the actual Lady of the Hunt, they still recognized her as Fae and assumed she also served their Lady.

"The lies bring strength. Not pain. Watch and learn." I drew a strand of falsehoods from the woman's mind and extracted it like sap through her skin, allowing it to soak into my own flesh and absorb into my blood. A satisfied sigh escaped my lips.

"How did you do that?" she asked, turning my hand over in hers and searching for the source of the trick.

"Try again." I set her fingers on the acolyte's temple. "Feel for the lies. Pull them to the surface."

She managed that much on her own, then hesitated. "It still feels like pain."

I moved one of my hands to grip her shoulder and squeezed, kneading into her muscles. "This is pain, as well." She tensed under my touch, then began to soften. "Until it's not." I began to tug at the thread of lies she'd pulled to the surface. But, this time, instead of absorbing it myself, I guided it to her fingers.

She sucked in a breath, then released a low moan that made me want to press closer. Suddenly the arch of her neck and the delicate skin of her ears demanded my full attention. They lured me in a way I'd thought only humans susceptible to. I allowed one finger of the hand I'd set on her shoulder to extend until the tip of my nail brushed against the side of her neck. She sighed and relaxed against me.

For a moment, I thought perhaps she wanted more of my

touch. Then the woman swayed, and I realized I'd let Sorcha take too much. I pulled her fingers away, enclosing them in my own. Then I wrapped my arms around her and tugged her backward.

She squirmed and pushed me away. "Why did you make me stop?"

"You said you didn't want to kill her."

The acolyte had collapsed, bent over her knees with her forehead pressed to the ground.

"Oh." Sorcha shuffled toward her, then froze. "Oh, no. Is she… Will she be okay?"

"She'll be fine in a moment." I closed a hand around Sorcha's wrist and guided her over to the trees. "Release the trap so she can go."

"How?"

"Same as before. In reverse this time." I steadied my breath and slowed my racing heart, turning away as she moved from tree to tree.

Her reaction had nothing to do with me. She'd never tasted that kind of power before and had been in a feeding daze. After more than twenty five turns, her Rogue magic must have been starved for it. If she'd tried to use those abilities without fueling them first, she could have tapped them dry.

The acolyte, trance broken, mumbled a prayer as Sorcha worked to release her.

"You may go," I said. "Tell no one of what you've seen."

She stumbled to her feet, caught sight of Sorcha, bowed again, and hurried back toward the temple.

"Does that work?" Sorcha asked.

"Does what work?"

"Commanding her to tell no one."

"Usually." My tongue flicked out to lick the taste of the woman off my fingertips. "How do you feel?"

Sorcha rolled her shoulders. "Refreshed."

"Good. Never take more than you need. At first, since you've gone so long with no nourishment, it will be hard to stop once you start. If you don't maintain control, you'll leave them a worthless shell, as good as dead, on the forest floor."

"You said it doesn't hurt them."

"Taking away the pressure of some of their lies is more relief than pain, but so much of the human mind is lies. They lie even to themselves. You'll paralyze them if you leave them with nothing but the truth, making them easy prey for any predator. A brutal way to die. You'd be better off slitting their throat and being done with it."

She tensed, eyes wide. "I could do this to Godda's human."

"Not yet, and not without my help." I beckoned to her. "Come. It's time that I returned."

"Teach me the rest of it."

I inhaled, considering the possibility. "While I appreciate your eagerness, you need to rest."

"I don't have time to rest. I need to learn so I can rescue Godda."

I couldn't have her running off on her own again. "If you return with me, we can try another lesson."

She extended her hand. "All right."

I closed my fingers around hers and transported us back to the lean-to, only to discover Rowan and Riagan outside, waiting for us. They'd both adopted High Fae forms, as though they'd just returned from Court. I'd studied them long enough to realize their appearance, paired with the way Rowan paced while Riagan lounged on a tree stump near the reflecting pool, glowering, meant trouble for me, and likely also for my Fledge.

5

Y skin tingled after absorbing all that power from the human. The energy surging through me erased any lingering reluctance to learn about Rogue magic and replaced it with eager curiosity. I wanted to learn out how to channel this energy into illusions, but, faced with my sire and uncle, I knew that wasn't going to happen anytime soon. So, I fought my heightened senses, struggling to compose myself and pretend these new sensations were entirely normal.

After a breath or two, I realized Riagan and my sire had both adopted High Fae forms. I blinked, trying to reconcile them with their earlier appearance. The forest around me slid in and out of focus every time my eyelids flicked open, a little like the summer after my tenth turn when Meara had dared me to drink an entire goblet of pixie wine at the solstice festival. My sire's pacing didn't help with my focus.

"Where have you been?" he asked, directing his annoyance at Bryn, even as his eyes flicked to me.

Bryn bowed. "Apologies, master. I've been giving Sorcha her first lesson."

That word still made my skin crawl. *Lesson.* Especially now that I knew that my mother might have faded just so I wouldn't have to be raised among the Rogues. I wanted to hate them, but after this small taste, I also wanted their power, and their help rescuing my sister.

My sire waved a hand in annoyance at Bryn's response and returned to pacing. "We have no time for that, now."

Riagan grinned. "What my dear brother means is that we've just returned from Court and have decided to take a more active role in this attempt to return the rightful queen to her throne."

Finally. "So you know that she abdicated?" I asked.

Bryn's fingers tightened on my arm. I must have forgotten to mention that when I'd said I was going to rescue her.

"Yes. We've heard." Riagan dipped a hand into the reflecting basin and swirled the water with his fingertips. "She's named Flida as regent queen to rule in her place. Unacceptable."

"Giving up her throne for a human." My sire shook his head. "Ridiculous."

At least we could all agree on that.

Riagan stood and brushed himself off. Unlike my sire, who'd chosen to adorn his High Fae form with the traditional court attire of breeches, blouse, vest, and cravat, Riagan wore only a loin cloth, wrapped low on his hips.

"Since Godda insists on marrying this human and has forbidden the Fae from killing him, we've decided to send her a wedding present." Riagan's sly grin implied that his idea of an appropriate present might not be so well received by his offspring and her lover.

My sire nodded. "You two will bring our present to Godda since Riagan promised Flida that the Rogues will not interfere."

"Yes. You must not mention where this present comes from." Riagan pointed a long finger at Bryn. "You will go in disguise. And my niece will glamour herself to appear human."

"Godda will recognize me, even with a glamour," I said.

"Of course she will. That doesn't matter. What matters is that her human know nothing of the Fae. For him, you will appear as one of them."

Riagan turned his back on me and focused his attention on Bryn. "Deliver the present. Once the human is out of the way, bring Godda home. If you succeed, we will consider that to be your Confirmation exam and will reward you by making you a Confirmed Rogue."

"What is this present?" Bryn asked.

I made a mental note to ask Bryn why becoming a Confirmed Rogue was so important. My uncle appeared to be dangling this as a reward, and Bryn wanted it. Perhaps as badly as I wanted Godda back.

"Bring them in." At Riagan's command, my sire motioned to a group of gnomes, clustered together near the base of a nearby tree. Their striped and spotted olive brown jumpers blended so well with the bark and moss that I wondered if they'd been standing there the whole time.

The gnomes scurried off into the brush and returned a moment later, leading two lumbering grey creatures with bat-like ears, beaked noses, and wings folded across their broad backs. Hunched over, they appeared no taller than me, but if they straightened, I knew they'd tower over all of us. I'd been so busy admiring their wings that it wasn't until the pair stopped next to my sire that I noticed their tails.

I'd heard whispers of gargoyles, but I'd never seen any in the flesh. And there was plenty of flesh visible between the two of them since they were both corded with muscles and devoid of any clothing or other adornments.

"This is Onfroi and Piers." My sire gestured to each in turn. I wasn't sure how he could tell them apart until I noticed a jagged, semi-circle chunk missing from Onfroi's left ear, as though someone or something had taken a bite out of it.

"They will be accompanying you on your journey and

have agreed to deal with Godda's human," my uncle explained.

I shook my head. "You plan to give our queen a pair of assassins? You think she won't realize what you're up to when we arrive with these two?" If I knew what they were, surely the Queen of the Fae would also know, and she'd forbidden us from killing her human.

"Sorcha has a point," Bryn said.

Riagan motioned to the gargoyles. "You'll deliver them in their dormant forms. They will appear as harmless stone ornaments, meant to adorn the human's manor."

I frowned. Unless I was missing some subtlety, there was no way this plan was ever going to work. "Godda intends to protect her human. She'll destroy them as soon as she gets a chance."

Riagan glared at me. His face rippled and shifted until his solid black eyes pinned me with an eerie stare. "That's why your job will be to protect them and distract her, until they can succeed."

I forced myself to hold his stare and not step back, even though my instincts warned me to flee.

"And what of Sorcha's training?" Bryn asked, pulling Riagan's attention away from me.

"If Sorcha hopes to outwit her sister, you'll need to complete it before you arrive. And once this is over, you'll still need to place her with a Confirmed mentor. If she doesn't succeed, you don't ascend."

My sire's narrowed eyes and the firm line of his mouth alarmed me, but I didn't understand his concern.

Bryn didn't respond.

Riagan stepped closer to Bryn. "Return with Godda once the human is dead, place your Fledge with a mentor, and you'll be Confirmed. It's as simple as that. Do you agree?"

"What about morphing?" Bryn asked.

"If you think you can complete the mission without it." Riagan shrugged. "Those are my terms."

I sucked in a breath. They were bargaining. Godda had warned me not to trust the Rogues or bargain with them. I held my tongue and glanced at my sire to judge his reaction, but his face revealed nothing even though his eyes were locked on Bryn and Riagan.

Bryn swallowed. "When I succeed, I want to be named a Rogue Leader."

Riagan laughed. "Allowing you to ascend without a test is enough of a reward. You know the only Rogue I've deemed worthy of sitting on my council is my brother. Why would I name a newly Confirmed Rogue a Rogue Leader? Do you think you're as good as Rowan, now?"

"No, Master." Bryn's chin dipped ever so slightly.

My fists clenched at my sides. It had been a bold play. Even though I wasn't sure I grasped the finer points, it did seem a stretch to be asking to advance from apprentice to re-spected elder just for managing to kill one troublesome human. On the other hand, we were being sent to rescue the Faerie Queen. I realized I'd wanted Bryn to succeed, maybe if only because I was growing to loath Riagan.

"I accept your terms," Bryn said.

Riagan nodded. "Good. Now that that's settled. You should go. Take the gargoyles and your Fledge and infiltrate the human's manor. He calls it Lydbury. You have three days until the wedding."

"Yes, Master." Bryn bowed.

Riagan waited until we were standing alongside the gar-goyles before calling out to us. "One last thing." He paused, waiting for our attention. "Godda has protected the manor well. Not only has she warded the perimeter of the grounds, she's also warded the walls of the manor itself. No transit onto the property or into the house. No Fae enters or leaves without permission."

"So how will we get in?" I asked, earning a glare from my sire.

"I would be less concerned about getting in, and more

concerned about getting out, my dear." Riagan smiled.

My mind filled with question after question. But, my sire caught my eye and frowned. I pressed my lips closed and nodded.

"Go on then," Riagan said. "What are you waiting for? An invitation?"

Bryn warped one hand around mine and tugged me into the forest. The pair of gargoyles who'd been silent as the stone of their dormant forms throughout our discussion, followed.

"Don't forget to ask him what happens to Fledges who fail, little Faerie princess." Riagan's laugh followed us into the trees.

Bryn released me. In a few strides he'd pulled far ahead. I hurried to keep up, even though it meant allowing the gargoyles to fall further and further behind. By the time Bryn stopped walking, the forest had swallowed their heavy footfalls. I'd thought we'd lost them, but when I turned, their two hulking forms loomed between the tree trunks behind me.

One of the pair whispered to the other, as though we couldn't hear him. "I still think this is a bad idea."

The one with the chunk missing from his ear, Onfroi, responded. "Why did you agree, then?"

I whispered to Bryn. "Do they know we can hear them?"

The other, Piers, stared at me. "Are you sure there's no other way?" He wrapped his tail around Onfroi's waist as he spoke.

Onfroi smoothed the tuft on the end of Piers's tail. "It's an easy job, and we need Fae magic to hatch our egg."

I inhaled a shocked breath. "So it's true then?" I asked.

"Yes. They agreed to a bargain with the twins." Bryn glanced between me and the gargoyles. "Now can we keep moving?"

"No." I shook my head. "I'm not talking about the bargain. I'm talking about the gargoyle curse."

"What curse?" Bryn asked.

"I thought every Faeling learned that story." I tried imagining Bryn as a Faeling and failed. Even a smaller version of the Fae who stood before me was nothing like what I was used to seeing running around the clearing near the Faerie Falls at festivals and feasts. In fact, now that I knew the true form of the Rogues, I realized I wasn't sure I'd seen any from their faction at our celebrations.

"Perhaps you might have already learned your Rogue lessons if you'd spent less time listening to nonsense stories in a creche," Bryn replied.

I shrugged, too excited about the gargoyles to bother arguing with him. "In this case, it appears it's not nonsense." I turned to the gargoyles to confirm my guess. "It's true. Isn't it?"

"They carry on like lovers," Piers whispered to Onfroi.

"We're not lovers." I crossed my arms. "Bryn's been assigned as my tutor. That's all." The thought of kissing that vicious mouth made me shiver.

Onfroi set one large, meaty paw on Piers's head and scratched behind Piers's ear. "Don't mind Piers, he's a bit of a romantic. Likes to think everyone's in love."

Piers flexed his wings, flapping them out before refolding them. "And here you have us signed up to kill some poor, helpless human and ruin a wedding. This can't be the only way to hatch an egg."

"Tell me about this curse," Bryn said.

I grinned, pleased to know something that Bryn did not. "The story claims that a gargoyle once kidnapped the Faerie Queen's Faeling. Filled with anger, she cursed the clan's eggs to stone. Only the touch of the Fae will release the hatchling from its prison and allow the gargoyle egg to hatch."

Piers nodded. "The bit about the Fae magic is true, at least. No one knows for sure if an ancient Faerie Queen's curse is responsible for the arrangement, or not." He shrugged his massive shoulders. "It's a theory."

"You just need any Fae to agree to free the hatchling?" Bryn asked.

"One who shares the blood of the Faerie Queen," Onfroi said.

Bryn looked at me.

"The Faerie Queen is my sister," I said. "I could help you."

Onfroi shook his head.

"Too late for that, now," Piers said.

"Hush," Onfroi hissed at his mate.

"As I said, they bargained with the twins." Bryn didn't seem at all bothered by the situation. Just as he'd dipped his chin at Riagan's taunts, he appeared to accept his master's cruelty to these sweet creatures.

Onfroi shrugged. "They've blocked our access to the queen for decades. We were desperate."

"What did you do to offend them?" Bryn asked.

"I just met that pair today." Onfroi shook his head. "It's not just us. It's all gargoyles. Though there aren't many left on account of not being able to get our eggs hatched."

"That's horrible!" I set a hand on Onfroi's arm to comfort him, but a low growl from Piers warned me away. As though I had any intention of seducing a gargoyle.

"Let's get moving," Bryn said.

"But it's not fair to involve them in this," I said. "Let's help them and send them on their way. We don't need assassins to rescue Godda. We can just lure her human away, drain him, and leave him on the forest floor to die." It would be one way of working around Godda's insistence that we not kill him.

"What we need doesn't matter any more. Each of us has been ensnared by some plot of the twins. We're in this together now, and it won't be over until we kill this Lord and return Godda to the Fae."

"The young Rogue is right," Onfroi said. "I appreciate your kindness, but there is no getting free of a deal with a Rogue."

Piers groaned. "I told you there had to be another way.

You never listen."

Onfroi turned and wrapped his wings around Piers, nudging his mate closer. "Yes. I know. You were right." He bumped his snout against Piers's, then nuzzled his neck. At first Piers tried to resist Onfroi's attention. Then Onfroi whispered, "I'm sorry."

I turned away to give them some privacy and found Bryn's eyes on me.

"And you'll listen to me next time?" Piers asked. Even though I could no longer see them, I imagined them making up.

"I will," Onfroi purred.

I grinned at Bryn. "They're adorable," I whispered.

Bryn's face remained expressionless. "We need to go."

"Can't we give them a moment?" I glanced behind me to peek at the two figures still embracing.

"We don't have time to spare. You've learned the very first step of the most fundamental ability. You still have to master feeding and trapping before you can learn the rest. If you can't feed, you'll never be able to manage illusions or transmutations."

"Are you doing this for Godda? Or are you doing this for yourself so you 'ascend,' whatever that means." I wasn't sure that I cared, and I was fairly certain I already knew the answer. But, if we were going to work together, I wanted to know for certain.

The lids of Bryn's eyes slid partly closed, leaving only a vertical slice of those black orbs visible. "Both lead to the same end, so what does it matter?"

"It matters because your priority seems to be lessons when it should be my sister." I wanted to know how to wield this Rogue magic, but Riagan said we only had three days. "The four of us can rescue Godda from whatever hold that human has on her without me learning any Rogue magic. I only need to know those things now so that you can earn your reward. This title you covet." I jabbed a finger into the center of Bryn's bare chest.

"The title I covet?" Bryn batted my hand away. "What about the title Godda bestowed on you, little hawk? Do you plan to rescue her only to fail to fulfill your sworn responsibility to her?"

"They argue like lovers." I wasn't sure which of the gargoyle pair said it, but the whispered comment caused me to take a step back.

My hands clenched and all that unused Rogue power surged within me. I couldn't control it. A wave of energy rolled off of me, rippling through the air in all directions. The trees trembled as the wave arched up and over my head until I was enclosed in a shimmering bubble, cut off from the others.

I inhaled, swaying on my feet, then collapsed. My eyes fluttered shut with my head pillowed by the mossy ground. Muffled voices, punctuated by thuds prevented me from drifting off, even as exhaustion pulled at my bones. I tried to push myself up on one elbow, but the effort was too much. I sank back to the earth, unable to remember what had brought me here and unable to care. With a sigh, I welcomed the sweet relief of sleep.

6

TRAINING an adult Fae to use powers they should have learned to control as a Faeling was proving more complicated than I'd anticipated. I had to wait until Sorcha hadn't passed out from accidentally casting an illusion years beyond her current abilities, before I could penetrate the shield she'd created. Whatever she'd done had added a solidity to the illusion that shouldn't have been there. The power she gained from feeding had somehow bled into her High Fae magic to create a dangerous and volatile mix.

In the end, my inexperience as a teacher cost us an entire day. Riagan had said we had three days, and the sun was setting on the first full day since leaving them. I wasn't sure how to interpret his guidance, so I wanted us to be ready to enter Lydbury at first light.

Once the sun set and the moon was the strongest light in the sky, the gargoyles would wake and depart, traveling ahead to spy on activity in the manor while I trained with Sorcha. Until then, the pair lay curled in an entwined lump near the base of a tree, looking more like a large boulder than two winged assassins. I had to admire their choice of ground. The section they'd chosen allowed them to blend into the scenery, but also exposed their rocky hides to whatever moonlight managed to filter through the overcast skies during the day.

Brilliant and deadly creatures with soft and sensitive hearts, they'd helped carry Sorcha until we found someplace safe to settle in for the night. Then they'd stood sentry while I rested and waited for Sorcha to wake. None of that had been part of their bargain with the twins, I was sure. If this pair were representative of their kind, I hated the twins for using them. Yet, I knew such was the way of the Rogue. They'd become a tool.

After a full day of feeding and resting, Sorcha huddled down next to the fire, warming her hands. She'd managed to trap and feed successfully without my help on the final two of the five attempts we made. The energy she'd absorbed from the humans radiated off her like the heat from the fire. Now that I knew what to watch for, it was easy to see. With nightfall almost upon us, it was time to risk another uncontrolled outburst. We only had a few hours for her to master illusions before we needed to be in position outside the gates of Lydbury.

"Come here," I said.

She lifted her head to stare at me through the flames. "Why?"

I wanted to snarl at her for asking questions and challenging my authority. That was how I'd been treated as a Fledge, but instinct warned me that wouldn't work with a student so close to my own age. Instead, I flexed my fingers and swirled my tongue behind my teeth, holding back the biting response Riagan might have offered and trading it for one more in line with words Sorcha would get from her Court-pleasing sire.

"It's time for a lesson."

She stood in one smooth, graceful motion and stepped around the fire to join me. I waited until she was next to me before I rose from my squat to stand at my full height. Just a hand's width from her body and nearly the same height, I didn't tower over her the way I did the humans I fed from. Still, I paused, watching to see if she'd pull back.

She raised her chin, angling it to match the slope of mine.

"Illusions," I said, the word forced through the choked sensation at the back of my throat. I blinked to clear my head. "Remember, think of it like a glamour, but rather than cloaking your own features to appear more human, you're projecting the illusion somewhere else."

She nodded. "All right."

"Start small or you'll eat through your fuel before you manage to cast anything properly." That seemed a safer warning than reminding her that if she wasn't careful, she might cast something so large she wouldn't be able to control it.

I paced away from the fire, to the opposite side of the clearing from the gargoyle lump. Something about Sorcha's eyes on me made me want to retreat to the shadows.

When I stopped and turned, I found she'd followed me on silent feet. "What are you doing over here?"

She shrugged. "I thought you meant for me to follow you."

"I meant for you to practice." I pressed my back against the bark of the tree we stood beneath and crossed my arms. The solidity of the trunk grounded me.

"You didn't tell me how." She stepped closer. The distance between us again reduced to what it was before.

My heart thumped against my ribs. My wrist bones absorbed the drumming, sending the vibrations up my arms and out across the surface of my skin. "I told you. It's like a glamour." I tried to put the bite of Riagan's voice into my own, but it came out sounding less like disdain and more like a plea for mercy. Like prey.

"Yes, but what should I do?" she asked.

I blinked to feel the clarity of darkness. I let the shadows fold around me like a cloak as my mind scrambled, trying to decide how best to teach something that now came as naturally to me as breathing. "Something simple. Create the illusion of a rock." I pointed to a patch of bare dirt behind her. "There."

She turned her back to me to look at the ground, and I exhaled. The thumping continued, but without her eyes on me, I could think.

She murmured words to herself. I could have caught them if I hadn't been forcing myself to stop noticing her. Her fingers flexed and curled at her sides. "A rock," she whispered.

Her long neck arced toward her shoulder as she tilted her head to the side. For a moment, she stood completely still. Then she growled. "It's not working."

I sighed. Her impatience would be the death of her.

She spun around to face me. "How can you cast a glamour on the ground? That's impossible."

Elementals and High Fae could cast a glamour on themselves to appear human, but Rogues were unique among the Fae because of what powered Rogue magic. "Use the lies."

"How?" Her brow wrinkled in frustration.

I leaned forward until my face emerged from the shadows. "Is there a rock on the ground there?" I asked.

She twisted to confirm what she already knew, then returned her little hawk eyes to mine. "No."

"If we were Elementals and could control earth magic, we could create one there. But we're not. We're Rogues. We can still make one appear there, but it won't be true. It will be a lie. Fae can't lie, but Rogues can borrow lies to fuel their magic. Use the lies."

"You said it was like a glamour. That's nothing like a glamour. That's not how glamours work."

A laugh bubbled up from my thudding heart and tumbled out my lips before I could catch it in my teeth and pull it back. "You are correct. But a glamour is the closest trick most Fae can pull, though it is nothing more than a defense mechanism meant to hide us in plain sight. This is a tool. Use the lies and learn it."

Her little hawk eyes narrowed at me. "Show me."

My nails dug into the flesh coating my ribs briefly before I let my hands drop to my sides. I pushed away from the tree and stepped toward her. She didn't flinch or back away, so I set my hands on her shoulders and turned her body to face the patch of dirt.

"There is a rock." I whispered the words past her ear as I stood behind her, holding her in place with the light pressure of my palms, feeling the power coursing through her body thrum beneath my touch.

"No there isn't." She tensed.

"Believe the lie. Show me the lie." My hands rose and fell with her breath. My eyes studied the curve of her ear, traveling up to the light dusting of pale hair that covered the pointed tip. My tongue darted out between my lips, wanting a taste.

Her body stilled. Her breath hitched, drawing me closer. "I think…" She paused. "Do you see it?" she asked.

I blinked. Darkness. I refocused on the ground just beyond the arc of her neck. "Good." I released her, stepping back into the shadow of the tree.

She was a fast learner. She was also the niece of the High Rogue. And the sister of the queen. And she'd shivered at my face. My true face. I swallowed my desire.

Sorcha turned to face me. "It wasn't even that hard." She grinned. "I just sort of plucked one of those little lies, just a tiny one, and sort of balled it up and—" She stopped her happy babbling and pounced on me. Her arms draped over my shoulders and her body pressed against me as she squeezed me and released a happy squeal. "I did it."

She pulled back and studied my face. "What's wrong? Did I do something wrong?"

"You embraced me."

She attempted to smother her laugh, but her breath escaped in short bursts through her nose, and her lips curved up in an amused smile. "You look terrified. I suppose Rogues don't hug? Is that it?"

Rogues did not hug. Still, the concept wasn't lost on me.

"Does my face no longer make you tremble?" I asked, trying to reestablish the distance between us.

Her mirth dissolved. "Do you wish it to?"

"Come." I paced away, then bent to retrieve an actual rock, setting it on a stump nearby. "You still have much to learn before dawn."

When I unfolded myself to standing, she was once again at my side. Her eyes hunted me. My heart lurched and pounded in response like a frightened rabbit.

"Can you change it?" she asked. "Your face? Like my sire and uncle do?"

I took a half step back. "That's morphing. Morphing is one of the endless tools of the Rogue." One she didn't need to learn, and one I had yet to master.

"Can you do it?" she asked.

I pulled my lips back into something resembling a smile, just so I could remind her of my sharp teeth and thick black tongue. "Would you prefer me with a different face?"

She hesitated. "I…" Whatever she'd started to say, her lips pressed together, sealing off the rest. She couldn't complete that thought without lying, and she couldn't lie without suffering Liar's Pains.

I lunged toward her, allowing my lips to part so my teeth would flash in the firelight. "You what?"

Her hand lifted until her fingers rested against my jaw. I tried to pull away, but she held my head still. Her forefinger shifted up to rest against the point of one of my front teeth.

"They're not even sharp," she said.

I sucked in air, willing my lips to close, but my tongue darted out instead, tasting. It flicked against the pad of her finger, just before my mouth responded to my command and closed, trapping the tip of her finger inside, replacing teeth and tongue with lips. Too much like a kiss.

She didn't react except to cock her head to one side like a curious bird.

My heart slammed again. One taste of her skin had flooded me with desire that refused to be ignored. She didn't want me. She was only taunting me. Tempting me.

She placed the palm of her other hand flat against my bare chest and stepped closer.

My skin warmed under her touch. Heat rose from that single point of contact, radiating up across my chest to my neck. The sensation reminded me of the ripples that skimmed across the reflecting basin, shattering the image of my face whenever the wind blew. I closed my eyes, picking through my gathered lies until I found a new face. A male face. A young priest from the temple who I'd touched years ago.

I imagined that face, scattered by the ripples, stilling as the wind calmed. When I opened my eyes, Sorcha stood before me, mouth open and eyes wide.

"How did you… ?"

It had worked. The corner of my mouth lifted the stranger's lips into a grin. "Like this a bit better, do you?"

She shook her head. Swallowed. Now there was real desire there. Written in her eyes. "It's not you." She couldn't lie.

"No, little Fledge." I stepped back to put more distance between us. The young priest had been beautiful enough to pass for Fae. I'd never seen him again, but I remembered his face. The face I wore now. The face she'd rather have as my true face. I allowed my features to morph back.

"That face… did you choose it because you're a male? Like my sire and uncle?"

"Rogues have no gender." I paced back to the tree stump.

"Oh." Her head tilted to one side as she considered that new information.

I turned to face her. "Rogues have all genders."

"Does that mean any Rogue can give birth?" she asked.

"Of course. If they choose that path."

"Rogues choose?"

"That is the power of the Rogue. To choose." This was hopeless. There was too much she didn't know.

"Have you chosen?" she asked, her voice barely above a

whisper.

"No." I paused. She would have to be satisfied with that simplified answer. There wasn't time for me to explain my choices or the choices of others. We needed to focus on the mission. "There is another type of illusion you still need to learn." I pointed to the rock I'd placed on the tree stump.

"Now what? Make it disappear?"

I shook my head. "Not yet."

Her eyes widened. "You mean you can do that?"

"Eventually you will learn to cloak objects, but first you will learn to enhance what is already there." The illusion she'd cast without guidance had been a cloaking illusion. If she tried that again and failed, we would lose another day and miss our chance to prevent Godda's wedding.

"Enhance it how?" she asked.

I studied the power radiating off of her and considered the options. She'd barely tapped into the lies she'd absorbed, so I decided to start small. "Mark it. A stripe of color will do for now."

"If I mark your silly rock, will that be all?" Her irritability hinted at the possibility of another uncontrolled outburst, but she needed to consume more of that power.

I nodded, silently sending a prayer to the Ancients that I was making the right decision. "For now. Then we feed and wait until first light."

Her eyes shifted to the lump of granite. Sweat beaded on her forehead as she concentrated.

As focused as I was on Sorcha, I failed to register the approaching hoofbeats as separate from the pounding of my pulse in my ears. It wasn't until the horses were close enough that the earth trembled under my feet, that I recognized the danger. I raised a hand and signaled for Sorcha to remain silent and glanced over to the spot where the gargoyles had been resting. The moon was bright in the sky, and they were already gone. They must have left at some point during her training, keeping quiet so they wouldn't interrupt.

"We have company," I whispered. I cloaked the fire in an illusion and pointed to the branches above us. "Fly."

"What about you?" she whispered.

"Illusions. You'll see." I stepped back into the shadows. "Hurry."

Sorcha transformed, flapping once to gain a bit of height, then soaring on silent wings to perch on a branch high above. I had only a moment more to cloak myself before the leader's horse burst into the clearing and drew up.

"The smoke was coming from here, I'd bet my life on it," he said as a second rider reined in his horse alongside.

"Nothing here now." The second of the men scratched his head as he glanced around.

Two more horses arrived, both carrying riders. The four animals spread out, circling the clearing. One shied as it neared the trees where I hid. Another tossed its head and veered away as it approached the illusion at the center of the clearing that hid our fire. The men glanced through my illusions and away.

The leader called out to his men. "Whoever was here can't have gone far. Lord Edric was clear, no one best disturb his wedding, or it'll be our heads on pikes at the feast. Hear?"

7

THE four riders criss-crossed the clearing below the branch I'd chosen as my perch. From the tops of their heads, I couldn't tell if any of them were among the group that stole Godda away. I only knew they were Edric's men, and they'd found us.

The leader of the group pointed to two of the men. "Davey and Gareth, you two head out along the south pasture. Murphy and I will go north from here to the far corner. Keep a sharp eye."

"Mite protective of that lass we scooped up in the woods, aye?" The one he'd called Davey sneered.

"Can ye blame him?" The one closest to Bryn patted the neck of his horse, trying to calm it. "I say we should have scooped up a few more while we were there. Enough of those lassies to have weddings all around."

"Too bad you're already married, Murph," said the one called Gareth.

My feathers ruffled and my beak snapped. I wanted to swoop down and gouge out his eyes, but there were too many of them. I would have to wait for my revenge. Instead, I memorized their names and promised myself that, if they had been involved in Godda's capture, I'd punish them all, but not until after the gargoyles ruined Godda's wedding.

Murphy's horse pranced nervously, coming within steps of Bryn before lurching away. In the moment before the horse reacted, I caught a glimpse of Bryn's hand reaching out to brush against the leg of the rider before it disappeared again into the cloak of illusion. If Rogues could adopt the face of any they touched, it would serve our mission well to have Bryn be able to impersonate one of Edric's trusted men.

The leader of the group reissued his command, and the pairs departed the clearing in opposite directions. Once they were gone, I circled up, high enough to mark their progress and check for any others who might be heading our way. Satisfied that we were safe for the moment, I glided down, transforming just before I reached the earth and landing with my boots on the ground to face an angry Bryn.

"They're gone," I said.

"I let my guard down." Bryn scattered the remains of the fire and doused it with dirt. "They should never have found us."

"Leave it," I said, motioning for Bryn to follow me. "We should go now, while Edric's men are out looking for us."

Bryn remained rooted in place at the center of the clearing. "There will only be more guards at the gate. And we should feed before we begin."

I grimaced. "We can feed once we're inside." While I loved the power rush that came from consuming human lies, I did not enjoy the process of feeding. We'd practiced five times already, and I'd had enough for one day.

"Too many people. Too risky," Bryn said.

There wasn't time to play it safe. "Let's at least go and check in with the gargoyles. Then I can get a sense of the wards to see what we're up against."

Bryn considered my suggestion, then nodded. "Then we feed."

I knew which way to go, but I let Bryn lead us through the dark forest, anyway. I'd seen the manor from above while I was circling the skies, watching Edric's men retreat. But, Godda's wards had prevented me from getting closer.

They were even stronger on the ground. The thrum and pulse of magic from her wards overwhelmed my senses before we reached the low iron fence surrounding the manor grounds. Only focused determination kept my feet moving toward Lydbury. It was hard to believe that humans could remain oblivious to this aching sense of wrongness that made me want to turn and run.

"This isn't Rogue magic." Bryn's shoulders hunched against the force of Godda's wards.

It didn't matter if she'd used Rogue or High Fae magic, no Fae could undo another's work. The best we could hope for would be to find an unprotected gap, or a loophole in her protections that would allow us to gain access.

As we followed the fence line around the edge of the grounds toward the main gates, I sensed for an opening. The entrance gate loomed ahead. Two stone posts each topped with a large metal globe. A sculpted dragon curled around each of the post tops, tongues flicking out of their open mouths.

The wards were different there, at the gate. I wanted to get closer to investigate, but Bryn pulled me away.

"There." Bryn pointed to a dark lump at the base of a tree nearby.

The lump shifted as we approached, and the silhouette of a pointed ear and beak-like nose lifted away from the hunched body. When the gargoyle's head turned toward us, one pointed ear became two, both whole and undamaged.

"You survived." Piers sounded a bit surprised.

"You could have warned us," Bryn snapped.

Piers shrugged. "Onfroi said we should stay at our posts."

Onfroi emerged from the darkness behind Piers. "What I *said* was there wasn't time to warn them." He flicked his tail at Piers as he glanced between Bryn and me. "And I assumed you two could handle a few humans."

I laid my palm on Bryn's forearm, hoping to prevent any further argument. "What else have you seen?" I asked.

Onfroi reached into a near-by bush and pulled out a bundle of fabric. "We lifted these from a laundry cart in town, as Bryn asked." He tossed the bundle at me. "There have been a few carts in and out. There's a guard stationed at the gate, but he hasn't been stopping the carts. He waves the drivers through, so he must recognize them."

I began to unravel the cloth and realize they'd stolen garments. A dress that I assumed was for me, plus a tunic and breeches to replace the simple loincloth that Bryn wore. I held up the dress and handed the rest to Bryn. The rough cloth had been sewn with a sleeveless bodice and long skirt, so it could be worn over my tunic and leggings.

Onfroi and Piers averted their eyes as I started unbuttoning the armored Queen's Guard vest I wore over my tunic. I tugged the dress over my head, adjusting it until the layers of fabric lay smooth against my torso. Then I reached for my vest to slip it on and fasten it over the rest.

Bryn caught my hand. "You can't wear that inside. It will give you away."

"No one in there will recognize the armor of the Faerie Queen's Guard." I scoffed.

"The fabric is too fine to pass as a ladies maid." Bryn released my hand and grabbed hold of the vest.

"I'm not going in without my armor." I tried to tug the fabric away, but Bryn wouldn't let go.

"Do you think they've kissed, yet?" Piers whispered to Onfroi.

"We can hear you," Bryn said to our companions, adding to me, "Riagan said you need to appear human."

The rattle of cart wheels trundling down the path on the other side of the trees, caught my attention. Bryn heard it, too, and stopped pulling on my vest long enough to listen. The clip clop of the horses' hooves were heading in our direction, accompanied by the tuneless whistle of the driver.

This was it. This was my chance. "I have an idea," I whispered, releasing my hold on the vest.

Bryn followed my gaze, then moved to block my path. "No."

"You need to feed before you can morph your face to pass for human, but I can do this, instead." I cast a glamour over my face and hands, making my exposed features appear more plain, my ears rounded, and my hands smaller with shorter, plumper fingers. Unlike Bryn's morphing, my real features were still there, only hidden from human eyes by Fae magic.

"It will be safer if we go together," Bryn warned.

"It won't." Adrenaline and excitement flooded my system. "Godda will sense my presence as soon as I cross that threshold. She'll suspect anyone with me. It's better if I go alone."

"But the plan—"

"Otherwise stays the same. You feed, then sneak those two in on a supply cart. But if I go first, I can distract Godda and keep her from finding you." I glanced over my shoulder. If I didn't hurry, I'd have to run after the cart and hope to draw the attention of the driver before he reached the gates. "I have to go."

Bryn's eyes narrowed. "Be careful."

"I will." I squeezed Bryn's hand once before hurrying out onto the path, ignoring the whispers from the gargoyles and waving my hand above my head to attract the attention of the driver.

The cart slowed as it approached me.

"Woah, there." The driver reined in the horses. Behind him, the load of barrels shifted and swayed. "You lost, lassie?"

A plan formed in my head, but it would rely on me casting an illusion. I batted my eyes up at the driver and sent a bit of Fae charm magic in his direction, hoping it would help. "I was supposed to be back before dark. The mistress of the manor is going to have me scrubbing chamber pots for weeks because I'm late. But my boot…"

I let my voice trail off as I lifted the hem of my long dress to reveal what I hoped would look like a worn through boot sole, if I'd succeeded in casting the illusion.

The driver shook his head. "Can't see nothing. Too dark. Where you headed?"

I sighed at the waste of magic, dropped the hem of the dress, and pointed behind me, toward the gates. "Lydbury, sir."

"Happens that I'm heading there as well. Hop on the back with the others, and I'll give you a lift." He waved toward the barrels behind him.

I hesitated. I hadn't realized there would be others. "Are you bringing supplies for the wedding?" I asked.

He nodded. "Wine and workers. Now, if you're coming, hurry up and hop on."

I grinned and made my way to the back, preparing to run if any of the humans on the cart happened to have the rare ability to see through Fae glamour. I relaxed when I spotted two young boys, both curled up against the barrels, asleep. The man who rode with them nodded to me, then helped me up. Once I was seated he slapped the side of the cart and the wheels started rolling again.

I inhaled and gripped the side rail, waiting to see what would happen when we reached the gate.

The cart slowed, and the guard waved us through, just like the gargoyles said he would. I kept my head down as we rolled past. Magic, unperceived by the humans, shimmered in the air around us as the cart penetrated Godda's wards. I exhaled the breath I'd been holding and grinned up at the receding gate posts. It worked. I was inside.

We continued to roll along the path, under trees that arched overhead, filtering the moonlight, until the trees stopped and the path widened. The cart slowed and then stopped outside the front of the manor.

I stared up at the building that loomed in front of me. A hundred of Godda's cottages could have fit inside this structure, but it lacked the warmth of my sister's home. Cold grey stone surrounded tall thin windows that provide a glimpse of darkness within. It looked like no one lived here.

The workers slid down from the back of the cart and busied themselves unloading supplies. I stood there for a moment, unsure what to do. I knew almost nothing about lady's maids, but I doubted one would climb the front steps and enter through the front door if she were sneaking home late. I started forward, remembering to limp a bit in case the driver was watching me.

I'd taken only a few steps when a figure appeared at the top of the steps. Her golden hair fluttered in the light breeze, and her eyes found mine in the darkness. She glanced past me to the supply cart, before returning her eyes to me.

I shivered under the fierceness of her glare. Part of me rejoiced at seeing her alive, even if she was dressed in human attire and glamoured to appear as one of them. The other part braced for her anger and the lecture I would no doubt receive.

"What are you doing here?" she whispered, when I'd reached the top of the front steps.

"At least one of your sisters should be here, to stand with you at your wedding."

She hushed me, glancing around to make sure that no one nearby heard what I'd said. She kept her voice low as she wrapped an arm around my shoulder and hurried me into the manor. "I told you to stay away. It isn't safe."

"You're here. Is it safe for you?"

"You were not invited."

"You don't want your sisters at your wedding."

She squeezed my arm. "Stop saying that word. I told you, little hawk, it's not safe." She pouted. "And now that you're here, I can't send you away again, or he'll know… But if you stay, you'll need a better glamour."

I remained silent, not daring to speak lest she change her mind and decide to turn me away, after all.

"If you go around looking like that, he'll know who you really are."

I thought of one of the women whose lies I'd consumed and adjusted my glamour to alter the color of my hair and dull the color of my dress. "Is this better?"

"You look like one of the peasants, but I suppose that's all right. He never pays much attention to them." She paused outside the door to a room and waved me inside. "Stay close and don't wander off."

My eyes roamed over the interior woodwork, the high ceilings, and the chandeliers. "If I did, I'd surely get lost."

She cut across the empty room, heading for the doors on the far side. "Not a word about who you really are, understand?"

"I promise." I hurried to catch up.

"Good. Now. Why are you here?" She ushered me out of the room and down another hallway.

"I told you. I didn't want you to be alone on your wedding day."

She stopped at the bottom of a wide stairway. "That's sweet of you, but I can take care of myself."

"Of course you can, you're—"

She cut me off before I could finish the thought. "I'm nothing. Not anymore."

I blinked at her. "You'd rather be Lady of this manor?"

"If you intend to stay, follow me." She led me up the stairs and down yet another long hall to a large sitting room that opened to a bedroom beyond. "This is my room. You'll attend me through the wedding. Then you'll return."

I turned in a slow circle, taking in the room. "Agreed." I stopped when I faced her again. "I only want you to be happy. We all do."

Her lips pressed together. "What did I say about who you are?"

I winced. "Sorry."

"Don't forget again. If you do, you could put everyone in danger." She pointed toward the far wall. "There's a small room through that door. You'll stay there. I'll go make the arrangements. Stay in here until I return."

I nodded.

She locked eyes with me, then turned and left the room, closing the door behind her. Once she was gone, I crossed to the windows and found that one actually led out onto a shallow balcony overlooking the front of the manor. I stepped out and searched the tree line beyond the gates for any sign of Bryn.

A hand closed around my arm, pulling me back inside. I turned to find Godda, back already, her beautiful face pinched in anger.

"When I said to stay in here, I meant inside. Are you trying to draw attention to yourself?"

"I'm sorry." I rubbed my arm where her hand had gripped me.

She glanced around the room, then stepped closer to me and spoke in a whisper. "He'll kill you all if he can't have me. I'd gladly trade my crown for my sisters. He's not unkind, he just knows more than he should. This is the only way to keep our kin safe. Do you understand?"

"So you don't love him?"

"Love." She laughed and waved a hand. "It's just a tool, little hawk."

I'd heard those words before. I wondered if she meant it the same way that Bryn did. Was love one of the tools of the Rogue? If that's what Godda believed, then maybe we were wrong to try to stop this wedding.

A heavy fist pounded on the door.

"That's him. Say nothing," she hissed at me. Then she turned to face the vibrating wood slab that separated us from her betrothed. "Come in."

The door opened and a dark-haired man wearing a tunic and breeches stepped into the room followed by two men with swords strapped around their waists. The men with swords waited by the door as their master walked toward Godda.

"The driver of that cart outside asked after a maid of

yours. Said she'd been caught out with a bad boot. He hoped you'd take it easy on the lass." His eyes slid past Godda and landed on me. "Is this her?"

My sister stepped aside so he could get a good look at me. "I was just sending her off to bed."

His eyes narrowed. "I don't remember this one."

"She's here to help for the wedding."

Edric stepped toward Godda and tilted her face up to his. "So you *will* marry me tomorrow?"

"I will marry you and stay by your side until death parts us, but only if you agree to the promise I asked of you." She stood still with her spine straight.

He twisted a piece of her golden hair around one finger. "You still insist on this promise?"

"Yes, my lord." She didn't smile or lean into his caress. Instead she continued to stand firm and unyielding.

Edric's jaw clenched. His eyes flicked to me, then back to my sister. "Right." He grimaced, then forced a more pleasant smile. "I promise, I will never threaten your kin folk or question you about them, ever again."

"Swear it in blood." She pointed to the knife sheath attached to his belt.

His dark brows pulled together, casting shadows across his eyes. He scowled at me, then glanced back at his guards before returning his attention to Godda. "Is this truly necessary?"

Godda reached out and removed the knife sheathed at his waist. "I insist."

"Out!" He barked the order at the guards, or so it seemed to me. They retreated to the hall, but when I didn't move, he pinned me with his stare. "What are you waiting for, girl?"

"She can stay." Godda said. Then she sliced the skin at the base of her palm and held out the knife for him to take.

He stared at the blood dripping down her wrist, threatening to ruin the embroidered cuff of her long-sleeved gown. His eyes flicked to me, then back to my sister.

Godda offered the hilt of the blade for him to take and waited, silently.

He hesitated only a moment longer, then swiped the blade against the base of his own palm and pressed his hand against hers. Their blood mingled, sealing the oath.

"Thank you, my love," she whispered, rising up on her toes to kiss him.

8

I WAITED until the cart rolled away, taking Sorcha with it, before retreating to rejoin the gargoyles.

"You know she's not coming back." Piers whispered to Onfroi as I approached. He didn't realize that, given his proximity to me and my Fae hearing, it was as though he was shouting his thought directly into my ear.

"She'll be back," Onfroi replied.

For a moment I wondered who the gargoyle intended to reassure, me or Piers. I didn't like that Sorcha had gone ahead without us. But there was nothing I could do about it.

She had been right about me being too drained to morph. What she didn't know was that I had only once successfully managed to completely change my face, and I'd done it for her. I hoped I could do it again. Any disguise I adopted would need to be convincing, and it would need to last for some time. If it slipped, I would be exposed. Glamouring my natural Fae form would not be enough to hide what I was from the humans.

"I need to feed now and find us a cart," I said. "You two wait here and keep an eye on the gate. I'll be back before daybreak." I started in the direction of the village, but didn't get very far.

Riagan appeared between the trees ahead of me. Then Rowan materialized behind him a moment later.

"Where is your Fledge?" Riagan asked.

I cringed. "Inside the manor, master."

"I see… Then why are the lot of you still lurking around out here?"

"The main gate isn't warded as thoroughly the rest of the manor, so Sorcha was able to sneak past the guard on a passing supply cart. She went ahead to distract Godda so she wouldn't sense our arrival."

"Has she completed her training?" Riagan asked.

"Yes, master." I'd taught her to feed and how to craft basic illusions. She needed much more practice to master all of it, but I'd taught her enough that, with luck, I might be able to place her with a willing mentor once this was over.

"She can cast an illusion and cloak objects?" Rowan surprised me by speaking up and asking after his offspring. I noted his interest and concern, which meant Riagan had as well.

I nodded. "She cast the illusion of a rock on the ground, then tricked the driver of the cart by disguising her boot sole."

Riagan scoffed. "That's barely different than a glamour and hardly demonstrates an ability to cloak."

"It's enough," Rowan said.

"We'll see." Riagan flashed me a sly smile. "Bryn still needs to find a mentor willing to take on such an unusual Apprentice. Until then, Sorcha remains a Fledge and Bryn cannot advance from Apprentice to Candidate."

I silently cursed my parent for ever placing me with such a sadistic and power hungry mentor. In her hubris, she'd born me of her own seed—something only Rogues could do—and tutored me herself before my power caught the eye of the twins. Then she'd lost a bargain with Riagan, and in the process, sealed my fate, making him my mentor. By Rogue law, I was stuck with him until I passed my Confirmation exam, or thanks to our bargain, until I completed this mission successfully.

He'd taken charge of me after my twelfth turn around the sun only to hold me back from advancing, turn after turn. My natural abilities threatened him so much that he'd refused to teach me morphing, insisting I should be able to figure it out on my own. Now, in my thirtieth turn, I was likely the oldest Apprentice Rogue in the history of Rogues. All because he had refused to assign me a Faeling to tutor, insisting it would distract from my training, until Sorcha came along.

Successfully training a Fledge and placing them with a mentor was the only requirement for advancing from Apprentice Rogue to Candidate Rogue. Most Apprentices advanced to Candidate before their fifteenth turn around the sun. So, even though I trained like a Candidate under Riagan, with or without his assistance, I remained an Apprentice. And now that I had managed to train a Fledge, he still refused to acknowledge my success.

Rowan stepped forward. "I will take Sorcha as my Apprentice."

I couldn't keep the shock from showing on my face. Luckily, Riagan didn't see my reaction. He had already spun away to face his twin.

"Impossible. She is your offspring. You cannot also be her mentor."

"What does it matter, brother?" Rowan held his arms out wide, pleading. "There is no rule against it."

"No. It isn't done." Riagan turned his back on his brother so he could face me. "You will have to place her with another Rogue."

"I am afraid that I cannot. Rowan has offered, and I accept." I bowed my head to hide my glee. I had waited too long for this. I didn't know why Rowan had chosen this moment to stand up to his brother, but I wasn't about to waste the opportunity he offered.

Riagan's bare feet paced the ground in front of me. As the

silence stretched, I dared to lift my head.

"Your mission hasn't changed, Candidate Bryn." Riagan used my new title as a weapon to remind me of my place and what I stood to lose if I failed. His manipulation succeeded.

"Deliver the gargoyles, kill the human, and bring Godda back to the Fae." As I recited the words, my joy shriveled under the pressure of the daunting task ahead. The title I'd finally earned suddenly meant nothing.

"Yes." Riagan extended a finger and set the sharp point of his nail against my bare chest. "Make sure the human dies, and be prepared. My offspring might try to protect him. She must not get in the way of this plan."

"Yes, Master." His advice made it seem as though he wanted me to succeed, but since I knew that couldn't be true, there had to be another layer to his plan.

His nail pressed into my skin. "If you don't bring her back, I'll make sure you never advance to the ranks of the Confirmed. Do you understand?"

I nodded. Hatred for him churned inside my chest, but years of practice kept me from showing my emotions.

"Good." He lifted his finger and dropped his hand. "You may go, now. I'd like a word with the gargoyles. Alone." He grinned.

I dipped my head and waited for him to move past me to join the gargoyles. When I started toward the village, Rowan laid a hand on my arm.

His eyes narrowed, and his voice dropped to an almost imperceptible whisper. "Do your best and let me handle Riagan."

His words reminded me why it was Riagan who had gained the title of High Rogue and not his twin. Rowan wanted me to feel relief, but he could not protect me. I was not one of the High Fae. I was a Rogue, and I would beat Riagan like a Rogue, even if it took me centuries.

I didn't want Rowan's pity or his help, but I needed him to continue to think of me as a meek and respectful Candidate.

"Thank you, Master."

Rowan released me, and I hurried away, eager to put distance between me and the twins. Eager to be done with this mission. *Deliver the gargoyles. Kill the human. Bring Godda back to the Fae.* The conditions of my freedom. *What could Riagan want with the gargoyles?*

My mind spun scenarios, concocting and discarding schemes, as my feet carried me closer to the human village. I could have transported myself there, but the rhythm of my feet against the earth helped me think.

The sky had gone from inky black to smokey grey by the time I reached the outskirts of the town. Birds chirped but no bodies roamed in the stillness of the pre-dawn. A good time for feeding, if I could find the right human to lure.

I needed to steal the face of one with a cart destined for Lydbury, if possible. If I couldn't find or lure a cart driver, I'd feed off what I could lure and use the face of Edric's man to gain control of what I needed.

I'd like a word with the gargoyles. Alone. Riagan's words haunted my thoughts as I sniffed the air, searching out my prey. I pushed them aside and focused my attention on the stables. A young human moved inside. Most children were too weak to feed on, and their lies weren't juicy enough to fuel much magic. I started to turn my attention elsewhere when another presence joined the boy.

Snippets of conversation drifted to my ears on the wind as I crept closer.

"…delivery…Lydbury…ready the cart…"

I licked my lips in anticipation. The lure for this one would be easy. I crouched outside the entrance and crafted the illusion of a basket of pastries on a table just inside the door. Then I waited for the man to notice.

"Who left these here? Did your Ma bring this for your breakfast?" The man stopped near the table and glanced around, perhaps searching the darkness for the boy's mother.

I was about to draw him closer when the boy stepped up

alongside the man.

"Where?" The boy was looking at my illusion, but didn't see it.

Icy fear crept down my spine. I scrambled back, pulling the shadows around me like a cloak, but it was too late.

The boy tugged at the man's sleeve and pointed. "There's something out there," he said, staring directly at me. He had the sight, or a charm of protection.

I disappeared, transporting myself back to the edge of the forest. I'd need to find someone else to lure, but at least I knew where to find a cart destined for the manor.

The sky had lightened by another shade, and more humans were up and moving around the village. A man stumbled out of a decrepit inn near the stables and tripped on the cobblestone path. I sniffed and scented his secret desires. A sheet fluttered on a clothesline alongside the inn, and I crafted an illusion that gave the hint of a matronly form. Enough to fool the bleary eyed man sneaking home in the pre-dawn. He hurried away from the form, and into the alley behind the inn where I transported myself to intercept him.

It didn't take long to extract his lies and send him on his way. Once he was gone, I closed my eyes and prepared to try on the face I'd stolen from Edric's man. When I'd succeeded before with Sorcha, I'd wanted to be that priest enough to believe the lie. I decided to take that approach again.

I thought of Riagan and the bargain we'd made for my freedom. I reminded myself of Sorcha, already inside the manor and depending on me to execute my end of the plan. Then I concentrated on the face of that rider and how it would bring me close to his master. The face that could bring me my freedom.

When I opened my eyes, I bent over a puddle to inspect my work. The rider's lips grinned back at me. But shouts from the stable drew my attention away from my new face. I hurried out of the ally and toward the commotion.

The boy with the sight might still see the truth behind the

lie of my face. So, I kept the two women who had also come
to investigate between me and the stable entrance until I could
be sure the boy was gone.

Outside the stable, a loaded cart and harnessed horse
waited for their driver. But the stable boy and the driver were
nowhere to be found, and the cart wasn't quite ready. One
barrel lay propped against the back of the cart, as though it had
slid off to rest on the ground. Except, it had come to rest on
something that looked like a sack of grain. The women in front
of me sucked in a breath just as I saw the problem.

The driver wasn't missing. He was pinned under the
barrel. I needed him alive. Elbowing past the women, I hurried
toward the driver and crouched down at his side.

"Can you lift it?" one of the women asked.

The pulse of life had thinned from a raging river to a frag-
ile thread. "Hurry and get help," I said.

"I think the boy went—"

I cut her off with a wave of my hand and a Riagan-like
command. "Go!"

The women scurried away. If I fed from this man, I would
take more than his lies. I'd likely take his life. But I'd also
have his face and his cart. There wasn't time to delay. Every
moment I wasted, the sun crept closer to the horizon.

I pushed the barrel off, hoisting it up onto the cart. Then I
bent and set the tips of my fingers against the man's temples to
relieve him of his burdens. His eyelids fluttered when I pulled
my hands away. I pulled him into an empty stall and left him,
reminding myself that humans lived and died in the blink of
a Fae eye, and they didn't require a queen's magic to safely
fade. If his death helped return Godda to her throne and kept
Fae magic controlled by the Fae, then it was worth it.

I settled myself on the driver's bench and guided the horse
out of the village before anyone could return. Once I passed
the guidepost marker, and the cobblestone path turned to gravel, I concentrated on shifting my features to match the driver's.
Then I urged the horse to pick up the pace. The gravel thinned,

replaced by packed earth, and the cart rattled along, bouncing over every rock and threatening to stick in every divot. I drove the horse harder until we traveled at a reckless pace, in a race with the sun.

The gargoyles would turn to stone when that glowing orb crested the horizon in the east. I needed to reach them before then. I didn't have the strength to lift the two granite statues they would become once they shifted. They would need to step up onto the cart themselves, or I'd have to wait until sunset to load them. By then, the gates would be locked in preparation for Edric and Godda's wedding.

I took the next turn too sharp, lifting the wheels up off the road. With one hand, I gripped the bench to keep from sliding. With the other, I yanked the reins to guide the horse. The cart wobbled beneath me, threatening to roll. The horse swerved under my direction. Then the wheels slapped down with a thump. My heart raced and my palms sweat, but I didn't slow our pace.

Another turn and the gates of Lydbury loomed ahead. I searched the trees that bordered the path, evaluating where I could stop and load two gargoyles onto the back without drawing the attention of the guard. As I considered my options, four riders galloped past the cart, two on each side, heading for the gates ahead.

The cart horse pranced and pulled. I called out to calm it, sending a bit of Fae charm along to ease the beast, as I kept my eyes on the riders ahead. One glanced back. I recognized the face I'd stolen.

I slowed the cart horse to a walk. I couldn't stop with their attention on me. So, I continued forward and waited for the riders to pull ahead. The one who'd looked back reined in his horse and called out to the others. They stopped and started to circle back toward me.

There was no way they could recognize me, not with this face. Realization dawned as they rode closer. It wasn't me. It was this face they recognized.

9

I WOKE before dawn in the little room adjacent to Godda's bedchamber. Even though the manor contained more
rooms than I'd been able to count, Godda had sent me to
bed in the smallest of the ones connected to her chamber,
and I didn't even have it all to myself. Two other maids, both
sleeping, occupied cots on the wall opposite from me. They'd
been in more or less the same position since I'd entered the
room a few hours earlier, and they didn't budge as I sat up
and pulled my dress over my head.

The room was barely large enough to contain the three of
us and our cots. A chest of drawers occupied the only remaining space along the windowless stone walls. If there had been
windows, particularly ones with a view of the gates, I wouldn't
have minded the sleeping arrangements. But without any way
to know what was going on outside, I'd barely been able to
rest as I laid on my cot and worried about Bryn's arrival.

Knowing he could be crossing through the gates at any
moment, I needed to keep a close eye on Godda. She'd been
alerted by my arrival, so I guessed that her wards would make

her aware of any Fae who crossed onto the manor grounds, even if they arrived through the gates. If that was true, I wanted to be there to distract her when Bryn attempted entry.

In my bare feet, I slipped out of the room and padded over to the large bed in Godda's room. The curtains were pulled, leaving only a small gap where I could glimpse my sister's sleeping form, curled under the blankets. I stood still for a moment, waiting to see if she'd wake. When she didn't, I crept toward the balcony window.

I didn't dare set foot on the balcony again, just in case she'd protected it with more of her wards that alerted her when someone crossed the threshold. I still hadn't determined how she'd known I'd crept out there the previous evening, but that seemed the most likely reason. Pushing aside the window covering, I squinted through the foggy glass to view the light grey morning.

I scanned the view until I located the gates and the path leading to the village. A low mist swirled around the treetops, but otherwise nothing moved outside. Then, four riders on horseback burst into view. They were too far away to make out their forms. I squinted at them, trying to find any sign that they might be the same four who had nearly found me and Bryn in the forest.

As I watched, one of the four turned to look back, down the road. I followed the direction of his gaze and spotted a cart loaded with barrels coming around the bend in the road. The four riders started back along the path to intercept the cart, but I didn't see what happened next. Godda pulled my hand away from the window covering.

"Get away from there." She kept her voice low, but her tone was fierce with warning.

"There aren't any windows in my room," I whispered.

"You don't need any windows. You need to stay where you cannot be seen." She tugged my wrist, pulling me away from the glass. Then she froze. Every muscle in her body tensed as she reached out with her senses.

"What is it?" I asked.

"Company," she said. "Get back in your room and stay there. If the others ask, say you're feeling ill." She released me and started toward the dress laid out on the chest at the foot of her bed.

More than anything, I wanted to know what had caused her alarm, but I couldn't ask without possibly giving away my own concerns. If she figured out there was a connection between me and Bryn, I wouldn't be able to deny it. I had to pretend I hadn't noticed her distress and find a way to distract her so that I could and delay her from finding Bryn.

"Let me help with that," I offered, reaching for her dress.

She froze again, her head cocked to one side, listening. "Here." She shoved the dress at me, then pulled her nightshirt over her head. "Hurry."

I helped her into the dress, but struggled while fastening up the back. My mind was on Bryn and the gargoyles, and I'd fumbled the laces by missing several holes. "Sorry."

She half-turned and batted my hands away. "I can do it. Go on and get your shoes. I've changed my mind. You're coming with me."

"Oh." I dropped my hands to my sides, but otherwise didn't move. "Are you sure?" If I went with her, I might be able to help Bryn. At least more than I could if I were forced to stay here.

"Go on." She waved me back toward the little adjacent room. "If I leave you here, you'll be back at that window the moment I'm gone. It's easier to protect you if you're with me. Then I don't have to worry about what he might do if he finds you alone."

If Edric was as dangerous as she claimed, Riagan was right to send the gargoyles to kill him. "You made him swear a blood oath—"

"That will only protect you so long as he doesn't know who you are, and it might not even if he does." She shook out a wool shawl and prepared to arrange it like a mantle around her shoulders. "Now stop standing there like a fool and finish getting dressed."

I didn't want her to change her mind again and leave me. So I hurried back into the small room to retrieve my leggings, untangling them from the knot of blankets I'd pushed to the end of my cot. I tugged them on under my long dress, then sat to fasten my boots, wishing once again that Bryn had let me bring along my armored vest. He was right, though. It would have been out of place here. But I didn't like feeling so exposed.

The two maids in the little room slept through my rustling about, or at least pretended to. When I rejoined Godda, I asked her about them.

"Leave them be. Best if you don't speak to them at all." She waved a hand in their direction. "Edric assigned them to me when I arrived. They're meant to keep tabs on me when he's out, like the pair of guards outside the door. So remember, not a word. Stay quiet and stay by my side."

I nodded. If Bryn had made it through the gate with the gargoyles, they must be on the grounds somewhere. I hoped they found a place to hide before Godda found them.

When we stepped out into the hall, the guards snapped to attention. Godda ignored them and turned left. I followed a half step behind, and the guards fell in a few steps behind me. We'd made it to the first turn when Edric stepped around the corner.

"Good," he said. "You're awake." His eyes traveled over Godda's body. "I was on my way to tell you we have company."

If Edric also knew about this 'company' arriving, then maybe it hadn't been Bryn after all. I should have felt relief, but instead skin prickled with worry. I twisted my fingers into the fabric of my skirt to keep them from curling into fists. For the first time, I considered what would happen if Bryn didn't arrive as planned. I'd promised Godda that I wouldn't harm Edric. I couldn't complete the mission and bring her home on my own.

"You'll need to go change into something a bit more… formal. The Bastard Duke William heard I was to be married and rode out with fifty of his men to attend our wedding." Edric's scowl gave no hint of how he felt about the arrival of these men. As though he knew I was studying him, his eyes lifted from Godda and fell on me.

My sister attempted to pull his attention away. "This is the only dress I have, my love, and the maids have been busy preparing another for our wedding."

His scowl deepened. Then a cunning smile curled his lips into a grin that reminded me of Riagan and sent a shiver down my spine. "Now that I consider it, I think that dress will do just fine for the Duke. Your beauty will shine through even in beggars' rags, and if you are too tempting, he might try to steal you away and forget how much he needs my allegiance. Then I would have no choice but to cut him down, and I would rather avoid bloodshed on our wedding day."

I shifted, impatient to get moving again and get away from this jealous man who thought he could own my sister. She was the Faerie Queen, and he a mere mortal.

Edric caught my movement and pinned me with his dark eyes. "Where are the maids I sent to attend you?" he asked Godda.

"They are still sleeping, my love." Godda placed her hand on his arm. "Let's not keep our guests waiting."

Edric glared at me a moment longer, then allowed Godda to turn him away and guide him down the hallway. I trailed along behind, keeping just ahead of the guards, but drifting farther and farther back, wanting to keep plenty of distance between me and Godda's human. Mortal or no, the menacing way he looked at me made me think he could see right through my glamour and knew exactly who and what I was.

The fact that William seemed to frighten Edric gave me some joy. Perhaps the presence of these men and their effect on Edric would distract Godda from Bryn's arrival. I hoped that they would hurry.

We entered the large room Godda had led me through after my arrival, only now it was no longer empty. Armored human males filled the room. They were packed too close together to count. The largest of them, in brawn if not in height, stood slightly apart from the rest. As Edric made his way toward him, the man turned his head on his thickly muscled neck and smiled.

"Lord Edric, the tales do not do her justice. Your Lady is perhaps even more beautiful than I'd heard." He reached for Godda's outstretched hand, cupping it in both of his, and dipped his head to kiss it.

Edric's hand twitched, then settled on the hilt of the sword strapped around his waist.

Godda curtsied. The sight of the Queen of the Fae bowing to a mortal man made my stomach turn. "Your Grace is too kind," she said.

William chuckled. "Well that is something I've never been accused of before. How refreshing. Wherever did you find her?" William asked.

"Lord Edric came across my cottage while hunting one day." Godda explained, even though William had directed the question to Edric as though my sister was a doe who'd suddenly learned to speak in the human tongue and not the crowned leader of Faerie, fluent in the languages of all beings.

I wanted to force the brute to his knees and insist he show my sister the respect she deserved. But, I'd promised Godda. Not a word. So I clenched my teeth to cage my tongue and kept my head down.

"Well, Lord Edric, you always were the better hunter. I'll give you that. Perhaps she has a sister I might claim?" William grinned at Godda's human.

I tensed.

Edric opened his mouth to speak, but Godda turned her head toward him. One look from her must have reminded him of his promise. "I'm afraid I cannot help you there, Your

Grace."

"Too bad. Perhaps when I am King you might change your mind." He released Godda's hand and reached into the leather pouch that hung from his belt. "And until I have a woman of my own to spoil, I'll just have to spoil yours."

"Your Grace's presence is gift enough." Godda's diplomatic words, meant to reassure Edric, appeared to have the opposite effect.

Her human took a step closer to their guest. Edric stood almost a full head taller than the burly Duke, but if he hoped that his height might intimidate the man, he was mistaken. William continued, undeterred.

He extracted a golden band from his purse and held it up so it might better catch the morning light streaming in through the tall windows. "Permit me the honor of presenting you with a small gift in celebration of this joyful day." He offered the hammered metal to Godda.

She extended her arm and allowed him to slide the band over her fingers until it dangled from her wrist. The golden metal matched the hue of her hair. Both gleamed with an otherworldly glow, lighting up the contours of her face, despite the glamour that hid her Fae features.

"Consider it a taste of what's to come once I'm King, should your Lord decide to ally with me." William tucked his thumbs into his belt and preened.

Edric grumbled his appreciation, then suggested William and his men retreat to the archery range for a bit of sport while refreshments were prepared and the musicians assembled to tune their instruments. With the promise of a competition, followed by food and dancing, and then a wedding, William and his men followed Edric out of the manor.

Once they'd left, Godda sighed with relief. "That went as well as could be expected." She held her wrist up to admire William's gift. "It's quite nice, don't you think?"

"For a human," I said. "I suppose it is." I resented the lengths she was forced to go to in order to keep up this charade, and I despised Edric for whatever he had done to keep her tied to him. These humans were all beneath her.

Godda scolded me with a look. "Come with me. I want to keep an eye on this group. There was something off about their arrival. I'm worried that…"

Her voice trailed off, and she left the rest unsaid as a cluster of women burst into the room and hurried toward us. The women all wore scarves draped over their hair, fastened in place with crown-like bands. The leader of the trio was a plump woman with smooth round cheeks and bright green eyes that matched the color of the shawl she wore over her plain wool dress.

She stopped in front of us and dipped a brief curtsy before speaking. "Lady Godda," she said. "We've been searching all over the manor for you."

The two women who stood behind her kept their heads down, but something about them seemed familiar.

"It appears you have found me."

"Emma and Rose were disturbed when they awoke and found you already gone." The woman gestured to the two maids behind her who I now recognized as the pair who'd been sleeping in the room with me.

"You may have noticed that we have company." Godda gestured to the door. "I couldn't keep them waiting."

"Yes, my Lady." The woman bobbed her head. "Now that we've found you, we've come to lead you back to your rooms. Your wedding dress is ready for a fitting."

"It can wait. I have other obligations. Our guests will need food and entertainment." Godda started forward, angling her body to walk around them.

The woman laid a meaty hand on Godda's elbow, preventing her from advancing. "Allow me to see to that, my Lady. It is your wedding day. You should be in your rooms, resting."

Godda remained silent a moment, staring down at the point where the woman's skin pressed against her sleeve and allowing the woman to squirm a bit for being so bold as to tell her superior what she should be doing.

The woman released Godda and opened her mouth to speak, but Godda silenced her with a wave. At least with these women she retained some semblance of the power she'd had as our queen.

"I think I would prefer a walk in the gardens. Alone." Godda paused, watching the woman for a reaction. "But first I will accompany Rose and Emma back to my room so that they may oversee the fitting. Then I will leave them there to assist with the final alterations."

"Yes, my Lady." The apple cheeked woman ducked her head and curtsied again.

Before she'd completed her bow, Godda turned and paced away. One of the maids hurried after her. The other hung back and fell into step beside me. I slowed, hoping she would continue ahead to join her friend, but she matched my speed. Annoyed, I turned my head to glare at her, only to find her grinning at me.

"Interesting. You don't appear to like this face as much as the other I borrowed."

10

SORCHA gaped at me. The fact that I'd tricked her, and hopefully tricked Godda as well, thrilled me. Sorcha didn't know this was only my fourth successful morph, nor did she realize this was the most complicated impersonation I'd yet attempted. The curves on this maid's body were so unlike the lean planes that comprised my own natural form that I'd needed to sculpt more than just my face to adopt her likeness. Given how much of our mission relied on me being able to accomplish this important bit of Rogue magic, I wasn't sure I wanted to share that with Sorcha. But this achievement wasn't the only thing that had my heart racing.

My body pulsed with the potential for magic. I'd fed well and escaped the scrutiny of Edric's men. I'd smuggled the gargoyles through Lydbury's gates, and there were still many hours until the gargoyles could shift out of their stone forms. Even though their power came from the moon, they could not walk the earth in the sunlight. So, I had time to share my good news with Sorcha. I wanted to let her know she was officially no longer a Fledge. No longer *my* Fledge.

Sorcha glanced ahead of us, then behind, making sure we wouldn't be overheard before speaking. "When did you…?" Her voice trailed off as she gestured to my borrowed face and form.

"That duke and his men arrived just in time to provide an ideal distraction, giving me time to load Riagan's gifts onto the cart I borrowed from a wine merchant. When I arrived, I found this maid lingering in the kitchen, alone." I gestured to the face and figure I'd adopted.

"Where is she now?"

I hesitated before responding, remembering how Sorcha hadn't wanted to harm the humans she'd fed from. I didn't think she would approve of the state I'd left this maid in, and I couldn't lie. The poor human's mind had been layered in lies and provided me with quite the feast in addition to a useful face.

"Do you really want to know?" I asked.

Sorcha frowned. "If we leave a trail of bodies, Godda is going to find out and know that something's going on."

"Well then, what do you suggest I do instead? Would it be better to have the maid running around while I'm impersonating her?" As the whispered words flew from my mouth, I realized I was snapping at her.

Sorcha glared at me out of the corner of her eye. "I suppose not," she muttered.

I offered hope in place of an apology. "She was still breathing when I left her."

Her gaze was fixed on Godda's back, ahead of us, and she didn't respond.

"If it makes you feel better, I'll check on her once Riagan's gifts are in place," I said.

She turned her head at that. "Where did you leave them?"

"With the cart."

"You left them alone? What if someone unloads the cart while you're gone? If they're moved and Godda finds them before we do, she'll destroy them." Sorcha managed to keep her voice low while still conveying her annoyance.

"I thought you'd want to know that we made it through the gates." This was not how I'd expected this conversation to go. My excitement drained away. I should have waited to find her until my portion of the mission was complete.

"Now I know, and now you should go." She waved me away with a flick of her wrist.

Ahead of us, the guards accompanying Godda had stopped outside a large oak door. Sorcha was right. If I didn't leave now, I'd be stuck inside Godda's chamber with the other maid. "Right. Stay close to Godda, and I'll find you at the feast."

"Wait." She reached out to grab hold of my sleeve, but stopped short of touching me once she knew she had my attention. "Will you look like that? At the feast?" she asked.

"No. It will have to be someone else. I'll find you." I pivoted, searching for an open doorway I could slip into to hide until the others were safely inside Godda's room.

"Be careful." Sorcha's whisper reached my ears just as I turned down what I hoped would be an empty hallway.

I paused and listened, waiting to see if I would be followed. I cursed Riagan for maneuvering us into accepting this mission. It wasn't as though either of us had any experience running Rogue missions to serve the Fae—especially not ones that involved assassinating the lover of an abdicated Faerie Queen. If he'd really wanted Edric dead and Godda returned to her throne, he should have sent a more experienced Rogue.

That thought nagged at me, begging to be examined fully. But, there wasn't time to think. I needed to get back to the gargoyles. Since the hall remained silent, I took another moment to get my bearings. We'd travelled up from the ballroom and down a long hall that led toward the back of the manor. I'd left the cart under a tree outside the stables, close to the entrance to the manor's kitchens, which were also on the back side of the house. If I could find my way back to the kitchens, I could find my way back to the cart.

Transporting myself there was out of the question. Even though it might be possible to move around like that within the confines of Lydbury, there were too many people out and about on the grounds at this hour of the morning to risk it. If a human saw me appear out of thin air, I would be forced to add to the body count. Sorcha was right to want to minimize unnecessary human deaths.

I started down a hall that appeared to run parallel to the backside of the manor. When it intersected with another, I turned right, hoping that would lead back to the main staircase at the front of the house. From there I'd be able to retrace my steps back to the kitchens. As I walked, I listened and practiced what I might say if anyone confronted me. That aspect of impersonation was one I'd almost failed already. I didn't plan to make the same mistake twice.

When Edric's men had spotted me on the cart, wearing the wine merchant's face, they'd decided to stop for a chat. They'd made it clear by their greeting that we were supposed to be old friends. If they hadn't been distracted by the unexpected arrival of the Duke's party, they would have discovered I was an imposter as soon as I opened my mouth.

Once this mission succeeded, I planned to send that Duke a bottle of Faerie wine to express my gratitude. Though he would never know what it was, where it had come from, or why it had been sent, his strength would increase from consuming it, and my debt to him would be repaid. But first, I had the not small matter of moving two stone gargoyles into position inside the manor so that, when they woke, they could execute their half of their bargain with Riagan. I would need help for that. And I would need a different face.

Using the face of one of Edric's men might allow me to command others without question, but it would also bring familiarity and attention. I wouldn't be able to keep up the facade in a household where many knew that face. Likewise, this maid's face would get me back to the kitchens without too many questions, but she would certainly be out of place

unloading a wine cart. I would have to return to impersonating
the wine merchant and hope I didn't encounter more of his
friends among Lydbury's servants.

I spotted the staircase just ahead and increased my pace.
At the bottom, I continued straight to another, narrower hall
that ended in a plain wooden door that swung on well greased
hinges and marked the entrance to the working portion of the
manor. Once I was through, I turned left and ducked into the
supply closet where I'd left the maid, shutting the door behind
me. She remained slumped on the floor where she'd collapsed,
but her heart still beat a faint rhythm. Sorcha would be pleased
about that. Unfortunately, there wasn't time to move the young
female or revive her.

I changed back into the clothes I'd been wearing when I
arrived and left the maid's long tunic and wraps in a heap near
her sleeping body. Then I slipped out of the closet, leaving the
door ajar so someone might notice and find the maid inside.

Nearby, the kitchen was bursting with activity. I wanted
to avoid it, but I didn't know another way out to the stables,
and I didn't want to waste time trying to find one. So long as
Edric was out on the grounds with the Duke, I would have
easy access to the area around his chamber and could hide the
gargoyles before he returned.

I hesitated a moment longer outside the kitchen door,
plotting a course through the madness. Then plunged inside,
planning to keep my head down and avoid all encounters. That
didn't last long.

"You, there!" A voice called out over the clanging of pots
and pans.

I hoped whoever it was had not been speaking to me, and
I picked up my pace.

"Hey! You!" The shouts were pitched in my direction, but
I didn't dare look up.

"Stop him." A woman chopping vegetables pointed to me
with her knife.

Someone nearby snagged my elbow and pulled me to a

halt. "Mama Marge is talking to you." The woman pointed behind me, toward the large hearth on the opposite side of the room.

I turned slowly and found the shouter had made her way over to me. I recognized her as the round-faced woman who'd brought me and the other maid to Godda. My pulse pounded in my ears as I panicked, expecting her to ask me why I wasn't up in Godda's chamber where I belonged.

The woman scowled at me. "Where's the wine? I was told you'd have it delivered first thing this morning."

I exhaled in relief, remembering I now wore a different face. "It's here. In the cart, outside. I was just looking for someone to help me unload it."

She shook her head, then waved at two young males who had been tending the fire. "Robert. Geoff. Come here."

The pair dropped their tools and scurried around the bakers, ducking under platters of chopped meat carried by cooks heading toward the stew pots.

"Take these two and get those barrels unloaded." She wagged a finger at me. "And be sure to stack them with the spout facing out this time so I don't have to send someone out there to do it again once you've gone."

"Yes, ma'am." I bobbed my head because it seemed the right thing to do in response to her command.

She narrowed her eyes and stared at me as though that wasn't the reaction she'd been expecting. Then she shook her head and pointed toward the door. "Out. We have work to do, and you're in the way."

I turned and hurried out the open door with the two young males following a half step behind me.

"Got out of that one easy, you did," one of the pair said once we were outside.

"Good thing ye kept yer mouth shut. Mama Marge has been lookin' for an excuse to lay into you after last time." The pair snickered.

I didn't respond because I didn't know anything about

what happened last time, and I was too busy preparing what I could say about the gargoyles that wouldn't be a lie, but would get me what I wanted. When we stopped next to the cart, I put my hands on my hips and puffed out my chest. "Right. Now, before we get to unloading these barrels, I've got a couple of statues in here. Pretty gruesome ones, at that. Someone's bad idea of a wedding gift, if you ask me. I want to get those unloaded first."

The young males craned their necks to see around me and the barrels. "Old Stewie says we're to stack all the gifts in the casino."

I lifted the back rail off the cart and propped it up against the outside of the stable. "Where's that?"

"It's one of the smaller rooms connected to the ballroom."

I clicked my tongue. Too far away. I needed to get them as close to Lord Edric's chambers as possible. "That won't do. These things are likely to frighten the guests if we put them in there. There has to be some place upstairs we can put them."

"Old Stewie won't like it. He doesn't let anyone upstairs except the Lord and Lady and their servants."

I gestured to the barrel closest to the back. "Help me lift this down."

One of them took an end, and I took the other. Together we slid the barrel off and set it on the ground. The young male who'd been watching stood with his mouth gaping. He tugged on his friend's tunic and pointed at the cart.

The gargoyles had arranged themselves in nearly identical crouched positions before freezing in place. Their stone faces stared out at us with open mouths bearing long pointed fangs.

"Still want to bring these to the casino to leave with the other presents?" I asked.

"You want us to carry those? Inside?"

"We can't take them through the kitchen. Mama Marge will have a fit."

"Is there another way inside?" I hoped this wasn't something they expected me to already know.

The young males looked at each other then began trading ideas too fast for me to get a word in.

"Maybe we could use Old Stewie's lift to get them upstairs."

"That way we wouldn't have to carry them."

"Probably should ask first."

"Nah. He won't care so long as we don't break it."

"Easy for you to say. He's your uncle."

I watched the two go back and forth until I grew impatient. "Enough."

They stopped their chatter and looked at me like they'd forgotten I was there.

"One of you help me grab hold of this one and the other lead the way to this lift." I gestured to the gargoyle closest to me.

"You'll want to use the servants' entrance." The one who was Old Stewie's nephew pointed to the opposite end of the manor.

His friend nodded. "Easier to drive the cart over so we don't have to walk as far."

"Hop on, then." I made my way to the driver's bench.

It took longer than I liked to position the cart, unload the gargoyles, set them on the platform, use the ropes and pulleys to lift them, then unload them and debate where best to leave them. The pair discussed the options while I poked my head into any rooms nearby with an open door.

"What's this one?" I asked, standing outside a wood-paneled chamber with an interior door that opened to another room, beyond. There was a table in the room, with a few wooden chairs scattered about.

Old Stewie's nephew shrugged. "It's a waiting room for Lord Edric's attendants."

Perfect. Aloud I said, "Let's leave them in here."

The young males shrugged, but didn't complain. They helped me lug the gargoyles inside the room. The weight of the first one threatened to collapse the table, so we set them on the floor, underneath. When that was done, I pressed a coin into each of their palms to thank them for their efforts. The contact with their skin also allowed me to add their faces to my growing collection. I would need to return once we were done unloading the barrels, and no one would bother questioning a familiar young male who appeared to have been sent on an errand.

11

GODDA remained in her room long enough for the maids to mark the final adjustments on the gown Edric had resurrected from an old family storage chest. The fabric draped in thick folds of creamy satin edged with lace around the neck and sleeves. Unfinished beadwork striped a sash that tied around her waist. Like all human fashion, it was overly fussy and entirely too ornate.

I tried to show some enthusiasm in order to blend in with the other maids who clasped their hands and sighed at the sight of the monstrosity. I'd seen my sister look more lovely in a shapeless white tunic. Godda caught me scowling and narrowed her eyes. I forced a smile and arranged myself in a chair with a bundle of discarded fabric to straighten and fold.

By the time I'd nearly completed my task, Godda was done with her fitting. She informed the others of her intention to have a walk alone in the gardens, then looked around for Edric's spies. The one called Emma had also found an unimportant task to busy herself with at the edge of the room. She set her embroidery aside and stood when Godda addressed her.

"Where's Rose?" Godda asked.

Emma shrugged. "I thought she'd returned with us, but I haven't seen her."

I considered remaining silent, but I was worried about the maid. Godda saved me from having to decide what to do by turning her attention on me.

"She was walking with you, was she not?"

"Near me." I didn't want Godda to think I'd been speaking with her spying maid, especially when that maid had actually been Bryn in disguise. "I saw her run off just before we reached the room. She was clutching her stomach and moaning. Perhaps she didn't feel well?"

Godda sent someone to check on Rose, then left Emma in charge of overseeing the remaining work on the dress and motioned for me to join her.

I followed my sister out of her room and down the hall. The guards trailed us, but kept their distance. This time, at the bottom of the stairs, instead of entering the ballroom, we turned left and started down another corridor toward a large oak door marked with a crest. The face plate of a helm had been carved above a shield displaying six rearing lions arrayed in three rows. One must not have been enough to convey the extent of their courage and nobility.

Godda ignored the fierce lions and turned left again, just before the door, leading our group into a small, unfurnished room. Unlike the rest of the manor, there were no rugs covering the floor or tapestries draped on the wall. The sheer emptiness startled me, but Godda didn't seem to notice or care. She continued across the small room to a pair of heavy doors fastened with an iron bar.

When Godda released the latch and pushed open the doors, a warm summer breeze blew in, caressing my skin and fluttering the hem of my dress. The green expanse of lawn stretched before us. Godda stepped outside and turned her face up to the sun, waiting for the guards to catch up. The pair of them stopped just inside the door and waited.

Without turning, Godda spoke to them. "I plan to walk

in the garden. My maid will accompany me. You will remain here."

"My lady—" One of the pair tried to speak, but she cut him off without hearing his complaint.

"Your orders are to watch me. We will remain within sight." She beckoned for me to follow, then stepped out onto the grass.

Ahead of us, low hedges marked the border of a rose garden. A gravel path wound between colorful bushes arranged in clusters around a reflecting pool that shimmered at the center of the square garden. All the vegetation had been clipped low enough to give a view of the entire area. It wasn't as beautiful as the garden outside of our mother's cottage, but I thought I understood the appeal. It was the first time I'd felt almost at home since arriving at Lydbury. I wondered if that was what drew Godda to this place.

She led me through the low hedge and onto the gravel path. We circled the pond once in silence. Then she stopped near a series of flat stones that led closer to the center. The path led to a stone bench, positioned so one could rest and watch the orange and gold fish circling just below the surface.

Godda turned to me. "Stay here and make sure I'm not disturbed."

I nodded. "Of course."

As she walked away, I wondered what she might be thinking. Perhaps she was having second thoughts about her wedding. I wished I could tell her why I was really here. She'd said that marrying this human was the only way to save the Fae, but there had to be another way. We'd find another way if killing him didn't solve the problem.

I kept watch, scanning the edges of the garden, ready to intercept anyone who dared approach, until a bright stab of sunlight reflected off metal caught my eye. My gaze fixed on Godda as my eyes hunted down the source of the flare. Her long neck bent, staring down into her palms where they curled open, cupped just below her chin. The bracelet from the Duke lay nestled in her hands. Her lips moved as though she were speaking, but no matter how hard I listened, I couldn't hear a word she whispered.

The band flared bright, then flickered out so quickly that I was sure I'd imagined it. Her shoulders lifted and dropped as she sighed. Then she slid the bracelet back onto her wrist and let her hands fall to her lap. She stared out at the ripples on the surface of the pond for a few more breaths, then stood, ran her hands over her dress to smooth the fabric, and picked her way back across the flat stones.

"Thank you," she said, touching my arm.

"What were you doing? Was that bracelet cursed or something?"

"No. It wasn't. It is now, though." She smiled.

I stared down at the simple gold band dangling from her wrist. "What? Why? What did you do?"

She shook her head. "Not now. Come. It's time for us to return."

I glanced around. We were still alone in the garden. The guards were still waiting at the door. The sun had started its descent toward the horizon, but surely there was no better time or place for her to explain herself. I worried that whatever she'd done, it might effect our rescue plans. Still, I couldn't ask her again. Not after she'd said no. As far as I was concerned, she was still my queen.

Unsympathetic to my obvious concern, Godda started back, picking her way through the clusters of rose bushes, pausing to admire a few along the way. She seemed more relaxed than she'd been since I'd arrived. I wondered what had changed.

When we reached the border of hedges she paused. "You are to depart immediately after the wedding. As soon as we retire to our rooms, you must go. I'll know if you don't."

"Are you sure? I could—" If our plan succeeded, I would be returning to the Fae, and she would be coming with me. Until then, I would pretend to be reluctant about leaving her here, alone with these humans.

"I've let you stay long enough. You're not safe here, and the forest isn't protected. Promise me. You return tonight."

"All right." I would go, but only because she would be leaving with me.

Godda nodded. "Remember. Not a word to anyone. Even Edric. Your tongue might give you away."

"Yes, my—" The word *queen* froze on my lips when she held up a hand.

"Not anymore." She said the words simply, without a touch of sadness or regret.

I pressed my lips together and frowned. Whatever she thought she was doing, I didn't like it.

"Now that that's settled." She turned away and started toward where the guards stood waiting for us.

We were both silent on the walk back up to her chambers. My heart beat in time with the thud of the guards' boots against the floorboards, ready for battle.

She must have sensed my disapproval. When we entered her rooms, she ordered everyone out. The maids spread the completed dress out on the chest at the end of her bed. They fussed over it and lingered, but Godda wouldn't budge.

Godda told them she would dress herself, and they were all to leave, even Emma and Rose, who had returned looking a little pale. I watched her for any sign that she might still be Bryn in disguise, but she appeared to be so weak that she could barely manage to lift a sewing basket. Emma had to take it from her and guide her out the door.

Once they were gone, Godda turned to me. "You, too."

"What?" I glanced over my shoulder at the open door behind me and lowered my voice. "I thought you wanted to keep me with you."

"Go down to the ballroom with the others and wait for me there. Talk to no one."

I hesitated. What had made her change her mind? Had she sensed something that I hadn't noticed? Now, more than ever,

I needed to stay close to her to make sure the gargoyles could complete their part of the mission.

"But the ballroom will be filled with the Duke and his men. How can I possibly avoid speaking with them?"

"You'll find a way." She wouldn't budge. "And remember what I said. You leave after."

I clenched my teeth and nodded. Then I stepped out into the hallway. Godda shut the door behind me, and the guards stepped into place to block me. I backed away but lingered, searching for an excuse or a hiding place where I could keep watch on her door.

"You, there." One of the guards called out to me. "Get a move on."

I glared at him and moved further down the hall.

Two young males ran up the stairs and past me, turning down a hall to the right. Their appearance reminded me that I was vulnerable alone in the hallway. Someone might question me and demand a response. They would be less likely to question my presence if I were lurking down in a room filled with others.

I retreated down the stairs and slipped into the noisy ballroom. The other maids had already disbursed to mingle among the cluster of the Duke's men. Rather than join them, I found a corner where I could watch the doors at both ends of the room to see who entered and left. Then I settled in to wait. As I searched the crowd to be sure that Edric wasn't present, I caught the eye of one of William's men.

I stared only long enough to admire his beauty. When I realized he'd seen me, I quickly looked away. I wasn't trying to attract attention. Unfortunately, he'd noticed and approached, anyway, weaving through the crowded room to reach me. I avoided his hazel eyes and the grin that peeked out from behind his close-cropped beard. I tried not to notice his long brown hair, pulled back and fastened with a leather tie so it curled at the nape of his neck, or how the fabric of his tunic stretched across his broad chest. This was no time to be distracted.

He stopped an arm's length from me and bowed as though I were the lady of the house, and still I ignored him.

"Would you do me the honor of dancing with me?" he asked.

I hadn't noticed anyone dancing, despite the soft lute music that filled the gaps in conversation. I'd also told Godda that I wouldn't talk to anyone. I shook my head and continued to scan the crowd.

He laughed. "You really don't recognize me?"

I turned my head to stare at his face. I couldn't be sure, and I didn't want to give anything away in case this was a trap. So I chose to remain silent.

The corners of the man's eyes wrinkled as his grin widened. "Come dance with me. I have good news I want to share." He held his hand out, palm up.

When I glanced down, his round tipped human fingers morphed into the long bony hands of a Fae. I blinked and the hand returned to its previous shape. For a moment I thought I'd imagined it. Then it happened again.

"Your hand." I kept my voice low in case anyone was listening.

"Take it, Sorcha."

I set my hand on Bryn's palm and stepped closer. "Is it done?"

"Soon, I think." Bryn led me in a slow circle.

We switched hands and turned the other way. "Then what is your news?"

"I've found you a mentor. You are officially an Apprentice now." Bryn released my hand and sent me spinning before catching me again.

My head spun as we took another turn. "Why?"

"You still have much to learn. The tools of the Rogue are endless and you've only just begun, my Rogue." Bryn spun me again, this time catching my hands so we stood face to face.

"I can't think about that now. I'm worried." I glanced

around the room. More couples were dancing, and there was still no sign of Godda.

"There's no reason to be worried." Bryn squeezed my hands. "Any moment now, Godda will come through that door. Then, when Edric does not appear, someone will be sent up to discover him. That's when we'll take Godda and run."

"You make it sound so simple. What about the gargoyles?" I whispered the last word, even though there was no way anyone might hear me over the music or be alarmed at my question. Humans didn't know the truth about gargoyles any more than they knew about faeries or demons. We were all just stories to them.

"They will depart on their own after they've completed their mission."

A commotion at the far end of the room drew our attention. The music stopped and the crowd parted. I expected to see Godda emerge to take her place in the center of the room, but it wasn't her. It was Edric, and he was very much alive.

I jumped at a tap on my shoulder and turned to find Godda clutching my arm and Bryn's. She wasn't wearing her wedding dress, nor was she wearing the simple dress and shawl she'd worn to greet the Duke. Instead, she stood there wearing a man's nightshirt that hung down almost to her knees with a dagger clutched in one hand. She'd belted the oversize shirt at the waist with the beaded sash from her wedding dress and wore it over leggings with no long skirt to hide her legs. She must have been in a hurry to find us if she was willing to risk the humans seeing her dressed in a way they would consider extremely inappropriate.

"Come with me," she whispered, tugging us through a door into a room filled with gifts. She shut the door and leaned against it. "You foolish Rogue. What were you thinking? Tell me you didn't involve Sorcha in your schemes. Does she even know what you've attempted?"

I swallowed. "I know."

12

GLANCING around the room at the assorted trinkets cluttering every available flat surface and the open crates shoved under every table, I realized Godda had led us into the casino where the young humans had said they were sorting the wedding gifts. My mind churned on Godda's questions and hung on the word "attempted," unable to acknowledge that her questions meant I had failed.

In my moment of hesitation, Sorcha spoke. "I know."

Godda's wrath had been focused on me, but she tensed at Sorcha's admission and turned toward her sister. "You knew?"

Before Sorcha could respond, I attempted to explain. "Riagan offered to help Sorcha return you to your throne, and—"

My words were swallowed by Godda's laughter. She locked eyes with me, and I recognized the look on her face as the one Riagan got just before he scolded me for being a useless idiot. Then a flicker of awareness softened her features as she studied my borrowed face, peering through the magic to discover my true form.

"Bryn? Is that you?"

I nodded, surprised that she recognized me underneath the magic and honored that she had remembered my name.

"You poor creature. I should have known." Her anger diminished a degree. "At least it appears that you have mastered morphing since I last saw you. Well done."

My pleasure soured a bit from her pity. "Thank you, my queen."

Godda shook her head. "I should have known Riagan would be behind this, and that he would be too much of a manipulative coward to do his own dirty work… What did you promise my sire?"

Sorcha spoke before I could answer. "We only promised to deliver his gifts and return with you."

Godda glared at her sister. "You promised, too? What did I warn you about bargaining with Rogues? Do you have any idea what would have happened if those *gifts* had succeeded in their mission?"

"How did you know?" I asked, once again drawing her attention away from Sorcha.

"I know everything that happens here. It's the only way to be sure…" She hesitated, then continued. "I found the gargoyles and froze them. If I hadn't and they'd succeeded, then you'd both be dead as well. If not here, certainly before you could return home." She paused, staring at each of us in turn, allowing her truth to sink in.

My mind tumbled back through everything Riagan had said and done since Sorcha's appearance in the twins' hut. He'd sent us, inexperienced as we were, on this mission. He hated Sorcha for what Maeve had done, and he feared what would happen if he didn't retain control over my power. It made sense. Godda was right, he would have killed us. He still might, even though we'd failed. I should have realized that was his true plan the moment he said: *I'd like a word with the gargoyles. Alone.*

"Why would they kill us? They liked us." Sorcha folded her arms across her chest.

Godda sighed. "Don't be naive, little hawk. Gargoyle assassins are ruthless, and this pair were desperate enough to bargain with Riagan who has no interest in allowing you to survive. Do you think he wants witnesses who might be able to tell the Queen's Court the truth of exactly who disobeyed my orders not to harm Edric?"

"Right." Sorcha shrugged one shoulder. "Then return with us and we won't hurt your human. I've seen how he looks at you. I know you're scared of whatever it is you think he can do to us. You don't have to stay here. Come home with us."

I knew that Godda would refuse, but I held my breath anyway, hoping Sorcha's plea might change her sister's mind. We hadn't killed the human, but if Godda agreed to return, I wouldn't have to face Riagan as a total failure. We might at least stop her from marrying and promising her life to the human. If we could manage that, I could always return to kill him later so I could honor my bargain, earn my Confirmation, and be rid of Riagan's control over me.

Godda stepped forward and cupped Sorcha's face in her palms. "I am staying because I love him, foolish as that may sound to you now. I was careless, and now he knows too much. He knows the Fae exist, and that's my fault. But it's all right. I promised him I'd stay so long as he never threatens the Fae or questions me about them. You witnessed our bargain."

Sorcha opened her mouth to protest, but Godda slid her finger over Sorcha's lips. Godda's body tensed, and she cocked her head like she was listening.

We stood in silence for a moment. Then Godda reached out and grabbed my forearm. Her other hand slid from Sorcha's cheek to rest on her shoulder. "Someone's coming."

The room with the gifts blinked out, and we reappeared in a cellar, surrounded by crates of root vegetables. At one end of the space, a ladder led up to a hatch cut into the ceiling. Godda released us and headed in the opposite direction, deeper into the cellar, toward the racks of wine extending from the far wall, out into the center of the room.

"Where are we?" Sorcha asked.

"Below Lydbury's kitchens." Godda gripped the edge of the rack next to one of the side walls and pulled. The rack hinged back, leaving just enough space for a body to slip behind, into what looked like a tunnel.

Sorcha pushed past me and rushed toward her sister. She grabbed Godda's arm and started pulling her into the tunnel. "Bryn, help me."

Godda twisted out of Sorcha's grip and shielded herself with magic. Sorcha ignored the shimmer in the air between them and ran toward Godda as though she intended to tackle her to the ground. Her body hit Godda's shield and bounced back, crashing into one of the tunnel walls.

I winced. As much as I didn't want to face Riagan without our queen, I knew better than to attempt to overpower her. My magic was no match against a High Fae, half-Rogue Faerie Queen, and Sorcha's wasn't either. If we hoped to lure Godda away from Lydbury, we would have to find a way to work around this bargain she'd made with Edric. It might still be possible, but I needed time to plan.

Sorcha glared at me from where she sat, slumped against the wall.

I shook my head and hoped she'd give me a chance to explain once we were away from this place.

Godda stepped forward and extended one hand to help her sister to her feet. With the other, she beckoned me closer. "Promise me you'll do your best to keep her safe."

Her binding words were kind, leaving me more than enough room to wiggle out, if I needed. She'd resisted asking for more, knowing what we would be up against now, returning to the twins without her. My initial assessment had been half right, so many days ago in the forest. Sorcha's impulsiveness was going to get us killed, but not in the way I'd expected.

I let my borrowed face fall away and settled back into my natural form. "I promise, I'll keep her safe."

Godda's eyes widened with surprise as she realized that I'd discarded her offer in favor of a much more binding commitment. She glanced at Sorcha, still sitting on the ground, then back to me. "Thank you. I am sorry that I can't help you with Riagan."

I spread my hands, palms up, and shrugged. "A bargain is a bargain… And you are right to be concerned for her safety."

"I wish you two would stop speaking as though I'm some delicate bloom that will wither in the slightest storm." Sorcha stood and dusted herself off. "Must I remind you both that I trained as a Queen's Guard before taking my place on the Court?"

"If you are so fierce, then do your part and watch out for Bryn." Godda stepped aside, allowing me to slide past and join Sorcha in the tunnel.

"Where does this lead?" Sorcha asked, ignoring or oblivious to Godda's attempt to reinforce the bind between us.

Godda flashed a pained look in my direction before answering her sister. "It ends near the temple."

I avoided Godda's eyes and kept my disappointment from showing on my face, certain that Sorcha didn't mean to leave me to fend for myself. She just didn't understand Riagan the way Godda and I did.

Godda bent and traced a rune in the packed dirt ground at the entrance to the tunnel. Then she tapped her knuckles against the stone wall. As she straightened, two goblins rose up out of the earth beside her. They unfolded their bodies and shook the dirt from their bald heads.

The goblins were short and thin and draped in rags. Both carried thick sticks that I mistook for clubs because of the way they held them with one end gripped in a fist and the other cradled in the opposite palm. When they bowed to Godda, I got a better look at the end of one and realized they were unlit torches, not weapons.

Godda stepped back and rested one hand on the wine rack. "I must go before they notice I'm not in my rooms.

These two will accompany you as far as the boundary of Lydbury's grounds. You'll be able to transport from there, if you choose, or stay in the tunnel until you emerge near the temple. Good luck."

The two goblins stepped in front of Godda, blocking our way back into the cellar.

I met Godda's eyes across the tops of their heads. An unspoken understanding passed between us as Sorcha lunged for the door. I nodded once at Godda, then wrapped a hand on Sorcha's elbow, pulling her back and guiding her deeper into the tunnel. Behind us, the door slid shut, plunging us into darkness. The goblins snickered.

I stopped, pulling Sorcha to a halt with me, and reminded the goblins of their duty. "Light."

They grumbled as they lit their torches.

Our shadows flickered around us as we started forward again. Dirt walls stretched before us with no end in sight. Beside me, Sorcha glanced back over her shoulder at the wall that was a door and the goblins blocking her path to it.

I caught her look and shook my head. "Don't."

"But we could—"

I cut her off and urged her forward. "It's done. Godda out maneuvered us." I dreaded facing Riagan and was in no mood for talking. I needed to think and plan while I had a chance.

"But, the gargoyles… We can't just leave them there. What about their poor egg?" She tried to resist the steady pressure I applied to her elbow to keep her moving.

"There's nothing we can do about that now. You'd be much better off focusing on what to do about your training now that your sire has agreed to be your mentor and your uncle wants us dead." I considered how much Rowan knew of Riagan's plans. Had he known when he told me he would handle Riagan? If he did, what had he meant?

"You can train me."

I glanced at Sorcha. "I am not qualified to train you. Only Confirmed Rogues can mentor Apprentices." And after this failure, Riagan would almost certainly never allow me to take my Confirmation test. If he couldn't kill me and make it appear to be an accident, he could at least make sure I would never be able to challenge him as a Confirmed Rogue.

"I'm not going back to the Rogues. Not after this. If I have to, I'll teach myself." She shook her arm free of my grip, but kept walking.

"I've tried that. It's not quite that easy, especially when you weren't raised as a Rogue."

"Then I suppose, since you've already promised Godda to protect me, that you'll just have to help me learn. Why bother with ridiculous Rogue rules anyway when they are what allow someone as awful as Riagan to hold the position of High Rogue?"

"The rules and traditions of the Rogues are a part of what hones our power and makes us unique among the Fae."

"The goblins are Fae and they're unique. The sprites with their wings and secrets are unique. Even the Elementals, with their ability to control nature are unique among the Fae. Your Rogue rules and traditions just keep you isolated and force you to succeed by being cruel to each other, and to the other Factions. Tell me, how have your rules ever served you, Bryn?"

Behind us, the goblins snickered.

The rules hadn't served me. They'd bound me to Riagan against my will, and they'd nearly gotten me killed for my efforts. Still, I wasn't ready to abandon them completely. It was too much to think about now, in the darkness under Lydbury Manor, but I could make a small concession.

I turned the idea over in my head, examining it from all angles. Then I cast an invisible illusion shield around us to block our conversation from the goblins and any other Fae ears that might be listening.

"I think it's best, once we leave here, that we not be seen together. If Rowan offers to train you, you should accept, but since we know we can't trust the twins, I will also train you. In secret."

"Why in secret?"

I hesitated, choosing my words carefully so that I didn't reveal too much of my own feelings when I suspected she didn't feel the same. "If Riagan can't kill me, he'll do everything he can to keep me from advancing and to make my life as miserable as possible for as long as he can. If he thinks there is any attachment between us, he'll think he can use you to get to me."

Sorcha scoffed. "I'd like to see him try. If he wants to punish you for this mission, he'll have to take me out, first."

A snort escaped my attempt to keep from laughing with relief at her reaction. "You are under no obligation to protect me from my mentor. The failure of this mission is not your fault."

"It's not yours, either. It's my stubborn, self-sacrificing sister's fault." She crossed her arms and her pace slowed.

The goblins urged us forward while grumbling their complaints in Ancient Fae.

I sensed a steady hum of magic up ahead. "I think we're close, now."

Sorcha looked past me, into the darkness. "I feel it, too."

We continued in silence. The sense of magic looming in the air increased with every step until it coated my tongue with a metallic tang. It was all I could think about. I dropped the shield illusion so I could concentrate.

After a few more steps, Sorcha's voice cut through the assault on my senses. "It's a good plan, Bryn."

I glanced behind us at the goblins. Their beady black eyes, so like my own, stared back at me. One of them lifted the corner of their wide mouth in a half grin.

Sorcha paused as the thrum of magic peaked around us. "This must be the boundary."

I nodded. There were no markings on the walls, floor, or ceiling to indicate as much, but the current of magic surrounding us had to be the same as the one surrounding the grounds above.

The goblins stopped just shy of the boundary. The one who'd grinned offered me their torch.

I took the flaming stick and thanked them, then I turned to Sorcha and caught the smile she was attempting to hide. "What are you thinking?"

"Come on." She waved me away from the goblins.

Together we walked past the invisible boundary and on into the darkness. When the pulse of the magic started to diminish, Sorcha glanced back.

She caught my arm and pulled me to a stop. "They're gone." She started back toward the boundary.

"Godda will sense it when you cross." I grabbed for Sorcha, but she slipped away.

"Even if she does, she'll be distracted with the wedding. She won't be able to do anything about it." Sorcha started running.

"Sorcha! Stop." I called after her, but she was already outside the halo of light cast by the torch I carried.

I hurried to catch up and found her slamming her fists against a solid dirt wall that hadn't been there moments ago.

"She's thought of everything. I hate her!" Sorcha's fists pounded against the wall once more, then she pressed her forehead against the dirt between them. Her shoulders shook.

I set one hand on the wall in wonder. I'd seen this mix of illusion and something else before. This was like what Sorcha had done after that first time she fed, but this illusion had been cast with purpose and skill. The possibilities of Rogue magic mixed with High Fae power stunned me. Could this be what the twins wanted to control?

Sorcha turned toward me. Her arms dropped to her sides as she leaned forward and set her head on my chest. My hand slid from the wall and wrapped around her waist. We stood like that for several breaths. Alone. Surrounded in silence.

I'd barely noticed that the hum of Godda's magic had disappeared, because I was too aware of every point where Sorcha's body touched mine and too terrified to move. I would not let Riagan harm her. Could I obey our Rogue rules and still break free of his control? The pieces of the puzzle twisted and turned, then began to assemble in my head.

Eventually, Sorcha's head tipped back and my tongue formed whispered words. "We'll find a way to get her back. I have an idea."

13

ROWAN had been steadily testing me all morning. He arrived at the cottage just as the sun lifted up above the treetops and didn't leave until the sun hit its peak height. The whole time, hinting and suggesting different approaches to the task he'd set for me. Approaches that would corner me into casting a solid illusion. But Bryn and I agreed, before that annoying Rogue went and disappeared, that I would not manage anything more than the most basic illusions while training with my sire.

Even though Bryn's disappearance was part of our plan, I hadn't expected it to last this long. It had been almost six years since Godda's wedding. Which wasn't very long considering Fae could live for millennia, but I was getting worried.

In Bryn's absence, I'd done my part. Training as much as I could with Rowan. Then, when I was alone, testing the limits of my Rogue magic. In secret, I'd patched up remote sections of the borders where the Fae forest brushed up against the edges of the human wilderness. But I couldn't keep my work hidden forever.

The section of border near the temple needed repairing. The Fae used that location to cross over into the human world too often, and the illusions had weakened to the point where a few humans were able to wander into our lands each moon cycle. The Rogues fed off them before sending them back across the border. But, if I didn't repair the illusions soon, more would come and eventually discover us.

"Sorcha!" Flida called out to me from the open door of the cottage, interrupting my thoughts.

When I turned to respond, I noticed another figure standing just outside the door. His brownish green robes blended perfectly with the colors of the forest. We had a visitor.

I hurried back through the garden, trying to control the hope building in my chest. I didn't think Bryn would be so bold as to appear at our cottage, unless maybe in disguise. I cringed and discarded that idea after realizing that Flida would be able to see through any Rogue magic. Bryn wouldn't risk that.

The robed figure dropped his hood when I joined my sister at the cottage door and any shred of remaining hope evaporated.

"Greetings, Cahal." I dipped my head to the Guardian of the Elementals.

"Sorcha." Cahal's blue eyes found mine when I looked up. The way he'd pulled his long brown hair back and secured it at the nape of his neck reminded me of dancing with Bryn at Lydbury. I stared a moment longer, trying to see if it really was Bryn in disguise, but Rowan had taught me what to look for, and there was no hint of Rogue magic around him.

"Cahal needs me to attend a meeting of the Elemental Elders." Flida had been spending more and more time with the leader of the Elemental Faction, and I suspected that there was more going on between the two than just politics. As acting queen, she had to be careful she wasn't seen as showing a preference for the Elemental Faction over all the others.

"All right." I shot her a questioning look. We shared the

cottage now that I'd returned home and Godda had left, but Flida wasn't in the habit of consulting me on all her comings and goings.

"I might be gone for a while." The intensity of the look she gave me communicated her unspoken hope that she would be spending some additional time meeting with the Elemental Guardian, alone, and didn't want to be disturbed. "Will you keep an eye on the cottage while I'm gone?"

"Of course." I grinned, casting my magic out to take control of the wards surrounding the cottage so that she could ignore them while she was gone. "Have a fun meeting."

Flida kissed my forehead, then set her hand on Cahal's outstretched arm. In a blink, they were gone. It wasn't until I turned to go inside that I noticed the scrap of paper laying on the grass where Cahal had been standing.

I bent to pick it up and realized there were words on it, but I hesitated before reading what was written. If the paper belonged to Cahal, it might be a private communication. I had almost decided that I should call a sprite to return the paper to him when I spotted the curve of an "S" followed by the rest of my name.

Sorcha, please return this to the cave at the base of the Faerie Falls.

The note wasn't signed. I searched both sides of the paper, then reread it.

I knew the location. It wasn't far from the cottage. The wards around the cottage would warn me if anyone arrived while I was gone. I folded the paper and tucked it into the woven armor belt that cinched my tunic around my waist. Then I jogged to the edge of the clearing and transported myself to the Faerie Falls.

It took a bit of searching to find an entrance to the cave that didn't require swimming across the lake and under the wide stream of cascading water. Eventually, I scrambled up and over a few large boulders to reach a shelf of rock that curved around the edge of the cliff and under the waterfall.

From there, I stepped into the damp cave and splashed through puddles as I made my way back, into the darkness.

"Hello?" My voice echoed off the stone wall.

A dim light flickered ahead, as though someone had left a fire blazing in one of the caverns. For a moment I regretted calling out and announcing myself. I had to be careful. I needed to consider that this might be a trap. I was fairly certain that I could trust Cahal, if only because he seemed to respect and like my sister. But, if I disappeared here, no one would know that he had been the one to leave me the note that led me to my death.

I paused to tap into what was left of my Rogue powers after my long training session with Rowan and spun a few basic illusions around me so that my body blended into the shadows. Then I crept forward on silent feet until I reached the cavern with the light.

When I peeked inside, I discovered a large space shaped like a bowl with a domed lid. A ledge circled the stone wall at the height of the opening where I stood. Below the ledge, a steep drop off sloped down to create a sort of room or workshop at the bottom of the bowl.

Down there, on a bench carved out of the stone wall, Bryn reclined near a small fire. A wave of relief hit me, followed by a surge of anger that I hadn't been the first to know of Bryn's return. We shared so many secrets and had promised to protect each other, like partners. *When had I started thinking of Bryn as my partner?*

My illusions flickered and my foot slipped. The toe of my boot kicked a loose pebble over the edge and down to the floor below.

"Come down from there Sorcha. I know it's you." Bryn's lips parted in a grin that showed those pointed teeth and black tongue that no longer frightened me.

I stepped to the edge of the ledge and dropped my illusions. "How long have you been here?"

Bryn waved a hand, beckoning me closer. "I've only just

returned, and I don't plan to put Cahal in any more danger than absolutely necessary, so I won't be staying here long."

I shifted into my hawk form, shedding the confusing flood of emotions clouding my thoughts, and circled the cavern once before swooping down to the floor below. I transformed back into my Fae body just in time for my feet to land on the cave floor. The brief period of hawk-mind focus brought clarity to my thoughts.

"Where were you?"

"It may be best if you don't know." Bryn stood and stalked closer to me. "Where's the note?"

I frowned as I pulled the paper out from where I'd tucked it behind my belt. "Here."

"Good." Bryn took the note from me.

"You've been gone for years. You left me alone to deal with the twins. Have you given up on the mission?" I set my hands on my hips and glared.

Bryn waved one hand over the piece of paper. The letters rearranged themselves, shifting shape and order. "It's not safe to talk here."

I plucked the paper from Bryn's fingers. But before I could read the words written there, the tug of one of the wards at the cottage alerted me that someone had arrived. "I need to go."

"Good. So do I."

I couldn't bring Bryn back to the cottage, and I didn't want to leave. We hadn't even begun to catch up on all that had happened. This was not at all how I'd imagined our reunion. "When will I see you again?"

Bryn reached out and set a hand over my fingers, pressing the paper deeper into my palm. "Soon."

"Can I transit from here?" I asked, trying to refocus and hoping whatever Bryn wasn't saying was on the note.

Bryn nodded. "Out but not in."

I scanned Bryn's face for any hint of what may be going on in that Rogue mind, but it was impossible to read anything in those black pool eyes. I slid my hand free, keeping a tight hold on the paper crumpled in my fist. "Soon, then."

I reached for the cottage and disappeared, ready to snap at whoever had bothered to come calling. But all that anger was erased the moment I realized it was Godda walking through the clearing with a young human boy at her side.

Tears welled behind my eyelids at the sight, and I ran to greet her. Godda had come home. I stuffed Bryn's note back into my belt, forgotten for the moment in the joy of seeing my sister, safe and healthy and home after all these years.

The boy hid behind her leg as we hugged. He stared up at me, his eyes fixated on my ears. I began to wonder if I should hide them with a glamour, but Godda had brought him to us with no warning, so I didn't think she cared.

Godda released me and pressed a hand between the boy's shoulder blades to urge him forward. "This is your aunt, my love."

He stepped forward and bowed to me, bending deep at the waist with one arm bent across his hips. "Your Majesty."

When I laughed, it sent him running back behind Godda's skirts. She wore long layers of them, with her shoulders and hair covered in embroidered shawls. She dressed like a human.

"Mamma." He whispered, tugging on the hem of her shawl. "She laughed at me. What did I do wrong?"

Godda bent down to his height. "Nothing, my love. Only, this is Sorcha. Your Aunt Flida is the Faerie Queen."

He cupped his hand against his cheek as he whispered in Godda's ear. "Are you sure Mamma? She's so pretty. She looks like you. She must be the Faerie Queen."

I covered my mouth to keep from laughing again.

"Your Aunt Flida is pretty, too, and being pretty isn't what makes a good queen or king, is it?"

"No, Mamma."

"That's a good boy. Now go run and play in the gardens while I talk with your Aunt Sorcha." Godda waited until the boy had run off, then she stood. "Is Flida here, too?"

"No. She's meeting with the Elemental Elders."

"What about the others?"

I shook my head. "It's still a few days until the new moon."

Godda frowned. "I know, but Edric is off on a hunt today. He won't be home until late. I took a chance because I wanted to introduce you all to Alned."

"If you can wait—"

She shook her head. "I can't stay. I'm sorry I couldn't give you more warning."

I glanced over my shoulder at the little boy chasing pixies through the garden. "He knows about us?"

"He has the sight."

"Does his father?" If Edric did, that would explain quite a lot.

Godda shrugged. "I don't think so, but I'm sure he suspects something. I'm still depending on his promise. He won't risk questioning me about my kinfolk, and that includes our son. Not if it means losing me forever."

"Does the boy have magic?" Fae females who chose to mate with humans couldn't give birth to Faelings, but the Fae blood in the veins of their offspring gave those human children the potential for magic.

"Nothing he's done has given him away, yet. I'm hoping he continues that way because it's best if he never knows. Having the sight is dangerous enough."

"You could leave him with us." I searched her face for a reaction. "Is that why you decided to bring him?"

She shook her head. "I can't send him away, yet. According to the humans, he's too young. But soon. Edric wants to send him to foster with one of the other local Lords who are loyal to King William."

The name sounded familiar. "Is this the same William who came to your wedding? The one who gave you that bracelet? Is he a king now?"

"Yes, and Edric has sworn fealty, even though he hates

him."

I remembered that. "Does this duke turned king still admire you? Does that have something to do with it?"

Godda frowned. "Perhaps. But if I can't send Neddy to Flida, I want him to go to William. There will be enough distraction at court to keep Neddy from talking endlessly about faeries, and Edric will be less inclined to pressure the boy, or attempt to question him, if it requires a visit to William."

As we watched, a group of gnomes emerged from their home under the rose bushes to chase the boy out of the garden before he could trample all the herbs in his quest to catch a pixie. The gnomes jabbed their thorny rose branch spears at the boy's bare legs, and the pixies cheered.

Godda's son stumbled backward, tripped and landed on his bum, then stood and raced across the clearing toward us.

Beside me, Godda laughed. "I suppose that will teach him to be cautious of even our smallest cousins."

I shook my head, remembering my own scars earned braving gnomes and pixies to eat my fill of summer fruit fresh off the garden vines. Godda's son belonged here. Flida would have known how to convince her to leave the boy, but Flida wasn't home.

"Will you walk with me back to Lydbury?" Godda asked, reaching down to rest a hand on her son's shoulder as he threw himself at her legs and buried his face in her skirts.

"If you're sure you can't stay… I know Flida will be sorry she missed your visit."

"We've stayed long enough."

"Then I'll walk with you as far as the temple."

Together we set out into the forest, walking in silence as Alned ran ahead, then circled back to show his mother some treasure he'd found, only to hurry away again.

After the boy had run off a second time, Godda returned her attention to me. "I noticed that the illusions near the temple need repair. Have you been training?"

"I have." I wanted to say more, but I held my tongue.

"Is Bryn your mentor?"

I cringed. "No."

Godda cocked her head and peered at me as we wove our way between the tree trunks. "Oh? What happened?"

"Bryn didn't return with me." I kept my eyes on the boy ahead so I wouldn't reveal anything more to my sister who'd raised me and knew me better than anyone. "Rowan is my mentor."

"Rowan?" Godda squinted at me. "Do you think that's wise?"

I shrugged. I didn't, but I'd had no choice in the matter.

"I wouldn't trust him if I were you."

I sighed and hoped she didn't truly think I was inexperienced enough to trust my sire, even though I had, once. "I don't."

"Where's Bryn? Are you watching out for each other?"

I thought of the note tucked into my belt. I wasn't entirely sure where Bryn was at that moment, but if I answered Godda's questions she'd see through my responses and know I was hiding something. "You are asking a lot of questions for someone who left us. Why do you care?"

"I never stopped caring." Godda's voice held a pleading note, but after she spoke she sucked in a breath and froze. Her body tensed as her eyes searched ahead for her son. "Alned! Come back."

The boy hadn't gone far. When Godda called him, he jumped down from the tree stump he'd climbed and ran back toward us. He'd made it halfway to Godda when a hunter on horseback emerged from the trees and scooped the boy up onto his saddle.

Godda winced and clutched at my arm.

The hunter reined in his horse, blocking our path. Up on the saddle, the boy looped his arms around the hunter's neck and kissed his cheek. The years hadn't changed the man's menacing face. I recognized Edric's watchful eyes as they settled on us, staring out from the shadow cast by his heavy brow.

"Where have you been?" he asked.

Godda stepped forward, angling her body to put me behind her. "Neddy and I went for a walk."

"And who is this?" Edric's unsettling eyes fixed on me. "What sort of creatures are you exposing our son to?"

I remembered that I hadn't glamoured my appearance to look human. We were still within the boundaries of the Fae forest. I assumed we would be safe here. The illusions near the temple were worse than I'd thought if Edric had found his way through.

Godda reached back and squeezed my hand. She angled her chin up, her eyes fixed on Edric. "You promised not to question me, my Lord."

Edric shifted in the saddle. One hand dropped to the hilt of the sword strapped to his waist. "How can I trust you when the moment I leave you alone you run away, back to them? And what were you thinking taking our son with you? This creature could have enchanted him. Did you consider that?"

"Papa." Alned tugged on Edric's breastplate. "It's okay. That's my aunt."

Godda glanced at me with sadness in her eyes. Then she turned her head up to face Edric. "You've broken your promise, my Lord."

I barely noticed when Godda released me. One moment she was there, and the next, she had disappeared.

"What did you do to her?" Edric growled as Alned screamed in his ear and beat his little fists against Edric's chest.

Faced with Edric's wrath, I called on whatever was left of my Rogue magic to cast an illusion that would force him back to the human lands. Then I circled the forest on hawk's wings, searching for Godda.

14

ORCHA sent me an urgent message after Godda disappeared, but I didn't discover it until a few days later because I hadn't expected her to contact me so soon. I responded, arranging to meet near the border where, if we were discovered, I could feign humanity and it would appear as though Sorcha only lingered there to feed. When I arrived at the agreed upon place and time, she was already there, pacing across a patch of mossy forest floor.

"Where have you been?" She waved a hand in the air as I approached. "No. Don't answer. I don't want to know, and it doesn't matter now. Edric has broken his promise to Godda."

"Has she returned?" Since leaving Cahal's cave, I'd kept to my hiding place, pacing the tunnel between Lydbury and the Lady of the Hunt's temple, far from the gossip of the forest. If Godda had returned, I intended to celebrate because it would mean half of my bargain with Riagan was fulfilled, and I would be that much closer to leaving the confines of that tunnel for good.

Sorcha's words put an end to that hope. "No. Godda just

disappeared. I was there, but I don't know where she went. And it's worse than just that." She paused, grimacing. "She has a son."

I knew about the boy. I'd seen him on the grounds at Lydbury. Godda may not have let me in, but she couldn't prevent me spying from the woods surrounding the property. "How does that make it worse?"

"He has the sight. And probably magic. And now Edric has him." She gestured toward the border where the Fae forest pressed up against the lands occupied by the humans.

"What does it matter?" I knew the High Fae raised their own Faelings, rather than sending them to a creche, but I didn't understand what they wanted with Godda's human son.

"The boy may be human, but he's still the son of the Faerie Queen. He should be raised here. By Flida."

"And what does Flida say about that?" If Godda had chosen to give birth to a daughter, I might understand the interest. A daughter, even a human one, might take some of the pressure off the sisters to produce a successor.

I hadn't been so isolated that I didn't know that gossip among the Fae had shifted away from Godda's abdication over the past few years. The debates between those who thought it was the human who had control over the former queen and those who believed the former queen had given up everything to satisfy some unnatural urge to mate with a human had largely ended. The conversations now centered on which of the sisters would be the first to produce a female heir. The forest was waiting for their Faeling Queen.

Sorcha shrugged. "She doesn't know."

"You didn't tell Flida about Godda's disappearance?" My mind raced. What did it mean that Sorcha had come to me first, before her sisters?

"I haven't even told her about Godda's visit to the cottage. There hasn't been time. I managed to shove Edric out of the forest with an illusion after Godda disappeared. Then I went searching, but I couldn't find her. And now I'm here." She stared at me as though she expected me to say something.

I didn't have an answer for her, and I couldn't focus while staring into her hope-filled eyes. So I glanced away, allowing my mind to work the problem as I studied the fading illusions that stretched along the section of border closest to us. They should have been strong enough to immerse any wandering human into a series of twists and turns, diverting them away from the Fae forest and spitting them back out on the human side. Instead, there were holes and gaps wide enough to allow even humans on horseback to find their way through.

My thoughts chased each other, fighting for attention. I pressed my palms together and tapped the tips of my nails against each other to help me think. "Do you remember what Edric promised? I need the exact words of the binding."

"Right." Sorcha pressed her lips into a firm line. She remained silent for several breaths. "I think he promised not to threaten Godda's kin or question her about them."

I nodded. "And what did she promise in return?"

"To marry him and stay by his side?"

"Hmm…" I inhaled deeply, sniffing out the strings of possibility as my parent had taught me. "She didn't say what would happen if he didn't keep his promise? Only what would happen if he did?"

Sorcha considered my question, then nodded, confirming what I'd begun to suspect. Godda had left her end of the bargain open. She could be anywhere.

"I can go and lurk among the humans to see what I can find, but you need to tell Flida and see if she has any way of searching the Fae forest." I remembered the magic surrounding the human's manor. "Have you checked the wards at Lydbury?"

Sorcha shook her head.

"I'll check those as well. As long as they're still active, then she isn't dead." I shook my head. "If a Faerie Queen died without a successor to capture her soul…"

Sorcha gave voice to my unspoken fears. "Demons. Or

worse."

The magic available to demons, usually tightly controlled by the Fae, expanded whenever a Fae soul wasn't safely returned to the ether. Demons mostly hunted humans and weren't much of a threat to the Fae, but if their numbers increased and they grew bold, humans might become aware of them. Then they might also become aware of the Fae, and humans, even though few knew how, had the ability to capture and control us. Worse than that, humans with Fae blood could use Fae souls to perform magic that would tether their lives to the earth, giving them a sort of immortality. I hoped, for the sake of our kin, that Godda was still alive.

My eyes drifted back to the patchy illusions. "Why haven't you repaired this section of the border?"

"If I fix it, the twins will notice. They'll know it was me."

"You're right to be concerned, but right now, I think Edric and the humans pose the greater threat." As I paused to consider the twins' reactions and what they might do in response, more pieces of the puzzle fell into place. "The twins will notice, and try harder to control you. They'll push you to take a Rogue mate in the hope that you'll produce the next Faerie Queen."

It was a logical conclusion, and one I expected would be met with disdain by Sorcha. I tensed, anticipating her reaction. She'd made it clear how she felt about Rogues when we'd first met. Even if she had come to me for help before going to her sisters, I didn't imagine that meant she'd changed her mind.

Sorcha started pacing. As she walked, she ticked her thoughts off on her fingers. "Riagan wants us dead because we know that he went against the High Court and plotted to kill Edric and bring Godda back. But we failed, so his plan failed, and Godda hasn't returned. Now I am their only chance to control the Fae." She paused, balling her hands into fists at her sides. "You're not safe, but I could be, if they thought they could control me. And if they want to control me, then maybe I could use that to protect you..."

This was not the reaction I'd expected. It took me a moment to realize that she'd stopped and was staring at me.

When I remained silent, she continued. "Godda told me something before her wedding. She said love is just a tool. It reminded me of what you keep saying about the tools of the Rogue." She hesitated. "If all they want is for me to produce a Faeling with a Rogue sire, I wouldn't have to take a mate to do that."

My mouth went dry. She couldn't be suggesting what I thought she might be suggesting. Even if the Rogues believed that love was a tool, she hadn't been raised as a Rogue. She'd been raised by a sister who had given up her crown because she'd fallen in love with a human. Godda may have said those words, but her actions proved that she didn't truly believe them.

"What are you suggesting?" I needed to hear her say it.

"Would it keep you safe from the twins if I agreed to a Rogue sire for my first Faeling, but only if it was you?" She paused. Her mouth twisted into a grimace. "I suppose… Would you even want that? To sire a Faeling? What would it mean for you, if you did?"

The Sorcha I had first met outside Riagan's hut wouldn't have cared what I thought. She would have assumed that any Rogues would beg for the chance to sire the Faeling of a High Fae. This evidence that she saw me, that she cared, made my heart melt. I had to remind myself that Rogues didn't fall in love, and Sorcha wasn't declaring her affections, she was using her tools, like a Rogue, to help me. She was offering a sort of bargain. Nothing more.

"If I give up my seed to sire another's Faeling, it means I can't carry a Faeling of my own." Each male Fae and every Rogue, carried only one seed. Male Fae needed a female to carry their seed, but Rogues could use that seed to carry their own Faeling, as my mother had done with me.

"Would that bother you?" She pinched her lower lip between her teeth, and a single crease appeared in her brow, between her eyebrows.

My eyes lingered on her lips. I reminded myself this was only a bargain and looked away. "I would trade my seed for my safety, if it came to that. But we should be cautious about how you make your demands. It will need to be carefully worded."

"All right, then. What should I say?"

My pulse pounded in my ears. I took a breath and forced the beats to slow. "Give me some time to think about it. In the meantime, I'll see what I can discover from the humans, and you fix the illusions. If the twins discover your work and pressure you before I return, tell them you'll need to get Flida's approval before taking a mate. I assume that will be true in any case."

Sorcha nodded. "How long will you be gone?"

"Perhaps only a few days. Perhaps longer."

We arranged a plan for exchanging information in my absence. Then I kept watch while she worked. I faced away from Sorcha so that she wouldn't distract me as I listened to the sounds of the forest and prowled around the trunks of the trees towering above us, letting my mind explore the possibilities of how we might use Godda's disappearance to work in our favor.

"Bryn." Sorcha's whisper cut through my thoughts. "I think I'm finished."

I turned to inspect her work, finding only the smallest of holes near the edge of a fallen tree that lay across the stream. I pointed. "There."

Sorcha sighed, wiping the sweat from her brow with the hem of her sleeve. "I'm not sure I have anything left."

"Use me, then." I offered her the inside of my wrist.

She stared at the pale patch of skin above the heel of my hand, then glanced up to meet my eyes. "How?"

"Rowan hasn't taught you to use another Rogue's power?" As soon as I asked, I realized that I already knew the answer. He wouldn't teach her something she might be able to use against them.

"You can do that?"

I reached out and took her hand, pressing her fingers against the pulse in my wrist. "You can't feed off a Rogue, but you can draw on my power to amplify or supplement yours. Press here. Sync your pulse to mine. Then pull."

To make it easier, I let my fingers rest on the inside of her wrist, using the steady rhythm of her heart beat to slow my own racing pulse until it fell into sync with hers. The press of her fingers, warm against my skin, hummed with an electricity that vibrated up my arm and swirled around my ribcage.

"That's incredible." She murmured the words, eyes fixed on where our hands connected.

I swallowed. "Now pull the power you need from me and direct it into the illusion."

The air above the fallen log shimmered, then it was done.

Sorcha released my hand, but didn't move away. She stared past me, at the log. "We don't have to, you know. If there's another way to keep you safe."

It took me a moment to understand what she was saying. "I'm surprised, that's all. I thought you hated the Rogues."

She shrugged. "You're a Rogue, and you're not so bad."

I grinned, showing off my pointed teeth on purpose. "I don't scare you anymore?"

Her eyes traveled across my face as her hand drifted up to glide against my cheek, then moved higher to skim my temple. She shifted closer until the fabric of her tunic brushed against my chest and the heat of her body erased the bite of the cool night air. "You don't scare me."

"Are you sure this is what you want?"

"If producing a Rogue Faeling will secure your freedom and safety, that's what I want. I don't think I care for love. Not if love is what drove my sister away from here and into Edric's world." Her hand dropped down to rest against my chest, above my pounding heart.

"Don't promise them anything, until I return."

"All right." Sorcha leaned in and brushed her lips against my cheek. "Safe hunting."

My heart stilled instead of sped. Sorcha's kiss shook me. It happened so fast, I could have imagined it, but she'd kissed me. Me in my true form. She hadn't lied when she said I didn't scare her. She didn't love me, but I'd been taught that love was just another tool of the Rogue. It was better this way. Partners but not mates.

"Safe hunting." I didn't trust myself to say more and disappeared to return to the safety of the tunnel where it would be easier to convince myself that Rogues didn't fall in love.

In the morning, after a long sleepless night, I made my way to Lydbury and then on to King William's castle. A few days turned into three years lurking in King William's court before my carefully chosen words whispered into the ears of influential Lords and Ladies paid off. I began hearing tales of "Wild Edric's Madness" and delicately pressed for more information. Once I had what I needed, I left the humans and returned to the forest to bring Sorcha the news.

Her desire to get Alned away from his father appeared to be justified. As soon as she arrived, I told her what I'd learned.

"Edric has been trying to hide it, but several of the Ladies have confirmed that Godda is no longer at Lydbury." We'd guessed at the truth, but now I had it confirmed.

"But where did she go?" Sorcha paced between the trees. "She didn't return to us, and the wards she cast to keep the Fae out of Lydbury are still in place. She hasn't faded, Bryn. She's just disappeared."

"It seems that way. Yes."

"What about the boy?"

"He's ten now. Old enough to foster, and I've sowed enough fear among William's Lords that none will take the boy unless William refuses. That much is good news."

"There's bad news, then?"

I pressed my fingers together under my chin and hesitated. What I said next would add to the pressure she already felt, but she needed to know. "He's coming for us."

"Edric?"

I nodded once. "He's coming for the Fae."

"How do you know?"

"William's Court may be laughing and calling him Wild Edric, but what they think is madness we know to be true. By all accounts, Edric has become obsessed with stories of faeries and magic. He's convinced that Godda is still alive. Here. Hiding from him because he broke his promise."

Sorcha opened her arms wide. "She's not. Flida's searched the forest. We would know if she was. Ancients be with me, I'd give anything to have her back, but she's not here."

"I know. But Edric thinks she is, and he's gathering his hunters. They're coming for us. They won't stop until they find her."

"We need to go get the boy and find a way to kill Edric." Her hand rested on the hilt of the knife sheathed at her waist.

"Godda made you promise not to kill him," I reminded her.

"Godda isn't here, and I don't have to be the one to kill him. I'll get the boy, if you can take care of Edric."

She had a point. Without Godda protecting Edric, he would be easier to kill. "All right. Get what you need and meet me here tomorrow. I think I know how we can get inside Lydbury."

15

BRYN'S plan was simple enough. We were going to walk into Lydbury through the main gate. The tricky part hinged on me being able to pass as Godda, but as long as we waited until after dark, I was fairly certain I could pull it off. Bryn would take the face of one of Edric's men, pretending to have found me. If Edric was as desperate to get Godda back as we'd heard, then the guard would just wave us through and not give us any trouble.

My faerie armor and weapons were hidden under a loose flowing dress and shawl, similar to what Godda had been wearing when she'd disappeared. If everything went well, I wouldn't need them, but if it didn't, I was ready.

Bryn crouched beside me, in the shadows of the trees outside Lydbury's gates. The familiarity of the situation reminded me of the last time we were here. The gargoyles had been with us then, surprised that we'd escaped Edric's men. They'd accused us of arguing like lovers.

I glanced at Bryn out of the corner of my eye. "Are you ready?"

"Hush." Bryn held up a hand. "Someone's approaching the gate."

I strained my ears to listen, annoyed that I hadn't noticed the approaching hoofbeats first. By the time I realized where they were coming from, the silhouettes of five men on horseback leaving Lydbury had ridden into sight. They hadn't yet reached the guard, and the sun had dropped low enough in the sky that I couldn't make out the details of their faces.

"Is it Edric?" I whispered.

"I can't tell. Watch the guard and tell me if he bows." Bryn crept closer to the gates, keeping close to the trees and remaining cloaked in shadow.

I stopped watching Bryn and shifted my eyes to the guard. He stood at attention, awaiting the approach of the riders. The horses trotted closer with the lead rider carrying a banner on a long pole. The guard immediately bent at the waist. I scanned the bodies of the riders, trying to pick out which of them was Godda's human, but it was impossible to tell in the growing darkness.

Bryn tapped me on the shoulder as the last of the riders passed through the gates. The group picked up their pace as they started down the road to town.

I stood and faced Bryn. "Where is he going at this time of night?"

Bryn stared after the riders. "I don't know, but I'll go after them and try to find out."

"You can't go after Edric alone. He has four men with him." I gestured toward the road. "And how do you plan to catch up to a group of humans on horseback?"

"Don't worry about that. If Edric is gone, that must mean the boy is alone. Go in and grab him. I'll attempt to delay their return so you have more time."

I grimaced. I had to admit it was a fair point, even though I would have preferred to work as a team. I didn't like the idea of returning to Lydbury alone. "Perhaps I should go after Edric and you should get the boy. If I shift into my hawk form, I can watch them from the skies."

Bryn frowned. "You could, but the boy knows you. He should come with you easily."

I shrugged. "Then take my face. Pretend you're me."

"No. It's better if I go after Edric. You can't do this." Bryn's face morphed to match the rider who'd come after us in the forest so many years ago. "Which means you won't be able to get close enough to distract them, if necessary."

"You had better not get close enough to distract them, either."

"If you stop wasting time and go, perhaps I won't have to." Bryn's borrowed face grinned at me.

I shivered. "All right, but if I'm going in alone, I'm flying instead of walking. We already know the wards won't stop me as long as I enter through the gates, and I don't want to risk questions from the guard."

"See? Another good reason for you to be the one to rescue the boy."

I scowled at Bryn. "Good hunting."

"Good hunting, my Rogue." Bryn disappeared before I could respond.

I might have some Rogue magic, but I was no Rogue. I was High Fae. To prove it, I did what only High Fae could do and shifted into my animal form, circling up into the starlight sky.

I found a current of air that would allow me to glide down, through the gate, on silent wings, and caught it. The guard might see me, if he was alert and his eyesight was keen, but he carried no weapon that might shoot me down. Fearless and free, I swooped and dipped my wingtip to skim past the tip of the bronze dragon's tongue before soaring up and heading toward the manor house at full speed.

I circled the manor once, taking note of the gardens and orienting myself based on what I remembered of the interior. On my second turn, I noted a balcony that had a view of the gate. I was almost certain it was the one connected to Godda's rooms. I transformed midair and landed in a crouch just outside the doors, waiting and listening to see if anyone moved inside.

There were no candles burning in the room and no sounds from within. So I pushed the doors open a crack and slid inside, shutting them softly behind me. On silent feet, I crept through Godda's room. I was almost to the door leading out to the hall when a man's voice broke the silence.

"Godda? Is that you?"

I froze in place. A chair scraped against the stone floor, and I tensed.

"Godda." The man sobbed before throwing himself at my feet. His hands clutched at my skirts and gripped my calves. "I'm sorry. I'm so sorry. Please don't ever leave me again."

Edric wasn't supposed to be here. If he was in the manor, then who had the guard bowed to? I didn't know what to do. If I pretended to be my sister, I would have to remain silent because I couldn't lie. But if I told him the truth, it might send him into a rage.

Even with my training and armor, I doubted I could fight him off, alone. Maybe I didn't have to. Maybe there was enough time for me to kill him before he noticed. I stared down at his back and slid my hand through the slit I'd made in the side seam of my skirt so I could reach for one of my knives.

Just as my fingers wrapped around the hilt, he turned his head up to me, dark eyes shimmering in the moonlight. "They took him. I couldn't say no. He's gone, and I thought I might die of loneliness. First you gone, and then our boy."

He rose up, onto his knees, so he could wrap his arms around my waist and bury his face in my stomach, forcing me to release my grip on my weapon and shift so he wouldn't notice the metal strapped to my hip. Then his words registered in my mind.

Alned wasn't here. That must have been William's men that we'd seen riding off with the boy. Bryn was following

Godda's son, and I was here, alone with the very dangerous human who had stolen my sister from the Fae. I needed to get away from him before he figured out who I really was, but he gave no sign that he planned to release me.

"Say something, please? Or do you plan to punish me further by remaining silent even after I've apologized?" He turned his face up to look at me. "So long as you have returned to me, I don't mind."

I pressed my lips shut, not even daring to smile, and hoped the room was dark enough that he wouldn't be able to tell the difference between me and Godda in the moonlight. I tried to take a step back, toward the door, but he held me tight.

"Don't go. Please. I've tried everything to get you back. I've searched out every mage and temple priestess within a three day ride. I've tried every trick they've suggested, but the forest won't let me in. Was it you? Were you keeping me out? Or was it those evil sisters of yours that kept you from me?" He winced and bowed his head. "I'm sorry. I know I promised you I wouldn't question you about your kin. Don't leave me. Please. I'll never do it again."

He begged and cried as his fingers dug into my flesh through the layers of thick cloth. His tears wet the front of my dress until the fabric grew damp and clung to my skin. I tried to hold still and give my mind time to come up with a plan, but when he started to pull himself up to his feet, I couldn't take any more.

I twisted my body, and he lost his grip on my dress. His hand slipped. The hilt of the knife sheathed at my hip brushed against his forearm. Before he could react, I pushed him away with all my strength, sending him stumbling back across the room.

He crashed into the chair he'd been sitting in and fell with his leg twisted beneath him. He howled in pain and followed the sound with a string of loud curses. I freed my knife and prepared to drive it through his chest before someone heard him and came to see what was the matter.

As I rushed toward him, his arms flailed out, searching for something he might use to pull himself up and away. Instead, one arm slammed into Godda's dressing table. The pitcher of wash water tumbled off the edge, smashing down on Edric's head. He wobbled and crumpled to the ground. When he fell limp, I rushed forward and ran my dagger through his heart, then danced back, out of reach, in case I'd misjudged my aim and missed the vital organ I'd been aiming for.

I crouched in the darkness and waited, counting my breaths and slowing my racing heart until I was sure that his was no longer beating. Then I crept forward and stretched two fingers out to feel for the pulse at his neck. His skin was warm, but his body was still. I exhaled in relief and sat down to rest beside the body, hoping Godda, wherever she was, would understand that I'd killed him in self defense.

"You're not Godda."

I spun around at the raspy sound of that now familiar voice and looked up at the semi-transparent figure floating above me. "You're not dead."

The spirit of Edric spread its arms wide as it released a cackling laugh that chilled my bones. It descended until its feet skimmed the floor. Then the silvery-grey form slowly solidified, gaining mass and color as I watched in horror.

"How?" I pulled my dagger from Edric's body and scrambled to my feet. The weapon wouldn't help me against a human spirit, but that didn't matter. I planned to flee and didn't want to leave my favorite blade behind.

"You're the one from the forest, aren't you? The one who was with her when she disappeared. The sister who looks like her." His spirit appeared almost human, if you didn't notice the shimmering aura that distorted the air around the edges of his form.

"Why aren't you dead?" I asked, both curious and attempting to distract him.

"Weren't you listening when I said I'd searched out every mage and temple priestess within a three day ride?" His leering grin sent shivers down my spine.

I edged closer to the balcony doors. "That explains nothing."

"Doesn't it, though?" His grin widened. "I wouldn't try that, if I were you."

The hand that I had been stretching toward the door behind me, hesitated. "What did you do?"

"You didn't think I was going to let her leave me a second time, did you?" He paused to study my reaction with his coal dark eyes. "I planned to get her back and keep her, one way or another. I still will, especially now that I know I'm right."

I shook my head. I'd listened to enough crazy madman talk for one night. At least I'd managed to kill him. I could deal with whatever was causing his spirit to linger some other time. I needed to escape and find Bryn so we could get Godda's son away from the human King and safely back to the Fae.

Raising my hands out at my sides to signal that I didn't plan to use them, I shifted my weight away from the door to throw him off my escape plan.

When his smile turned into the satisfied look of a hunter with its prey trapped and begging for mercy, I threw my weight back against the doors, hoping it would be enough to push them open. Once the cool night air hit my skin, I would transform and fly after Bryn. But the cool air never came. Instead, my body arched in pain as it crashed against the threshold, and I fell forward, onto my knees.

"Silly Fae. You won't escape me that easily." He laughed. "You won't escape me at all."

"What did you do?" I sat back on my heels and wrapped my arms around my waist, feeling up and down my ribs and back for the source of the stinging agony that had dulled but hadn't yet disappeared.

"I've created a cage for my beautiful bird, but alas she's not here." He bent at the waist to bring his eyes level with mine. "You are, though. And since I have you, you're going to help me get her back."

I winced. "You're dead. Why aren't you dead?" Tears welled in the corners of my eyes. I swallowed them down so they wouldn't escape.

"A little gold in a mage's pocket will buy all sorts of useful lessons for a young wizard, and healthy, strong animals given up for sacrifice will coax many a secret from a temple priestess. Now that I know for certain that my love does not lie underground, I will not go from this earth until I can take her with me." He crouched down in front of me and hooked a cold, damp finger under my chin, tilting it up so I would be forced to look at him. "You are my prisoner now, and if you value your life, you will help me find Godda."

16

ORCHA didn't return that night. She never sent a message. I'd gotten close enough to the riders to realize our mistake, but by then it was too late. When I arrived back at Lydbury, I realized I couldn't get past the gate without risking discovery. Even the most trusted servants were being questioned, searched, and scrutinized when they arrived and departed. It didn't take very long to learn the reason for the additional security from the gossips at King William's court.

They'd found Edric's body in Godda's rooms. He'd been murdered. The rumors claimed that he'd caught Godda with a lover. The two men had fought over her, Edric had been killed, and the lovers ran away. Several days after the whispered stories began spreading in King William's court, Edric's death was confirmed, though the circumstances were still a mystery.

The King called Alned to the throne room to inform the boy that he'd inherited his father's title and lands, including Lydbury Manor. Alned remained stoic as he accepted his fate and expressed his desire to remain at court and complete his

training. I considered removing him from the castle and returning him to the Fae, but decided he would be safe enough at
court, at least until I could figure out what happened to Sorcha.
I guessed that she had been the one to kill Edric, but I needed
to know if she had died in the process.

When I arrived at Lydbury, the iron gates were closed and
barred. The guard post had been abandoned, but I lacked the
Elemental magic needed to remove the lock on the gate. The
only other way I knew to get in was through the tunnels. If I
tried hard enough, perhaps I could find a way through Godda's
illusion.

I began by casting every sort of shield piercing magic available to the Rogues, but Godda's barrier held. I tried
transporting myself past it, into the tunnel I knew lay beyond,
but nothing happened. Days passed as I poked and prodded
at the magic. Then one day, while I was laying on the floor of
the tunnel staring up into the darkness, thinking of what to try
next, the muffled sound of singing reached my ears.

I sat up, turning my head in different directions, searching
for the source. The singing stopped. I was about to lay down
when it started again. I crept closer to the barrier and pressed
an ear to the dirt wall. There was someone on the other side.

I beat my fist against the solid illusion. The singing
stopped.

"Hello?" I called out, feeling like a fool.

Whoever or whatever was on the other side scurried closer. "Hello?"

"Who are you?" I asked.

I was answered by the thump of a fist hitting the wall.
"Bryn? Is that you?"

"Sorcha?" The word escaped my throat on a wave of
hope.

"I'm trapped. He's using—" Her voice cut off abruptly.

"Sorcha? Sorcha!" I banged on the wall again.

A silver mist seeped up from the base of the barrier, rising
to form a column beside me. As I stared, it took the shape of a

man. Edric.

"Aren't you an interesting faerie." His voice was rough and grating. "I thought your kind was supposed to be beautiful and charming, but you are nothing of the sort, are you?"

I bared my pointed teeth in a snarl. "Release her."

"Or else, what? You can't harm me. You'd have to get inside Lydbury, first. I welcome you to try." His lips curled in a sly grin.

If Edric's spirit still walked the earth, then he must have found a wizard who knew how to use soul magic to bind his life force to an object. "What do you want?"

"I want my wife returned to me. Bring her here, and I'll exchange her for her sister."

I tapped the tips of my fingers together, considering the bargain. "Godda is not among the Fae. We've searched and cannot find her."

"Then search harder if you hope to get your dear, sweet, Sorcha back." He sneered, not allowing me a chance to respond before disappearing in a shimmering haze.

Sorcha was alive. That fact fueled me as I worked to form a plan that would get me into Lydbury so I could find whatever object tethered Edric's spirit to the earth and destroy it. But Sorcha's warning made me think that Edric must have found a way to bind Fae within the boundaries of Lydbury. That meant I would have to also find a wizard willing to help me break the spell.

Since Godda's son had magic, and a claim to Lydbury, I decided to start with him. I returned to the King's court, borrowing a face I hoped would allow me to get close to the boy and earn his trust. It took a few years to accomplish that goal. Even then he wouldn't engage in any discussions of magic. He hid any abilities and refused to return home until he reached his maturity. So I returned to the tunnel to hide, only venturing out to spy on the gate once it was reopened.

Servants and supplies arrived to prepare the manor when it was time for Lord Alned's return. A feast was scheduled to celebrate the Winter Solstice. On the night of the Solstice, I watched the guests flood through the gates to partake in the festivities. In the distance, a hunting horn called out across the hills, and a band of human spirits, led by Edric, rode along the edges of the Fae forest on ghostly steeds.

A girl from the town went missing that night. So did three Elemental females who had been sent by the Regent Faerie Queen to her temple priestess to bestow blessings on the faithful. But there were no rumors of otherworldly happenings among the servants that came and went from Lydbury.

Edric's spirit either no longer lingered in the manor, or Godda's son had decided to use his magic to banish his father's spirit from the grounds. Regardless, every Solstice after that one, the ghostly band returned, taking more Fae with them each time they disappeared. Even though I tracked them, I could not uncover where they hid their prisoners.

The Regent Faerie Queen ruled that the Fae were no longer allowed to interact with humans. She hoped closing off the Fae forest would keep Edric's spirit from capturing and killing all the Fae. Any human who learned of the existence of Fae would be killed to protect our secrets. Rogues were allowed to feed to maintain their magic, but they had to take extra precautions to ensure that the humans did not remember the encounter.

I used my Rogue exception as an excuse to keep watch over Lydbury and the Wild Hunt. Centuries passed and Edric's terror continued. Then, someone from the village found a tapestry depicting the Faerie Queen rumored to have married Edric Sauvage. They brought it to the manor and presented it to the Lord. He began to take an interest. He started asking questions. He sought out a wizard. My hopes soared, until his car hit a tree, killing him and his wife.

For the first time, their son, the new Lord, picked up where his father left off. I lurked in the woods as the young Lord attempted to lure faeries and make contact with the Fae. He claimed their family was cursed and swore off marriage and children unless the Fae intervened. I scented the threads of fate shifting and prepared.

On the night of the summer solstice, those threads led me to a chapel in the countryside, near Lydbury. Just before sunset, a young woman emerged from the chapel and wandered into the field. She wore a long white gown and hummed to herself as she bent to pick flowers. Deciding I might use this opportunity to feed, I lured her further away with the illusion of more beautiful wildflowers. She picked dandelions that appeared to her as delicate blooms and wandered closer to the trap I'd laid for her in a circle of ancient oaks.

I waited in the shadows while the young woman stepped into the circle and turned, admiring the gnarled and twisted trees. Once she looked away from where I hid, I dropped the illusion cloaking me. When she faced me again, her body jolted back and her eyes went wide with shock.

"Are you lost, human?" I asked.

"What are you?" She took a step backward.

I crept closer to her. "You've entered my home and haven't guessed?"

"You…" She started to name me as a faerie, but held her tongue. Instead, she shook her head in denial as she stared at the tips of my ears, then blinked at me as though she didn't trust her eyes. "But that's impossible."

"Quite possible. After all, you came to me." I gestured toward the chapel where I'd first spotted her.

"I did no such thing. I merely wished to have a closer look at these trees. How was I to know that a…a faerie lived here?" Her face had gone pale, and her breath came in shallow bursts.

I interlaced my fingers as I inhaled the scent of her fear along with the scent of fate's possibilities. "So you do know what I am."

Her hands curled into fists at her sides. "I'm sorry to have bothered you, but I must be going." She turned and started to walk away.

I disappeared and reappeared in front of her, blocking her

path. "Not yet." The trap I'd set would prevent her from leaving until I released it, but if she tried to escape, it would knock her unconscious, and I needed her awake for my plan to work.

She glanced around, then up, then back at me. "Please?"

I laughed. It was a valiant attempt at winning my favor, but I couldn't let sentiment sway me if I hoped to take control of fate's threads. "First, I demand payment."

"Payment? For what?"

"You trespassed, human. Now you must pay the price." I grinned at her, enjoying this game where I decided the rules. She was the first human I'd toyed with in this way. If I wasn't careful, I'd become drunk and reckless on her fear.

"I didn't know this area was off-limits. It's not like there's a sign. How about we make a deal—"

I laughed again. "You'd like to make a deal with me?"

"Let me past, and I'll never come here again." She folded her arms across her chest.

I waggled a finger back and forth in the air between us. "That's not a deal, human. There's nothing in it for me."

"Of course there is. I won't bother you again. See? We both win." She shrugged, opening her palms to the sky.

I didn't want to make a deal with this human. I only wanted to force her onto a different path. "If you want to make a deal, we must both give something up. I have you. If you leave, I'll be giving you up. I'd rather not give you up. I have use for a human like you."

I sniffed the air. The young Lord was close.

The young woman shivered.

I needed to stall her and keep her from running away. "Why are you in such a hurry to leave, human?"

"I need to return to my fiancé. I've been gone too long. He'll be looking for me."

I cocked my head to one side and closed my eyes, searching for the thread that tied her to the chapel. It was already loosening. I only needed to strengthen the potential tie to the young Lord to shift fate's threads in my favor.

I opened my eyes and grinned. "How easy it would be to make him forget you. To make all of them forget you. Who would come rescue you, then?"

"What do you want?" She wrapped her hands in the long silky skirt of her white dress.

"To taste your lies." I crept closer. I didn't need to feed, but it would buy me some time and make her slightly more easily influenced.

Her body stilled and tensed. "What? No."

I shrugged. She appeared to be determined to do this the hard way. "Then bargain with me for your life, human."

"Okay."

I sighed, disappointed that she'd agreed so easily. I was hoping she would argue to buy a bit more time. The sound of my frustration was drowned out by a rustling in the hedge just beyond the circle of trees. I twisted my head in that direction, knowing what I'd see. Right on time, Edric's descendant jogged toward us, brushing leaves from his hair.

"Stop." I called out to him.

He paused outside the cluster of trees, gripping the strap of the canvas bag he'd slung over one shoulder.

"Who are you to interfere here?" I asked, even though I already knew the answer.

The young Lord straightened. "I'm Oscar Sauvage, descendent of Godda. I seek an audience with the Faerie Queen."

"Come closer." Interesting that he claimed Godda as his ancestor when speaking to me. I beckoned him closer, willing him to step inside the ring of oaks.

Rather than obeying me, he reached a hand inside his flannel shirt and extracted a piece of twine tied around his neck. After fumbling with the clump of braided herbs that hung from the twine, he held it between two fingers so that I could see it clearly. "You cannot charm me, Fae."

Feigning disappointment, I stretched an arm toward the young Lord and flicked my wrist. The trees obeyed my command, sending roots up from the ground to wind around his legs and pin him against the tree trunk. I didn't need him in the circle to strengthen the potential for a bond between these two.

"No matter. I can grant you no audience, and you are interfering." I knew he sought out the Faerie Queen, but I didn't plan to help him with that. If Flida knew I was breaking her laws, she'd kill this pair of humans, and I'd lose this chance to influence fate.

"Leave him alone." The young woman picked up a handful of pebbles and threw them at me.

"You must not deal with this trickster." The young Lord shouted at my captive as he strained against the vines that bound him.

I held up two fingers and swiped them through the air, creating an invisible shield that would allow them to see each other, but would prevent him from hearing what we said. "He'll stay where he is until our deal is complete. He may watch, but he must not interfere."

The woman's shoulders slumped. "Okay. Let me think."

"Think, human. What is it that you desire?" The sun was setting, and I wanted to be gone before the Wild Hunt appeared.

"Be careful!" The young Lord twisted and pulled against his restraints. "You can't trust this creature."

I hissed at him to be quiet. "Silence. Another word from you, and I will take you as well."

The young woman paced as she considered what sort of deal to propose. "I'm ready. But first I want to know what will happen if I stay with you."

"I will feed off you." I hoped that she'd agree that was the better option and give up on bargaining.

She glanced at the young lord, then back at me. "Will I die?"

I tapped one impatient finger against my lips. "No."

"Okay. Then here is what I offer you: let me return to my family and my life with no interference of any kind from you or any of the Fae, and I will return to you once a year for one day and one night."

I groaned. For a moment I'd thought she would agree to let me feed so I could release her into the arms of her waiting hero, but apparently she'd misunderstood. She'd presented me with a bargain instead of agreeing to let me feed, and the terms she offered went well beyond what I would have taken. Now I was forced to negotiate.

"Your bargain is tempting, human, but not sufficient. One day and one night each year is not enough in exchange for what you ask. However, I would take another in your place." I glanced at the young Lord to make sure that he couldn't hear us and wasn't trying to escape.

"Will two days and one night each year satisfy you?" Her counter-offer was of no interest to me. The only use I had for her was to bind her to Lydbury.

"No." I glared at her. "I will let you go free to enjoy a long and happy life with your husband, but in exchange, I will take one of your heirs." She thought I meant the man who waited for her at the chapel, but if this worked, she wouldn't be returning to him.

"What?" She shook her head. "No."

"It must be you or one of your heirs. Decide, human." If I succeeded in binding her to the young Lord who'd sworn off marriage, and I controlled their heir, I would control Lydbury.

The young woman glanced over at the current master of Lydbury as thought he might be able to help her. He strained against the roots that held him against the tree trunk, and she worried her lower lip with her teeth. The thread between them grew stronger.

After a few moments of silence, she presented new terms. "I will not hand over a child to you. If you want one, you must lure it yourself. And if you are successful, you must allow them to make the choice to stay with you or to return. If they choose to return, you must let them go and never bother my kin again. But it must be their choice."

I stalked toward her. "I will let them choose, if you agree

you will not warn them or attempt to intervene."

A horn blew in the distance. Edric and his riders were on the hunt. We didn't have much time. I set a hand on the young woman's shoulder so that she wouldn't run. Then I turned my head toward the sound. Once I was sure that they weren't yet within sight, I returned my attention to the human.

"I must go. Do we have a deal or are you coming with me?" I needed her to agree to our terms before I could leave. This was one of the many reasons I had hoped to avoid a bargain.

Her eyes sought out the young Lord, but I stood between them, blocking her view.

She grimaced. "You'll let me go free to live a long, healthy, happy life with my husband. You and your kind will stay away from me and my kin."

"Unless I succeed in luring one of your heirs to me. If I succeed, I will give it a choice to stay or to return, and in exchange you will not tell anyone about the Fae or our bargain." I silently sent a prayer to the ancients that she would hurry up and accept these terms. I couldn't risk being caught by the Hunt.

"If they choose to return, you'll never bother us again." She stared at me with a fierceness in her eyes that wasn't there earlier. She wasn't half bad at bargaining, and I almost felt sorry for leading her away from her safe future and onto this more dangerous path.

The horn sounded again, this time closer. It was time to go.

I squeezed her shoulder, sinking my long nails into her bare skin. "With what name will we seal this bargain? And speak the truth. I'll know if you're lying."

"Vivian."

"Bryn the Rogue accepts your bargain, Vivian." I grinned as I released her and the magic that held the pair apart. Then I disappeared, retreating to the safety of the tunnels with the hope that the events I'd set in motion would indeed lead to the future hinted at on the winds of fate.

17

WHEN the demons discovered that Edric was to thank for the sudden abundance of Fae souls, they built him a dungeon. He left Lydbury to his descendants and moved us underground, away from the humans, where I lost touch with my Rogue magic and lost track of time.

As Edric's band of vengeful spirits grew, more and more Fae were caught and paraded before him, then tortured for any knowledge of Godda, and killed to feed the demon hoard's expansion. I wondered how long it would be until my soul joined theirs, but Edric never touched me. Instead, he kept me in steel shackles, milled by mages using potions that prevented me from using my powers. Chains connected my ankles so I couldn't run and my wrists so I couldn't fight, but otherwise I was free to roam the dungeon, so long as I tended to the Fae prisoners.

The first time I refused was when I discovered Isleen among the captives. She'd begged me to kill her, but Edric demanded I keep her alive. When I resisted his order, he made me watch as he tortured her.

After Isleen came Rionach. By the time the Hunt brought in Meara and Niamh, I'd stopped paying attention to the faces. I almost didn't recognize them. Once they were gone, I lost all hope of escape or rescue. With how many Fae Edric's Hunters caught each solstice, I doubted there were very many left. I wouldn't let myself think of Bryn.

Then, one night, when I made my rounds, bringing nourishment to the new batch of captives, I sensed a difference. As I approached the next cell, I allowed myself to look closer at the captive and realized she wasn't Fae. She was human. A tiny seed of hope unfurled in my chest. She might be a Rogue in disguise, or she might be an opportunity to feed my Rogue magic.

I stopped in front of her cell and extended the bowl toward her, slipping it between the bars as I examined her face from under my hood.

"What is this?" she asked.

She didn't appear to be a Rogue, so I kept my head down and glamoured my Fae features to appear human, just in case she caught a glimpse of my face. "Food."

When she reached for the bowl, she trapped my hands and held them pressed between her palms and the rough ceramic. Shocked that she would be so bold, my head snapped up, and my hood fell back.

"Where are we? Who are you?" she asked. The woman was pretty, for a human. She had long, straight dark brown hair that she'd pulled back to show off her smooth, pale face. Even bundled in layers it was obvious that she had a lean, athletic build.

I shook my head to signal that I didn't plan to answer her questions.

"Eat." I pulled against her grip on my hands and caught the glint of gold wrapped around her wrist. I stared at it, not quite believing what I saw.

When she caught me looking, she released me and backed away from the bars with one hand clutched over the bracelet. Godda's bracelet. I studied her through the bars. She was human and didn't possess the halo of magic that surrounded those with wizard blood, but she had been marked by magic. Fae magic.

I spoke to her in the language of the Fae to test her. "Where did you get that?"

When she didn't respond, I set the bowl on the ground inside the bars and retreated down the hall. Hope filled my body with an energy I hadn't possessed in centuries. A human with a connection to the Fae had found Godda's bracelet. This was a gift from the Ancients. I would feed, and I would escape.

I tended to the other two captives quickly so that I could have more time with the human before Edric called for me to bring them up. One was a powerful Elemental with bright red hair. I cautioned her to dull the color so that she wouldn't attract Edric's attention. Then I helped them clean and dress in the simple white gowns Edric insisted the captives wear in his presence. When I was done, I made my way back down the corridor to check on the human.

The spirits had left her separate from the others, and I wondered why. When I heard voices, I realized she wasn't alone. The spirits must have brought another captive in. I allowed the chains that bound my ankles to drag across the stone floor, announcing my presence.

"Shh," I warned, keeping my own voice to a whisper.

She turned her attention away from the body the spirits had dumped in the cell across from her and focused on me. "Help him! Can't you see that he's hurt?"

"Eve?" The body moved, and a young male's head lifted. I could tell from the magic enveloping him that he was Fae, not human, and glamoured. He pushed himself up until he could look around.

The young woman curled her fingers around the bars of her cell and called out to him. "It's me, Liam. I'm right here. What happened? Are you okay?"

"Hush." I stepped between them, facing the woman. "You

shouldn't talk to him. It will only make it worse for you both."

"Make what worse? How could it be worse?" She shook the bars.

I placed my hands over hers, glancing once at the bracelet before cautioning her again. "Hush."

She slid her hands out of my grip and wrapped her fingers around my wrists, holding me in place. "Tell me where we are."

"I can't."

"Why not?"

I shook my head. I couldn't lie, and I wasn't allowed to tell her the truth. I shouldn't even be speaking with her, but if she kept making a fuss, someone might notice she was human, and I'd lose my chance to feed.

"Why am I here?" she asked.

"The Master will make it clear when he sees you. But first I must ready you."

Behind me, the young man rattled the bars of his cell. "Let her go! Take me instead."

I turned my head to get a look at him. He was kneeling at the front of his cell. Edric rarely bothered with male Fae. He feared them because he assumed incorrectly that they were more powerful than the females. This one must have put up a fight instead of running away.

I pulled against the woman's grip and twisted, trying to get a better look at him. Then I spoke in our language. "What is your name?"

"Liam of Flida. Who are you?"

My only living sister's son. I released a keening sob and dropped my head to my chest as tears streamed down my face. I hadn't been able to save the others, but I had a source for my Rogue magic now. I wouldn't let Flida's son die here. I couldn't.

The woman looked past me. "What did she say?" she asked my nephew.

Liam responded before I could choke back my sobs. "Eve,

tell me what she looks like."

I glanced up and met her eyes. Had Liam been the one to mark her with his magic? Did he trust her?

She spoke. "Golden-blond hair. Blue eyes. Do you know her?"

Now it was my nephew's turn to moan. "We thought you were dead."

I tried to bite back another sob. "Let me go to him," I begged.

The human woman let go of my wrists, and I spun away, falling to my knees in front of my nephew's cell. I reached for his face. "Who is your sire?"

"Cahal of the Ancients."

I grinned through my tears, happy for Flida. "How is she?"

"Fading. But she's determined to hold on until we can destroy Edric."

"Do you know how?"

"I've found the artifacts at Lydbury. Arabella of Rionach destroyed them."

A niece. I had a niece. Rionach hadn't mentioned a Faeling before she died. "Will she be queen?"

"No. The eldest is Fiona of Isleen."

There was more than one, and they'd kept the Faelings hidden from Edric. We might be saved after all.

Behind me, shuffling steps retreated to the back of the cell.

Liam glanced past me, calling out in his English tongue. "Eve. Wait."

"It's all right." Her voice was soft, her tone resigned.

"No, you don't understand." He looked pained, and I realized that he loved this human. He must have been the one to mark her. Didn't he understand that falling in love with humans was what had gotten us into this mess to begin with?

I shook my head and stood. "He is my kin," I explained.

She turned her head to look at me. "Kin?"

"Eve, she's going to help you," Liam said.

His trust in me warmed my heart, but it was unjustified. I'd promised no such thing. If he'd asked, I would have told him that I intended to feed off her so I could use my Rogue magic to help us escape.

The young woman folded her arms across her chest. "But I'm not leaving without you. And you're hurt. She should help you."

Liam shook his head. "I'll be fine. Just promise me you'll listen to her."

The distant echo of laughter caught my attention, and I glanced down the corridor to see who was coming. "I must go. They must not find me here. Stay quiet. I'll return soon."

I hurried away to gather what I needed to prepare the woman to meet Edric. When I returned, the pair were busy discussing how they'd ended up in Edric's dungeon. Their voices carried through the maze of stone and iron cells. It was clear from what Liam wasn't saying and what the woman was asking that she didn't know about the Fae.

"I think they took you to get to me." Liam's truth was only partial, unless he didn't realize that they took her because he'd marked her with his magic.

"They took her because they think she's one of us," I said, stepping out of the shadows.

"One of you? You mean part of your family?" This woman was either stupid, or naive. Had humankind grown so distant from magic that she truly didn't realize she'd been captured by spirits and thrown into a demon-built dungeon tended by one of the last of the High Fae?

Before I could respond, Liam spoke to me in our tongue. "She doesn't know. She can't know. They'll kill her if she knows about us."

"Who will kill her? Flida?"

He nodded.

I wondered what had happened to cause Flida to prohibit interaction with humans. If that was her wish, I would abide by it, if only because it was clear how much the idea of this woman's death pained my nephew. I stepped closer to the woman's cell and raised my hand to unlock the door.

"What are you doing?" She glanced at the bowl in my hands. "I don't need that. He's the one who's been bleeding. Help him."

I shook my head and unlocked her cell, then chose my words carefully to keep Liam's secret. "I need to get you ready to see the Master. He'll be calling for you soon."

"But Liam—"

"It's okay," he said. "I'll be fine. Whatever happens, listen to her. Do what she says."

"Fine." She voiced agreement, but she looked like she would run at any moment.

My fingers tingled in anticipation of absorbing her lies. I stepped inside her cell and shut the door behind me. It wasn't locked, so I took care to keep myself between her and the door. She glanced at the key in my hand.

"There's nowhere to run," I warned. "They'll catch you before you even make it down the hall."

"I doubt that."

"Your overconfidence will get you killed. When you see the Master, you must be silent. Invisible."

"Listen to her, Eve, please." Liam sounded like he was in pain.

I walked toward her, holding the bowl of water out between us. "We need to get you clean."

"Why?"

"The Master is very particular." I handed her the bowl. "And we need to do something about that." I pointed at Godda's bracelet dangling from her wrist.

She set the bowl down on the stone floor and hugged the bracelet to her chest. "You can't have this."

"She's right, Eve. If anyone here sees you wearing that bracelet, they'll never let you go."

"How am I going to explain to Uncle Oscar that I lost his

family's precious heirloom?"

I spoke in the Fae tongue to Liam. "She wears my sister's bracelet on her wrist and says it is her family's heirloom. She's lucky I asked and didn't just rip it from her arm. Edric will not be so kind when she goes before him with the other captives. He'll single her out for torture, convinced she stole it from Godda herself."

Liam responded in a soothing tone. "She'll give it to you. Just please promise me that you'll make sure she isn't selected and help her escape."

I narrowed my eyes at the young women. I'd do what I could, but I was leaving this dungeon with or without her.

"Give her the bracelet," Liam said.

"Why can't I just give it to you?" she asked.

"It will be worse if they find it on me. Please, Eve. She'll return it once we're free. You need to listen to her."

I held out my hand, and she slipped the bracelet off her wrist. After a quick glance at Liam and then down at the gold band resting in her palm, she handed it to me. The way her lip curled, I could tell that she was not happy about this plan.

"Quickly, now." I wrapped my fingers around the bracelet and slid it over my fingers, pushing it up until it stuck at the widest part of my forearm where it would be hidden from view by the sleeve of my robe. "We don't have much time."

I washed the young woman's face, using the act as a cover to steal some of her lies, and helped her change into a simple white gown that would help her blend in with the Fae prisoners. Then I brushed out her long dark hair, again using the excuse to touch her temples as another opportunity to feed. When I finished, I locked her cell behind me, nodded to my nephew, and disappeared down the corridor to examine Godda's bracelet.

In an alcove, far from the prisoners and the spirits, I held the band up to candlelight to get a closer look. The markings etched into the gold formed words in the language of the Ancients, but the way they were ordered made no sense. I whispered one aloud and the band warmed. I spoke the next word, but nothing more happened.

The call of Edric's horn interrupted my experiments. It was time. I returned the bracelet to my arm and went to collect the captives.

As I approached Liam's human, she rushed to the bars, her eyes wide with fright. Liam was already gone. I'd planned to free him when it was time to escape, but Edric had wasted no time sending him to fight the demon hell beasts. I should have warned him when I had the chance.

"Where did they take him?" she asked. "Is he okay?"

"Hush." I unlocked her cell and beckoned to her, unable to reassure her without lying. "It's time. Follow me."

I led her through the corridors of the dungeon to the cells that held the two Elemental females. The red-haired one had taken my advice and dulled her color to a light reddish-blond. I opened their cell, and they fell into step behind me without a word. Unlike the human, they understood what was coming.

I led the three captives up the curved staircase to the large chamber above, then paraded them between the line of stone pillars that held up the arched ceiling. Edric and two of his Hunters waited at the far end of the room. When we reached them, I motioned for the captives to form a line.

They stood shoulder to shoulder with their eyes on the stone floor as Edric waited for me to present them.

"Master, these three were captured by your Hunters this evening." I dipped my head and hoped this was the last time I would have to serve him.

Edric paced along the line, examining each of them in turn. He stopped in front of the powerful Elemental first. "Her hair reminds me of summer." He stepped closer. "Let me see your face."

She tilted her head up, but didn't meet his eyes. The way she shivered and shook, she seemed weak and already broken.

He grumbled and moved on to the other Elemental. "Look at me."

The brown-haired Fae tilted her chin up and glared at Edric. For a moment, I was sure he would pick her just because she dared to challenge him.

"Not highborn, but might be useful." He let the Elemental glare as he continued on to Liam's human. "Look up."

She did as she was told, but stared past him, avoiding eye contact.

"Well, look what we have here. Something new." Excitement crept into his voice. He'd said the same thing about Isleen before choosing her. "Look at me, girl."

She turned her face toward him but kept her eyes downcast. I braced for the selection I knew was coming.

Edric's feet barely touched the floor as he circled her, studying her from every angle. "I think I'll start with this one. Take the others back. I'll deal with them later."

"Yes, Master." I had no choice but to leave Liam's human behind as I ushered the Elementals away. At least I would be able to save our kin.

The red-haired Fae didn't stop shivering even after I returned the pair to their cell. I wanted to give them hope of our escape, but I didn't dare speak a word of it while so many spirits and demons lingered near-by.

I secured the Elementals and cloaked myself in shadow, using the smallest possible amount of Rogue magic necessary. I would return for them, and my nephew, once I freed myself from my shackles and found a way out.

18

VIVIAN thought she'd found a way around our bargain by not reproducing, but her heir did not have to be a child of her loins. I selected her favorite niece and sent the young woman dreams of the Faerie Queen to lure her to England. After she arrived at Lydbury, nearly all the pieces were in place for me to take control of the manor. But fate had other plans.

Inside Lydbury, the young woman's thread tangled with Flida's son. Then the Hunt captured them both. Her by mistake, and him because he'd chased after her like a fool. Flida would be livid when she discovered that her only child had been taken by the Hunt. None of the captured Fae ever returned.

I tried to follow the spirits who had ridden off with Vivian's niece, but I lost them near the temple ruins. Flida's son had also followed her trail. He arrived shortly after me. I hid when a young demon and several spirits appeared. Liam of Flida could have run, but he fought them, even though he was outnumbered. I cringed as I watched. Then he fell and they disappeared with him.

I escaped to the tunnels, seething with frustration. Plan after plan had failed, and I was unsure what to try next. I'd spent centuries trying to rescue Sorcha, relying on the thin hope that Edric would keep her alive. All the plans I had made to topple Riagan's rule had been left to rot when my effort shifted to banishing Edric.

As much as I didn't want to admit defeat, Vivian's heir had been my last hope. I was going to have to give up and go back to the Fae. I'd distanced myself from my kin to avoid having to face the twins. Better that they thought me dead. But now I'd have to return and accept whatever punishment awaited me.

I paced to help me think. When that failed, I sat with my back to the wall and closed my eyes. I let my mind drift, shifting ideas around and trying to form a new plan. I lost track of time and startled when a broken sob pulled me from my thoughts.

The sound echoed down the tunnel, coming from the direction of the temple ruins. I assumed it was a child who had stumbled on the forgotten door, now buried beneath the stone slabs, and gotten lost. I refocused, intending to ignore the interruption. Before I could sink back into my mind, the whisper of muffled voices filled my ears.

Never, in all the centuries I'd spent lurking in the tunnel, had any soul disturbed me. I considered fleeing before I was found, but the only safe place for a Fae on the night of the Solstice was deep in the Fae forest, and I wasn't ready to return. So I stood and wedged myself into the corner where Godda's illusion met the tunnel wall. Pulling the shadows around me, I hid and waited to see who or what would appear.

Three figures shuffled into view a few moments later. The one in the lead wore a long hooded robe. The two who followed wore thin white gowns that hung in a sheath from the straps on their shoulders, extending to their ankles and leaving their arms bare. They were Fae females.

The one in the robe stopped when she spotted the solid

illusion that blocked the tunnel. Her companions halted behind her. The dark-haired one who had cast a small ball of fire to light the way, directed the light ahead so they could get a better look at the obstruction.

The red-haired Fae straightened her shoulders and stepped forward. She shook as she called on her Elemental magic to no effect. The dirt wasn't swallowed back into the earth, because it wasn't dirt. It was an illusion.

The robbed figure stepped forward. She raised an arm and reached out to touch the wall.

"I know this place. I've been here before." Her hood dropped back, revealing blond hair and a face I'd feared I'd never see again.

"Sorcha?" I stepped out of the shadows and into the light cast by the Elemental.

Three heads turned to look at me. The Elementals shrank back, but Sorcha rushed forward. She threw her arms around my neck.

"You're alive." I whispered the words as my arms wrapped around her waist. I'd wished that to be true for so long. She was here. She was free. "How did you escape?"

She pulled back far enough to look into my eyes and laid a palm against my cheek. The joy that had been there a moment before drained from her face, replaced by sadness and fear. Her cool hand slipped from my skin as she slid out of my grasp, melting back toward the others.

"They brought in a human." She paused. "And Flida's son. My nephew."

"Where are they now?" My heart pounded against my ribs. The threads I'd shifted had led to Sorcha's freedom after all.

"They are still prisoners of the Hunt." She pointed back down the tunnel toward the temple ruins. Toward where I'd lost the trail of the spirit who'd captured Vivian's heir. Toward where Liam had been defeated by the demon and disappeared. The Hunt had been hiding right under my nose.

"Alive?" I asked.

She nodded. "When I left them."

"Show me where." I started back down the tunnel.

Her hand grasped my arm. "No."

I turned to argue, but my eyes caught a glimpse of gold on her wrist. It glowed in the light cast by the Elemental. Sorcha hadn't been wearing any jewelry on the night we'd gone to fetch Alned from Lydbury.

"Where did you get that?" I asked.

"The human was wearing it when she arrived." Sorcha twisted the band around her wrist.

"May I see it?"

She slipped the bracelet off and held it out. The metal was warm to the touch, possibly from contact with Sorcha's skin, but possibly something else.

"There's writing on the band," she said.

I angled the surface toward the light source so I could read the words etched into the surface.

Sorcha looked over my shoulder as I examined the bracelet. "It was Godda's, given to her by William at Lydbury."

The two Elementals moved closer. The brown-haired one spoke for the pair. "We should keep moving. It may not be safe here."

I kept my focus on the carvings, narrowing my eyes to block out the others. There was something there. I almost had it.

Sorcha touched my arm. "I'll bring them back to the forest and return for the bracelet. Be careful."

I nodded, and she moved away from me to talk with the captives she'd freed. I didn't want her to go, but it would be easier to concentrate without an audience.

Once they disappeared, I refocused. I read the words again, painting them against the blank canvas of my mind. Envisioning them so I could absorb them and distill their secrets.

When I considered them as a whole, the bracelet warmed in my hands. I picked one of the words at random and concentrated on it. The bracelet cooled. I expanded my focus to encompass them all, and it warmed again.

Sorcha reappeared before me. "Any luck?"

"Perhaps." I closed my eyes and repeated the process until I found a word that warmed the metal. Then I found another and another. Soon the order began to make sense.

I opened my eyes and moved toward Godda's illusion. I touched the illusion with one hand and gripped the bracelet in the other. Carefully, I drew power from the band, as though it were another Rogue. Then I commanded the illusion to dissolve.

The obstruction shimmered and faded, revealing iron bars that stretched from the floor to the ceiling of the tunnel. Beyond them, the tunnel had been boarded up. The bars and boards were no illusion, and they'd been warded. The additional layers of protection must have been added sometime after Godda's wedding.

Sorcha sucked in a breath behind me. "How did you do that?"

"Godda." I held up the gold band. "You found her. She's right here."

Sorcha snatched the bracelet from my hand and cradled it in her palms. "Is she…alive?"

"No." I paused, knowing that wasn't the answer Sorcha wanted to hear. "I'm sorry."

"But why?" She stared down at the gold band as though willing it to respond.

"I don't know why she did what she did, or even how, but the words etched into the band are scrambled. I think you can use them to free her soul when you're ready."

"I need to bring this to Flida." Sorcha's fingers curled around the bracelet as she turned away from me.

"What about Liam?" I asked.

She shook her head but wouldn't look at me. "I can't go back there."

"I'll go."

"No." The word echoed off the walls, sharp with fear. "There's nothing you can do to help him. No one returns."

"You returned." I kept my voice soft.

"I used the human to escape. I…" Her voice drifted off. She shivered. "I need to go."

I stepped closer to her. "Let me help you, then. If you won't let me help Liam."

"You've helped me enough already." She turned her head to glance back at me. Then she disappeared.

I stared at the place where she'd been only a heartbeat before. I wasn't sure what I'd expected to happen. I'd never let myself think beyond my plans to free her and banish Edric. In my mind she was the same High Fae who had asked me to sire her Faeling in order to protect me from the twins.

Riagan and Rowen.

The pieces of the puzzle that I'd been trying so hard to arrange suddenly fell into place. Edric had been killed, if not banished. Godda had been returned to the Fae. Soon she would rest with the Ancients. But, the twins didn't know.

I transported myself to the woods near Riagan's lean-to hut. I wasn't even certain the twins would be there, but if I thought too long about it, I would lose my chance. I didn't have much time to negotiate before they realized what I planned to offer was already done.

When I arrived, I crept toward the clearing. The lean-to was there, still standing but barely. The roof sagged and the pillars were covered in moss. It appeared as though it hadn't been visited since before the temple collapsed. I lifted a hand to call a sprite, hoping one might tell me where I could find the twins.

Before I could send the signal, a pair of figures stepped out from behind a nearby tree. Their faces were in shadow. I could only tell they were Fae from the silhouettes of their ears in the moonlight.

"What do you want?" The voice that spoke was low and slurred.

"I'm looking for the High Rogue and his Rogue Leader."

"Who are you, and what business do you have with them?" The voice that asked had a harsher and sharper tone than the first.

"I am Bryn of the Rogues, and I bring them a bargain."

Laughter followed my announcement. Then one of the pair stepped forward, allowing the moonlight to fall on his face. Rowan stood facing me in his natural form. He slurred when he spoke. "You live."

"I do."

The voice from the shadows that I suspected belonged to Riagan responded. "You are in no position to bargain. You already have a bargain with me."

"I come to offer new terms." I kept my voice flat and my face blank. I would show no fear.

Riagan laughed again. He still wouldn't show his face. "We made a deal. Kill Edric, and return Godda to the Fae. I will not accept anything less in exchange for your Confirmation."

Rowan stared at me, but remained silent.

"I do not ask for anything less, Master." I forced the last word out, as much as it pained me. Better that he think he still had the upper hand. "Edric is dead. It is only his spirit that still walks the earth. I will banish that spirit and return Godda to the Fae, but I want more than my Confirmation."

Riagan scoffed. "Fool. You didn't kill Edric. Why do you waste my time?"

"Sorcha killed Edric." I directed my words at Riagan, but kept my eyes on Rowan's face.

"You cannot prove that," Riagan barked from the shadows.

Rowan straightened at the sound of his offspring's name. When he spoke, the slurring was gone from his speech. "Sorcha is gone. Captured and killed by the Hunt, most likely."

"I can prove that she killed Edric, and I will. But first, I want to agree on new terms."

Riagan clicked his tongue against the roof of his mouth, scolding. "If you want me to grant you something more, then you must give me something more."

"It is not you I wish to bargain with." I kept my eyes locked on Rowan. "I wish to bargain with the Rogue Leader to take your place as High Rogue."

"You will not." Riagan lurched forward into the moonlight. He stood, hunched and wrinkled, in his natural form. He'd aged in my time away and no longer wore his Court-ready face.

"I will." I kept my spine straight and my face blank. Inside, shock and excitement warred in my belly. *This is what I'd been scared of? This might actually work.*

"What is your bargain?" Rowan asked.

I offered him the one thing I knew he couldn't refuse. "I will honor the terms of my bargain with Riagan, and I will return Sorcha to her seat on the Queen's Court. When I do, you will make me High Rogue."

Rowan's lips pressed into a line. He knew I wouldn't offer if I didn't believe it possible. If I didn't know that she lived. "Sorcha will confirm your claim that she killed Edric?"

"She will."

"This is madness!" Riagan's fists clenched. "How do we know you haven't been hiding her this whole time? You could have captured her yourself and hidden her away somewhere, only to come back and offer this as your way to usurp me. I will not allow it."

Rowan shifted to face his twin. "It is not yours to allow. Rogue Rule states that the challengers for the seat of High Rogue bargain with the Rogue Leader."

Riagan bared his chipped and yellowed teeth. "The Rogue Leader serves the High Rogue."

Rowan's eyes narrowed to vertical slits. "The Rogue Leader serves the Rogues, as does the High Rogue."

"You will not accept this bargain." Riagan hissed at his twin.

"You will not interfere." Rowan cast a shield around Riagan, containing him and cutting off his complaints. Then he returned his attention to me. "Sorcha will confirm that she killed Edric. You will return Godda to the Fae. Sorcha will take her place on the Queen's Court, and neither of you will ever speak a word about your bargain with Riagan."

I admired that he'd added a term of his own, especially one that showed how well he served the Rogues. It would only make the rest of the Fae hate us more if they knew that the Rogues had a hand in creating the Hunt.

I nodded. "Once Godda is returned to the Fae, I will receive my Confirmation. Then, after Sorcha confirms that she killed Edric and swears her Oath to the Faerie Queen, you will make me High Rogue."

Riagan pounded on the invisible wall separating him from his twin, and I realized he could hear us, even though we could not hear him.

"If you fail to meet these terms, you will be banished," Rowan said.

I grinned. "Bryn of the Rogues agrees to these terms."

Rowan nodded. "Rowan of the Rogues accepts your bargain and wishes you good hunting."

19

I STOOD by myself at the edge of the woods, watching the rest of my kin celebrate the coronation. My sisters were gone. Flida and Godda's souls had been returned to the ether. Their strength now helped fuel our magic.

I was alone. One of the last from our generation. Flida's partner remained, but even he was planning to pass his responsibilities as Guardian of the Elementals on to a younger Fae. And there was Bryn. We had been partners once, but we'd been united by a mission, not by love. That was over now.

"There you are." The voice came from the shadows at the edge of the forest.

I turned toward the sound and stepped closer. A face that had haunted my dreams, reminding me of my failure, stared back at me. Shoulder length auburn hair, curling in waves and tucked back behind round-tipped, human-like ears. Dark eyebrows and wide hazel eyes contrasting with pale skin above a close-trimmed russet beard. When I blinked, that face was gone, replaced with another. The nose was the same. Odd that I'd never noticed that before.

"It's done." I said and looked away. Tree trunk. Fallen

leaves rustling in the breeze. Dirt beneath my feet.

"You killed him, and you brought her home." Bryn remained in the shadows, face just visible, lit by moonlight filtered between the bare branches above.

I shook my head, still not meeting Bryn's gaze. "The human did. With Liam's help." Liam. My nephew who hadn't even been born when I was captured. Flida's son. *May she rest with the Ancients.*

"They may have been the ones to banish him, but you killed him." Bryn's eyes searched the clearing behind me where our greatly diminished kin had gathered to see the new Faerie Queen crowned. My niece. Fiona of Isleen. Raised by Flida. *May her force strengthen us all.*

"The human did what we could not." I'd seen the evidence of our failure when I went to fetch Evelyn from Lydbury, the place where I'd lost my freedom. That poor frozen gargoyle, still trapped. My sister lost forever. All because I'd agreed to a bargain with a Rogue.

"Ah, but she is here because of you." Bryn's fingers pressed against each other. The sound of those long nails clicking against each other brought back memories. "You and me. Us."

My eyes found Bryn's. "Who is here because of me? The human? What do you mean? What did you do?"

"When I couldn't find you, I acted on the scent of possibility." Bryn paused, head tilted, waiting for me to understand.

"You still speak nonsense and riddles. It appears some things never change."

Bryn blinked and stepped closer. "You haven't changed."

"But I have." I searched Bryn's face, eager to see the judgement there. What I found instead made me look elsewhere, anywhere to avoid what I hadn't earned.

"It's over." Bryn took another step, emerging from the shadows to close the gap between us.

My lips twisted, and I started to turn away.

Bryn caught my chin. Nails caressed my cheek, and my

eyes met those ink black wells I'd once shrank away from in fear.

"It's over," Bryn said, again.

I closed my eyes against the truth. "It will never be over."

Bryn's hands smoothed my hair back from my face. "It's not your fault."

"It is." I swallowed, squeezing back the tears. "I failed."

"He's dead." Bryn's nails traced a familiar pattern across my skin.

I imagined Godda's face, bright behind my eyelids, just as it had been when she walked the earth. "Did she know what he was capable of?" An anguished moan escaped my lips before I could bite it back. "We should have killed him before he could betray her." I whispered.

"Look at me." Bryn held my face.

I shook my head, trying to escape. I'd expected to see the judgement I deserved. I could even bear Bryn's pity. Just not the other emotions I'd seen there. Ones I didn't dare name. Ones that shouldn't be on offer to me. Not after what I'd done.

"Open your eyes, Sorcha of Maeve, my Rogue." The first time Bryn had called me that was the night of Godda's wedding feast. Instead of warmth, the memory only brought me more pain. I'd never earned that name.

"She's gone. They're all gone. I'm the only one remaining." I kept my eyes pinched shut.

"You're not. I'm here." Bryn's nail sketched a rune against my skin. *Endless*. "And we have a new queen. Do we not?"

My eyelids flicked open so I could glare at him. "It's not over. The demons still hunt us." It was the threat to our kin that was endless, not our partnership.

"Then we'll fight them together." Bryn smiled, revealing those wicked sharp teeth. "You still have me. You have always had me."

"No."

"If that's your wish." Bryn released me. Cool night air

replaced warm palms as Bryn took one step back, into the shadows, and then another.

"No." I reached out. My fingers circled Bryn's wrist. That wasn't what I wanted. It was what I thought I deserved. Punishment for my failure.

"No?" Bryn paused, features flickering in the moonlight. Hairless with bottomless black pools for eyes one minute, auburn beard and human features in the next.

"Don't." I tightened my grip. "Don't waste your lies on me." I'd buried that part of my past centuries ago. I'd burned that part of me and left the ashes in the dungeons. Only the emptiness remained.

Bryn's features shifted once more, returning to the form I'd once found so terrifying, but that now felt like coming home. "As you wish."

I relaxed my grip and let go. "Tell me what you mean. About the human."

Bryn nodded once, then moved closer until we stood shoulder to shoulder. Bryn faced the coronation celebration behind me, while I kept my gaze fixed on the darkness of the forest. "Possibilities. Threads on the wind. Do you remember your lessons?"

I clenched my teeth. "I'm no Rogue."

Bryn clicked his tongue, scolding. "The unraveling that began when Godda was captured. I may have found a way to weave the threads together again. Now that the human has chosen us, she gives me hope."

"She swore the Oath." I didn't understand why one human, a human I'd left to die in Edric's dungeons, could be so important to the future of the Fae. "Liam's claimed her as his mate."

"Good." He inhaled, breathing deep. "Yes. The threads are aligning. All that remains is to give them a push."

I twisted to face Bryn. "What are you planning?" I remembered enough of what I'd been taught to know I couldn't change any bargains that were already set in motion. That didn't mean I wouldn't do whatever I could to protect my charges. I'd sworn an Oath to serve and protect the new Faerie Queen, and before Flida faded, I'd promised her that I would look after her son and our nieces.

Bryn turned to face me, our bodies close enough to be dancing. My memories reminded me that I'd never danced with this face. Only the other.

"Do you really want to know?" The moon reflected in Bryn's eyes, creating the effect of white pupils swimming in a sea of black.

I set my hand to rest on the hilt of the knife in my belt. It was a threat with no teeth. Injuring Bryn would be like carving out a piece of my own flesh. "I won't let you hurt them."

Those black eyes followed the movement of my hand. "The human and her mate?"

"My nephew and nieces." If Bryn intended to cross them, I wouldn't hesitate, regardless of the link between us.

"I don't want any harm to come to them. I seek to strengthen them." Bryn lifted my hand from the hilt of my knife and pressed our palms together, interlacing our fingers.

"That is your plan?" I needed to hear it. Bryn was Fae and couldn't lie.

"Yes." Bryn stepped closer, pinning our entwined hands between our hearts.. "I found a thread with the potential to repair the rupture caused by Godda's abdication."

"Let Fiona fix the rupture." Nothing good came from Rogue meddling. Not that I'd seen. "Our time is over."

"If you truly believed that, you would not have Sworn." Bryn's head tilted as though listening to a distant voice on the wind. "You will play your part. I will play mine. Only now we can work side by side. Together. Like before."

"My place is at the side of my queen." I pulled away.

Bryn released me. "You feel nothing for me, then?"

I froze at the question. Emotion swirled in my gut, rising like a wave to crest in my chest. "My feelings are what caused this disaster in the first place. I was hurt and thought I knew what was best. I agreed to Riagan's bargain, and look what that did to our kin. My feelings can't be trusted."

"You are more Rogue than you realize. Edric started this. Now he's gone. We made that happen. Together. Rogue meddling returned you to me." Bryn reached out, unfurling the fingers of one hand and offering it for me to grasp.

The gesture pulled at the hollow emptiness inside me. "You have no idea what I did to survive."

Bryn's tongue clicked. "You're a Rogue. You did what you had to do."

"I'm no Rogue." I clenched my hands against my sides to resist the urge to take the lifeline Bryn offered me.

"Did you learn nothing from me?" Bryn stepped closer, hand still outstretched and waiting for mine.

I fixed my gaze on Bryn's bare chest, not daring to look into those black pool eyes and unable to respond. When we met, I had thought I knew everything.

"Tell me. How did you find the bracelet?" Bryn asked.

"The human…" I lifted my eyes, realization dawning. Bryn had said she was here because of me.

Bryn nodded. "What are the tools of the Rogue?"

"Endless." That word. A lesson. A promise.

"You've not forgotten, then."

"The things I did…" I pressed my palms flat against Bryn's chest.

Bryn's fingers lifted my chin. "You did nothing more than you were taught. You used the tools of the Rogue. You survived."

I'd thought my life would end in those dungeons, alone, after I'd watched all my kin die at the hands of that madman and the demons who'd joined forces with him. I thought I'd been forgotten. Left for dead. But, Bryn had never given up on me. Warmth poured into that empty place in my chest, the one surrounding my heart.

"Thank you," I whispered, allowing my hands to slide down and around Bryn's waist.

Bryn inhaled a shuddering breath and traced the curve of my lower lip with one thumb. "Partners?"

I nodded. "Partners."

The corner of Bryn's mouth lifted up into a grin. "Good. Because our work is not quite done. Are you ready for a new lesson?"

20

THE morning after Fiona's coronation, I brought Sorcha with me to visit Rowan. We found the twins together in their usual hideout.

Rowan paced, still wearing his Court face and attire, unchanged from the coronation festivities the previous evening. His tunic was wine-stained and rumpled. His boots were caked in mud.

Riagan lounged in his Rogue form on the stump where I used to practice and wait for his commands. He appeared to be lecturing Rowan about something, but we were too far away to make out his words. Even though I brought evidence that would satisfy my bargain end his reign as High Rogue, I knew he wouldn't relinquish his power easily. I would need to be careful.

Rowan walked forward to greet us as we stepped out of the forest and approached the lean-to. Riagan scowled, but otherwise didn't acknowledge our presence.

"High Rogue, Rogue Leader." I bowed to them. "I bring you a Sorcha of Maeve to confirm Godda's return and Edric's death."

"Sorcha." Rowan's eyes glistened with unshed tears. "It is true. You have returned."

"I have." Sorcha dipped her head out of respect. "And I brought the soul of our former queen with me."

"You returned with her soul? How is that possible?" Rowan asked.

"Godda made a bargain with her human. She arranged it so that, should he ever break his promise to her, she would disappear, and her soul would be captured in a bracelet until it could be returned to the Fae."

"How did you know where to find this bracelet?" Riagan turned his head to glare at Sorcha.

She was not intimidated by him. "I was with her when she enchanted it."

"So she told you what she'd done?" he asked, narrowing his eyes to vertical slits.

Sorcha stood tall under his scrutiny. "No. I didn't know what she'd done until after she disappeared. When I saw the bracelet again, I suspected. Flida confirmed it. She used the last of her power to free Godda's soul. Then I guided both of my sisters to the ether."

"But only a queen can do that." Rowan spoke in a reverent whisper.

"When I returned, Flida informed me that all the High Fae have the capacity to perform that rite. It is up to the queen to choose who learns to use that power. Godda taught Flida before she left to live with the humans. Flida taught me before she faded. Now Fiona gets to choose which, if any, of the other remaining High Fae will learn to use that power."

This secret of the High Fae was new to me, as I assumed it was to the twins. I scanned their faces to confirm my suspicion. Riagan appeared unmoved, but Rowan pressed his lips together as he studied Sorcha. I recognized that look. He was considering how he might use this knowledge to his advantage. Riagan was probably doing the same, but Rowan chose not to guard his reaction.

"Rogue Leader." I drew his attention to me to distract him. "I believe this satisfies the first requirement of our bargain."

Rowan nodded. "Bryn of the Rogues, I now pronounce you Confirmed. You are a full Rogue with all the rights and responsibilities that come with that title."

"Thank you, Rogue Leader. As a Confirmed Rogue, I wish to proceed with the second part of our bargain." I hadn't warned Sorcha about what I hoped would come next.

She turned to me, a question on her lips, but turned away when Riagan reached out suddenly to wrap his fingers around his brother's wrist. I tensed, waiting to see what he would do before I reacted.

Riagan dug his nails into Rowan's skin as he spoke. "Rowan, I beg you, if you go through with this, you will lose me forever."

Rowan winced. "If you attempt to flee from your fate, I will stop you."

Riagan scoffed. "You don't have the power to stop me."

"So certain, are you?" Rowan twisted his arm free.

Riagan straightened his spine and squared his shoulders. "I have always been the stronger twin."

"I feel compelled to test that theory." Rowan faced off with his brother as I worked to keep my jaw from dropping open in surprise.

"Be my guest." Riagan took a step forward.

"I will." Rowan lifted one long finger and held it between them. "But first, Sorcha of Maeve, did you kill Edric Sauvage?"

"It was an accident, but I did." Sorcha's voice trembled only slightly, enough for me to notice, but not so much that the twins, so focused on each other, likely did.

"And you have sworn your oath to serve the new Queen of the Fae?" Rowan asked.

"I have."

"Don't." Riagan commanded.

Rowan continued to ignore his twin. "Then, by the rules of the Rogues, I must pronounce Bryn of the Rogues our new High Rogue."

Sorcha gaped at me, but I couldn't look at her. I kept my eyes on Riagan.

"Fools." Riagan cackled. "Goodbye brother."

I lunged forward, expecting that Riagan would disappear, as he'd threatened to do, and not trusting that Rowan would catch him before he did. But Riagan remained standing there. I caught myself and pulled back before I crashed into him. We stared at each other for a moment.

Then he turned to Rowan and screamed. "What did you do to me?"

"I bound you to me." In the confusion, Rowan had drawn his knife. He pushed me aside and plunged his weapon into his brother's chest. Then he curled his other arm around Riagan's waist and held him in a tight embrace as Riagan gasped for air.

Rowan's eyes searched for Sorcha until he succeeded in meeting her gaze. "Our time is over. I wish for you to free us both." This was what he'd been planning.

Sorcha's hands shook as she stepped forward and set one on each of the twin's shoulders. "As you wish, my sire. I will do for you what I could not do for so many of our kin in Edric's dungeons. May you find peace. May your souls rest with the ancients."

She closed her eyes. A moment later I closed mine against a blinding flash of light. When I blinked them open again, the lifeless bodies of the twins lay crumpled on the ground.

Sorcha turned to face me with tears in her eyes. "You should have warned me."

"I'm sorry." I stepped forward to brush the drops from her cheeks. "I should have guessed that was what he was planning."

"No. You should have told me you made a bargain to become High Rogue. This changes everything." She shook her head.

"This changes nothing." I clasped my hands around hers. "I will swear my oath to the Queen of the Fae, and together we will show the Fae that the Rogues are not to be feared. We will work with the High Fae to rebuild and strengthen the Fae. Together. As partners…or, if you'll have me, as my mate."

Sorcha stared up at me. Her expression revealed nothing of her feelings, and I began to fear that I might have asked for too much. Her body leaned toward mine for a moment, then she pulled back.

"I will go to Fiona and let her know what has happened here. I will ask for her blessing, then give you my answer." She disappeared before I could respond.

I agonized for days as I laid the bodies of the twins to rest and waited for Sorcha to return. I paced and schemed and swore and thought of a million ways I should have done things differently, or what I would say if she refused me. I wasn't asking for love. I only wanted her by my side. Forever. I'd thought she wanted that, too.

After a week passed, I could wait no longer. I went to the Faerie Queen to swear my Oath. She accepted my fealty, but said nothing of Sorcha. I returned to the Rogues, fearing that I would never hear from my partner again. I ignored that fear and guarded my hope, choosing to believe that Sorcha would reappear when she was ready. Then I turned my attention to my kin.

Weeks later, a Sprite appeared, carrying a message. I tensed, wondering if it would contain Sorcha's response, but the paper said nothing of Sorcha. It contained only a request from our queen.

High Rogue, I need you to confirm that Liam's mate, Eve, truly has no magic.

The note reminded me that I hadn't released Vivian from our bargain. It was time to pay a visit to her heir and collect what was promised. When I examined Eve's lies, I would be able to tell if she was hiding a heritage of magic, even if it was a lie she herself believed to be the truth.

I tracked Eve to Liam's cottage, but he had warded it so that they wouldn't be disturbed. I followed Eve when she returned to Lydbury, but Liam had warded the manor as well. The protection was meant to keep the demons out, but it also kept me from entering. So, I waited for an opportunity to lure Eve away from her mate and her family.

When she next accompanied her uncle to the university, I pounced. A slight illusion drew her into an empty stairwell. I waited for her to come close, before stepping out of the shadows and speaking.

"We meet at last." I grinned, revealing my pointed teeth. "I've come to collect what I'm owed."

"Do I know you?" she asked.

"We have not yet been introduced, but I've been watching you for many years, Evelyn, heir of Vivian." I paced toward her and cast an invisible shield to block our conversation from being overheard. It would also prevent her from running. "You may call me Bryn."

"It's lovely to meet you, Bryn. Unfortunately, this isn't the best time for a chat." She glanced behind her as she backed away.

"I believe it is past time we met." I flicked my tongue out to taste the faint hint of fear in the air. "After all, you made your choice. Thanks to your aunt and our queen, we're linked now, you and I."

"What do you mean? What does my aunt have to do with this?"

"Ah-ah." I waved a finger back and forth in the air between us. "First a taste, then I will explain."

"A taste of what?" She scrambled back and slammed against the wall.

I disappeared, transporting myself closer. When I reappeared, I stretched my fingertips up to press against her temples, trapping her head between my hands. My eyes blinked closed as I searched her mind.

"Yes. So many delicious lies." Most were her efforts

to hide the truth about Liam and the Fae from her aunt and uncle. Once I was sure none of them were about magic, I fed on a few of her harmless lies to free Vivian from our bargain. Then I opened my eyes and released my hold on Vivian's heir. "Thank you for that refreshment. It has been too long."

"What lies? What did you do to me?" Eve touched the sides of her face, where my hands had been.

"What all Rogues do. Make bargains and feed off human lies. Just ask your aunt. She knows." I grinned, this time without teeth. "That's right. You can't ask her, can you? Secrets and lies. So many secrets and lies."

"Are you trying to say that my aunt made a bargain with you?" She was a fast learner.

"Oh, yes. She bargained her life for yours."

"That's impossible."

"I'd think you'd know better by now then to claim a thing to be 'impossible.'"

Right on time, Liam of Flida appeared behind his mate, interrupting our discussion.

"Get away from her!" He rushed forward to embrace his human and protect her.

I clicked my nails together. "Now, now, Ambassador. Is that any way to speak to a respected Rogue Elder?"

Liam inspected his mate as though I would have been idiot enough to harm her. "She's off-limits to you and your kind."

"Too late, mate." I chuckled, no longer able to contain my amusement as the first pieces of a new plan clicked into place. "I've been waiting many long years to receive my end of the bargain I made that brought her here. You have me to thank for that. Did you know?"

"Enough nonsense." Liam stepped toward me. "I don't care what you think you did to bring her here. You will leave her alone."

"We'll see…" I slid back into the shadows beneath the stairs. "But even you cannot stop her if she decides to come to me…"

I disappeared into the darkness, not thinking and choosing where to go by instinct. For once, the thrill of success and the sustenance of human lies had left me feeling empty. That word—mate—that I'd used to taunt Liam, haunted me.

When I materialized again, I realized I'd transported myself to the place where Sorcha and I had left messages for each other when it was still unsafe for us to communicate via sprites, and I wasn't alone. Sorcha was there, waiting for me.

21

I HADN'T come to the old oak overlook to find Bryn, but somehow Bryn had found me. We stared at each other in silence, unsure how to proceed. I owed Bryn an answer, but I'd spent so long considering my response that I worried what sort of reaction I would receive now that we were finally face to face.

Flustered, I blurted out the first thing that came to mind—an explanation for my delay. "I've been traveling, trying to determine if Niamh or Meara had mates, or any offspring, before they were captured and killed by Edric. Fiona needs Faelings if she hopes to rebuild what Edric tried to destroy. She especially needs ones who will carry on the High Fae bloodline. As far as we know, there are only four of us left—my two nieces, my nephew, and me. There may be more, but until we find them, one of those three will have to produce an heir."

"What about you? You could give birth to an heir." Bryn's tongue flicked out, tasting the threads of fate.

I already knew the answer. "My offspring could give birth to an heir, but I could not. The crown will pass to the eldest female of the next generation. Fiona made that clear when she gave her blessing on our partnership."

"On our *partnership*." Bryn twisted the word so that it sounded more curse than blessing.

I looked away from Bryn's intense gaze and bent to inhale the scent of a flower, caressing the velvety soft petals between my fingers and thumb. "She left it to me to decide how it would be between us."

"And you wish to be my partner, but not my mate?" Bryn spoke without a hint of emotion.

I plucked the flower from the branch and spun it between my fingertips. "You have stood by my side for centuries, even when I was trapped in Edric's dungeons. You never gave up on me. Why?"

"Riagan may have forced us into a partnership I didn't want, but you stood up to him. You stood up for me. In the face of every obstacle, we have been better together than apart. You are the only one I trust enough to call my partner. I…" Bryn paused, blinked once, and swallowed. "I love you. Edric kept us apart for centuries, and I don't want to spend another moment without you by my side."

I dropped the flower stem I'd been squeezing between my fingertips, but Bryn reached out and caught it before it could touch the ground.

Bryn offered me the flower, head bowed. "If that is not what you want, I will honor your decision."

"That *is* what I want."

Bryn's head lifted until our eyes met. "It is?"

"I told you once that I didn't want love, at least not the kind that had stolen Godda from the Fae. But your love isn't like that. Even when I didn't believe in myself, you believed in me. And you're right. We *are* better together. I've been frightened of love consuming me, but your love makes me more, not less. I would like very much to remain by your side as your partner *and* mate, forever."

Bryn tucked the flower behind my ear. "Then let that be our arrangement. Partners. Mates. Devoted to one another.

Loyal to our queen and kin."

A thought occurred to me. "Piers was right."

"Who?"

"Onfroi and Piers. The gargoyles. When I went to Lydbury to collect Eve for Fiona's coronation, I saw them, still frozen in stone. I wish they could see us now. Perhaps we could free them." I rested my palms on Bryn's chest.

Bryn's head tilted to one side, but I didn't wait for a response. I leaned forward until my lips brushed against Bryn's. For a moment my heart stilled. Then Bryn responded, pressing into the kiss, deepening it until our lips parted and something in my core snapped taut.

"There's one more thing." I whispered the words against Bryn's mouth.

Bryn's arms tightened around my waist, pulling me closer. "What more do we need?"

I leaned back until our eyes met. "If we truly hope to unite and strengthen the Fae, it will take more than our union."

It took only a moment for Bryn to realize what I was saying. "You still want a Faeling with me?"

"Our Faeling will fulfill the promise my mother made to the Rogues."

"But that promise died with Maeve."

I shook my head. "Perhaps, but with our Faeling, there will be no mistake. Our Faeling will be born a Rogue."

"What do you mean?"

"Our Faeling will have the power to choose."

"You would do that?"

"I wouldn't have it any other way."

Bryn kissed me, and my heart filled with love. I was finally home.

VIVIAN'S PROMISE

1

I LOVE him. I love him not. I love him.

Damn. I tossed the stem into the grass at my feet. Did every single flower in this field have an odd number of petals?

Of course I loved him. That's how I'd ended up in this thrift-store wedding dress, picking flowers for my bouquet in a field outside of an idyllic chapel in the English countryside in the first place. The question I'd been struggling with for the past half hour was more complicated.

Alex and I had only been engaged for a month, but we'd dated all through high school. Stumbling across the perfect dress while on our families' summer vacation to England seemed like a sign that we should get married now, even though it wouldn't be legal, and we'd have to put off the honeymoon because Alex was flying home tomorrow to get ready for cadet training. All that royal wedding excitement we'd encountered must have infected our spontaneous decision. Except I was no Diana, and Alex was much cuter than her prince.

I wandered farther from the chapel, kicking at dandelions

just to watch the seeds scatter, until the structure I'd fled disappeared behind one of the rolling hills. I slipped through a gap in the hedge at the edge of the field and found myself in another nearly identical green pasture. Only, this one had even more bright blooms swaying in the breeze. And sheep. I bent and studied a trio of delicate purple flowers, wishing I had my camera with me to capture the soft petals in this light. Instead, I yanked them from the earth and began to assemble a new bouquet.

Alex claimed if he was old enough to go to war, he was old enough to have a wife. I couldn't argue with that logic. And if I changed my mind and backed out now, I'd have to sit through another lecture from my parents about the consequences of my flighty, irresponsible behavior. My stomach churned with anxiety. But I didn't turn around. I followed the pull that led me away from that chapel instead of running toward it.

The sun crept toward the horizon as I gathered up the pink and purple wildflowers. If I didn't turn back soon, I'd ruin our plans for a sunset ceremony. But I couldn't go back without a bouquet, and I'd ruined the first batch in my sad attempt at fortune-telling. So, I followed the line of pale-pink blossoms to a clump of gnarly old trees, stopping to pick the colorful blooms every few steps. By the time I'd reached the circle of thick, twisted trunks, I'd collected a respectable bouquet. No excuses remained. Time to turn around. But the patterns created by the light as it penetrated the trees in the clearing enchanted me, and I wanted a closer look.

Lifting the hem of my long milky-white gown, I stepped over an exposed root. Summer-evening sunlight filtered through the branches. A breeze ruffled the leaves above my head. I turned in a slow circle, marveling at the natural beauty and wishing I'd thought to bring my camera to capture the texture of the tree bark, the curving roots, the way the sun filtered down onto the carpet of moss at the center, and the lichens that dangled from the branches above. I longed to be rooted like this, to weather with time and age while growing strong and healthy, surrounded by my family and friends. Who knew what this circle of oaks had seen, had survived.

Finally prepared to return to the chapel and take my place at Alex's side, I completed my circle, turning once again to face the way I'd come. Only, now a figure stood blocking my path. Tall and lean, wearing a tunic and leggings that nearly blended with the tree it leaned against. The creature cocked its hairless head and twitched its long pointy ears as it regarded me.

"Are you lost, human?" it asked.

"What are you?" I took a step backward, away from this strange being that had appeared from nowhere.

It stepped toward me. Large dark eyes, with no visible pupil, narrowed as the corners of its mouth tilted upward. "You've entered my home and haven't guessed?"

I swallowed, then blinked, convinced what I was seeing couldn't be real. With those ears and those eyes, and how it called me "human," I could only guess that it wasn't. I'd read my fair share of fantasy stories, but never in my life had I thought I might stumble into one. "You...but that's impossible."

"Quite possible. After all, you came to me." It waved a hand in the direction I'd approached, as though it had been hiding and watching me the whole time.

"I did no such thing. I merely wished to have a closer look at these trees. How was I to know that a...a faerie lived here?" Perhaps it would let me go if it knew I'd only stumbled into this place on accident.

"So you do know what I am." It laced the long, bony fingers of its hands together in front of its chest. Sharp nails arched from the end of each finger, making them seem twice as long as a normal human's.

It had been a lucky guess. I gulped and decided to try to make a run for it. "I'm sorry to have bothered you, but I must be going." I turned to exit the circle of trees between a different pair of trunks. Only, when I started forward, it appeared before me again.

"Not yet."

I glanced in the direction of the chapel, which was no longer visible beyond the hedge and over the horizon. Then I checked the position of the sun in the sky. I hadn't worn a watch because wearing a watch with a wedding gown seemed ridiculous. But, now I wished I knew the time. If it was late enough, perhaps someone would come looking for me. Except they wouldn't know where I'd gone.

"Please?" I asked, hoping the use of that so-called magic word might allow me to pass.

The faerie laughed, an eerie sound that sent shivers down my spine. "First, I demand payment."

"Payment? For what?" My palms began to sweat. One fist clutched my new bouquet, and I clenched the other at my side, resisting the urge to press my hand against the silk of my dress.

"You trespassed, human. Now you must pay the price." One half of the faerie's large mouth pulled up into a grin.

"I didn't know this area was off-limits. It's not like there's a sign. How about we make a deal—"

Eerie Fae laughter cut short my proposal. "You'd like to make a deal with me?"

I had no idea why the idea was so amusing. "Let me past, and I'll never come here again."

The faerie waved one thin finger back and forth. "That's not a deal, human. There's nothing in it for me."

"Of course there is. I won't bother you again. See? We both win."

"If you want to make a deal, we must both give something up. I have you. If you leave, I'll be giving you up. I'd rather not give you up. I have use for a human like you." It sniffed the air around me.

I shivered.

"Why are you in such a hurry to leave, human?" it asked.

"I need to return to my fiancé. I've been gone too long. He'll be looking for me."

The faerie cocked its head to one side and closed its eyes like it was listening to something I couldn't hear. When it opened its eyes, it grinned. "How easy it would be to make him forget you. To make all of them forget you. Who would come rescue you, then?"

My skin tingled from hairs rising in alarm on my forearms. "What do you want?"

"To taste your lies." It crept closer to me.

I froze. My breath caught in my throat. "What? No."

It shrugged. "Then bargain with me for your life, human."

I considered my options. If no one came for me, I would likely die at the hands of this creature. If I bargained for my life, I might find a way to get back, but at what cost? I took a breath. The only way I was getting out of here was to agree. "Okay."

The hedge beyond the circle of trees rustled. The faerie and I both twisted toward the sound.

A man jogged toward us, brushing leaves from his hair. "Stop." He paused outside the cluster of trees, gripping the strap of the canvas bag he'd slung over one shoulder. He wore simple clothes, brown moleskin slacks and a flannel shirt. I was sure I'd never seen him before.

"Who are you to interfere here?" The faerie asked the question on both our minds.

The young man straightened. "I'm Oscar Sauvage, descendent of Godda. I seek an audience with the Faerie Queen."

"Come closer." The faerie beckoned to the young man, coaxing him inside the ring of trees.

Oscar reached a hand inside his flannel shirt and extracted a piece of twine he wore tied around his neck. He fumbled with the clump of braided vegetation hanging from the twine, then held it out for the faerie to see. "You cannot charm me, Fae."

The faerie stretched an arm toward Oscar and flicked its wrist. Vines twisted up from the ground, winding around the young man's limbs and pinning him against one of the tree trunks. "No matter," the faerie said. "I can grant you no audience, and you are interfering."

"Leave him alone." I picked up a handful of pebbles and tossed them toward the faerie, hoping to distract it. Whoever this man was, he might be able to help me. If he could get away, perhaps he could tell my family what had happened to me.

"You must not deal with this trickster," Oscar said, straining against the vines that bound him to the tree.

"He'll stay where he is until our deal is complete. He may watch, but he must not interfere." The creature held up two long fingers and swiped them through the air between us and Oscar. The space between the trees shimmered for a moment, but when I blinked, the effect had disappeared.

My shoulders slumped. "Okay. Let me think."

"Think, human. What is it that you desire?"

To return to the chapel, for starters. But, what if I could bargain for more? If I must give this faerie something in exchange, perhaps I could argue for more than just my safe return.

"Be careful!" The young man strained against the vines. "You can't trust this creature." His thigh muscles bulged as he pressed against the trunk with his boot and twisted.

The faerie hissed at the man. "Silence. Another word from you, and I will take you as well."

I paced while I considered my options. The man's warning made sense. Every faerie tale I'd ever heard spoke of wishes granted in unexpected ways, all because there had been a loophole in the wording. I must get this right, or I'd surely suffer undesirable consequences.

It wouldn't be enough to escape from the clutches of this faerie. I must make sure it could never harm me, or my loved ones, again. But I'd need to offer it something in return, something it would value at least as much as my life.

I stopped in the middle of the tree ring and turned to face the Fae. "I'm ready. But first I want to know what will happen if I stay with you."

"I will feed off you."

I glanced over at Oscar, but he made no move to indicate whether or not what this faerie said was true. "Will I die?"

The faerie laid one extended finger against its lips as it considered my question. When one half of its otherwise smooth forehead wrinkled, I noticed that the creature lacked eyebrows, or any hair on its face. The expression appeared odd without the effect of a quizzical arched brow. "No."

"Okay. Then here is what I offer you: let me return to my family and my life with no interference of any kind from you or any of the Fae, and I will return to you once a year for one day and one night."

A rumble vibrated from the faerie's throat. "Your bargain is tempting, human, but not sufficient." It licked its lips. "One day and one night each year is not enough in exchange for what you ask. However, I would take another in your place." Its eyes cut toward the young man.

Oscar scowled but didn't speak. Though he was a stranger to me, I hoped he knew I would never bargain with his life, not after he'd revealed himself in an attempt to save me. "Will two days and one night each year satisfy you?"

"No." The faerie pinned me with its icy gaze. "I will let you go free to enjoy a long and happy life with your husband, but in exchange, I will take one of your heirs."

"What?" I shook my head. "No." There was no way I could ever agree to giving up one of my children to this creature.

"It must be you or one of your heirs. Decide, human."

I glanced over at the young man. He strained against the vines that held him but didn't meet my eyes. Perhaps this is why he'd tried to warn me. This horrible creature had trapped me in an impossible choice. I chewed on my lower lip as my mind scrambled for another option. Then, I had an idea.

"I will not hand over a child to you. If you want one, you must lure it yourself. And if you are successful, you must allow them to make the choice to stay with you or to return. If they choose to return, you must let them go and never bother my kin again. But it must be their choice."

The faerie stalked toward me. "I will let them choose, if you agree you will not warn them or attempt to intervene."

A horn blew in the distance, interrupting our negotiation. The faerie's pointed ears twitched toward the sound. It clamped a bony hand on my shoulder and turned its gaze toward the horizon. I looked as well, trying to locate the source. That's when I noticed the sun had dropped below the treetops. I needed to return soon, or Alex would think I'd abandoned him.

The faerie turned toward me but didn't release me from its

grip. "I must go. Do we have a deal or are you coming with me?"

Oscar kicked his boot against the tree. The faerie stood between us, blocking my view of him. "You'll let me go free to live a long, healthy, happy life with my husband. You and your kind will stay away from me and my kin."

"Unless I succeed in luring one of your heirs to me. If I succeed, I will give it a choice to stay or to return, and in exchange you will not tell anyone about the Fae or our bargain."

"If they choose to return, you'll never bother us again." I locked eyes with the faerie and hoped I'd thought of everything.

The horn sounded again, this time closer. The faerie squeezed my shoulder, sinking long nails into my bare skin. Its all-black eyes remained locked with mine. "With what name will we seal this bargain? And speak the truth. I'll know if you're lying."

"Vivian," I said.

"Bryn the Rogue accepts your bargain, Vivian." It grinned and lifted its hand from my shoulder. I blinked, and it disappeared.

"You're lucky. The horn must have scared it off," Oscar said. The vines binding him had fallen to the ground at his feet when the faerie disappeared. He beckoned to me. "Come on. We have to get out of here."

I walked to the edge of the circle, and the faerie did not reappear to try to stop me. Hiking up the hem of my dress, I took a tentative step over the exposed tree roots. Then, when nothing happened, I lifted the other foot and crossed out of the ring.

"Hurry," Oscar said. "We don't have much time." He started across the field, in the opposite direction of the chapel, glancing back at me over his shoulder after a few steps. "What are you waiting for? Let's go."

"I'm not going with you. I have to go back."

"There's no time."

"I know. I'm already late to my own wedding. I need to go." I turned away from him and gripped the skirt of my dress, bunching it up in my hands without letting go of the flowers I'd picked. Just as I stepped forward, preparing to run back to the chapel, appearance be damned, a hand gripped my arm, holding me back.

My heart raced and my mouth went dry. I twisted my head, expecting to see boney fingers gripping my arm. Instead, Oscar's smooth, warm hand held me and prevented me from bolting toward the chapel.

"If you go that way, they'll get you for sure."

I stared at his hand, then glanced up to take in the worried lines on his forehead. "Who?" The horn sounded again—only, this time it was louder and very near. A shiver ran down my spine.

"You can hear them, then?" His accent reminded me of the boarding-school boys in one of my favorite movies.

"That horn, you mean?"

He nodded.

"Of course. It's loud as hell and getting closer. I'm not deaf, I'm late for a wedding. *My* wedding." I shot a pointed look at his hand, which was still clinging to my forearm. "So let me go already. I'm not about to wander into a pack of hunters. I'll be fine."

He shook his head. "It's no good if you can hear it. You should stay with me until they've gone. If we can get to that cottage there, we should be able to miss them." He pointed to a leaning structure that appeared as though it might fall down in a stiff wind. "But we have to hurry."

"You must be joking. Look, I appreciate you trying to help me before, I really do, but I'm not about to follow you to some abandoned building just because some hunters chasing a helpless deer are blasting a horn. I may be an American, but I'm not an idiot, regardless of what you Brits think." I twisted my arm loose from his grip and stomped toward the hedge.

Oscar came jogging after me. "Sorry. Perhaps I wasn't clear. That's no ordinary hunt." He cut me off and stood blocking my path.

"Unless they're hunting brides, I don't think I'll have a problem." I veered around him, but he held out his arm.

"Right. See, that's the thing." His cheeks colored in the fading daylight. "Legends say that's exactly the sort of thing they're after."

I cocked my head. "Are you teasing me?"

"No. Sorry. I just…it's the summer solstice, right? Sunset." He pointed to the horizon.

"Exactly. My wedding day and time." I glared at him. "You're welcome to join me. It's not like the chapel will be full. But I really have to go."

The words were barely out of my mouth when the first rider leapt the hedge. The hooves of his black horse hit the ground but didn't make a sound. Oscar grabbed me and pulled me against him as he edged us closer to the bushes.

Five more riders followed the first over the hedge before continuing on across the field, galloping away from us on silent mounts.

"What was—"

Oscar's hand covered my mouth before I could get the rest of my question out. But, it was too late. A final rider, the one carrying the horn, cleared the hedge and pulled up short. He turned his mount to face us.

"What do we have here?"

Oscar released the hand he'd had covering my mouth and reached for my hand. His fingers closed around mine, warm and somehow reassuring, as he stepped alongside me to face the rider.

"Two lovers out for an evening stroll?" The rider slid from the saddle, keeping one hand on the reins of his mount.

"Apologies for getting in your way," Oscar said. "We'll just be going."

"Nonsense." He walked toward us with his eyes fixed on Oscar. "You look familiar."

It should have concerned me that this mysterious sunset hunter recognized the guy who'd earlier attempted to rescue me and now held my hand like we'd been dating for years. But I couldn't stop staring at the rider's clothes. From the leather armor vest to his breeches and boots, the entire ensemble made him look like he was returning from a Renaissance fair, or a reenactment of some type. Perhaps that was why Oscar wanted to keep me from getting in the way.

The rider stopped in front of Oscar. "Yes. I know who you are."

Oscar tightened his grip on my hand. "You must be mistaken."

"No. I'd know that face anywhere." He scrubbed a hand against his own chin. "You're a Sauvage. Is this your lady?" He turned his eyes on me and caught me staring at him.

For a moment, it appeared as though I could see right through him to the trees in the field beyond. But it must have been some trick of the fading daylight, because when I blinked, the effect was gone. I opened my mouth to respond and clear up the confusion, but Oscar beat me to it.

"Yes. In fact, we were heading up to the chapel. We're about to be married. We should really be going, if you'll excuse us." He tugged my hand and started walking toward the hedge.

I glared at him. He'd just tried to save me from bargaining with a faerie, only to try to keep me from returning to the chapel. Now he was pretending we were a couple. Perhaps there was something more to this strange rider than I understood. I decided to trust him and follow his lead.

"Stop."

Oscar froze, and I halted alongside him, but that command caused something inside of me to snap. I'd had to make a terrible deal that I would likely regret forever, the sun was setting on my wedding, and my fiancé probably thought I'd abandoned him. Whoever this hunter guy was, I'd had enough. I'd gone along with Oscar's polite English attempt at an exit. Now it was my turn.

I spun around to face off with Mr. Creepy Renaissance Fair. "Look, I don't know who you think you are." I pointed my finger at him as I lunged toward him. "But, I've had about enough. Whatever you and your friends are up to, we want none of it. Do you hear me? We're getting out of here. Right. Now. So, don't try to stop us again." I gave him the glare I saved for my brother when he'd gone too far, pausing just long enough to show I wasn't scared of him. After that, I'd planned to pivot and march away, all the way back to the chapel.

Only, the creep stared back at me for a moment, then he had the nerve to start laughing. "Oh, she is a feisty one, isn't she?"

Oscar's hand gripped my shoulder. "Sorry. Sorry about that." He tried to pull me back, but I wouldn't budge.

If he thought this was feisty, he hadn't seen anything yet. I shrugged off Oscar's hand and executed my practiced older sister "you're going to get it now" look before flinging my hair over my shoulder and pivoting toward the hedge. I'd managed a few angry steps before I sucked in a breath and froze in place from what felt like a bucket of cold water thrown at my back. Except, I wasn't wet, and somehow that creep was standing in front of me instead of behind. His brows shadowed his eyes as he scowled at me, and I shivered.

Oh, no. Not another faerie. Please don't let him be another faerie.

2

THIS petite fireball with her dark hair and tanned skin had managed to attract the attention of possibly every supernatural being in the county, and was going to get us both killed. Somehow, she had accomplished what I'd been unable to do, after all my research and preparation. Even given my family's heritage and the curse I sought to break, I'd never stumbled into a faerie trap or encountered a spirit.

"Sauvage." The spirit's voice snapped me out of my reflections. "While I admire your taste, do get your woman under control, or I'll be forced to take care of her for you."

Before she could plunge us further into danger, and while she appeared to be still in shock from the spirit transiting right through her, I hurried forward and wrapped my arm around her. "Be still," I whispered. "And please do shut up and let me handle this." Perhaps if this woman had grown up listening to the stories of trickster Fae or of the Wild Hunt, she might not be acting quite so brave at the moment.

She elbowed me in my side and twisted out from under my

arm, but remained silent.

"You mentioned you were to be married. Did I hear that right?" the spirit asked.

I nodded.

"Right. Well, come along, then, and we'll have ourselves a bit of a celebration. I'm in the mood for a party." The spirit skimmed across the earth in a way that resembled walking, if you didn't look too closely. He hoisted himself up into the saddle, returning to the back of his deceptively alive-looking horse. If the horse had been any other color besides black, it might have appeared more ghostly. As it stood, the fading daylight did much to obscure the fact that this mount was no more alive than its rider.

The spirit waved us along, signaling that we were to walk ahead of him. Adrenaline pulsed through my veins along with a measure of caution. I didn't think I had anything to fear from this spirit, or the Wild Hunt. If the legends were to be believed, young women who heard the horn of the Hunt didn't fare well once they'd been captured. I had an obligation to do what I could to keep this woman alive. If I succeeded, perhaps she could help me figure out why the Fae had favored her over me. I reached for her hand and set out across the field, as directed by the spirit riding behind us. As long as he continued to believe she was with me, she'd likely be all right.

Our path took us past the collapsing cottage I'd thought might provide us shelter from the Hunt. I glanced at my supposed bride-to-be out of the corner of my eye as we walked, hand in hand, across the field. She'd pinched her mouth shut in a way that made it clear she had words she wanted to spew at me, and possibly also our captor, but was doing her level best to honor my request. I squeezed her hand. In response, she glared at me from the corner of her eye.

She finally broke her silence, but she managed to keep her voice to a low whisper. "Where is he taking us?" I still worried he could hear us.

I shook my head. "I'm not entirely sure. Sorry. I don't think he means us harm. We'll probably be fine as long as we play along. I'll come up with something to get us out of here."

The spirit on the horse behind us started to hum an old drinking song. I hoped it meant he wasn't listening.

"You'd better," she said. "I'm going to have some serious explaining to do when I get back." She fixed her glare on the trees rising up at the edge of the field and trudged along beside me. Not exactly the friendliest response, but under the circumstances, I supposed I should be happy she wasn't quaking in fear or confronting our captor, insisting she had no idea who I was and demanding to be released.

"Right." Keeping my voice low, I leaned closer to her and whispered, "Since we're supposed to be engaged, it might be good to know your name, at least."

"My name?" She raised her voice a bit in surprise but lowered it again when she noticed the look I gave her. "Shouldn't you already know that?"

"How would I?" What did she take me for, a psychic? It's not like we'd had time to become properly introduced while I was lashed to a tree by Fae magic, or while I was trying to avoid this encounter with the Hunt entirely.

"What's the fuss up there, lovebirds?" the spirit called out to us. "Not getting cold feet, are we?" He laughed, then let out one long blast on his horn. I had a feeling I knew who this was, and his reputation preceded him.

"No," I called back. "Just having a chat. That's all."

"Good. Wouldn't want anyone running off and ruining the festivities, now would we?" He started humming again.

My companion waited a few bars before continuing our whispered conversation. "Weren't you listening when I made the deal with that faerie?"

Oh. So, that was why she'd got all ruffled about me not knowing her name. "You made a deal with it?" So, she hadn't been as lucky as I'd thought. The horn hadn't scared off that trickster Fae in time to save her from whatever sacrifice she'd made. "I didn't hear that part, no. That's odd." Odd but not unheard of, and clearly something not prevented by the charm I wore. Interesting. I'd have to add that to my notes.

"Could it have blocked you from hearing?" She kept her voice to a whisper, but only just. Her shock confirmed that she had no idea the extent of Fae magic. The poor girl.

I nodded. "Possibly. Or it erased my memory of the words spoken." Trickster Fae were the worst. If only she'd stumbled into one of the High Fae, or even an Elemental, perhaps I could have been of more help to her.

She groaned. It must be sinking in that this night had been a right botch up for her. "My name's Vivian," she whispered.

I felt bad for her. I did. But nothing I could say would undo whatever promise she'd made. "It was brave of you to make a deal with that trickster." Brave and idiotic.

"It's not like I had much of a choice." She paused. I thought that would be it, but then she spoke again. "It seemed pretty spooked by that horn. Who is this guy, anyway, and why is everyone so scared of him?" She motioned to our captor, still humming away on his spectral ride behind us.

I chanced a glance back at him over my shoulder before responding. "I'm not scared, just properly cautious. You would be as well if you knew anything about the Wild Hunt."

"The Wild Hunt? Is that what they're called?" She huffed. "At first I'd thought they were part of some sort of reenactment drama. Can you believe that outfit? He looks like he just stepped out of a Renaissance fair." She shook her head. "'The Wild Hunt,' huh? They sound like a biker gang that opted for horses instead of Harleys."

I snorted. "Right. Well, that about sums it up. Except they're not bikers, they're spirits."

"Spirits?" Her voice squeaked and she stared at me with wide eyes. "Of dead people?"

I nodded. "Quite."

"Well, that at least explains that awful wet feeling I had back there when he suddenly materialized in front of me. I thought I'd just imagined it, but it's really not my night, is it?" She sighed.

"Sorry." We walked a few more steps as I debated if I should tell her more or leave it alone. "I don't know if this makes it better or not, but I think that one back there happens to be my great-great-too-many-to-count-properly-grandfather."

"You don't say." She stayed silent for a few more paces. "You think he insisted we come along because he has some sort of bone to pick with you?"

"I'm not sure, though I will say I wasn't keen on meeting him." Despite the fact that this particular ancestor didn't hold much interest for me, I had to admit that having firsthand knowledge that truth lay behind at least one of the local legends had my historian heart all aflutter.

"And now that you have?" she asked, pulling me back to the reality of our situation.

"I'm not keen on seeing where he's taking us, or finding out what he wants. We need to tread carefully if we want to return to our homes." At least I was still close to my home. Even now, as we approached the clump of trees that marked the start of the forest bordering the edge of this property, we remained within a short walk from Lydbury.

If I was right about the spirit that had captured us, Lydbury was his home as much as mine. He'd seen it built. He'd brought his Faerie Queen wife there after he'd captured her, on a night not unlike this one. And yet, the route he'd chosen for us to walk had skirted that property. Perhaps there was a connection. Something I was missing about this night, this spirit, and our situation. I longed for the books and papers I'd left scattered across my desk in my study. The few I had with me weren't likely to be of much help. While they might tell me something of the Faerie Queen, they were more storybooks than history books.

Still, I'd been captured by one half of the ancestral pair I believed to be at the root of the family curse I sought to break. Perhaps it hadn't been mere chance that I'd encountered him this evening. Perhaps this had more to do with me than with the woman who walked by my side. But if that was true, why had the Fae come for her and not for me?

"Here we are." The spirit stopped us at the edge of the forest and dismounted. He left the ghostly beast and led us into the forest. When I glanced back over my shoulder, the horse had disappeared.

We followed a narrow path with only the moonlight to guide us until we reached a clearing where other spirits already huddled in small groups. All talking and laughing stopped as soon as our host appeared before them.

"The Master has returned!" one spirit called out.

"All hail Lord Edric, leader of the Hunt!" another shouted. The others responded with boisterous cheers. My suspicions were confirmed. Our captor was none other than the spirit of Edric Sauvage. My distant relation and the original owner of Lydbury.

"Men," Edric called out as the cheers died down. "Let's hear the report. How fared the Hunt?"

The spirits shifted, clearing away to reveal a long, lean figure tied to a tree at one edge of the clearing. It twisted against the chains that held it, then dropped its head to its chest, exhausted. That's when I noticed the points on the ends of its ears. I stepped forward at the same time that Vivian pulled back, causing me to drop her hand.

"Ah!" Edric moved closer to the captured Fae. "This is cause for celebration. Excellent work, men." He paced in front of the faerie. "Has she revealed anything?"

"Not yet, my lord," one of the spirits said, bowing slightly. "We haven't had much time to question her and wanted to leave some of the fun for you. We know how much you enjoy it."

Vivian moved closer to me, her body warm against my back as she stood on tiptoes to whisper in my ear. "Is that another faerie? Or a human with abnormally pointy ears?"

"Faerie," I whispered. Two faeries in one night. What were the odds?

Edric reached out and lifted the faerie's chin, forcing her to look into his eyes. "What do you know?" he asked. He caressed a lock of the faerie's hair.

The faerie winced away from Edric's touch and spat at his feet. "Nothing, Hunter scum."

"This one looks different than the one we met earlier. Why are they hunting faeries?" Vivian asked in a hushed voice so only I could hear her.

The Fae chained to the tree wore a similar tunic to the trickster that had ensnared Vivian, but the trickster had been hairless and this female wore long hair tied back in a braid. She appeared more human in general, so long as you didn't pay any mind to the ears. When she twisted against her chains, I caught a glimpse of a symbol embroidered in silver thread on her chest. I'd seen that symbol before, but I couldn't place it.

Before I could get a better look, Edric's hand clamped around the faerie's neck. Vivian sucked in a breath behind me. The faerie choked and gargled as Edric squeezed. The sound made my stomach twist. If he harmed this creature, I might not get another chance to get answers to my questions. My mouth opened to yell out for him to stop, but Vivian's fingers dug into my shoulder.

"Don't," she hissed into my ear.

"He's going to kill her," I whispered back.

"Weren't you the one who told me to be quiet and play along? Would you rather he do that to us instead?" She had a point.

Whatever deal she'd made with that faerie had apparently not caused them to be deserving of any favors in her eyes. Not that I could disagree. I had no love for the Fae, only reasons to distrust and possibly hate them. But until my questions were answered, I didn't wish them harm.

"I can't stand here and let him kill her." I searched for a distraction, anything that might pull Edric's attention away from the faerie.

I pried Vivian's fingers off my shoulder and wrapped my hand around hers. Holding on to her, I edged closer to the spirits. They were all captivated by Edric, who had relaxed his hold and was saying something into the faerie's face too quietly for me to hear.

Sliding up next to one of the spirits, I leaned over and spoke in a low voice, loud enough to be heard by Edric if he was paying attention. "So, this is what you lot do, then? Hunt Fae?"

The spirit I'd addressed turned toward me. His dark eyes

glowed with an otherworldly menace. "Who's asking?"

I stepped back, trying to ignore the pain of Vivian's nails digging into the palm of my hand. "All right. I'll just wait over here for Edric, then."

Two other spirits nearby overheard and turned toward me, hovering just behind the one I'd addressed. "Show some respect to the Master. That's 'Lord Edric' to you, human," one of them said. He was the skinniest of the three, and the tallest.

The other's eyes slid past me to land on Vivian. He hissed at his friend.

"What are you doing here, human?" The one I'd addressed wore the nicest armor of the three. Aside from a gaping wound at his shoulder, he'd retained his noble stature, even in death. "The likes of you aren't welcome here."

"But she is." The one who'd first noticed Vivian leered at her from between strands of greasy hair that hung in clumps on either side of his face. "Come closer, pretty girl." When he smiled, he revealed several wide gaps where teeth should have been.

Vivian tugged at my hand. My eyes darted to Edric. I couldn't tell if he'd noticed that some of the attention had been drawn away from him and onto me.

Raising my voice a bit, I said, "I don't think I'd try that if I were you."

"What are you going to do about it?" the skinny one asked. He laughed as he lunged toward me.

Edric appeared between us, and the three spirits backed off a bit. "I'll ask that you leave these two alone, men," he said to the three spirits who'd engaged with me when I'd provoked them. Then he opened his arms to address his hunters.

"With all the excitement, I neglected to mention that I've also had a bit of luck on this evening's Hunt. Except, instead of the lovely prize you've found me, I've had something of a family reunion, as it turns out." He gestured to me. "My many-times-great-grandson here was about to wed and bed his lovely bride when I came across them near the chapel."

The spirits hooted and whistled. Their attention turned away from the captured Fae and fully onto us, instead. Edric moved among them as they shifted, blocking my view of the creature. Just before I lost sight of her completely, I saw her head jerk toward me and her eyes narrow. Did she know who I was? Part of me knew I needed to keep my focus on Edric; he was the danger here. But, the rest of me wanted to shove through the crowd and find out what that Fae knew.

Vivian edged closer to me, rooting my focus back on the immediate threat of the spirits we faced.

"Yes!" Edric's voice rang out above the cheering, and the spirits quieted. "That's right. I rescued him just in time. Given the prize you've found, we deserve a bit of a celebration, don't you think?"

The spirits roared in response. Some banged on the breastplates of their armor. Others lost touch with the ground entirely and lifted up to hover with head and shoulders above the others. Their excitement concerned me.

"Father Buck? Where's Father Buck?" Edric searched the assembled spirits until one portly fellow stepped forward. "There he is! Come up here. Your services are needed."

I worried where this might be heading. The spirit of Father Buck hiccuped as he stumbled to the front of the gathering. His comrades propped him up and patted him on the back as he made his way toward Edric. When he reached his master, Edric threw an arm around his shoulders.

"What do you say we have ourselves a little wedding?" Edric asked.

I cringed, and not only because Vivian's fingers were digging into my palm again.

Father Buck rested his hands on his round belly and grinned. "Lovely night for a wedding, I'd say."

As all the assembled spirits cheered, Vivian began to back away. She pulled against my grip, but I wouldn't let go. If she ran, they'd go after her. If we didn't play along, they'd figure out we barely knew each other. While I might escape with my life because my ancestor happened to be the head of this menacing crew, I couldn't be sure of what they would do to her. The stories of the Hunt all agreed that anyone who saw them ride disappeared, never to be seen again. But she didn't know that. I needed a way to tell her so that she understood what was at stake.

I had to try to get her away from the others, just long enough to explain my plan. She wasn't going to like what I had in mind, but I couldn't see any other way out of this situation.

3

"CAN we have a bit of privacy to talk?" Oscar asked. He kept a firm hold on my wrist, not too tight, only enough to keep me still and by his side.

It was as though he knew how badly I longed to bolt from the clearing. Every instinct told me to get far away from this gang of soulless horsemen. But Oscar held me here. He'd kept us safe so far, and I was inclined to trust him. After all, the leader seemed to favor him, to a point.

Edric studied Oscar with his hooded eyes. "I suppose that's fair." He pointed past his gathered men. "There's a smaller clearing just through those trees, there. Perfect for a honeymoon suite, if you don't mind fresh air on your backside and dirt on your knees. Have your talk, but don't stray far. We'll know if you do."

He really had a way with words, this one. Made me want to punch him. I wondered what would happen if I punched a spirit. It probably wouldn't get me back to Alex.

Oscar ran his thumb over the skin on the inside of my wrist, sending a jolt of sensation up my arm. The distraction focused my attention away from thoughts of causing Edric pain and onto the point where our bodies touched, reminding me that we'd been in near constant physical contact since we'd been captured. My brain rationalized the touching as a necessary part of pretending to be in love with Oscar, but I feared my body had started to forget that this man was not my real fiancé.

"Thank you. We won't be long," he said.

The spirits parted to offer us a path through to the trees at the far side of the clearing, opposite of where they'd chained that faerie to the tree. Oscar started walking, and I followed. The spirits leered at me as I hurried after Oscar. One even licked its bloated lips. After that, I focused on the slightly frayed strap of Oscar's bag and watched it rub against the material of his shirt, bunching up the bit between his shoulder blades and releasing it with every step.

Once we reached the trees, Oscar picked a path through the undergrowth. I set my slippered feet down where his boots had squashed the vegetation, taking slightly larger steps than normal to avoid tripping or further ruining my shoes and dress. Hoping with every stride that brought me farther from the chapel that Alex would understand. As promised, not far from the edge of the clearing, we found the moss- and dirt-covered opening Edric had mentioned, under an ancient cedar tree.

Oscar looked back toward the clearing, and I followed his gaze. We could still make out the shapes of the men in the moonlight through the trees, but only barely. The leaves of the trees and the ferns growing up off the forest floor did a good job of shielding us from view.

"We should run," I said. "Now, while we have a chance."

Oscar shook his head. "We won't get away from them.

They're not limited to walking and running like we are. They have an advantage."

"So you want to go along with this ridiculous plan of his?" Tension edged my shoulders up toward my ears. I clasped and unclasped my hands as I started to pace.

"I don't think we have much of a choice. According to the legends, people who witness the Hunt don't return. If we go along with this, maybe they'll agree to let us go. I don't think they'll harm you as long as they think you're important to me." He sat down on a fallen log and twisted his bag around until it rested in his lap. He unlatched the buckles and flipped open the flap that covered the opening.

I stopped in front of him, hands on my hips. His head was nearly eye level with mine now that he was sitting and I was still standing. "I can't marry you. How am I going to explain that to my fiancé when we get back?"

Oscar searched in his bag for a moment, then lifted out a thick, leather-bound book. "You won't have to. It's not a real wedding, Vivian." He ran a hand over the cover but didn't look up.

I kicked a small rock into the forest. "That Father Buck is a priest. At least, he used to be, before he, you know, died. Or that's what Edric implied, anyway." The words kept tumbling out of my mouth. If there was a babbling stage of fright, I'd reached it.

Oscar didn't respond right away. He only opened the book in his lap using the ribbon marker. I glanced over, trying to figure out how he could remain so calm in the midst of this crisis. That's when I noticed there was something heavy and round tied to the end of the marker. I stepped closer.

"What are you doing?" I asked.

"If we were really about to be married, I'd have had rings.

Luckily, I happen to have these with me. They will have to do." His fingers worked the knot, untying what looked like a man's gold ring from the end.

"These? That's only one ring. Where's the other one?" I angled my head to get a closer look.

He inserted the tip of his thumb into the ring and slid the metal against his forefinger until there was a soft click. Then, he deposited two rings into the open palm of his other hand. "They nest," he said. "They were my parents' rings."

I took a step back. This gruff and matter-of-fact man, who from the looks of it wasn't much older than me, had lost his parents, and he kept their rings attached to a book in his bag. I wasn't entirely sure if this was odd or sweet. "You carry them around with you?"

He closed his fingers over the rings and looked up at me. "Not always." He grinned. "You're in luck today—"

"Yes, today has definitely been my lucky day, hasn't it?"

"Right. Well, I supposed not. But, in this case, I needed them for some research I was doing before I ran into you."

I couldn't think of any reason why he'd need his dead parents' rings for research, but I had bigger concerns than his explanation at the moment. "You seem to still be assuming that I'm going to let them go through with this wedding."

"Don't worry, Vivian. I'm not interested in marrying you any more than you're interested in marrying me." He slipped the rings into the breast pocket of his flannel shirt and finally looked up to meet my eyes.

I winced. "That isn't what I meant." Not that I was interested in marrying him. Only, the way that he said it just made it sound so certain. I hadn't really considered it. Perhaps if I wasn't already engaged. I sighed. This line of thinking wasn't getting me anywhere and was precisely the sort of indecisive, flighty thing that I was supposed to be getting a handle on.

"I understand what you meant." He rubbed his palms against his pant legs. "You want to get out of here. I want to get out of here. Trust me when I tell you this is going to be the easiest way for us to both get out of here without joining the Hunt."

I wondered if you had to be dead to become a member. Probably. That was not an outcome I was interested in, though it would solve the problem of my bargain with the faerie. "Won't we have to get an annulment or something when we get back?"

Oscar tilted his head to one side. "And tell them what, exactly? That we were married by the spirit of a priest in a forest with no paperwork or witnesses to prove it? I'm fairly confident there wouldn't be a court in the country, mine or yours, that would hold us to our vows."

A nervous giggle escaped my lips. "Well, when you put it that way, I suppose it does sound a bit ridiculous."

"They're not human anymore, Vivian. They'll disappear at sunrise, and likely won't return until the next solstice. Your secret fake wedding is safe with me." He raised his eyebrows in silent question.

"Okay. I'll do it."

He stood and set his hands on my shoulders. "Let's go then before they change their minds and come up with a plan we actually need to worry about."

My head tilted back so I could look up at him. So close, I realized he smelled like campfires and fresh air. His brown hair and brown eyes were the opposite of Alex's sun-kissed blond hair and blue eyes, but they were nearly the same height. I caught myself before I could continue comparing them. This was a fake wedding. Oscar didn't want to marry me. He'd just said so. And I wanted to marry Alex.

I ignored the voice in my head that whispered how if I'd

really wanted to marry Alex, I wouldn't have wandered off from the chapel in the first place, and then I wouldn't be in this situation at all. Instead, I nodded and let Oscar lead me back out into the clearing where the spirits waited for us.

"Oh, good," Edric said. "You've returned. What will it be, then, Sauvage? Are we to have a wedding?"

"Yes." Oscar placed an arm around my shoulder.

The spirits hooted and hollered until Edric's voice called out, "Enough!" They quieted.

"Let them through," he commanded.

The crowd parted, and we made our way back toward the priest who hadn't moved from his place next to his master.

Edric stepped in front of Oscar, blocking his path. "As your ancestor, I'll do the honors of giving away the lady. Unfortunately, I'm afraid we don't have any maids in our company this evening." The spirits grumbled. A few booed. "So, your bride will have to do without an attendant."

"I'll manage," I muttered.

"Good." Edric sneered at me.

I hadn't really intended on him hearing my response.

"Shall we begin?" Father Buck asked, his words followed by a hiccup.

The spirits gathered around us, enclosing us at the center of a soulless circle. I kept my eyes on Oscar to avoid thinking too much about the fact we were now surrounded. At a signal from Edric, Father Buck began the proceedings.

The spirit of the dead priest said a few words of introduction, mostly to warm up the crowd. Then he got down to business. "Who here gives this woman to be married?"

"I do," Edric said.

Fake wedding or not, this felt very real, and it should have been with Alex. My heart twisted as I stared into Oscar's eyes, trying to decipher what he might be thinking. At least that kept my mind off the words I was about to speak, promising myself to a man I'd only just met.

Oscar slipped the smaller of the two rings onto my finger, and I repeated the words the priest recited. Then, it was his turn. Oscar winked at me as he promised to love me in good times and in bad. I smiled. Now that I was considering it, in another situation, perhaps if I didn't have Alex, I wouldn't mind flirting with him and seeing how things went. Throughout everything, starting with his brave attempt to help me with that faerie, he'd stayed by my side. He could have abandoned me. The spirits probably would have let him go.

I was so lost in thought that I barely heard the words, "You may kiss the bride." My heart pounded. I hadn't thought about this part. I would have to kiss him. In front of all these spirits. I had a moment to recall that, aside from our brief breakup in the fall of our sophomore year, I hadn't kissed anyone but Alex since middle school. I could count the number of boys I'd kissed in my entire life on one hand and still have fingers left over. And now I was going to have to break my promise to my fiancé in order to complete this sham marriage that I hoped would be all it took to get me safely back to my family.

He must have read the panic on my face, because Oscar raised an eyebrow before slowly leaning toward me. I pulled the corners of my mouth up into what I hoped resembled a smile, the best I could do to let him know that I was okay. I closed my eyes as our mouths aligned.

My lips tingled when they touched his, and the sensation radiated all the way down to my fingertips. Oscar started to pull away, but the spirits chanted for more. His eyes fluttered open to meet mine. He grinned and released his grip on my hands so he could wrap his arms around my waist and pull me up against him. The silky material of my gown rubbed against the rough flannel of his shirt as he held me.

"All right?" he whispered.

I nodded.

I barely had time to inhale before he covered my mouth with his. My lips parted and my head tilted back. My body responded against my will. I pressed my hands against his chest for balance and soon found them wound around his neck. The pounding of my heart and the roar of blood in my ears drowned out the whistles and calls from the hunters.

Oscar scooped me up in his arms and set off for the secluded spot we'd escaped to earlier. I buried my face against the flannel covering his chest, breathing in the woodsmoke scent that lingered there. My cheeks burned and my conscience chided me as he carried me to the far side of the clearing.

He set me down once we were safely inside the trees. The calls from the spirits grew louder and more graphic as they encouraged Oscar to "seal the deal."

"Sorry about that," he said. "I thought it best to give them a bit of a show."

I nodded. My mouth had gone dry and my cheeks burned. I paced a bit, trying to force my heart beat back to a normal tempo. He'd just said it had all been for show. There was no sense in getting worked up over a meaningless kiss. The entire charade had been in the hope we'd escape with our lives. I thought of Alex waiting for me, worried about me, and banished all thoughts of Oscar's lips and hands from my mind.

I took a breath. "So, now what?" I asked.

He sat on the fallen tree. "Now we wait, I suppose."

I gestured to the chanting coming from the clearing. "Do you suppose that will stop anytime soon?"

"Possibly, but it might be best if they keep it up for a while."

He started digging through his bag. He pulled out what looked like a large pocketknife, slipped it into his back pocket, and buckled the flap closed. "I need to go see if I can free that faerie before they get back to what they were doing before they decided to marry us."

"You can't be serious." If we couldn't save ourselves, we had no business trying to save a faerie, especially after the bargain I'd been forced to make earlier in the evening.

"I have to try. Just stay here and wait for me to get back. All right?" He stood, lifting the strap of his bag over his head.

"No way. I'm not staying here by myself. Not with that group sounding like they're ready to barge in at any moment to see what we're up to." I moved closer to him.

"But if they do come check on us, it will be better if at least one of us is here." He placed his hand on my shoulder.

"No. Nope. Definitely not." I crossed my arms. "If you're going, I'm going with you."

"It's safer for you if you stay." He took a step back and his arm dropped to his side. The night breeze cooled my skin where his palm had warmed it.

"It's safer for me if you stay. What am I supposed to do if that faerie decides to take off with you, or capture you? What if Edric and his hunters find you trying to free her?" I gestured toward the clearing. "I'll be stuck here in the forest, alone, with no idea what's going on. Nope. You go, I go."

He arched an eyebrow. "For better or worse?"

I nodded. "Exactly." Only, not exactly. Just for tonight. But, it didn't seem like the time to argue the point.

He grinned. "All right. But, if we're caught, I'm going to have to make it look like you were trying to run off, and I went after you."

"That's your plan?"

"My plan was to go alone. This is the revised plan. Unless you have a better one?" He cocked his head, waiting for my response.

"No."

"Brilliant. Then, let's go." He gestured for me to follow and set off into the trees.

Oscar pushed aside branches as he made his way along the edge of the clearing. I followed close behind, once again stepping where he stepped as he picked a path through the moonlit woods that kept us close enough to the spirits that we could hear them, but far enough that they wouldn't be able to see or hear us. Every few minutes he paused to listen. Each time, the celebration seemed to still be in full swing.

I didn't understand why he thought wandering off and attempting to rescue a faerie was a better idea than just escaping into the woods. If we weren't being watched, then we should be making our way back to civilization. I was just about to suggest that when he stopped suddenly in front of me.

My hands landed on the back of his shirt as I stumbled to a stop behind him. He held out an arm, signaling me to keep back. Then he crept forward, pausing after each step to listen and look around. We were closer to the edge of the clearing now. Dark shapes and flashes of silver moved just beyond the trees ahead.

If they found us here, I'd have to run blindly into the woods behind me. I wasn't likely to get far before either I fell or Oscar caught me. After that, we'd have a lot of explaining to do.

Oscar walked to the left, then back to the right, searching the trees ahead of him. He took a few more cautious steps toward the edge of the forest, then froze. My heart raced as I listened and waited. Finally, he started to back away. When he turned toward me, I searched the trees directly behind him, trying to figure out what had spooked him.

"What happened? Is this the wrong spot?" I asked in a whisper when he'd come close enough to hear.

"It's gone." He frowned. The wrinkles that formed above his brow illustrated his confusion.

I squinted into the darkness beyond him. "What do you mean? How could she be gone? Maybe we're just not in the right place."

He shook his head. "This is definitely the right spot." He half turned and pointed toward the trees. "Look at that tree there. Can you see the chains?"

Shifting closer to him, I followed the line of his finger and stared at the shapes of the tree trunks near the edge of the clearing. They just looked like silhouettes of trees to me.

"No." I moved closer until the flannel of his shirt rubbed against my bare arm. I flinched away, even though I wanted to lean into his warmth.

"Trust me, they're there. But, from the sound of it, I don't think anyone's noticed yet. We should get back before they do."

I shivered. "Okay."

"Are you cold?"

I nodded and rubbed my palms against my bare biceps, trying to generate some heat that didn't begin or end with the man standing in the forest with me.

He lifted his bag from his shoulder and began unbuttoning his shirt.

"What are you doing?"

"Giving you my shirt." He flicked open the buttons on the cuffs before shrugging it off his shoulders to reveal a plain dark-colored T-shirt. He handed me his flannel, the one I already knew smelled of woodsmoke and cedar.

I pushed his offering back toward him. "If you give me that, then you'll be cold."

"I'm fine." He shook the shirt out and draped it across my shoulders. "Take the shirt, Vivian."

Even with only a T-shirt and trousers, he was still wearing more clothing than the silky, spaghetti-strap dress I'd intended to marry Alex in, the one that was now probably ruined from trudging about in fields and through the moonlit woods. I slipped my arms into the sleeves and hugged the fabric to my chest.

"Thanks."

He stepped closer and reached for the button that lay just below my collarbone. My hands dropped to my sides, and I barely breathed as his fingers skipped down my front, fastening the buttons.

"All right?" he asked.

I nodded.

"Good. Let's get back, then."

My fingers curled to rub against the soft flannel cuffs that fell across my palms. The campfire smell wafted upward to fill my nostrils with every step. I focused on where I placed my feet and not on my growing awareness of every movement made by the man in front of me. I had to get out of this forest and back to my family soon, before I did something impulsive and foolish.

He stopped suddenly, and my arms wrapped around his waist as I failed to steady myself. His large, warm hand engulfed both of mine, holding me in place. I waited and listened and tried not to notice how our breathing fell into sync. His chest rising and falling under our joined hands. The cold metal of his ring pressing into my skin.

"Do you hear that?" he asked.

A flutter of wings in one of the tree branches above our heads made me look up. "That?" I whispered.

"No." He followed my gaze up into the tree. "I thought I heard something up ahead."

"In our clearing?" *Our clearing.* I sounded ridiculous.

He nodded. "Stay here." He patted my hand and took a few steps forward. My arms fell from his waist and wrapped around my own body. Safer this way.

I studied the tree line, listening to the voices of Edric's hunters and watching their dark shapes. As much as I wished they would go and leave us alone, they were still there.

"Come on," Oscar called in a low voice, catching my attention. "I think it was just an animal."

I pushed through the shrubs, re-emerging in our clearing. He set his bag on the mossy ground, up against the fallen tree, then sat down in front of it and leaned back. "It's too dangerous for us to try to find our way back through the forest in the dark. I suggest you get comfortable while we wait for sunrise."

4

THE first rays of sunlight filtered through the leaves, waking the birds and me. My arm had gone a bit numb where Vivian's head rested as she curled against my side to keep warm. I shifted, hoping I'd be able to extract myself without waking her, but she lifted her head when I moved.

"Good morning." I spoke the words toward the sky to avoid assaulting her with the smell of my breath.

"Oh, God! I can't believe I fell asleep." She scrambled to her feet, kicking small rocks and branches up under the smooth leather soles of her shoes. "We need to get back. We have to hurry." She shoved the sleeves of my flannel farther up her forearms before reaching up to tidy her hair.

I stood and brushed myself off. The honeymoon was over. Time to return to reality. "It's all right. I don't think we walked that far last night. There should be a field just beyond those trees there." I pointed in what I believed to be the direction of the chapel. "If we cut across that, we should be back to the chapel in less than an hour."

She frowned. Not quite the reaction I'd been expecting. "I doubt anyone will still be there waiting for me. I should probably go directly to the hotel." She ran her fingers through her hair, smoothing it and extracting the plant matter that had settled there in the night.

"Where are you staying?" I shook leaves and dirt off my bag, then checked the contents to make sure I hadn't crushed anything while using it as a makeshift pillow.

"At a hotel in town. I suppose that's too far to walk from the chapel, isn't it?" She groaned. "I'll never make it in time."

"In time for what?" I checked my watch.

Her brow creased with worry. "Alex—that's my fiancé—was scheduled to fly home today." She wrapped her arms around her waist.

"All right. Well, it's still rather early." I tapped the face of my watch. "Just past five."

"Oh. Good." She sighed. "If only we had a car. I would be able to catch him before he has to leave for the airport."

"My house isn't far from here. We can get my car, and I'll drive you." Something about bringing her home after the spirit of a dead priest had pronounced us man and wife made me squirm a bit. But, it wasn't as though I'd be carrying her over the threshold or anything. She wasn't interested in seeing Lydbury. She wanted to return to her fiancé. "You're quite sure your fiancé would leave without you?"

"Oh. Yes. He's starting his first year at the Air Force Academy, and he needs to get back for cadet training." She didn't seem bothered by this in the slightest. One thing I had to give her, she didn't ruffle easily.

The fact that he'd planned to just leave the morning after their wedding didn't sit quite as well with me. "But you were supposed to get married last night."

She shrugged. "It was sort of an impulsive decision. We were here with our families on vacation. Our parents are old friends. Then I found this dress in a shop, and we thought it would be fun to get married now instead of waiting until he graduated."

While she talked, she slipped her arms out of my flannel and brushed it off before handing it back to me. Then she got a good look at her dress in the morning light.

"Oh, dear. I'm kind of a mess. How am I ever going to explain this to Alex and my family?" She rubbed at a streak of dirt that ran from her hip to her knee.

"Leave it," I said. "A good cleaner should be able to fix it up for you." At least, the woman who looked after Lydbury's housekeeping had managed to get worse out of my clothes.

She glanced up at me, her eyes wide. "Be honest," she said. "Aside from the dirt, how do I look?"

Like a woodland sprite who'd crossed the leader of a supernatural biker gang and won. I grinned. That thought I decided to keep to myself, lest this situation become even more awkward. "Like you slept in the woods," I offered instead.

She scowled, then started laughing. "Well, I suppose there's no disguising that, now is there?"

I stepped closer to her and reached out to pluck a leaf from her hair. "There. That's a bit better."

Standing this close to her, as she looked up at me with her eyes sparkling, reminded me of our kiss the night before. Our eyes locked for a moment, and I wondered if she was thinking of it, too. Her cheeks began to flush.

"What about you?" I asked, breaking eye contact as I secured my flannel around my waist. I wanted to reassure her that it was all right. That she could trust me to keep secret the events of the previous evening, supernatural and otherwise. But I also didn't want to assume the kiss mattered to her. It wasn't as though, after this morning, we would ever have reason to meet again.

"What do you mean?" she asked.

"It sounds like your fiancé is going off to university. What are your plans?" She was much younger than I'd thought, barely old enough to drink in a pub. I had close to ten years on her. Despite her small stature, I'd assumed she was at least in her mid-twenties, likely because of the wedding dress.

"My plans. Oh. Sure." She looked down and scrubbed the toe of her shoe against the mossy ground. "I'm not much of a scholar. I...well, art is my best subject, really. So, I thought I'd try photography. It's my favorite." She shrugged, then looked at me out of the corner of her eye like she was judging my reaction. When I didn't respond, she continued. "I put together a bit of a portfolio my senior year of high school. I thought I might try art school, but I didn't apply in time."

Even after just one night with her, I was beginning to realize that she talked a lot when she was nervous or scared. "What sort of photography do you like best?"

"Textures," she replied immediately and with confidence. Then she added, "I mean, I love capturing details, and how ordinary things can look extraordinary if you look at them from a slightly different perspective." After a breath, she added, "And faces. I love capturing faces when the person is occupied with something they love and not thinking about the camera." She glanced down at the hem of her dress. "I know I sound silly, but..."

"You don't sound silly at all." I walked past her, toward the path that would lead us back to the clearing. "Come on. Let's get moving. You can tell me more about it while we walk."

I cut a path through the trees, lifting branches out of the way and offering her a hand to help her climb over a fallen tree blocking our way. All the while, I asked her questions about her art and let her talk about her dreams. I kept her talking and didn't give her much of a chance to ask me any questions. That worked until we emerged from the forest and she got her first glimpse of Lydbury.

"Wow. That place is huge." She stopped to take in the view. "Do you think they'll mind that we're cutting across their property?"

I grinned. "No, I think it will be all right." I kept walking. The morning fog, burning off to reveal the manor house, was a sight I'd seen too many times to count. Though I had to admit, it was grand when the morning sun lit up the stone and the green grass sparkled with dew.

"Do you know the people who live here?" She lifted the hem of her skirt and jogged to catch up with me.

"Person. Just one person. And you know him as well."

"Wait." She stopped walking and stared at me. "This is where you live?"

"I'm afraid so." I stopped as well, turning to face her.

"By yourself?" Her eyes were wide with disbelief.

I hated talking about this part. "Only for the past year. I inherited the house after my parents died, and I don't have any siblings." I braced myself for the outpouring of sympathy.

"I'm so sorry." She clutched the hand that still wore my mother's wedding ring.

"Thanks." I started walking again, cutting a path across the lawn toward the old carriage house.

She turned toward the house, taking one last look before hurrying after me. "It's beautiful."

"Thanks. I can't take any credit for that, though. It's chock-full of art and antiques. It's really too bad we don't have more time for me to give you a tour. Given that you're an artist and all, you'd probably enjoy what's inside even more than the exterior."

"I'm not really an artist."

"Right, then. Haven't you just spent the past quarter hour telling me about your portfolio?"

"Well, sure, but they're mostly just from homework assignments. It's not like I've sold anything or had any shows, or even taken more than a few art classes."

"Don't sell yourself short, Vivian."

She kept quiet for a while after that. We'd nearly reached the carriage house when she finally spoke. "Thanks." The single word had been uttered so softly that I almost missed it.

"You're welcome."

I propped open the doors to the carriage house while Vivian wandered inside. I waited for a moment while she explored, seeing the space through her eyes. It wasn't much. Just the one car in a run-down old stone building that used to hold a carriage, a pair of horses, and a loft for a coachman to spend the night when he couldn't get home to his own cottage. Mum and Dad had turned the old stalls into a storage area, I kept my Rover parked in the main area, and the loft had been left to mostly rot. I kept meaning to get up there and fix it, but it always seemed like a good project for another day.

"I can't believe you actually live here." She turned to face me. Dust from the dirt floor swirled around her feet. Her poor dress had seen better days, but she glowed in the golden morning light. *Sod it.* She'd glowed in the moonlight last night as well.

I cleared my throat and dragged my eyes away from her. "Right. Well, your chariot awaits. Let's get you back to that fiancé of yours. Shall we?" I waved her around to the passenger side of the Rover before climbing in behind the wheel. I hoped that would give me a moment to collect my thoughts before she joined me.

Nothing about last evening had been easy, except that kiss. I'd had to go and show off by amping up the volume. Idiot. Now I'd be lucky if I ever forgot the taste of those lips and the feel of her body pressed against mine. And once I dropped her off at her hotel, I'd never see her again. Those lips and that body, that artist soul that I had only managed the tiniest glimpse of, were soon to belong to another man until death do they part.

Who was I kidding? They'd always belonged to another man, regardless of what she'd been forced to say to save herself last night. I was dwelling on a moment that had meant nothing to her. It was time to move on.

The door latch clicked, and a burst of fresh air blew into the car as Vivian slid into the seat beside me. I slid the key into the ignition and started the engine. Time to get her back where she belonged. Then I'd just have to get her out of my system.

I backed out of the carriage house, pivoted the car to face down the drive, and shifted into park. "Hold tight for a moment." I jumped out and jogged over to the carriage house doors to close them and latch the bar across.

Once I was back in the car and buckled in, we set out in silence for her hotel. Vivian stared out the window, taking in the view along the gravel drive that led from the house to the road.

"It's so peaceful here," she said.

"And still rather close to town. I should have you there in about fifteen minutes."

I felt her eyes on me, though I didn't take mine off the road ahead. "Thank you for all your help. Last night. This morning. After seeing how they were treating that faerie... Well, I don't think I'd be heading back to my hotel this morning if you hadn't come to my rescue."

"You did all right." I grinned, remembering how she'd stood up to Edric before she knew who and what he was. "You certainly don't rattle easily."

She laughed. "I suppose not. Though, it's a good thing I can't tell anyone about what really happened last night. They wouldn't believe me. My family doesn't believe in that sort of thing." She paused. "Honestly, I wouldn't have believed it, either. Not without seeing it all firsthand." She shivered.

"I grew up wanting to believe it all. In a house like mine, you can't get away from the stories. But, it wasn't until just after my parents died that I truly started to believe it was possible that there was more out there. Then I went searching for it."

"Well, you certainly found it."

"That's the thing. I hadn't found anything. Not in all my searching. Not until you stumbled into that faerie's trap."

"Now what will you do?"

"Keep looking, I suppose. For the faeries, at least."

"Ugh. I never want to see another one of those creatures for as long as I live."

I smiled. "Understandable. But I have some unfinished business with them." I had no reason to think highly of faeries, either.

To her credit, she didn't ask or try to pry. She sat quietly, watching the fields rush by outside the car windows.

"What will you tell your family?" I asked. If I ran into them while dropping her off, I should probably be prepared so our stories would match up.

"I think I'm going to tell them I got lost and couldn't find my way back in the dark. So, I stayed out in the woods all night. Then, you found me in the morning, since I'd ended up on your land. How does that sound?" She glanced over at me to judge my reaction.

I nodded. "All right." It was probably for the best that she'd minimized the amount of time we might have spent together. Fewer questions that way. I wasn't convinced that they'd all believe she hadn't spent the night with me. Still, it was worth a go.

We crested a hill and the town came into view in the valley up ahead. "I'll just see you into the lobby, and be on my way, then."

"Okay. I suppose that's probably best." She returned to staring out the window. "It's too bad you can't stay, really. I think you'd probably get along with everyone. But, it doesn't look good, does it? Me returning with you after missing my wedding last night."

"No. Not really." My lips twitched up at the corner, but I held back my grin. If her fiancé took her back after this, he was either supremely trusting or a complete idiot. For her sake, I hoped he was a decent bloke. I also hoped I wouldn't have to meet him.

I steered the car toward the center of town. She'd said they were staying at the Golden Lion, one of the nicer establishments. The closer I got, the more Vivian fidgeted in her seat. I wanted to reach over and lay my hand over hers to keep her from twisting them together in her lap. Instead, I gripped the wheel with both hands and focused on finding a place to park.

Just past the lobby entrance, a spot opened up. I backed in, positioning the car neatly between its neighbors, then cut the ignition.

I squeezed the keys inside my fist and pressed it against my leg before looking over at her. "Ready?" I asked.

Vivian nodded but didn't reply. She unlatched the door and slipped down onto the pavement. I did the same, catching up to her near the back of the car where she'd paused to wait for me.

"Lead the way." I waved her ahead but stayed close behind her shoulder.

We entered the lobby to find a small group surrounding a pair of constables. The group consisted of two older couples and a young man with close-cropped hair, talking in animated American accents. A few younger, smaller versions of these adults lounged on armchairs near the fireplace. The two older ones, a boy and a girl, had their noses buried in their books. The youngest one sat up as we entered and pointed at Vivian.

"She's right there, Mom. Look!"

All eyes, including those previously absorbed in paperback dramas, turned toward us.

"Vivian! There you are! We were worried sick!" An older version of Vivian came rushing toward us, her arms outstretched to embrace her daughter.

"Thank you, Officers," the man who I'd guessed was her father said. The constables exchanged a few hushed words with the remaining adults, but I didn't catch what they said. My attention was focused on the young man, who had left the group and started walking toward us. He locked eyes with me in a silent challenge. I took a step back, away from Vivian and toward the door, and slipped my hands into my pockets.

"I should go," I said.

Vivian was still absorbed with her mother's questions and tears, but she heard me. "No, wait. I should—"

What she had planned to say was interrupted by her fiancé's arrival. "Vivi, who's this?" Alex asked. Not even a "hello, how are you" first. This guy was all business.

"Alex, I'm so sorry. You'll never believe what happened." I caught sight of my mother's wedding band as her hands reached for him, and my stomach dropped. This was not going to go well.

"Hey there, mate," I said, stepping forward to intercept Alex. I slipped my own ring off into my pocket before extending my hand to greet him. "You must be Alex. My name's Oscar. I found your fiancé wandering on my property this morning and wanted to see her safely back to her family."

Alex shook my hand, using only slightly more pressure than necessary, then draped his arm across Vivian's shoulders and hugged her to him. "Well, thanks for that, man. We were worried about her."

The constables walked up to us, and in the shuffle to allow room for them to pass, I caught Vivian's eye. Once I had her attention, I glanced down at her left hand, the one still wearing my ring alongside her engagement ring. She sucked in a breath, and I turned my attention back to the others to distract them while she removed it.

"Yes, well, I need to be going. It was nice to meet you all." I shook hands with Vivian's parents. Then turned to Vivian.

"Thank you," she said. She hesitated.

Alex hadn't let go of her, and I wasn't about to insert myself. This would have to be goodbye, then.

"Don't mention it," I said. "Safe travels." I smiled, trying to show her it would be all right. Then I waved at the others and pushed through the door, onto the street.

In a few steps, I was back to my car. I collapsed in the driver's seat and ran my hands through my hair. I'd spent less than a day with her. Leaving her with her family and the thought of never seeing her again shouldn't hurt this much. I jammed the key into the ignition and started the engine.

I needed to get out to the pub more. I may have sworn off marriage because of this bloody family-curse business, but that didn't mean I needed to remain celibate. Not if it had me this messed up over a pretty face and a few kisses. Even if she had promised to love me forever in front of a pack of vengeful spirits, she'd only said what she had to in order to return to her family and her fiancé.

A night out might get Vivian out of my system, but first I wanted to retrace our steps and see if I could find some answers that could finally lead me to the Fae. Shifting the car into gear, I headed back toward the chapel and the location where I'd first set eyes on Vivian.

When I'd overheard her conversation with that faerie, I'd been on my way back from meeting with a local hermit who called himself a wizard and swore he could work some Midsummer magic that would tell me something more about the circumstances around my parents' deaths. I should have known better than to trust him. He'd smelled of whiskey when I'd met him, and whatever herbs he'd singed and spoken over had given me no answers and hadn't even been able to clear the stench from his cottage.

I parked on a dirt road that bordered the far edge of Lydbury's grounds. Then, grabbing my bag from the back seat, I set off toward the trees where the faerie had ensnared Vivian. I circled the trees once, searching for any obvious Fae sign, but saw nothing. Either I was missing something, or this place no longer held any power. Cautiously, I stepped over the ring of entwined roots and into the center of the tree circle.

"Come on out, faerie." The wind swallowed my words, but nothing appeared or answered my challenge. "Right. I'll just be going, then." I glanced around as I crossed to the far side and lifted my foot to step over the exposed root that crossed my path. No faerie appeared to stop me.

Anger raced through my body. They'd shunned me. The

bastards. I ripped the cord that I'd wore knotted around my neck and crushed the charm in my fist, letting the dried leaves crumble to the earth at my feet. Let the faeries come for me now with no protection.

Following my boot tracks across the field proved easy in the daylight. In no time, I'd arrived at the clearing where Edric and his hunters had lingered the previous evening. I cut across to the tree where they'd chained the faerie. It took me a few minutes to make sure I had the right location, because the chains had disappeared. Once again, there was no sign of the Fae and no blood. Nothing to show that anything unusual had happened here. I was just about to give up and return to my car when a flash of silver in the dirt caught my eye. I kicked at it with the toe of my boot, then bent to examine the small knife I'd uncovered.

5

I PARKED my borrowed bicycle near the bushes clustered around the front steps of Oscar's mansion. Three stories of stone, capped with peaked dormers popping out from the roofline, towered over me. It was no less impressive than it had been the first time I'd seen it, and no less intimidating. If only I'd had a chance to return his ring before he'd left. I took a deep breath before climbing the stone steps leading to the large oak door.

A knocker in the shape of a lion's head greeted me as I confronted the door. I wished I'd thought to write a note. Then I could have left the ring in the mail slot. But my conscience wouldn't let me off that easily. I needed to thank him, in person, for all he'd done to return me safely to my family. And I needed to make sure I returned his mother's ring with the same care he'd shown me.

I lifted my hand and reached for the cold iron ring, knocking once, twice, and a third time for luck. Then I waited. And waited. I hadn't considered the fact that he might not be home.

If he'd gone out, how would I find him?

I searched my pockets for a scrap of paper that I might scribble a note on. I'd worn cutoff jean shorts and a loose blouse, and I'd left my tote at the hotel. Aside from about ten pounds in cash that I'd brought just in case of emergency, I didn't have anything in my pockets. That way, if my family returned before I did, I could say I'd just left the room to get some soda for the stomachache that was supposedly keeping me from touring with them today.

Just as I'd decided to leave and return later, perhaps after I tried calling ahead, the door creaked open. Oscar's ruffled brown hair and sleepy brown eyes appeared in the opening.

"Vivian?" He blinked at me, squinting in the sunlight.

"Hi. I... Oh. Um." I scuffed my toe against the stone step. "You left before I could return your ring." My heart raced and my chest ached with nerves at the sight of him. I stuffed my sweaty palms into my pockets and pressed the cotton against my thighs to dry them.

He swung the door wide open and waved me inside. "Come in." His shirt was rumpled and untucked, and his feet were bare against the wood floor. He looked like he'd just woken up; only, it was nearly ten in the morning.

"Oh. That's okay. I don't want to bother you." I slipped his ring off my finger. I'd put it on after leaving the hotel this morning. It seemed safest to wear it so I wouldn't lose it, but I'd put it on my right hand. Wearing it next to my engagement ring didn't feel right. "I'll just..." I extended my hand, offering him the ring.

"Come inside, Vivian. I'll put on some tea." He turned and walked down the hall, away from me, and left me standing in the open doorway.

I stepped over the threshold and glanced around. A wide

staircase with a carved wooden railing ascended along the wall on my left. It stopped at a landing before continuing up to the second floor. A golden-haired woman, sitting on a throne, surrounded by vines and flowers, with animals gathered around her, stared down from a tapestry on the wall overlooking the landing. On the opposite side of the entry, to my right, a parlor containing polished furniture with velvet seats appeared untouched and meant solely for entertaining guests.

As I made my way down the hall, I glanced into the open doors of each room I passed. So much space, and no other people. It was hard to believe someone as young as Oscar lived in a house this large and impressive, by himself. I entered the bright, modern kitchen at the back of the house where he was busy preparing refreshments. Water hissed in the kettle on the stove as he arranged mismatched teacups, cream, and sugar on a tray.

"It's not too early for biscuits, is it? Or would you prefer bread? I think MaryAnn left some around here somewhere." He rummaged through a few cabinets and came out with a few packages.

"Oh. Is MaryAnn your girlfriend?" He hadn't mentioned a girlfriend, though I hadn't asked. My stomach clenched. I'd been so concerned about getting back to my own family that I hadn't even thought to ask him if anyone would be worried about his safe return. "She must have been worried when you didn't return last night."

He snorted. "Not likely. She's nosy, but I don't think she keeps close tabs on me." He unrolled the top of a paper bag and extracted a few sticky pastries to arrange on a plate. When he caught me staring at him with narrowed eyes, he put the bag down and stared back, confused. "MaryAnn's the neighbor. She comes by from time to time to bring me groceries and such. Doesn't believe a young man can live on his own in a big old house like this without the help of a woman. That sort of thing."

"Oh. That makes more sense." Now I felt like an idiot. An irrationally jealous idiot, at that.

"You thought I was calling my girlfriend nosy?" He laughed. "I don't have a girlfriend, Vivian. I'd have said something if I did. In fact, the only other woman I've spoken with outside of work in the past few months, besides you and MaryAnn, is the housekeeper who comes by to help with the cleaning and such." He shrugged. "I tend to get a bit wrapped up in my work. Probably a good thing MaryAnn stops by with food." He held up a box. "These have become my favorite biscuits. Don't know where she finds them. I'll have to ask." He deposited a few onto a plate, started to close the box, then changed his mind and shook a few more out.

"Biscuits?" I stared at the mound of chocolate-coated disks on the plate. "Those are cookies."

"Right." He grinned at me. "What did you think I meant?"

I shrugged. "Biscuits are like little rolls. You put butter on them, or maybe honey or jam, but they're definitely not the same thing as cookies."

"Right, then. If I ever get to America, I'll keep that in mind." The kettle whistled, and he busied himself pouring the hot water into a ceramic teapot. "I hope tea's all right with you."

"Tea's fine. I don't drink coffee, if that's what you're asking. But you really don't need to go to all this trouble. I just wanted to—"

"Return the ring." He carried the teapot over to the counter and set it with the teacups and plates on the tray. "So you said." He lifted the tray, balancing it with ease as he made his way around the long wooden slab of a table, heading toward the door to the hallway.

I followed him out of the kitchen and into a room lined with bookshelves. He set the tray down on a low table between two leather armchairs near the empty fireplace. "Have a seat. You can at least tell me about how things went with your family before you run off." He sat down and began pouring tea into the teacups.

"Oh. Okay. As expected, everyone was really worried when I didn't return to the chapel. Turns out they went out into the surrounding fields looking for me, but never found me. Do you suppose that faerie kept them from discovering me? Is that possible? I've been wondering about it, but there's been no one to ask." Mostly because I'd sworn not to speak of the Fae to anyone.

I sank into the seat across from him, realizing that I'd gone into jabber-mode again. Only, I couldn't figure out why. There wasn't anything to be nervous about. I was just having tea with a friend. I may not have known him long, but after all we'd been through together, I supposed I'd earned the right to call him a friend. Even if I couldn't tell him about the awful deal I'd made, he was the only person I could talk with about this strange supernatural world I'd uncovered.

"What do you take in your tea?" he asked, interrupting my thoughts.

"Oh, um." I considered the options arrayed on the tray between us. "A lump of sugar, I guess." I reached for the sugar spoon at the same time he did, and my fingers brushed against his. I glanced up, only to find myself staring into his eyes.

"All right?" he asked.

"Oh. I can do it," I said at the same time.

One corner of his mouth pulled up into a lopsided grin. "Of course you can, but I'm serving."

I lifted my hand away and tucked it alongside the other, then wedged both between my kneecaps. My heart slammed against my rib cage and my palms began to sweat. I rubbed my lips together, capturing the bottom one under my front teeth, as I watched him drop one brown cube into my cup.

He set a spoon on the saucer, alongside the cup, before lifting the set and offering it to me. I extracted my sweaty hands from their hiding place and focused on accepting the teacup, saucer, and spoon without shaking and spilling the contents.

"From what I know of the Fae," he said, "it's entirely possible that it kept them from finding you." He stirred a bit of milk into his own teacup.

It took me a minute to realize that he was responding to my earlier question. I'd lost my train of thought when our hands collided.

"What did you tell them?" he asked.

"What I'd planned to. That I wandered off and got lost. It seemed like the sort of thing I would do." I started to shrug, then remembered I had hot tea in my hands. I took a sip instead.

"Is everything all right with your fiancé?" He dunked a cookie into his tea and took a bite.

I nodded. "I went with his family to drop him off at the airport yesterday. He wasn't thrilled about how I disappeared, but he was mostly just happy I was okay." I took another sip of tea, savoring the rich, slightly sugary taste as it rolled across my tongue. Something about the tea in England made it a million times better than the tea we drank back in California.

He nodded and finished chewing, then asked, "What about the wedding?"

I frowned, remembering how Alex had been more concerned with packing than with picking a new date. He had four years of hard work ahead of him. I supposed it only made sense. The wedding could wait. "I guess we'll wait until after he graduates, like we'd originally planned." I set my teacup and saucer on the table. "I don't like keeping secrets from him. It doesn't feel right."

"Will you tell him, then?" He took a sip of tea.

"I can't. I swore an oath to that faerie." I selected a cookie off the plate and took a bite. The chocolate coating melted on my tongue, giving way to the satisfying crunch of a graham cracker beneath. "Wow. These are good."

Oscar grinned and grabbed another one for himself. "I'm glad you agree."

We chewed in contented silence for a moment, listening to the ticking of the clock on the mantel. It reminded me that I should be getting back to the hotel. Only, now that I was here, I didn't want to leave. The moment I stepped out of this house, I would have no one to talk with about what had happened. Even if I hadn't sworn to never speak of the Fae, no one would ever believe me.

"We'd always planned on having a big family. Three kids, at least. But that probably won't happen now." It took me a moment to realize I'd said that out loud and not just thought it in my head.

Oscar shifted in his chair. "I'm sure you'll get it sorted."

He didn't understand. The only way out of the bargain I'd made—at least, the only one I'd thought of so far—was to never have children. If I didn't have any, there would be none for the Fae to lure away from me. How would I ever be able to explain that to Alex? Perhaps I had four years to come to a different conclusion, but I would be lying to him that whole time.

"I was going through some papers yesterday, and I found a flyer you might be interested in," Oscar said. "The university

I work at is hosting a summer program in the arts. There appears to be a unit on photography. I thought of you when I saw it."

"Are you a professor?" I wondered if I'd guessed his age wrong. Maybe he was much older than I'd realized.

He scratched the stubble on his chin. "I teach a few classes, but mostly I do research. My specialty is local history."

"Is that how you know so much about the Fae?"

"I suppose." He took another cookie from the tray. "But most of what I know about the Fae is from research I've done into my own family history."

"What does your family have to do with the Fae?"

"Right. You remember that Edric fellow?"

I nodded. How could I forget the glowering leader of the band of spirits that had kept me from attending my wedding and forced me into a sham wedding instead. With Oscar. My eyes flicked to his lips as I remembered the kiss we'd shared. I glanced away, down at the tea tray, and busied myself selecting another bite to eat in order to avoid eye contact until I got my pulse under control. "Did Edric have some connection to the Fae?"

"Yes. His wife. There's a legend about him marrying the Queen of the Fae. I've always been curious about it, but no matter what I've learned or tried, I've never managed to encounter one outside of a book or diary. Until I found you ensnared by one."

I shivered. "Why would you want to meet one on purpose? I could have lived happily without that encounter."

"Right. You happened to stumble across one of the nastier types of Fae, at least according to local myths and legend. That one wasn't the sort I've been after."

"But why would you want to encounter any of them?"

He tapped his fingers on the arm of his chair. "This may sound a bit dodgy, but...I think Edric's wife, Godda, cursed my family."

"Cursed them?" My first thought was of his parents and how they'd died. Only, I didn't want to bring that up first, in case that wasn't what he'd meant. "How?"

"It doesn't matter. I'll probably never find the answers I'm looking for. I'm only telling you this because of that ring you want to give back to me. You can keep it."

"What? No. I couldn't. It was your mother's. Don't you want to give it to your wife or your children someday?" I twisted the metal band on my finger.

"No." He frowned.

"No?" My voice nearly squeaked in surprise.

He shook his head. "No."

"Why not?" He'd been carrying his parents' rings around with him. They must have meant something to him. Unless whatever research he'd been doing had to do with selling them. Though why he would do that, I had no idea; there had to be a hundred things more valuable than two plain gold bands in this room alone.

He sipped his tea. "I've sworn never to marry. I won't continue our family line so long as this curse hangs over our heads."

"Wow. Okay. Now you have to tell me." I sat back in my chair. "What could be so bad that you would swear off companionship for the rest of your life?"

He blushed. "I didn't say that, exactly."

My cheeks warmed as I realized what I'd implied. "Oh. I just meant—"

"It's all right." He laughed. "I know what you meant." He shifted in his chair. "All right. If you must know. Edric and his wife, Godda, had one child. A boy. As did every pair through-out the centuries after them. One child. Always a boy. Creating a straight line down to me."

"There's nothing wrong with boys." Especially not when they grew up into men who were as kind, brave, and attractive as the one sitting across from me. Or like Alex, who was also kind and brave and attractive—and my fiancé.

"I'm not saying there is. I'm only noting that it's highly un-likely for this pattern to continue as it has across centuries. I'm certain it has something to do with the Fae, only I hav-en't been able to determine what's causing it. Regardless, I've sworn that this curse will end with me. Either I find a way to break it, or I will not have a family." He took an aggressive bite out of the last cookie on the tray.

"It still seems a bit dramatic, if you ask me." Having only one child and knowing it would be a boy still seemed better than having any number of children and knowing one of them would be lured away by the Fae. "And what if you do manage to break the curse? If I keep your ring, you won't be able to change your mind and give it to someone else."

"I already gave it to you." He stared at me, as though daring me to be so impolite as to return a gift.

I bit the inside of my lip. "Only to help me escape from a band of evil spirits."

"Keep it, Vivian," he nearly growled at me before taking an-other sip of tea.

I hesitated. I didn't want to make him mad, but it seemed like he was making a decision that he would later regret. "I can't exactly wear it, you know."

He waved his hand. "Wear it or don't wear it. It's nothing to do with me. Why should I care?"

"So you don't?" I squirmed. I wanted to run. His indifference stung.

"Would it make a difference?" He spoke the words softly. His eyebrow arched.

My heart thudded. I blinked and looked down into the liquid in my cup, as though that held the answer.

He cleared his throat and set his cup down. "Let me find that flyer for you. It's around here somewhere. If I'd known I'd be seeing you again, I'd have left it out, but I'm certain it's buried under a stack of papers on my desk…" He placed his hands on the arms of the chair.

"That's okay." My hands had started to sweat. I gripped the saucer tight to the bottom of my cup to keep it from slipping and scooted to the edge of my chair. "I'm sure I've already missed the deadline if it's taking place this summer. Besides, I'll be leaving soon."

"It will only take a minute." He stood. "I'll just pop across the hall to my study and fetch it for you."

I stood up as well, my shins rubbing against the low table between us. "Really, you don't need to do that. I should be going, anyway. I've taken up too much of your time already." I started to move away, but my knee nudged the tray and set everything clattering.

We both reached down to steady the plates and teapot at the same moment. Our hands ended up tangled. Our heads bumped together. My cheek brushed against his stubble. He clasped a hand over my wrist, and I turned my face toward his. In a breath, the space between us collapsed. His fingers slid across my cheek, and I couldn't take my eyes off his lips.

The electricity that had surged through me when we'd first kissed returned full force. My lips parted and then collided with his. Dishes rattled and my heart raced and all my senses jumbled together until the taste of chocolate on his tongue mingled with the scrape of his calloused thumb against my skin. Then we were standing, and somehow he'd managed to step around the table and pull me against him.

His fingers pressed the soft cotton of my blouse against my skin. The button of my jeans rubbed against his pants, catching on his fly. The rough fabric of his wrinkled button-down shirt scraped against my chest, and his lips danced over mine, pressing and teasing and questing for more.

I couldn't stop. I had to stop. This wasn't supposed to happen. Again. The last time we'd kissed, we were just acting to save our lives. This time we had no excuse.

Hyperaware of every point where our bodies connected, I forced myself to pull away.

"Sorry." Oscar let go and took a step back, putting more distance between us.

"No, I'm sorry. I..." I glanced behind me at the table. Miraculously, nothing had spilled or broken. "I should go."

"Vivian, I didn't mean to... Sorry. I shouldn't have... I'll just get that flyer for you before you go." He ran his hand through his hair and hurried out of the room.

The ticking of the clock kept me company in the silence and steadied me as I caught my breath. I couldn't stay. If I stayed, I'd be likely to give into this bizarre attraction again. I needed to leave, now, before he returned. If I saw him again, I'd lose my nerve.

I pulled the ring out of my pocket and glanced around for a pen and paper. I scribbled a quick note on a pad I found near one of the bookshelves. Then I ripped off the page and left it on the table with the ring on top. Before I could change my mind, I fled down the hall toward the front door.

Just as my hand touched the knob, I heard Oscar step into the hall behind me. My heart clenched, but I fixed my resolve and cracked the door open so I could slip out into the bright sunlight. I jogged down the front steps, hopped on the bike, and peddled down the long gravel drive. With every pump of my legs, I willed my heart to calm and my brain to forget the thrill of Oscar's lips against mine.

6

S HE'D left the ring behind. My fingers rubbed the curved metal I'd stowed in my pocket as I set out across the field toward the temple ruins. I'd thought a walk might clear my head after her visit. So, I'd grabbed the silver knife I'd found near the clearing where Edric and his hunters had kept us and that faerie captive. Digging further into my search for the Fae seemed like a good way to distract myself from thoughts of Vivian.

The opposite proved to be true. Walking several miles, alone, only gave me more opportunity to replay her visit in my head. No matter how many times I tried to steer my thoughts toward the Fae, they circled right back to that petite American woman. The one who'd patched things up with her fiancé and returned my ring. I had to admit, I was the idiot now, thinking she might hang on to it for sentimental reasons. She had no reason to be sentimental about me. Except, that kiss had definitely made me think otherwise.

"Argh." I released the ring, letting it fall to the bottom of my pocket, and ran my hand through my hair. *Enough. Focus on the knife.*

I slid the silver object out of my back pocket. The knife blade shined in the afternoon sunlight. I gripped the weapon at the metal guard where the blade met the wooden hilt and ran my thumb over the carvings in the handle. A leaping stag curved around the grip while a cloaked hunter held a bow and arrow aimed directly for its heart. Leaves and vines adorned the area surrounding them, giving the scene a woodland setting.

Nothing about the blade seemed extraordinary. It could have belonged to one of the hunters. But I knew I'd glimpsed this scene before in a display at the old temple ruins. There, the same leaping stag and archer had been painted on an urn, one that had been found among the ruins. Still, that coincidence alone wasn't enough to make me think this knife belonged to the faerie. It had been the tapestry my father had hung in the entry at Lydbury that convinced me there might be a connection.

I stepped across the stream that bordered my field and started the climb up the hill on the other side. My muscles were burning by the time I reached the top. A thin film of sweat covered my brow. I wiped it away and used my hand to shield my eyes so I could gaze down at the large stones that littered the field beyond.

A gravel drive led from the road to a small visitor center, likely closed this late in the evening. But, that wasn't the destination I had in mind. The worn path that wove around and between the tall stones didn't require admittance. They were the main attraction, some lying on their sides, others standing upright, all still forming the general shape of an ancient temple that used to stand in this spot, now ruined by time and neglect.

I picked my way down toward the temple ruins, around the low bushes that dotted the hillside, searching the scattered stones for a place that might have matched what I'd seen in the tapestry. Lush greens and bright jewel tones had been woven around the golden-haired Faerie Queen on her throne, depicting vines and flowers. But in one half they wound their way around stone pillars inside a structure. On the other side, those plants grew under an open sky in the company of songbirds and a great brown stag.

A sliver blade lay on an alter just behind the throne in the tapestry. Symbols circled the edge of the stone slab. If there was a connection between that tapestry and this temple, I could prove it by finding that alter stone. My fingers rubbed the carvings in the knife handle as I walked the worn path, examining each stone I passed for any visible carvings that might have lasted through centuries of weathering in an open field.

The more I walked, the less likely it seemed I would find anything. Long shadows cast by the setting sun made searching for details even more difficult. After thoroughly exploring over half the ruins, I came upon a patch of yellow star-shaped flowers. I pulled up a fistful of the herb and carried it over to the nearest stone slab.

I sat, setting the knife beside me on the stone. My fingers began to weave the stems into a fresh protection charm. I placed my mother's wedding ring at the center and wove the herb around it. Faerie lore claimed that charms like these were enhanced by the addition of something of personal value. It couldn't hurt that the ring was made of a metal alloy. A pure, naturally occurring metal would do nothing to repel a faerie. But man-made metals would.

My mind wandered as my fingers worked, and I waited to

see if the colors would deepen. Residual heat radiated up from the slab as I watched the sun sink toward the horizon. Only a few strips of peach and orange streaked the blue-gray sky this early.

As I watched, a flutter of wings caught my attention. What appeared to be a large gray bird tumbled out of the sky and turned into a breathtakingly beautiful woman walking across the field. I blinked to clear my vision, but the she remained.

She walked directly toward me with her head held high. A cascade of dark-brown hair tumbled down over her long charcoal cape. Something about her posture and appearance compelled me to stand. It wasn't until she'd come much closer that I spotted the twisted iron circlet crown set atop her head and the points of her ears that rose up on either side of it.

"Oscar Sauvage," she said when she stopped in front of me.

"Yes, my lady?" The title fell from my lips in response to her regal bearing, though I had no idea who she could be, aside from one of the Fae. She almost appeared human, aside from her ears and the fact that I'd seen her transform from bird to woman. I knew I had never met her before. I would have re-membered if I had. I was sure of it.

"My name is Flida, Queen of the Faeries and Huntress of the Fae. This was my temple, once." Her eyes scanned the scattered stone slabs before returning to lock with mine. "You've been seeking us, and now you've met our enemy. I felt it was time to answer your questions about the other half of your heritage."

"Enemy?" I shifted, trying to position myself so I could look at her without staring directly into the sun setting behind her. I couldn't tell if the glow that surrounded her like a halo was an effect of the sunset or something to do with her and her magic. "Edric is your enemy?"

Her mouth pulled down at the corners. "I'm afraid that he

has become our enemy, hunting us and torturing us these past centuries, ever since his wife, my sister Godda, the true Queen of the Faeries, disappeared. So you see, the two halves of your ancestry are at war. It would be best for you to choose a side, but I thought you should at least know how things stand with us."

"What if I don't want any part of this war? Why should I bother taking sides when none of this affects me?"

"It affects you more than you realize. Why do you think the Hunt has stayed away from Lydbury when that was once Edric's home?"

I considered her question, remembering how Edric had skirted the land belonging to the estate on the night he'd led me and Vivian into the forest. "I don't know."

"There is much you don't know. The Fae have been keeping it safe from him. Our spells have prevented him from returning." She walked toward one of the standing stones nearby and placed her palm against it.

"What difference does it make to you if he comes to Lydbury?" Not that I wasn't thankful to the Fae for keeping him out. Now that I considered the possibility of sharing the grounds with a band of vengeful spirits, the prospect had no appeal.

She turned to face me, leaning her back against the face of the stone. "Edric may be able to draw power from that place, and he is powerful enough as it is. If we can't banish him, we can at least keep him from gaining strength."

My fingers rubbed the nearly completed charm I still clutched in my hand. "If he hadn't found me first, would you ever have come to me?"

Her lips pouted when she frowned. "It is unlikely. We have sworn off communication with the humans to preserve our safety."

"And yet you will appear to young women wandering in fields?" I wrapped the unfinished ends of the herb stems around the charm and tucked it into my pocket.

Her eyes narrowed as she cocked her head slightly, the movement reminding me of a curious bird. "What do you mean by this?"

"A...friend of mine... She was trapped by a trickster Fae on the night of the solstice and forced to made a bargain in exchange for her life. How is that allowed, but answering my questions is not?" I watched her face for a reaction, but she revealed nothing.

"The Rogues are allowed things that are forbidden to other Fae." She pushed off the stone and paced to where I stood. "They have requirements that make them dependent on humans in a way that is very different from others of our kind. We've made...allowances for them."

I'd never considered it, but there were different types of Fae mentioned in the legends and stories I'd read. "What sort of allowances?"

"This is precisely the sort of thing humans are not meant to know."

"How can I side with creatures I know nothing about? Creatures that might harm me, or people I care about, without thought or repercussion." Not that there was anyone left in my life to harm. The Fae had already gotten to Vivian, and possibly also to my parents. That question remained unanswered.

She fisted her hands, then flexed them. Her long, thin fingers arched like claws before relaxing against the sides of her cloak. "Bargains are allowed, but the Rogues must ensure no human they encounter or treat with be allowed to speak of the bargain, or of the Fae, to anyone."

"But I was there, too, and it didn't swear me to secrecy."

She waved a hand, dismissively. "You are a descendent of Godda."

"How would it have known that?" I'd given it my name. Could that have been enough for it to know my heritage?

"All Fae can sense what's in your blood." Her bony fingers reached out and clasped my wrist, pulling it toward her. She twisted my arm so my wrist faced the sky and traced the veins beneath my skin with her long thumbnail. "Of course it would know, just as I knew."

I froze like prey before a predator, unable to move or think clearly until she released my arm. I sucked in a breath, remembering eyes, not unlike hers, snapping to meet mine across the clearing. "And the faerie that Edric captured. That must be why it looked at me like it did, just before..." Recalling what had happened next brought my thoughts back to Vivian. "My friend won't tell me what she promised that Rogue, as you call it, but she seemed bothered by it. Is there anything you can do to help her?"

She stared over my shoulder with unfocused eyes. "I'm afraid that, even as acting queen, I am unable to interfere in another Fae's magic."

"I see." Perhaps I could make my own bargain. I retrieved the knife from my back pocket and held out my hand with the blade laid flat across my palm. "Is this one of yours?"

She reached for it, but I shifted it away. Her hand hovered in the air above it. She flexed her fingers and it rose up, twisting and tilting in the air between our two hands. "Yes. Where did you find it?"

I watched her face as she studied the knife. "Edric's hunters captured a faerie the night he captured me. I tried to free it, but when I reached the tree where it was chained, there was no sign of it. I found this near that spot when I came back to search the next day."

"That is troubling." Her thin lips pressed together.

"It had a silver crest on its tunic. Does that mean anything?" After what she'd said about Edric hunting the Fae, his actions made more sense. If the creature had not managed to free itself, then it may already be dead.

She pushed aside her cloak to reveal the silver embroidery on her own tunic. "Like this?"

I nodded. It was not a crest, as I'd imagined. Instead, it appeared to be a vine pattern that curved from her collar and down under her arm like an aiguillette.

"One of the High Fae, then. Possibly one of my Queen's Guard." She winced. Her fingers curled into her palms, and the knife glided down until it rested on my palm again.

"Do you think it escaped?" I asked, running my thumb over the carvings in the hilt.

"I don't know." She pressed a hand against her chest. "But I thank you for trying to help."

I balanced the knife at the blade guard and offered her the hilt. "I'll give this to you, if you'll agree to help my friend."

She shook her head. "Keep the knife. I cannot interfere. I will make you no promises, but I will do what I can to ensure she is dealt with fairly by the Rogues."

I returned the knife to my back pocket. "Thank you." Disappointment mixed with dread. Whatever happened to Vivian, whatever deal she'd made, I couldn't help her. And I'd never know if anything did happen to her because I had no role in her future.

"If you tried to help this Fae, does this mean that you've chosen to side with us in this war?"

I still didn't understand why I needed to choose a side. I

didn't even understand why Edric was at war with the Fae in the first place. It seemed like an ill-advised quest to me. "Can you tell me why he is hunting you?"

She sighed. "He wants Godda back, and he thinks we're keeping her from him."

"But he's dead." A chill cut through the air as the sun dipped below the trees in the distance.

"Yes. And Godda has disappeared." She paced to the standing stone and rested her palm against its face. "No one knows where she is, including me. But that hasn't stopped him." She leaned against the stone as though drawing strength from it. "Even after hundreds of years, the only thing keeping him from decimating us has been the limited window he has to walk the earth."

"The solstice." This matched what I'd read about the Wild Hunt.

"Yes. The longest and shortest nights of the year." She pushed away from that stone and placed her hands against the one next to it. "But the Hunt is strongest at each solstice."

"What do you mean 'Godda disappeared'?" I sat on the stone slab I'd been resting on when she'd arrived, absorbing whatever warmth remained, as I watched her move between the other stones nearby, pressing her hands to each. "Did she run away?"

"No. She vanished." She glanced over her shoulder at me. "And that is not how Fae die, if that's what you're thinking. Edric broke his promise to her, and she vanished. I was her second-in-command, and even I know nothing more than that."

I waited for her to complete her circuit of the nearby stones. Then I stood to face her. "Before I can promise anything, I need to know...did Godda curse my family?"

"Why would you ask such a thing?" She stepped toward me,

her eyes flashing as they caught the last rays of sunlight. "Did Edric tell you that?"

I shook my head. "No. This is based on my own observation. I've studied our family history. It's statistically unlikely for every generation, tracing back to Godda and Edric, to only produce one child, a boy, and no more."

"Ah. I see." She turned toward the sunset, putting her back to me.

"Is it a curse?"

She spoke without turning. "I don't believe it is a curse, though it may be a spell she cast to protect the Fae." She turned her head to the side to glance at me over her shoulder. I could just make out her profile in the dusk. "You see, daughters of her line might be considered queens in their time, depending on when they chanced to be born. She likely understood that a mortal daughter could never lead the Fae, and such a disturbance in the succession might lead to discord among our kind." She turned away again. "Perhaps she though it better that no daughter be born."

I stepped forward until I stood next to her, shoulder to shoulder. "But why only one child?"

"She could have had many, had Edric honored their agreement. But our males can only sire one child. While the Fae blood continues to be diluted by hundreds of generations of mortal ancestors, perhaps that bit of genetics remains. I cannot say for sure. It's not often one of our kind chooses to give up their powers to live a mortal life."

She'd revealed so much to me about her kind, about the extremely diluted Fae blood that still coursed through my veins. But there was still one more thing I needed to ask before I could agree to take her side. "There's something else I'd like to know."

She turned toward me and placed her hand on my shoulder. "What's that, Nephew?" Her thin fingers curled around until I could feel her nails scrape against the cotton that covered my skin.

"My parents." Her eyes mesmerized me. The bright blue distracted me from the question I wanted to ask most. "Were their deaths truly an accident?"

One wrinkle formed in her smooth brow as her mouth pulled into a frown. "What do you think happened?"

"I don't know." I remembered the call and MaryAnn telling me I needed to come home from university right away. I let the pain give me the courage to continue. "But, it feels like more than a coincidence that my father found that tapestry of Godda just before he crashed his car into a tree."

She grinned. This close, I noticed her inhuman teeth. "You think the Fae had something to do with their deaths?"

"Did you?" I studied her face, watching closely for a reaction.

Her brow smoothed and her lips pulled into a line. "Why would we meddle in human affairs? What difference is a tapestry to us?"

"So it was only a coincidence?" I wanted to believe her, but I needed her to speak the words.

"I cannot say. I cannot claim to know everything that happens among my kind." She released my shoulder. "The factions are currently united and ruled by my court, but each group has its own secrets, like the Rogues. This is allowed, so long as these secrets don't bring harm to our kind and don't alert humans to our presence. All I can tell you is that I know nothing of your parents' deaths. I know of no reason why the Fae would wish your family harm."

"I suppose that is enough." I had so many questions.

Before I could ask anything more, she tugged the hood of her cloak over her head and said, "It's late. I must go. But, before I do, you must tell me. Which side do you choose, Oscar? Will you pledge yourself to the Fae?"

"Yes, my lady." I knew Fae couldn't lie. So long as she claimed the Fae had not played a role in my parents' deaths, the decision was easy.

"Good. You must never speak of our meeting. You must never tell what you know of our kind. Do you swear to protect our secrets with your life?"

"I do."

"Thank you, Nephew. In turn, we will do what we can to keep you and Lydbury safe."

"Will I ever see you again?"

"No one knows what the future holds. Perhaps." With a flip of her cape, her body twisted into a flutter of cloth, then feathers, finally taking the shape of a great gray owl before flying off on silent wings into the sunset.

I sat to consider what I'd learned as I finished making the charm I'd started. My vow to never marry seemed silly now. I had no one and nothing to blame for my parents' deaths but pure chance or misfortune, and the Fae appeared to be more complicated than I'd ever imagined. Factions. A court and queen. Succession rules that favored daughters. Instead of having my questions answered, my curiosity had only been stoked. I wanted to know more, and I doubted I would ever have the opportunity. Just like with Vivian.

In only a few days, I'd been given a glimpse of two things I ached to explore in more depth, but both were off-limits to me. My fingers tucked the loose ends of the weaving into the body of the charm.

I'd have to let go of my fascination with the Fae in order to keep their secrets, but I could dedicate my work to engaging others with the local history. Perhaps that would be enough to keep places like this decaying temple from being destroyed. They may be able to draw strength from their places of power in the way Edric did. If they could protect Lydbury, I might be able to help protect them.

Similarly, I'd done what I could to protect Vivian. I closed my fist over the charm. But perhaps there was something more I could do. I hurried up the hillside in the fading daylight, a plan taking shape in my mind. I couldn't see her again. She'd made that clear when she'd left Lydbury. But, I didn't need to see her to do what little more I could to help her.

7

MY dreams since leaving Lydbury had been exceptionally vivid and relentless in their exploration of my
chemistry with Oscar. Sharing a hotel room with my
younger brother made the whole thing worse. Every night, I
woke in fear that I'd called out or made some revealing noise
in my sleep that would give me away. Luckily, my brother slept
like the dead, or, at least, he slept the way I'd thought the dead
slept until I'd been kidnapped and married off by a particularly
nasty gang of them.

He banged on the bathroom door, interrupting my thoughts
to complain I was taking too long in the shower. I let the cool
water cascade down on my head and over my ears to drown
out his yelling. This was my last shower in England. When I
left this hotel room today, it would be with my suitcase packed
for our afternoon flight back to California. Goose bumps prickled my skin, but I couldn't make myself turn off the water.

I rubbed my hands over my face, scrubbing away the tears
that had mixed with the water. Then I counted to five and

turned off the tap. Grabbing my towel off the rack, I yelled out to Brian: "Be out in five."

His response was muffled by the door and the bathroom fan, but he managed to make it clear that I should have been out ten minutes ago. I scraped my toiletries off the counter and into the ditty bag I'd inherited from my father the last time he'd upgraded. Then I pulled on the hotel bathrobe, leaving my towel tied around me underneath.

With one last glance to make sure I hadn't left anything behind, I grabbed my ditty bag and opened the door.

"Finally. Geez, Viv." Brian pushed past me into the bathroom and slammed the door shut.

I counted down the seconds until I heard him yell.

"Ugh! You used up all the hot water, too!"

I couldn't take all the blame for using up the hotel's hot water. I just happened to get my shower in before it ran out. Benefits of being the older sister, and of being awake first and badly in need of some personal space due to hotter-than-average nighttime entertainment.

Even though he wouldn't be inclined to linger in the cold water, I knew he still had to shave. If I hurried, I could finish what I needed to do before he returned to stick his nose in my business. I pulled on my clothes, dumped the rest into my suitcase, and sat down at the small desk. Then I set to work writing out the letter I'd been composing to Alex in my head for the past ten minutes.

> *Dear Alex,*
> *I'm so sorry, but I can't marry you. Something happened that night in the forest. Something that I can't explain. It changed me, and you deserve so much more than I can offer you now. I'll always love you. Always. You're going to be an amazing pilot and husband and father.*

With much fondness and sorrow,
Vivian

I folded the letter, slipped it into an envelope, and sealed it before I could second-guess my decision. I couldn't lie to him. I had to let him go. Breaking it off with him just as he was starting cadet training was probably a terrible thing to do, but it would only be worse if I waited. Now I just needed to figure out how to return his engagement ring, but that could wait until after we got home.

The phone rang as I was zipping up my suitcase.

"Hello?"

"Vivian, your father and I are almost packed. Are you and Brian ready to go?"

"Almost," I said. "Brian's just finishing up in the shower."

"Well, tell him to hurry up."

"I will."

"And don't forget to bring your luggage with you when you come down for breakfast. We'll be waiting for you in the lob-by."

"Okay, Mom. See you in a bit." I hung up the phone, then walked over to the bathroom door and knocked. "Brian, that was Mom. She says hurry up."

He opened the door to the bathroom, already dressed from the waist down and toweling off his hair. "Did you tell her it's your fault we're late?"

"Just pack your stuff and let's go already."

"Girls, man. What do you even do in there that takes you so long?" He pulled his shirt on over his head.

"What do you do in there that stinks it up so bad?" I waved a hand in front of my nose.

"Ha. Ha. Ha."

"Come on," I said. "Last chance for all-you-can-eat bacon.

You know they'll never let us eat that stuff when we get home."

"You're right." He slammed his suitcase shut, secured the latches, and tugged it off the bed. "Let's go."

"You sure you've got everything?"

He unlocked the door. "Roger that. Let's bust this joint." He slipped out the door and headed for the stairs.

I took one last look around, trying to memorize everything. Then I grabbed my things, shut the door behind me, and lugged my suitcase down the hall after him. By the time I reached the staircase, my arms were burning. I set my suitcase down with a thump and readjusted the strap of my tote bag, which had started to slip down my arm.

"Seriously, Viv. What's up with you?" Brian stopped on the landing and looked up at me.

"What do you mean?" I groaned as I lifted my suitcase and started down the two flights of stairs to the lobby.

Brian waited for me to catch up to him. "You've been acting strange ever since you left Alex at the altar. Did you hook up with that British guy or something?"

"What?" My head snapped toward him. "Why would you say that?"

He held up his free hand. "Hey, don't look at me like that, man. I'm just asking."

"Did someone else say that?" I glared at him.

"Not really. I mean, Jenny said he was cute, which, ew. But it would explain why you keep disappearing and acting all moody."

We reached the next landing, and I paused to rest my arms. "I'm not acting all moody."

Brian continued walking. "It would be cool if you did, you know," he said as he started down the second flight of stairs.

I hurried after him. "Why would you say that?"

He shrugged. "Just...you don't have to marry Alex, you know."

"I thought you liked Alex."

"I do. I mean, Alex is cool. But you don't have to do stuff just because you think it's going to make Mom and Dad happy."

I blinked. When had my sixteen-year-old brother grown up?

He reached the bottom of the stairs and stopped to look up at me. When he saw my face, he gaped at me and made a choking, gulping noise. "You look like a fish." Then he laughed and set off for the front desk.

So much for thinking he was mature. I rolled my eyes and followed him.

"How may I assist you?" the man behind the desk asked when we approached.

"My parents said we could leave our luggage here while we ate breakfast?" I smiled and hoped he wouldn't tell me to get lost.

"Of course, miss. What name should I leave with your luggage?"

"Vivian Serra."

"All right, Miss Serra. Just leave your bags here, please. I'll fetch some tags." He turned and started to walk away, then stopped. "Wait. Miss Serra?"

"Yes?"

"I think we have a letter for you behind the front desk. You said your name was Vivian?"

"Yes. That's me."

"Let me check. I'll be right back." The clerk disappeared through the office door.

"Do I have to wait for you?" Brian asked, tapping his fingers on the counter. "Or can I go grub some bacon?"

"Go. Please. Just leave me a few pieces." I gripped his fingers to make him stop, then released him and gave him a shove toward the breakfast room.

"You snooze you lose, sista." Brian shot me with his fingers, then took off to find our parents.

The man behind the desk returned, holding a letter. "Yes, here you are." He handed it to me and began tagging our luggage. I took the letter from him and slid it into my tote, then pulled out the one I'd written to Alex.

"Thank you. Do you know where I can mail a letter of my own?" I asked, holding up the envelope.

"I can take it, miss. Do you have postage?"

I gave him the letter, plus enough money to cover the postage, and he took it and our suitcases off into the office. After he'd gone, I pulled the envelope he'd given me out of my tote and stared down at the neat letters scrawled in blue pen in the center of the envelope. My name and the name of the hotel. It was a wonder the envelope had even found me. Something lumpy inside puckered the cream stationary and roused my curiosity.

"What time will you return for your luggage?" the man behind the desk asked. I hadn't even noticed him approach.

"Hmm?" I glanced up. His words took a moment to register. "Oh. Um. In a few hours, I guess? Will that be okay?"

"Of course, miss."

I wandered over to the nearest chair and sat down before tearing into the envelope. An object that looked like a clump of grass on a string, but heavier, fell out into my palm. I set the envelope down in my lap and studied it. My heart sped up as I realized where I'd seen something like this before. Clutching it in my hand, I checked the envelope to see if it contained anything else. Inside I found a card and a folded brochure.

Vivian,

You left this behind, but it's yours now. I know you can't wear it, so I made it into a charm for you, instead. Whatever agreements you made, hopefully this will offer you some protection. I look forward to the day I see your work hanging in a gallery.
All my best,
Oscar

I set the card down and studied the heavy lump in my palm. He'd woven some sort of grass around a ring. I tensed. He was giving me his mother's wedding ring. To keep. I glanced down at the glossy brochure that had fallen open in my lap. It was for the classes he'd told me about. They'd be starting in a few days, not far from here, and they were pay as you go, no portfolio required.

"Vivi, what's taking you so long, love?" My mother's voice snapped me to attention. She hadn't quite reached me yet.

I shoved the note, the brochure, and the charm back into the envelope and stuffed it into my tote. By the time she'd stopped in front of me, her arms folded across her chest, I'd stood and pulled myself together.

"Sorry. I didn't mean to keep you waiting." I took a step forward, angling past her, and headed toward the hotel restaurant.

She caught my arm and held me back. "What's going on with you? You haven't been acting like yourself. First you wander off and leave us all waiting at the chapel. Then you stay back from sightseeing claiming you have a stomachache. And now you're sitting here in the lobby while the rest of your family is eating breakfast and worrying about you." She cocked her head, inclining it so she could get a better look at my face, which I hadn't turned toward her.

"I'm fine, Mom. I just saw something I wanted to read real quick, and it took longer than I thought it would. You can let me go now." I narrowed my eyes at her.

"Would that something be whatever I saw you shoving into your purse just now?"

"It's not a purse. It's a tote bag. It's what I carry my camera in, Mom."

"Yes, love. I know. Your precious camera. The latest in your never-ending stream of hobbies and obsessions." She shook her head but released her grip on my arm. "It's a good thing Alex loves you. Your irresponsible behavior would drive a saint mad. At least I know he'll take care of you."

I spun around to face her. "I don't need him to take care of me, Mom. Thanks a lot."

She laughed. "What? You think your father and I are going to take care of you for the rest of your life?"

"What's going on, Maddie?" My father stepped up alongside me. So much for breakfast.

"Nothing. Your daughter was just about to tell me who she thinks is going to take care of her now that she's grown, with no plans for college, no job, and no husband."

"I'm going to, Mom. I can take care of myself."

"I see. And how do you plan to do that?"

"Well, for starters, I'm not coming home with you. I'm staying in England." The words were out of my mouth before I realized what I'd said. Perhaps my mom had a point about my impulsiveness. Not that I planned to admit that anytime soon.

"Come on, Bibi. Let it go." My father's use of my childhood nickname softened me a bit. Then he offered me a bundle enclosed in a napkin, already spotted with oil, in an attempt to lure me with food. "Brian brought a croissant and some bacon for you."

My mouth watered and my stomach rumbled as I unfolded the napkin to reveal delicious strips of bacon laying on top of a perfect buttery, flakey croissant. I pinched a slice between my fingers and was about to raise it to my lips when my mom crashed the party.

"Put it away until we're in the cab. If we don't hurry, we won't have time to tour the history museum before we have to leave for the airport."

I glared at her. "I'm not going."

"This is not the time to act like a spoiled brat." My mother hissed the words at me in a low voice. It was too late, though. The other guests in the lobby had already been glancing over and trying to make it look like they weren't interested at all in whatever was going on between me and my mother.

Brian walked up behind my mom and plopped down in the chair I'd been sitting in. He crossed one leg over the other and smirked at me as he bounced his foot up and down. The perfect son. He never argued with our parents. He just did as he was told, aced all his classes, and scored high enough on his placement tests that colleges were already beating down the door to recruit him. Absolutely no one would dare to call him flighty or impulsive.

"Your mom's right. We should get going." My father edged closer to me and added in a low voice, "You were the one who wanted to see that medieval armor exhibit after all, right?"

He had a point, though that was before I'd seen more than enough—worn by spirits who probably died wearing it—to last a lifetime. Still, going with them to the museum might give me more time to think through my plan. Now that I'd said the words aloud, I realized how much I wanted to take this chance. What else was I going to do with the rest of my summer? I just needed to prove to them that I had a plan. That I could take care of myself.

"Fine. Let's go."

"That's my girl." My dad patted me on my back, then walked toward the lobby doors to catch us a cab. My mother let her breath out in a huff and followed him.

"That was a rush," Brian said. He stood and tugged on his shirt. He'd just received it for this vacation, and it was already almost too small for him.

"Thanks for saving me some bacon." I lifted a piece to my mouth and took a bite. Then started to walk toward the door.

"No prob." He fell into step next to me, but neither of us was in a hurry to catch up to our parents. "Are you really planning on staying here?"

"Is it really so crazy?"

"If I were in your shoes, I'd do it."

"No, you wouldn't."

"No. I wouldn't." We laughed.

"What's so funny, you two?" my dad asked as we approached.

"Nothing," we said, nearly in unison, which only made us laugh harder.

My mother, who had been talking with the doorman while my dad flagged down a cab, waved to us. "Cab's here. Hurry up."

I took another bite of bacon and followed my dad and brother. I finished the rest in the cab while my mom talked the driver's ear off, and I stewed on how I could manage to stay the rest of the summer and take art classes at the university. I didn't have enough saved to cover classes plus lodging and food for the rest of the summer, and I certainly couldn't ask my parents for the money. I needed a job.

At the museum, I trailed after my family. The displays had nothing on Edric and his Wild Hunt crew. When I spotted a concession vendor, I stopped to get something to drink to wash the taste of croissant and bacon out of my mouth. I read through the offerings. While I was waiting for my turn and trying to decide what to order, a small sign below the menu caught my eye. "Now Hiring." My pulse raced and my mouth went from sticky to dry.

"How can I help you?" A young woman, about my age, stood behind the cash register, ready to take my order.

"I'd like a lemonade, please." She punched the order into the cash register as I worked up the courage to ask about the job. "And, I was wondering about the sign, there." I pointed.

"You mean the menu?" She raised an eyebrow at me.

I released a nervous chuckle. "No. Below the menu. You're hiring?"

"Oh, that!" She grinned and turned to open the cooler to retrieve my drink. "Right. The manager's looking for someone to take my place. I just transferred over from the concession at the university."

"You're kidding?" This was a sign. It had to be.

She took my money and gave me change. "It's not a promotion or anything. Don't get the wrong idea. I just wanted to be closer to town for the summer."

I realized I must have been looking at her like she'd won some sort of grand prize. "It's just, I'd love to have a job near the university. That would be perfect."

"Are you interested, then?"

"Definitely."

"I'll let my manager know. You can meet him at the concession at the university when it opens tomorrow, if you like. He's been taking my shift. He'll be thrilled to get back to sitting around on his duff."

I laughed. "If you talk to him, tell him I'll meet him there in the morning."

"I'll ring him at my break. Good luck!"

"Thanks!" I grinned as I sipped the cool sweet-and-tart beverage and waited for my family to finish browsing the gift shop. If this worked, I might be able to earn the funds I needed to stay. If it didn't, I'd be stuck here without enough money to do much, and I'd end up having to turn around and fly home.

On the cab ride back to the hotel, I imagined different ways I could convince my parents that I was responsible enough to stay. I tried to anticipate their arguments. I didn't have a place to sleep. That would be a problem. The hotel was way too expensive for me to afford alone. Just one look at the uniform on the man who fetched our bags from the storage room was enough to realize that. I'd have to find a hostel, but I didn't know how much that would cost, either.

While my parents were busy fussing with their luggage and checking the plane tickets, I slipped my engagement ring off my finger and passed it to Brian. "Give that to Alex for me next time he's home from school, okay?"

Brian stared at me with wide eyes. "You're serious."

I appreciated that he didn't ask it as a question. He just believed me. "Yeah. I'm staying."

"Wow, sis. That takes balls."

"Um, clearly it doesn't." I motioned to my figure. No balls here. Still capable of taking risks.

He shrugged. "You know what I mean."

"What's going on?" my mom asked, handing each of us our plane tickets.

"Good luck," Brian whispered. Then he continued through the doors and out onto the sidewalk.

I bit my lip. Then I took a breath and went for it. "Mom, Dad, I'm not going with you."

My mom sighed. "We're not doing this again, Vivian. Let's

go. We have a plane to catch." She started to turn away.

"No. Really. I'm not kidding." I pulled the brochure for the art program out of my tote and held it out to them.

"What's this, Bibi?" my dad asked. He took the brochure. My mom leaned over his arm to read it.

"Out of the question," she said. There was no way she could have read more than the title on the page before coming to that conclusion.

"I think I have to agree with your mom on this one, hon. Even if we agreed to pay for this, where would you stay? How would you pay for food and lodging? Supplies?"

"I know. But I'm not asking you to pay. I applied for a job. I'll find a place to live. I'll take care of it myself. I'll even talk with the airline to change my plane ticket to return home at the end of the summer instead."

"You applied for a job? When? Is that what you were doing when you ran off from the chapel that night?" My mom's eyes narrowed, causing a crease to form between her brows. "And who are you going to stay with? That man who brought you back? Is that what this is about?"

"Maddie." My dad put a hand on my mom's shoulder. "Watch your tone."

Her face twisted toward my father. "I suppose you're just going to let her do this?"

"She's an adult. If this is what she wants to do, I'm not going to stop her."

"Thank you," I said.

He snorted. "Don't thank me. Being an adult means that you're responsible. Are you responsible? If you do this, I don't want you calling home tomorrow saying you changed your mind. And don't be calling asking for money, either."

"Yes, Dad." Luckily, I hadn't spent much of my graduation

money during our vacation. I'd planned on buying a new camera, but that would have to wait. I could do this. I had to prove to them, to myself, that I could do this.

I walked to the lobby doors with them. By the time the cab arrived to take them to the airport, my mom had started crying.

"I want you to call and tell us where you're staying. I expect a message on the machine when we get home."

"Yes, Mom."

"And you'll call us every week." My dad slipped me money for a phone card.

"I promise. I'll be fine."

"I just can't believe you're not coming home," my mom sobbed.

The driver closed the trunk and came around to hold the door open. I hugged each of them, waved until the cab drove out of sight, then carried my luggage back to the front desk one last time.

"Can you give me directions to the nearest hostel?"

8

PREPARING to teach a new school year meant ending my summer with meeting after dreadful meeting. Once I was done for the day, I headed straight to my office. Cutting across the quad with my eyes on the gravel walk seemed the best way to get there with the least chance of making eye contact with one of the senior professors who loved to hear themselves talk and had a way of not taking the hint that I wasn't interested in another story about the good old days.

Unfortunately, that strategy left me vulnerable to summer students who weren't watching where they were going. A dark-haired young woman walking toward me, deep in an animated conversation with her friend, slammed into my bag as I tried to pass.

"Oh! I'm so sorry!" Her tote fell to the ground but somehow remained upright. She ignored it and spun toward me with arms outstretched. "Are you okay?"

When I reached out to steady her, I got a look at her face and stared as recognition hit me.

"Vivian?" It couldn't be. I curled my arm around her waist and pulled her into a hug.

Her head tilted up as her face aligned with mine. Her wide eyes, still filled with surprise, stared up at me. "Oscar." Her mouth slightly parted.

I longed to kiss her lips but settled for her cheek instead. Then I let her go.

She glanced over her shoulder at her friend. "I'll catch up, okay?"

"Is this...?" her friend asked, lifting up Vivian's tote and handing it back to her.

Vivian nodded.

"Got it. Catch you in the canteen later, then?" Vivian's friend asked, raising her eyebrows in a silent communication that I wasn't certain how to interpret. But I didn't have much time to think about it.

"See you there," Vivian replied. After her friend waved and continued on her way, Vivian turned to face me.

"You're still here," I said. "I thought I'd never see you again." I adjusted the strap of my bag until the weight of the books and paper inside rested on my hip again. Now that we were finally face-to-face, after all this time imagining what I'd say to her if we ever met again, words were failing me.

She checked the contents of her tote, lifting out a camera to inspect it. A relieved sigh escaped her lips as she realized that it had miraculously survived intact. "I decided to stay," she said, returning the camera to her bag. "I've been working and taking classes."

"I see." She was wearing an apron from the university concession over cutoffs and a blouse with a wide collar that exposed one of her tanned shoulders. "Are you on your way to work now?" I asked.

She grinned. "No. I just left. I was headed home."

"Home?" My fingers dug into the strap of my bag. She'd been here long enough to have a home, and she hadn't come to me.

She nodded and tucked a strand of hair that had fallen loose from her ponytail back behind her ear. "I've been staying with some friends I met in one of my classes. They convinced me to leave the hostel and take their roommate's spare room while he's gone for the summer."

"You've been here for weeks. Why didn't you let me know? You could have stayed with me." As soon as the words left my mouth, I realized how ridiculous they sounded. Of course she couldn't stay with me. How would she explain that to her fiancé?

"I..." She glanced away. "I needed to do this on my own."

My eyes darted to the ring finger of her left hand; only, she'd already tucked it into the pocket of her cutoffs. "How's Alex?"

"I ended it." She caught her bottom lip between her teeth, still not meeting my gaze.

I struggled to keep my voice even and calm as excitement and hope raced through my veins. "When? Why?"

"The morning we were set to leave." She met my eyes for a moment, then shrugged and looked away. "I decided I couldn't lie to him. He deserved better."

Warmth rushed to my cheeks. "Can I... Are you busy now? Perhaps we could go somewhere and talk?"

She smiled and ducked her head. "I'd like that."

"I was just heading back to my office. We could go there. Or maybe to the pub?" I wanted to be alone with her, but maybe it was too soon. Maybe that wasn't what she wanted. I tensed, waiting for her response.

"Wow. You have an office here? I mean, of course you do.

How silly of me." She'd started babbling again. I took that as a good sign. "Sure. I'd love to see your office. I mean..." She bit her lip again. "That sounds good." A pink blush crept up her neck toward her cheeks.

I wanted to pull her into my arms right there in the quad, but I managed to maintain some professional dignity. "Right. It's this way." I gestured in the direction I'd been walking before we'd collided. From this spot, I could throw a rock at my office window and nearly hit it, but right now it seemed miles too far away.

She fell into step beside me. This time, though, she wasn't as animated as she'd been with her friend. We walked in silence, both lost in our own thoughts. When we reached the door of my first-floor office, I managed to unlock it without much of a fumble.

The room wasn't much bigger than the pantry at Lydbury, and most days I had to keep the door closed because it opened onto a high-traffic corridor, but it was all mine. I'd had to share with another assistant lecturer when I'd started. It had taken three long years before I'd carved out my own space here. In many ways, I was more proud of this office than owning Lydbury. I'd earned this.

I left Vivian to browse my shelves as I set the electric kettle to boil. At least I'd had the forethought to refill it before locking up and leaving to attend those beastly meetings this morning. I glanced at her out of the corner of my eye. She'd set her tote on my guest chair, and she had her back to me, head tilted to the side, reading the spines of the books on my shelf.

"So you decided to take the arts workshops?" I wiped down two of the university mugs I'd collected from functions over the years and set them on the desk.

She removed her work apron and stuffed it into her bag.

"Yes. I suppose I have you to thank for that." She met my eyes. "Thank you, for leaving that flyer for me. I'd already decided to break it off with Alex before I got your note, and I was feeling a bit lost, I think. So, it was perfect timing."

The burst of curiosity, hearing that she'd called it off with Alex, got squashed by the thought of her feeling lost or alone. At least I'd been of some help to her. That was all I'd wanted when I'd decided to leave the envelope for her at her hotel. "Which course are you doing?"

"Photography." She pulled a thick black notebook out of her tote and held it out to me. "And a bit of sketching, just for fun."

I took the book from her. "Are you sure?"

She nodded, blushing. "It's not much. But, if anyone might appreciate them, it would be you. Everyone else thinks I'm some sort of fantasy nerd."

I flipped open the cover and turned the first blank page, to reveal a pencil sketch of a faerie. She'd captured the smooth, hairless face, pointed ears, and dark, stringy hair of the trickster who had ensnared her. It wasn't a perfect reproduction, but it was close enough that I recognized it immediately. As I turned the pages, I found more of that faerie, plus Edric, some of his hunters, and the face of the faerie they'd captured, twisted in pain. "These are quite good."

"Oh, they're okay. You should see Donna's work. She's the girl I was with just now in the quad. She's easily the best in our sketching workshop."

"Is she your flatmate?" The kettle clicked off. I set her sketchbook on the desk and turned to fill the teapot.

"No." She frowned. "My...I mean... I live with two guys. Brad and Tom."

"Right. I see." Perhaps she hadn't come to find me because she'd already found a new bloke to date. Someone closer to her own age.

She lifted her tote and placed it on the floor next to my desk before collapsing into my guest chair. "It's not like that. Everyone always thinks I'm dating one of them or the other and that's why I'm living there. It's so awkward whenever I tell people where I live."

"Right. Well, it is a bit of an unusual arrangement." I poured tea into the waiting mugs and placed one down in front of her. I carried mine over to my chair on the opposite side of the desk. As soon as I sat, I regretted my decision. This was how I met with students. Too impersonal for the sort of conversation I wanted to have with Vivian. Even though I'd found the smallest desk in the building to fit inside this space, there was still too much surface area between us.

"I haven't told my parents. They would freak out and order me to come home immediately if they knew. But, the guys are both really nice. One has a girlfriend nearby who I've become good friends with. The other has a boyfriend who reminds me of my brother." She grinned. "But the best part is I get to have my own room, even if the walls are covered with posters for metal bands." She tugged at the fringe on the raw edge of her cutoff jeans while she talked. "Of course, their roommate, or flatmate, I guess is how you call it, comes back next week. And, classes are ending soon. So, I'll be moving out and heading home to California."

"When?" I set my mug down on the desk and leaned forward in my chair.

"I'm moving back to the hostel this weekend. Then I fly home at the end of next week, after classes are done. I still have to put my portfolio together. And finish my final project. And—" She'd started ticking items off on her fingers as she talked, but I held up my hand to stop her.

"Don't go back to the hostel. Come stay with me. I won't even charge you rent. It would just be nice to have you around."

She stared at me in silence. The fingers she'd been counting on drifted to the handle of her mug, and she traced the arc with her thumb.

"Sorry," I said. "That came out wrong. I should have asked. Would you like to stay with me instead? I'll understand if you'd rather not. I wouldn't want you to be uncomfortable."

"Oh, Oscar. It's not that." She sighed. "It's just..." She bit her lip again when she paused to think. "I don't want to be your flatmate."

"Right, well, I don't have a flat, so there's that sorted." I smiled, hoping she'd laugh.

"'Housemate,' then?" she asked, eyebrows raised.

"It's fine, Vivian. I'm sorry I pressed you. I just hate to think of you having to spend money on a room when I have more space than I can use." I waved a hand, dismissing the topic. "Why don't you tell me more about your classes?" I sat back and took a sip of tea, hoping I'd managed to hide my disappointment.

"You don't understand." She lifted her sketchbook off my desk and shoved it back into her bag. "I don't want to be *just* your housemate. And I certainly don't want to be your charity case."

"My charity what?" I shook my head. "I'm not asking you because I think you can't afford it, if that's what you mean."

"I should go." She stood. "I told Donna that I'd meet her for dinner." She lifted her bag to her shoulder. "Thank you for the tea. It was nice catching up with you."

She hadn't even taken a sip, and now she was about to walk out of my life, again. Somehow, this had gone completely sideways.

I stood and walked to the other side of my desk, taking care to give her space. "Perhaps we could get dinner before you leave?"

"Okay. Sure." She glanced at the desk, grabbed one of my pens, and scribbled her number on a scrap of paper. "I'll see you around?"

I took the paper from her and glanced down at the digits scrawled in her handwriting. "I'll call you."

"Bye, Oscar." She reached for the doorknob and slipped out before I could think of anything to say to stop her.

I stood in the doorway, watching her hurry down the hall until she disappeared among the other students. Then I backed into my office and shut the door, a touch too hard, but given the noise in the hall, I suspected no one would notice.

Damn. I glanced down at the scrap of paper she'd handed me, then shoved it into my pocket. Slouching in my chair, I drank the rest of my tea, then hers as well, as I replayed the conversation in my head, trying to figure out where I'd gone wrong.

She didn't want to be my housemate. No. She'd said she didn't want to be *just* my housemate. *Bloody hell.* How had I missed that?

I grabbed my bag and my keys and hurried to lock up. She'd said she was going to the canteen. With any luck, I might be able to catch her there and apologize for being a complete idiot. Maybe I could even set things to rights.

Setting a brisk pace across the quad, this time with my head up and eyes searching for any sign of her, I brushed past anyone in my way. But when I reached the canteen, there was no sign of her or her friend. I let my breath out in a huff. Panic swept over me. What if I'd missed my opportunity to tell her how I felt?

I'd have to give her enough time to get home and call her later. If I stopped at the pub for dinner and a pint before returning to Lydbury, then she might be home when I called. I backed out of the canteen, just missing some students on their way in, and started the long, slow slog to my usual dinner alone.

* * *

A roar of laughter escaped from inside the warmly lit stone building when I pulled open the thick wooden door. Without glancing around, I placed my order at the bar and waited for my pint. Beer in hand, I made my way to my usual table near the back, only to find it already occupied by a group of women. Rather than turn around and take a seat at the bar, I slid into the narrow booth near the loo. Possibly the worst seat in the pub, but I didn't plan on staying long.

While I waited for fish-and-chips, I scanned the crowd for any familiar faces. I'd been just about to take a sip when my eyes landed on the group gathered at the table next to me. One petite young woman with her hair pulled back in a ponytail had been just about to slide out of the booth when she glanced over and locked eyes with me. Her mouth dropped open.

I set my glass down on the table, suddenly frozen. What were the odds of running into her twice in one day after I'd spent half the summer pining over her?

She stood and crossed over to sit with me. "I was just on my way to find you," she said.

"That's funny, I was planning on coming to find you." I leaned forward, closing the distance between us. "I wanted to say I'm sorry. I don't want you to be just my housemate. That wasn't what I meant."

She glanced down at the tabletop and rubbed at a bit of graffiti carved into the wood. "I shouldn't have run off like that."

"I also wanted to tell you that I've changed my mind." I gripped my cold glass with both hands to steady my nerves. "About marriage and family."

She glanced up, her eyes wide as she stared at me. "Did you break the curse?" she whispered.

"No. I...I got some answers. But, it's more than that." My hands slid down the sides of the glass until they rested on the table. "I've had a lot of time to think about what you said. You were right. I was being dramatic."

"Oh." She bit her bottom lip.

"Vivian." I slid around the table and onto the bench next to her. "I haven't been able to stop thinking about you." I set my hand on top of hers where it lay between us on the tabletop.

She stared down at the back of my right hand, which was engulfing hers. On my right ring finger, I wore my father's wedding band. I'd been wearing it since the day she'd rushed out of Lydbury, but I wasn't sure if she'd noticed earlier.

"Oh," she said again.

"I thought about it a million times since you left Lydbury that day. What would I say if I ever saw you again? Then, when I did finally see you again..." I shook my head. "Right, well, I think I managed to say everything wrong." In all the times I'd imagined this conversation, she'd said more than just that one word. I waited and hoped for a longer response this time. One that wasn't the rejection I feared.

"I've thought about you, too." She twisted her hand beneath mine until our palms were pressed against each other.

"Why did you stay away?" I ran my thumb along the edge of hers.

"I wasn't ready." She leaned her head against my shoulder.

"And now?" My heart beat faster, hoping I'd been right and

that she did fancy me as more than a housemate.

The fingers of her free hand fluttered to her neck. She pulled a chain from beneath her blouse and held it up so I could see the charm on the end. Most of the herbs had frayed and were beginning to unravel. She'd worn it. Every day, from the look of it.

"You gave it to me anyway, didn't you?" she asked. Her fingers rubbed against the dried herb stems I'd woven around my mother's wedding ring.

"That's how those charms work." I twisted on the bench so that I faced her, and took both of her hands in mine. "Are you going to try to give it back to me again?"

She flashed me a lopsided grin. "No."

"Does that mean you might consider staying in England, to be with me? I'd very much like to have a real relationship with you." What I wanted was to marry her for real, but I thought I might scare her off if I suggested it this soon.

She leaned forward and pressed her lips against mine. The rowdy pub fell away. All my senses focused on her. The soft dampness of her lips as they slid against mine. The fruity scent of her lip gloss. The taste of cider that lingered on her tongue as it tangled with mine.

Someone shoved a basket onto the table, and the crinkle of the paper against my sleeve reminded me we weren't alone.

"Get a room!" the bartender jeered as he walked away.

Her friends at the table across the aisle from us cheered.

Vivian pulled back from our kiss. She covered her mouth with her hand as she dissolved into giggles. "Oops," she said.

"He's just jealous." I grinned at her.

She scooted away from me a bit. "I should tell you something first." She gripped my wrists to twist my hands palms up between us. She traced the lines on my hands with her fingertips rather than meet my eyes.

"What's that?" I extracted one hand so I could lift her chin.

"I've decided I'm not having any children." She set her mouth in a firm line.

"But I thought you wanted children. You said…"

"I've changed my mind." She scooted away from me on the bench.

Perhaps this had something to do with the Fae. Or with Alex. I didn't want to ask. If she wanted to tell me, she would. "That doesn't bother me, Vivian. It changes nothing about how I feel."

"Are you sure?" She snuck a chip from my plate and glanced at me out of the corner of her eye.

"Of course I'm sure." I snagged one of the chips for myself. "Remember, I was the one who told you I didn't plan on having children."

"But, you said you'd changed your mind." She waved her chip at me before taking a bite.

"I'd be all right with just the marriage part." I brushed a crumb from her lips. "But, I think only if it's with you." The words had left my mouth without thought. For a moment I froze. Since I couldn't put them back in, I stuffed in a chip, whole, instead. I chewed, hoping I hadn't revealed too much, too soon.

"What did you say?" She gaped at me.

I swallowed before plowing ahead with the truth, even though it seemed absurd that I could have fallen for her this hard, this fast, or that she might not run at what I was about to propose. "I think we should get married. For real this time. No hiccuping spirit of a priest."

"But…"

"We can wait until you're ready. Or, if you decide you'd

rather not, I suppose that's fine, as well." I tensed as I waited for her response.

"You're asking me to marry you?" Her eyebrows rose.

I gulped and nodded. "I love you and thought maybe we could try it for real this time. Will you marry me?"

She slid toward me and threw her arms around my neck. "Yes. My answer is yes."

"You don't want to think about it?"

She leaned back to look me in the eyes but left her arms around my neck. "I've been thinking about it. A million times since I walked out of Lydbury. Every time I touch this charm around my neck. We don't have to rush out and do it tomorrow, but if you're asking me, my answer is yes."

I wrapped my arm around her waist and pulled her in for another kiss. Now that I had her with me again, I was never letting her go.

Eve the Immortal

1

THE bright flash of light outside the cottage door tore my attention away from the knife-wielding Fae I was supposed to be battling, just long enough to allow her inside my defenses.

"Pay attention, human. You make this too easy." Arabella gripped my upper arm with one hand. The point of her knife hovered inches from the fabric of my tunic, which was stretched tight across my abdomen.

"I'm sorry. It's just..." I glanced over to the tiny faerie fluttering near the basket of honeysuckle hanging outside the front door of the cottage. "Be right there!" I shouted.

Arabella squeezed my arm tighter. "Ignore the sprite. I'd hope your life would be more important to you than the mail delivery." She released me, pushing herself away as she sheathed her knife.

"It's just practice. You're not actually going to try to kill me. Again." It had been a few months since she'd tried to eliminate me for knowing too many of their secrets. Our relationship had improved since then, but not so much that I had full confidence she wouldn't try to kill me again if I gave her half a reason.

"And I suppose you think a real opponent would just hold on while you check your messages? Fiona made you immortal, Evelyn, not invulnerable." She paced over to where she'd left her cape.

"Just give me a moment to deal with this, and then we can go again. I'll do better this time. Promise."

"Can't." She swung the cape across her shoulders and flipped the hood over her head. "Private lessons are over for the day. Time for me to get back to my duties."

"Okay. I'll practice that new attack before our next lesson." I rotated my shoulder to relieve an ache that had developed there.

"You'd better. I don't plan to go easy on you just because you're my cousin's mate." The words were barely out of her mouth before she'd disappeared in a blink of bright-blue light.

I hadn't gotten used to that term, "mate." In their world, there wasn't any place for boyfriends and girlfriends. You were either paired, or not. That pairing didn't have to be a permanent arrangement, or even an exclusive one, but it did imply a mutual commitment. I didn't mind the commitment part, but every time I heard someone use the word "mate" to describe my relationship with Liam, I cringed a little. Just another odd faerie thing that would take some getting used to, I supposed.

"Hello, there." I stopped below the hanging basket and waited for the sprite to finish feasting on the honeysuckle nectar. Its mothlike lime-green wings beat as fast as a hummingbird's against its back as it hovered just above my head, making it difficult to get a good look at its tiny body.

The key to transactions with sprites seemed to be persistence. Any Fae home adorned with sprite-friendly flowers could receive messages. But, as I'd begun to realize after three months of trying and failing to get the little brats to hand over my messages, they were mostly in it for the sweet nectar. If I waited patiently for this one to finish, I'd be here all day. But I couldn't nag it, either. The key to getting messages delivered, as much as I hated it, was small talk.

"Lovely weather we're having today, don't you think? Just a few more weeks until it's officially spring." I paused. "I've heard the Fae have a charming spring festival. What's it called again?" I tapped my finger against my chin, feigning forgetfulness. I knew perfectly well what they called their beloved spring festival, and I'd not yet met a faerie who could resist talking about it.

As expected, the sprite extracted its long nails from the petals, licked the dripping ends, and turned toward me. A miniature humanoid male torso, naked to the waist and attached to ridiculously muscular thighs for so small a creature, hovered in the air at eye level. He angled his beaked nose at me as he jabbered in a tongue I hadn't yet learned. When he paused, he grinned at me with a flash of sharp teeth, waiting for a response.

"That's nice." I smiled back.

His tiny eyes narrowed, and he huffed his displeasure, then disappeared in another flash of blinding-white light. Two envelopes floated to the ground at my feet. I still couldn't quite make sense of the message system the Fae had developed. Apparently, they had a fondness for written correspondence. My cell phone had no reception anywhere in their realm, but I could receive e-mail. Only, there were no computers. My e-mail came handwritten and sprite delivered. How it got off my phone and onto paper, I still hadn't figured out.

I scooped up the envelopes and headed inside to find Liam. One envelope had his name written on the back, the other had been addressed to me. I itched to open mine, especially once I read that the sender was my best friend, Angie. I wished I could tell her that her e-mail had been transcribed into formal written correspondence delivered by a nectar-loving winged creature not unlike those depicted in children's stories. Sprites were possibly a little more frightening in the flesh, but they were still diminutive and magical. She'd love it, and I could never tell her.

Liam caught me around the waist and pulled me to him as I entered the room that served as the cottage's kitchen. "There you are." He swept my low ponytail aside so he could kiss my neck. "Mmm. Sweaty."

"Eww." I pushed him away and handed him the envelope that had been addressed to him.

He took one look at the writing and dropped it onto the table. "Not 'eww.' I was watching you out there. You're definitely improving. Nice work." He plucked my envelope from my hand and set it next to his on the table.

"Hey. I wanted to read that." I faked a pout as I linked my arms around his neck.

His hands gripped my hips as he pulled me tight against him and leaned down to kiss my lips. My fingers curled through the long locks of hair at the nape of his neck, and I fell into his touch until the room seemed to disappear. Letter forgotten, all I wanted was to be closer to him.

A beam of sunlight cut through the window, making me squint to block out the brightness, and reminding me that the morning was slipping away. I broke off the kiss, but Liam continued to trail kisses down my jaw and along the side of my neck. A quick glance at my watch, possibly the only clock in the faerie realm, confirmed that I needed to be at Uncle Oscar's lecture in an hour.

"So...I need to be back at Lydbury soon," I said. My body did not want him to stop, but if he kept going, I wasn't going to be able to resist the temptation to skip class.

He leaned back, meeting my eyes. "Are you sure?" He raised an eyebrow.

"If your cousin hadn't kept me drilling all morning, we might have had more time." My hands slipped down until they rested against his chest.

He kissed my forehead. "It is important that you learn to defend yourself."

"Ugh. You sound just like her." I pushed against his chest, and his arms released me.

He grinned. "Well, don't tell her, but this one time, I think we're in agreement." He swatted at my butt as I walked away to get a glass of water.

I flashed him a fake-surprised look over my shoulder. "Shocking."

"Unheard of, really." He picked up his letter from the table and stared at the handwriting on the back of the envelope. "I suppose I should see what our queen wants from me."

I set my glass down so I could rip open the envelope that contained Angie's message. Reading it through once, quickly, was enough to make me suck in a breath. I scanned through it again to make sure I'd read it right. "Crap."

"My thoughts exactly." Liam tossed the parchment down onto the table. He ran a hand through his hair, sighing.

I caught a glimpse of her signature before Liam retrieved the letter, folded it, and stuffed it back into the envelope. "What does Fiona want?"

He shrugged. "The usual ambassador stuff. I'll go visit her

after I drop you off and get it sorted. What's yours say?" He peeked over my shoulder at the letter I held.

I held it up for him to read. "Angie is coming to visit."

"Oh." He took the paper from me, frowning as his eyes scanned the page.

"Yeah. And she wants to meet you." I stood on tiptoes to reach over his arm and point out the relevant section.

"I see." He handed the letter back to me. "It's not that I don't want to meet her. I really do. It's just…" He waved a hand toward his head and wiggled his finger at the points of his ears.

"Yeah." I folded the letter and set it in the compost bin. I'd respond to her actual e-mail when I got back to Lydbury and my laptop. "I guess you'll glamour up, and we'll hope she doesn't ask too many questions?"

He laughed. "Right. This should be interesting."

"You don't say." Keeping my life in the world of the Fae separate from my life in what I kept thinking of as "the real world" had been getting increasingly complicated. I started down the hall that led to the cottage's two small bedrooms.

He followed me. "Would you like to clean up a bit before I drop you at Lydbury?" He reached out to run a hand along the curve of my hip, which was still covered by the running tights I'd put on for my sparring session with Arabella.

I buried the urge to respond to his touch. "I think I'll just shower and change there." I shoved dirty clothes and toiletries into my overnight bag. "If you can drop me in my room, they might not know I was gone last night."

He stepped up behind me and wrapped his arms around my waist. "Are you still sneaking out to see me?" he asked, nuzzling my neck.

"What am I supposed to tell them? That I'm going to your place for the night, but I somehow don't need a car to get there?

It's not like I can explain to them where it is you live, or how they can reach me if they need to get in touch." I sighed and leaned against him, letting my head fall back onto his shoulder.

He smiled against my skin. "True. That does make it a touch more difficult." His words breathed warm air across my collarbone. "You could just move in with me, you know. There's plenty of room here for both of us now that Ari and Fi moved out."

Fiona had taken Flida's room when Liam moved back in, but Arabella and Liam hadn't lasted long as roommates. Shortly after Liam returned, Arabella took to spending her nights in the barracks with the Queen's Guard, satisfied that Liam, and the two guards who patrolled outside the cottage, could keep Fiona safe in her absence. But that arrangement didn't last long, either. Now Fiona had her own cottage, complete with an office and a receiving room to meet with her Court, or her subjects, and Liam lived alone in his mother's old cottage.

"I'm not sure how I'd explain that to my aunt and uncle, or to my parents, for that matter," I said. As much as I wanted to move in with Liam, my new secret life with the Fae had made everything in my old life much more complicated. It didn't help that I couldn't even transport myself between Lydbury and the cottage without one of them taking me. In theory, I could just hike to the cottage after a long trip by train from the small town near Lydbury. Except, I didn't know where exactly to find the entrance to their realm.

"I suppose just running away to live with me is out of the question?" He knew the answer to that.

"Definitely." There was no way I was going to abandon my family and friends, no matter how much I loved Liam.

"Just thought I'd ask in case you'd changed your mind."

"If I change my mind, you'll be the first to know. Most likely because I'll be standing around with my bags packed, waiting for you to pick me up." I couldn't hide that tiny bit of frustration that seeped into my voice.

He stepped around me until he stood between me and my overnight bag, then tilted my head up until my eyes met his. "I'm sorry it has to be like this. Would you have been happier if I'd given up my place among the Fae to live with you?" He paused, then added, "I still could, you know."

I shook my head. "We each swore an Oath to serve and protect the Queen of the Fae. You know we're not backing out of that." This was what I wanted. I'd chosen to be part of this world. Now I just needed to figure out how to manage my life in both places. Keeping secrets wasn't one of my strengths, and I didn't want it to be, but that's what I'd agreed to do. I rose up on my toes to press a kiss to his lips.

He cradled my face in his hands as his mouth met mine. I relaxed into him, savoring the way our bodies fit together like we were made to do just this, forever. And we would, too, long after my family and my friends were gone from this world. It was a thought that frightened me a bit, and one that snapped me out of the pleasure I'd found in Liam's arms.

"We should go," I said.

He groaned. "Whatever Oscar's teaching today, I'd be happy to review with you. Here. In bed. Preferably naked." His thumb found the strap of my sports bra peeking out of the collar of my shirt, and he slid both the strap and my shirt down to expose my shoulder so he could kiss it.

I laughed. "Despite your very tempting offer, if I don't return to Lydbury soon, they're likely to figure out I'm not in my room and start worrying."

"All right." He looped his arm through the strap of my overnight bag, then snuggled me into his arms. "Ready?"

I nodded against his chest. "Ready."

Air disappeared, sucked from my lungs like I'd been dunked in freezing water. When we resurfaced in my room at Lydbury, I filled my lungs and opened my eyes. Liam dropped my bag on the floor and toppled us onto my bed. He leaned over me, propped up on one arm.

"As much as I would love to stay and help you clean up, I shouldn't keep our queen waiting." He kissed my forehead and then the tip of my nose.

"I understand. Tell her hi from me, okay?"

"I will." He pushed himself to standing, straightened his tunic, then ran a hand through his hair. "I think she has a diplomatic assignment for me. I'm not sure how long it will take, but I'll be back as soon as I can."

"More than a day or two?" I asked, sitting up.

"Maybe. I'll try to send you a message if it will be longer than that. You'll be all right?" He caressed my cheek, and I leaned into his touch.

"I doubt anyone will try to attack me at the museum or the university, and you've restored all the protection spells around Lydbury." I pushed off the bed and placed my hands on his shoulders. "I think I'll be fine."

"He can still—"

I held up a hand to cut him off. "I know. But he doesn't scare me." Nigel hadn't returned since the night before Fiona's coronation. I didn't think he would, either.

"He should scare you."

I rolled my eyes. "He helped us." No matter what I said, I hadn't been able to convince Liam that Nigel wasn't that bad.

"Just be careful." He gripped my waist and tugged me closer.

"I will. I promise."

"Right. Well, I'll be back soon." He leaned down to kiss me, then let go and took a step back.

"Liam?"

"Yes?"

"Try to use the door when you come back? You know…instead of just appearing somewhere in the house? It makes it way easier to explain how you got here when you arrive like a normal guest."

His cheeks shaded pink. "I'll try to remember."

"Love you." I pounced forward to give him one last kiss.

"I love you, too, Princess." His nickname for me brought a smile to my lips, as always. He squeezed my hand, then disappeared in a blink of light.

I sighed. My Fae time was over for a bit. Time to switch back to being Eve in the Real World.

2

CCORDING to Fiona, one did not just appear in the queen's chambers unannounced. I expected that some things would be different now that my mother was no longer serving as Queen of the Fae—not that I would have ever dropped into my mother's cottage unannounced—but dropping in on each other was something my cousins and I had always done. We'd never warded buildings against each other's entry.

Of course, there were a few times while I'd been staying at Lydbury that I'd wished I'd warded against Arabella dropping in on me. And she might have thought the same about me after that one time I appeared in her room while she was otherwise occupied with a female Elemental who happened to be apprenticing with my sire, Cahal. That was awkward, but only because I'd also been attempting to charm that same female and hadn't picked up the hint that she wasn't looking for male attention. Maybe it was better to arrive "like a normal guest," as Eve put it.

Arriving outside Fiona's new cottage, positioned on a hill with a view of the Faerie Falls, I presented myself to Fiona's guards. They knew me. Both were new recruits, but they'd been stationed outside my mother's cottage more than a few times before Fiona moved. One left her post to duck inside and let Fiona know I'd arrived. The other scanned the surrounding area and ignored me.

The first guard reappeared, followed by Fiona. Framed in the doorway of her cottage, the filtered sunlight illuminated Fiona's dark-brown skin and reflected off the angles of the iron crown she wore nestled into her tight curls.

"My queen." I bowed to Fiona, then flashed her a smirk as I stood.

She waved a hand at me and grinned. "Enough of that. I see you got my message. Come in."

I followed her into the cottage, breathing in the fresh pine scent from the wood that had been used in the construction. She'd already settled in. Shelves lined one wall of the main room. A few armchairs surrounded a low table piled with papers. The wall overlooking the back garden was almost entirely glass. Outside, a long stone table surrounded by high-backed stone chairs waited for meetings of her Court.

"Take a seat." She motioned to her assortment of plush armchairs.

I picked the one closest to me and slid into it. "Too busy to come talk with me in person?"

"You have no idea." She scowled at me. "Perhaps if someone were spending more time doing their job, and less time romancing their mate, I might have a bit more time on my hands. As it is, I've got complaints stacking up from nearly every faction." She lifted a stack of messages off the low table, revealing a teapot and cup that were hidden behind it. Then she waved the papers at me to illustrate her point.

"Complaints?" I took the stack from her and started flipping through them. "No one brought any complaints to me." I glanced up at her.

She sank into the chair across from me and reached for her teacup, pausing only to flash me a glare out of the corner of her eyes. "Mm-hmm." Lifting the cup, she raised it to her lips and took a sip.

"You think they haven't been coming to me because I haven't been reaching out to them like you wanted me to." I returned the papers to the table.

"All the factions?" She raised an eyebrow. "Even the goblins?"

I nodded. "Of course. I talked with the goblins last week. They seemed fine."

She reached for the papers and set them in her lap. Paging through them, she extracted one cream-colored sheet of parchment and handed it to me. "They didn't mention any of this?"

I scanned the page. "What? No. This is..." I rubbed a hand over the stubble along my jaw. The more I read, the more annoyance turned to anger that simmered in my veins. "Those wee rock-crushing lump heads."

Fiona snorted. "I might suggest a different tone than that when you meet with them next." She took another sip of tea. "But, as much as I'd love to continue to guide you in the ways of diplomacy, we have bigger issues to discuss."

I set the complaint back on the stack, making a mental note to take all of it with me when I left, and sat back in my chair. "Is it the demons?"

She sighed. "Not this time. We have no word yet from Arabella's spies about what they might be up to since leaving the

Wild Hunt." She set down her teacup and pressed her palms against her thighs. "No. I was referring to your sire."

"My sire? What about him?" My fingers flexed, nails biting into the upholstered arms of her chair.

"He's retiring." She frowned.

"Oh." I sighed, relaxing a bit. Only a few months had passed since my mother faded, and she had been younger than my sire. For a moment, I'd thought Fiona was about to tell me that I was going to lose Cahal as well. I didn't understand why she was so concerned with him stepping down as Court Elemental.

"Yes." She tapped a nail against the porcelain cup as she lifted it from the table. "According to the memory keeper, he's held the position of guardian on the Court since Godda's reign, may her force strengthen us all."

"May it be so," I responded automatically, hoping I wouldn't have to ask her to explain why that was a problem.

"He says that seeing Flida fade made him realize he's too old for this 'Court nonsense'—his words." She rolled her eyes.

I grinned. She'd executed an excellent impression of him. "Sounds like him."

"Yes." She pressed her lips together, and her eyes narrowed at me over the lip of her cup. "I can't help thinking it's me that he's opposed to serving. You remember the coronation? He never swore his Oath."

The Cahal I'd known as a Faeling and apprentice had been distant, even though he was my sire. He was a loner by nature. "I don't think it's you," I said.

It had always surprised me that Cahal had ended up as leader of the Elementals, their guardian. He'd bested the strongest of his kin to earn the title and a place on the Court. We hadn't had much contact since I'd left his service, aside from the visit I'd paid him before my mother faded. Based on that encounter,

I had no reason to conclude he'd changed.

"Whatever it is, his retiring means I'll need to call a Conclave for the Elementals." Her frown shifted into a grimace.

I could tell this situation troubled her, but it didn't appear dire. "Aside from the fact that he's my sire, what does this have to do with me?"

Her eyes narrowed. "You try my patience sometimes, Cousin."

"Sorry. I don't get it. I'm not the one with access to the queens' memory keeper, and the Conclave that gave us Cahal was well before my time. And yours. As far as I know, it's an Elemental thing, isn't it?" She couldn't seriously think that this was something I could help with.

"Conclaves are a serious matter to the Elementals." She'd adopted the voice I'd heard her use when instructing Faelings. Clearly, I'd stepped in it this time. "The competitions can breed tensions within their faction. Especially if there's no clear favorite among them." She leaned toward me, raising one perfectly arched eyebrow. "Is there a clear favorite?"

"How would I know?" I grumbled.

"Perhaps because you are half Elemental, and their guardian is your sire." She set down her cup. "Not to mention, you are my ambassador to the Fae factions. I need you to know these things. And this shouldn't be nearly as difficult as getting a bunch of disgruntled goblins to open up. These are your kinfolk."

"I haven't spent time with the Elementals since I was an apprentice, and you know that." Elemental Faelings were raised in a common crèche, but High Fae females raised their own Faelings, or sent them to be raised by their mother's kin. My young life had been no different, which was why I'd been raised by my High Fae mother, and my cousins were raised alongside me after their mothers, may their forces strengthen us all, were killed by Edric.

"You've spent more time with that faction than anyone else on my Court. Consider this your first priority." She fixed me with her stare as though I'd dare to do anything but agree.

I could never refuse her. Arabella and Fiona were my closest kin. They were like sisters to me, and I'd do anything for them. "I am at your service." I grinned at her, but instead of smiling back, she scowled. There must be something else on her mind if she still hadn't relaxed enough to be in a joking mood.

She shifted a bit in her chair. "Good. Now...about Evelyn... how is she adjusting?" She tapped her long ebony fingers against the arm of her chair.

I shrugged. "All right." I leaned forward and palmed an ore that had been set out as decoration on the low table between us.

Fiona stood and snatched the sparkling rock from my hand. "Put that down. Do you have any idea what this is?" She placed the egg-shaped lump on one of the shelves before returning to her chair.

I held my hands up. "No. Should I?"

She cocked her head at me. "How is it that you never saw Flida using the memory keeper?"

I squinted at the rock, then at her. "That thing holds the memories of all our queens?" I'd heard my mother mention the device, but I'd always envisioned it as a glowing golden orb, for some reason.

Fiona nodded. "Yes. There's a powerful crystal inside that ore. We have the Elementals to thank for the magic behind it. Earth magic, as I understand it. But the memories themselves are encrypted in a language only known to the queens."

"Fascinating." I'd been away from my kin studying human

culture and history for too many years. The fact that Fiona knew more about my Elemental kin than I did frustrated me.

She cleared her throat. "I've been thinking about your mate's role on the Court."

"What about it?" Mention of Eve focused my attention back on Fiona.

"As one of the Sworn, she should have an official role on the Court. I have an idea about something that I might like her to do for us," she said, returning to her chair.

"What sort of thing would that be?" I couldn't help the hint of excitement that escaped in my tone.

"I'm still deciding, but I wanted to check with you first to see if you thought she'd be interested in taking on more responsibility."

"I think she'd love to be more involved."

"Ari reported that Eve is still working with Oscar and spending significant portions of her time at Lydbury. Should I be concerned about that?"

I shrugged. "It might be easier on her if she could talk with Oscar. Let him know where things stand. That sort of thing. He does know about us, after all."

"I'll consider it." She stood and walked over to the memory keeper, reaching out to lay one hand on the uneven surface. "Flida was the first to meet with him, you know. She may have been the only one until I talked to him after what happened with Edric. Her memory of it is all here."

"It's a bit strange knowing that you now share all my mother's memories." I realized that meant she probably now knew much more about me than she had before. An uncomfortable amount more. "A bit creepy, actually."

She grinned at me. "It's not everything, you know."

I let out a breath. "Thanks. That does make it a bit better."

She laughed. "Worried that I've been exposed to memories of your naked Faeling bottom?"

Heat warmed my cheeks. "You haven't, have you?"

"No, silly." She left the ore, crossing over to stand in front of me. She crouched until we were eye level, then tugged on a lock of my hair. "You may think you're the center of the universe, but your bum isn't worthy of making it into the queens' memories." She cocked her head and narrowed her eyes. "Yet." Standing, she tugged her tunic to straighten it, then repositioned her crown. "Now, get out of here and get to work. I want that report before I announce the Conclave."

I stood to face her. "Yes, my queen." I was halfway to the door when she stopped me.

"Oh, and Liam?"

"Yes?"

"Don't forget to spread the word about the repopulation effort."

I turned slowly. A knot formed in my gut as I prepared to respond. "Right. I meant to speak with you about that." She'd included the word "repopulation" in her note to me, and Eve had almost seen it. If she had, she'd have asked questions I wasn't prepared to answer, and I couldn't lie to her.

"Do you have a problem with my decree?" Her arched brows dared me to disagree.

"No. I agree with it. Edric and the Hunt decimated our numbers. We need to rebuild. Repopulation is part of that." I had no issue with her plan, or the incentives it offered.

"What's the problem, then?" she asked.

I rubbed my palm against the back of my neck. "It's...a little personal."

"Ah." She nodded. "I see. You want to know if I expect you to help with the effort?"

She'd guessed correctly without much of a hint. That's how well she knew me. "Evelyn..."

"Is a human." She nodded.

"Yes. Right. And she's also my chosen mate." My arm dropped to my side, and I squared my shoulders.

"You could sire another's child," she suggested. "You wouldn't even have to mate with the chosen female, should you choose to remain faithful to your mate. There are ways, you know."

"That's not..." Heat rose up my neck and crept toward my cheeks. "Humans can be a bit possessive about this sort of thing. But, even if she agreed, I wouldn't want to."

The arch in her eyebrows returned. "You'd sire a human child, instead?"

"Then...there's no chance for a child of ours to be Fae?" I frowned. I'd been holding out hope that might be a possible solution.

"None. The genetics are clear on that count. Even Godda could not have produced a Fae child with her human." I detected a small amount of pity in her voice.

I took a breath. I'd already made my decision. Now I just had to tell my queen and hope she understood and accepted my choice. "If I sire a child, I want it to be with my mate."

"All right, Cousin. Don't worry. I won't ask that you comply with my decree." She crossed the room until she stood in front of me. Reaching up, she placed a hand on my cheek. "I only ask that you communicate it to the factions."

"You know how much I want to see our kind flourish again, don't you?" I searched for any hint of disappointment in her eyes.

"I do. Honestly. I understand. I'll do my best to have enough for both of us." She hugged me.

"And Ari, too?" I asked, squeezing her back.

She released me, shaking her head. "You let Ari worry about Ari. She can make her own decisions."

The entire topic of Fae genetics served to highlight how much I stood to learn about my own kind. I'd been away for years, studying Edric's life, searching for a weakness, and perfecting my ability to pass as human. My mission had forced me to disconnect from my life among the Fae, from what it meant to be Fae. I barely knew what it would take to rebuild and make life safe for the factions. The least I could do would be to help our queen with the one responsibility she'd delegated to me.

"Give me those complaints, and I'll work on those as well." I held out my hand to take them from her.

Fiona glanced at the stack of papers, then waved off my offer. "Don't worry about those. I'll take care of them. For now, just worry about the Elementals. I don't have much time before I need to announce the Conclave."

We said our goodbyes, and I left. If I hurried, I could drop in on Eve and let her know I'd be gone longer than I'd planned. And somewhere in there I had to figure out how to tell her about Fiona's repopulation decree.

3

AFTER my shower, I jogged down the front steps, past the tapestry of Godda, only to find Uncle Oscar waiting in the foyer. "Sorry. I'm running a bit late today."

"Spending time with Liam again?" He grinned at me.

"Yes. You don't mind, do you?" My stomach twisted with guilt.

He laughed "Mind? Of course not. Why would I mind?"

"It might be a bit weird, that's all. Me dating your former secretary." On the other hand, based on his reaction, perhaps I was being oversensitive.

"I don't see what's odd about two young people who fancy each other spending time together." He placed a hand on my shoulder and leaned down to kiss the top of my head. When he leaned back, he stared into my eyes and added, "I understand. I may be old, but I remember."

I smiled at him to hide the thoughts running through my mind. How could he possibly understand the situation I'd put myself in?

"Right then. Let me grab a few things and we'll be off." He turned and started down the hall to his study, then paused. "Oh. Almost forgot. I left a stack of books on the table in the library. Would you mind shelving those for me when we get back?"

"Of course." I slipped my phone out of my pocket, checked that it was still working, then added a reminder about the books. By the time I'd sent a quick response to Angie telling her I'd call her later to talk details and finished checking my messages, Uncle Oscar had returned, coat and briefcase in hand.

"Ready?" he asked.

I grabbed my jacket off the coatrack and followed him out the door and around to the carriage house. Uncle Oscar remained quiet and pensive for most of the drive to the university. I attempted to ask him about his agenda for the lecture, but he kept his answers brief. Even though he'd said he didn't mind me spending time with Liam, I worried he was just being polite.

He pulled the car into an open stall in the car park, and I followed him to his tiny first-floor office. He'd been teaching here since before I was born, yet he refused to take advantage of his seniority and upgrade to a better location with more space, closer to his peers. Instead, he chose to remain crammed in this tiny room, not much bigger than a closet, located in one of the busier hallways in the building. He claimed to have a sentimental attachment to it, though he'd never explained why.

A flash of light in one of the dark corners of a stairwell caught my eye, and I froze, wondering if it could be Liam. If it was, he likely had something urgent to share; otherwise, he'd never risk materializing at the university.

"Uncle Oscar?"

He turned and noticed I'd stopped. "What is it?"

"I just... There's something I just remembered." I glanced between him and the stairwell, trying to determine if a figure lurked there in the shadows. "Go on ahead, and I'll meet you in the lecture hall."

"Are you sure? Is everything all right?" He took a step toward me.

I waved him off. "I'm sure. I just need to make a quick trip to the ladies' room." I patted my bag and faked a sheepish grin.

A light blush colored his cheeks. "Oh. Yes. I see. All right, then. Carry on." He hurried away.

I hated lying to him, but I couldn't think of how else to get away without questions. As I cut across groups of students in a hurry to get to class, I remembered Liam's warning. Faeries weren't the only creatures able to transport themselves in the blink of an eye. And, since I'd been on my way to class with my uncle, I wasn't carrying the knife Arabella had given me. I hadn't had any contact with Nigel since before Fiona's coronation, and I didn't think his awful mother would try to abduct me from such a populated location. But just in case, I ran through Arabella's lessons on self-defense as I approached the stairwell.

"Hello?" I crept closer. If there wasn't anyone here, I was going to feel like an idiot. Just as I was about to turn around and leave, a figure stepped out of the shadows to face me.

I recognized it as Fae, only, not one I'd seen before. This creature stood as tall as a human but didn't have any hair. Its ears and hands resembled those of the High Fae I'd met, but its eyes were almost entirely black, and I couldn't tell where pupil ended and iris began, or if it even had an iris.

"We meet at last." Its mouth pulled back into a grin, revealing pointed teeth. "I've come to collect what I'm owed."

I kept my weight on the balls of my feet, ready to push off and flee if I sensed this creature meant me any harm. "Do I know you?"

"We have not yet been introduced, but I've been watching you for many years, Evelyn, heir of Vivian." The creature laced its long fingers together as it paced toward me. "You may call me Bryn."

My instincts screamed that I should run, but if there were Fae who might harm me, surely Liam or his cousins would have warned me. So, I pushed down the adrenaline spiking pins into my muscles, prompting them to action. "It's lovely to meet you, Bryn. Unfortunately, this isn't the best time for a chat."

I glanced behind me, but the hall had cleared of students and professors, even though I hadn't heard the clock chime. My foot scraped against the stone floor as I backed away, and I realized all the normal sounds of the university had disappeared. In their place, an eerie quiet engulfed the stairwell. Goose bumps prickled my forearms.

"I believe it is past time we met." The creature's thick gray-black tongue flicked out to lick its bottom lip, then disappeared again behind those daggerlike teeth. "After all, you made your choice. Thanks to your aunt and our queen, we're linked now, you and I." Eerie laughter bubbled from its lips.

"What do you mean? What does my aunt have to do with this?"

"Ah-ah." It waved one long finger between us. "First a taste, then I will explain."

"A taste of what?" I scrambled back but slammed against the wall.

The faerie disappeared, then reappeared before me. It reached out and touched the tip of its nails to my temple. I tried to pull away, but the nails of its other hand pressed against the opposite side of my face, pinning me between them. A grin stretched across its face as its eyes blinked shut between vertical eyelids. "Yes. So many delicious lies." When its eyes flicked open, it released me. "Thank you for that refreshment. It has been too long."

"What lies? What did you do to me?" My fingers brushed against my temples, then down the sides of my face. I hadn't felt anything aside from the points of its nails, but the look on Bryn's face made it clear that something had transpired.

"What all Rogues do." It pressed its fingertips together beneath its pointed chin. "Make bargains and feed off human lies. Just ask your aunt. She knows." Its mouth stretched into a sly smile. "That's right. You can't ask her, can you? Secrets and lies. So many secrets and lies." Its dark tongue flicked out to lick its pale, thin lips.

"Are you trying to say that my aunt made a bargain with you?" As far as I was aware, Aunt Vivian knew nothing of the Fae.

"Oh, yes. She bargained her life for yours."

"That's impossible."

"I'd think you'd know better by now then to claim a thing to be 'impossible.'"

A flash and bang behind me tore through the unnatural silence in the stairwell and drew my attention away from the faerie.

"Get away from her!" Liam said. He closed the distance between us in a few long strides and folded me into his arms.

The faerie clicked its nails together. "Now, now, Ambassador. Is that any way to speak to a respected Rogue Elder?"

Liam held me at arm's length as he inspected me for harm. Once he'd reassured himself that I appeared unhurt, he stepped between me and Bryn, leaving one hand resting lightly on my waist. "She's off-limits to you and your kind."

"Too late, mate." The faerie executed a little hop as it tapped its fingers together and chuckled at its rhyming joke. "I've been waiting many long years to receive my end of the bargain I made that brought her here." It cocked its head to one side. "You have me to thank for that. Did you know?"

"Enough nonsense," Liam said. "I don't care what you think you did to bring her here. You will leave her alone."

"We'll see..." Bryn turned and sauntered back into the shadows beneath the stairs. "But even you cannot stop her if she decides to come to me..." It disappeared into the darkness.

Once it was gone, Liam turned toward me, placing a hand on each of my shoulders. "Are you all right?"

"I'm fine. I think." I rubbed my temples again, but Bryn had left no mark I could feel.

Liam hooked a finger under my chin and tilted my head from side to side, examining me before centering my face and locking eyes with me. "Stay away from those Fae, do you understand?"

"I didn't seek it out. It found me. Babbling some nonsense about a bargain with my aunt and delicious lies. What's a Rogue, anyway?"

"Rogues are trickster Fae. They're dangerous for humans, but not deadly. The more a Rogue feeds on a human, the more enthralled that human becomes." He glanced past my shoulder into the darkness where the faerie had disappeared.

"*Now* you tell me that there are some Fae I should keep away from? I thought they all respected the rule of the Faerie Queen. What would one of these Rogues want with me, anyway?" I knew I still had a lot to learn about the Fae, but it didn't help when Liam conveniently forgot to tell me basic things like "beware of the dangerous faeries."

He tore his eyes away from the shadows long enough to realize I was glaring at him. "Whatever else you may be, you're still a human, and that may be too tempting to resist for faeries like the Rogues." He looked past me again. "I should go after him."

Sounds of doors opening and closing and students shouting to each other down the echoing stone halls signaled that whatever magic had enveloped us had disappeared with the Rogue. I gripped Liam's hand. "No. You shouldn't." I tugged him away from the shadows beneath the stairs. "What you should do is tell me why you never mentioned anything about faeries who might harm me. If these Rogues are dangerous, don't you think it might have been a good idea to let me know?"

He cradled my cheek in one hand as he stared into my eyes. "I'm sorry. I didn't think you'd ever encounter one. That's why I placed wards around Lydbury and around the cottage. To alert me to danger and to protect you from harm."

I placed my hand over his and slid it down, off my face, until I grasped both his hands between mine. "I appreciate your vigilance, but I need to be able to take care of myself."

"It's my fault you're in danger. So, it's my responsibility to protect you." He shifted his hands so they engulfed mine. "Just promise me you won't go wandering off without me while I'm gone. All right?"

"I already promised you I'd be careful. What else aren't you telling me?" I tugged my hands free, hitched my bag up on my shoulder, and wrapped my arms around myself.

He frowned. "There isn't anything else specific you should be watching out for besides demons and Rogues, if that's what you mean." He sighed. "But there is something else I wanted to mention before I run off again."

"What's that?"

"It's what Fiona wanted to see me about... Well, part of it, anyway." He ran a hand through his hair, something he only did when he was worried or frustrated.

I tensed but didn't say anything. Waiting for him to continue, I tried to anticipate what could have him this worked up. Maybe his odd behavior wasn't just a response to his concerns about my safety.

"I need to meet with each faction's Elders to communicate Fiona's repopulation decree."

"Okay." That didn't sound obviously awful. "What does that mean?"

"The number of Fae have decreased over the past few centuries due to Edric and his Hunters. Now that he's gone, Fiona believes it's time for us to rebuild."

"That sounds like a good thing."

"It is." He rubbed his palm against his chin. "It's just...I told her I wasn't going to participate in the repopulation effort."

"Oh." The thought that he'd be expected to contribute in that way hadn't even crossed my mind. We'd only been together a few months. I was just getting used to the idea of being his mate. I certainly wasn't ready to have a half-Fae baby. But I was also a little offended that he'd refused outright without even discussing it with me first. "Why?"

"Fae males can only have one child. I'd like that child to be with my mate."

"Oh." My cheeks warmed and my heart raced. That wasn't what I was expecting. "I'm not...opposed to having children... or a child, I guess, if you can only have one. Just...maybe not right now?"

Liam grinned. "I know. Or I guessed that's what you'd say." He stepped closer and placed a kiss on the burning skin of my cheek. "There's no rush. One of the benefits of immortality. Assuming I can keep you out of danger long enough to enjoy them."

I shook my head. "It's not your responsibility to protect me. I need to learn how to protect myself." He started to respond, but I held up a hand. "Let's not argue about it now. I still don't understand why you had to tell Fiona you weren't going to participate if you plan to have a child with me someday."

"Right." He grimaced. "The problem is that any child of ours..." He hesitated. "It would be human, not Fae."

"What? Why?" That didn't seem fair.

He shrugged. "That's the way things work. The line follows the females."

Understanding dawned on me. "And if males can only sire one child... Fiona needs all the males, really. To help with re-population."

He nodded. "Exactly."

"I see."

"Right. Well. Now that I've delivered that news to you, and chased away a Rogue as an added bonus, I'm off to make sure the Elders in each faction understand and agree with the decree."

My mind had stuck on the choice he'd made. I needed more time to decide how I felt about it, but even after his explanation, it didn't sit right with me. "Duty calls."

"It does." He pulled me into his arms. "But I was thinking I might come by Lydbury tonight to see you. I have another assignment that may keep me away for a bit, but I think it's fair if I don't start that until tomorrow."

"See you later, then?" I pressed my lips against his for a quick kiss. When I opened my eyes, he'd disappeared.

I checked my watch. If I hurried, I might be able to sneak

in to Uncle Oscar's lecture and be only a few minutes late. Sparing one more glance into the shadows under the stairs, I shook off the creepy feeling of being watched and set out at a fast walk toward the lecture hall.

4

FTER meeting with the sprites, the goblins, and the brownies to discuss Fiona's decree, I decided I was free to spend the evening with Eve. I still needed to pay a visit to the Rogues, but I wanted to talk with Fiona about Bryn's visit to Eve before I did that. Then there was the matter of reintegrating with the Elementals long enough to reacquaint myself with their politics. But all of that could wait until tomorrow. Bryn had unsettled me, and I wanted to reassure myself that Eve was all right.

In my rush to see her, I nearly forgot the promise I'd made to show up at the front door like a "normal boyfriend." Instead of Eve's bedroom, I pictured one of the least visited places I'd found during my time at Lydbury, and materialized in the loft of the carriage house. Judging from the level of dust covering the boxes stored up there, I was fairly confident nothing had been moved since I'd done my inventory of artifacts at Lydbury months ago.

I gave the carriage house a quick sweep with my magic to

make sure I was alone before bypassing the ladder and transporting myself directly to the garage floor below, just in front of the cars, where I used to park my motorcycle. Rather than stay and linger on memories, I slipped out the side door and made my way to the front of the house. All these precautions ate at the time I'd rather be spending with my mate. I could only hope that Fiona would decide to eliminate her demand for secrecy so that I might avoid these roundabout maneuvers in the future.

Knocking on the door seemed particularly absurd considering the fact that I'd lived and worked here for months. I knew that if I turned the knob, I'd find the door unlocked, as always. I knocked anyway, fixed my glamour, and waited to be let in.

The door swung open, revealing Vivian swathed in a halo of light. "Ah, Liam. Come in. Come in." She stepped aside and waved me past, into the foyer. "I believe Oscar and Evelyn are in his office. You're just in time for dinner."

"Sorry to just drop in like this. I told Evelyn I'd come by once I was done with my work."

"You're always welcome here." She stepped aside and waved me in. "Besides, I could use the help getting those two to stop working and come to the table."

"I think I can manage that."

"Oh!" she said. "I almost forgot. If you can herd them to the table, there's an extra-large piece of pie in it for you."

"I'll drag them there, if I have to." I'd missed Vivian's pies. Fae weren't much for baking. We didn't even have an oven in the cottage.

"Good boy." She patted my arm and then headed toward the kitchen.

I poked my head into Oscar's study and found Eve, mug of tea in one hand and the other pressing buttons on the scanner. She looked up from her work when she spotted me in the doorway. Her eyes darted from me to Oscar, who appeared to have nodded off while reading a journal at his desk.

"Did you use the door?" she whispered.

"Of course." I crept closer to her, capturing her waist between my hands while using my magic to make sure her tea didn't spill. "Your aunt says there's pie."

"I'm going to need to go for a run tomorrow, if that's the case."

I pressed my lips against the bare skin on the side of her neck, then whispered, "If I catch you, can I have my way with you?"

"Shh..." She glanced toward Oscar, giving me even better access to the tender skin just under her earlobe. My efforts produced a soft moan, and her fingers squeezed my arm. "Not here."

My hand slid across her waist and up, under her sweater. "How about here?"

She giggled, and Oscar shifted in his chair, then coughed. Eve jumped away from me. I slid my hands into my pockets and turned to face her uncle. "Dinner's ready."

He grinned at me. "Right."

Eve reached for her mug and placed it on the tea tray. "I'll just bring this into the kitchen and see if Aunt Vivian needs any help." She collected Oscar's mug and the teapot, then carried the tray out of the room, shooting me a pleading look that I interpreted as instruction to behave.

"Shall we head to the dining room, then?" I asked.

"Yes. Only...does she know?" he asked.

I had an idea about what he might be implying, but confirming would definitely break Fiona's rules. "She does."

"Is she safe?" He stood and placed both hands on his desk.

"I won't let anything happen to her, sir." If he had any idea about Eve's role in banishing Edric, he'd probably never allow me to set foot on the grounds of Lydbury ever again, let alone go anywhere near his niece. Good thing Fiona had been able to keep that bit under wraps.

"Right. See that nothing does."

I waited as he walked around his desk to join me near the door. "I promise."

He nodded, then clapped me on the back and led me out of his office.

Dinner felt a bit like an inquisition, but I muddled through, politely answering questions about my "new job." Between evasive responses, I managed to savor the excellent roast and potatoes Marge, their chef, had prepared for dinner. After scraping my plate clean of any residual pie crumbs , I offered to help Eve clear the table as a means of escape. As soon as the dishes had been safely returned to the kitchen, I snagged Eve and tugged her into the study.

"I know it helps you keep up appearances for me to drop in for dinner with your aunt and uncle like a 'normal boyfriend,' but I thought that would never end." I sighed, collapsing into one of the leather armchairs near the fireplace.

"Oh, stop." Eve wandered over to a stack of books set out on one of the tables. "It wasn't that bad."

I followed her with my eyes. "It's easier for you. You can lie. What am I supposed to say when Vivian asks me what sort of research I'm working on for my new boss?"

"I think you did great." She lifted the book on top and paused to read the title. "Huh," she said, setting that book down and reaching for the next.

I stood and wandered over to see what had drawn her curiosity. "Are these Oscar's?"

She flipped open the cover of the book she held. "I think so. At least, he asked me to shelve them for him. I almost forgot." Her face scrunched into a scowl.

"What's the problem?" I asked, leaning over her shoulder.

"Look at these." She passed the book she'd been flipping through over to me. Then she reached for another.

I read the titles of both, then scanned the rest. With the exception of a leather-bound journal that had no title on the spine, all of them had something to do with faeries and folklore. Eve had just opened the journal, so I leaned closer to read over her shoulder as she turned the pages.

"I think this must be an old journal of his." She paused on a page with sketches of a plant I recognized.

I pointed to the flowers of the herb he'd sketched. "I think the humans call that faerie wort."

She turned the page. Notes in Oscar's scrawling handwriting shared the page with another sketch, this one of a weaving pattern. The heading read: "Protection Charm."

"You said he left these out for you?" I asked. The questions he'd asked me before dinner came rushing back to mind.

"Not exactly." She paused to skim the next page. "He said he'd left some books out and asked if I'd shelve them for him."

I knew Oscar. There was no way this was a coincidence. "He meant for you to see this."

"Do you think he suspects something?" She closed the journal and set it on the table. "Fiona told me he knew about the Fae."

I frowned. "I think he's worried about you." I hesitated. If Fiona hadn't told her that Oscar knew about me, then it wasn't my place to tell her, at least not without Fiona's permission.

"I wish I could tell him that I'm okay."

I wanted to tell her it would be all right, but I couldn't lie, and I couldn't see into the future. I could only promise to protect her, as I'd promised to Oscar. But if she knew I'd done that, she would probably get angry and insist she could take care of herself, as she had at the university. "Do you want me to help you put these away?"

Eve stacked the books and pulled them toward her, setting her palm protectively on top. "No. I think I'd rather have a closer look at them first. If you're right and he meant for me to find them, then he probably also meant for me to read them."

"All right, but maybe not tonight?" I set one hand on top of hers and put my other arm around her shoulders so I could pull her against me.

She grinned. "Are you saying you don't want to spend a quiet evening reading with me?"

I glanced back toward the fireplace. The memory of the night of our first kiss was still fresh in my mind. I wondered if she remembered, too. "Reading's nice," I said. "But I just realized I've been here for hours and haven't managed to give you a proper kiss hello."

"How tragic." She tilted her head back until our faces aligned, her eyes wide with mock horror.

"Quite." I leaned in and captured her bottom lip between mine, sliding my tongue over the tender, plump skin. She tasted like the pie's sugary fruit filling.

Eve twisted toward me, wrapping her arms around my neck and leaning against me as we kissed. When she paused, I thought she'd suggest we take this upstairs. Instead, she said the last thing I would have expected her to say.

"About that repopulation thing..." She remained quiet for several heartbeats. Her front teeth captured her lower lip, then released it. "I've been thinking... I mean, I suppose it's okay if you need to—"

I pressed my fingers to her lips, anticipating what she was about to offer. "I don't. I chose you. Remember?"

Her eyes glimmered. "How can I forget? After all, it's your fault I ended up caught by the Wild Hunt in the first place."

"Ah, but if you hadn't been caught, you wouldn't have been able to use your quick-thinking mind to rid us of Edric." I hugged her against my chest.

She snuggled against me, wrapping her arms around my waist. "How are we ever going to make this work?" she whispered.

I kissed the top of her head. "We'll figure it out. We have time."

She tilted her head back, meeting my eyes. "I suppose, in that case, maybe we go and not read in my bedroom." The corners of her eyes crinkled as she smiled.

"I thought you'd never ask." I glanced around to make sure we were still alone. "Stairs? Or faerie express?"

"We can skip the stairs," she said. "But let's take the books. For later."

"I suppose." I curled one arm around Oscar's stack of recommended reading and curled the other around my mate. Then I transported us directly into her room.

After magicking the books onto her bedside table and reaching out with my mind to set the lock on her bedroom door, I turned my attention to Eve. Gathering the hem of her sweater in my fists, I worked it up and over her head.

Her fingers unfastened the buttons on my shirt while our lips feasted on each other's skin. As much as I wanted to use my magic to make short work of our clothing, as I'd reminded her downstairs in the library, there was no reason to rush. Besides, I loved watching her shimmy out of her jeans.

"How long will you be gone this time?" she asked, running

her hands across my bare chest.

"A few days, I think." I slid my hands down her back, my finger tips slipping inside the waistband of her underwear, shifting them down until they fell to the floor.

"Too long," she grumbled, stretching up on her toes, her breasts and belly sliding against my skin as she captured my earlobe between her lips and teased it with her tongue.

I groaned. "Come with me."

"I can't," she whispered into my ear. "Angie's visit. Remember?"

I lifted her up and she wrapped her legs around my waist. In two strides, we were tumbling naked onto her bed, and her whispers turned to moans as I used my tongue in a new, wordless campaign to convince her to join me, move in with me, leave Lydbury behind, and continue on as my mate for the whole of our immortal lives.

5

$\mathcal{A}$RABELLA arrived at the cottage the next morning, banging on the door to drag me out of Liam's arms to train. I initially thought it was Aunt Vivian trying to wake me up, but when I blinked my eyes open, I realized at some point in the night Liam must have had transported us back home. I didn't have much time to dwell on the idea that I'd started to think of his cottage as home. If I wanted Arabella to quit pounding down the door, I needed to pull on some training clothes, and fast.

"Enough, Ari. We're up," Liam yelled before rolling over and tugging the blanket up over his shoulder.

"I'll get rid of her." I shoved my arms into my favorite warm-up top and yanked it over my head, then started searching for my running tights, hoping Liam hadn't forgotten to bring my clothes.

He sat up and rubbed his eyes. "No. It's all right. You train. I need to get to work on this assignment that Fiona gave me, anyway."

I glanced over and caught him watching me walk about naked from the waist down. "I don't suppose you've seen my running tights?"

The distracted look vanished from his face. "Oh." My overnight bag materialized at the foot of the bed. "Sorry about that."

The thumping of Arabella's fist on the door paused long enough for her to yell, "I'm giving you one more minute, and then I'm coming in! Don't think I don't know what you're up to in there." She punctuated her warning with a final thump.

Seconds began ticking down in my head as I tugged on my running tights and gave Liam a quick kiss. "How does she even know we're back?" I asked as I pulled my hair into a ponytail and shoved my feet into my shoes.

"Who knows?" Liam sighed. "She's paranoid. She has spies everywhere. I wouldn't put it past her to have paid the pixies in our garden to tip her off on cottage-related activity."

"Well, that doesn't creep me out or anything." I kissed him one more time, using up my last remaining seconds. Then I rushed to the door and swung it open just as Arabella reached out to grab the knob.

"Good morning," I said.

She retracted her hand, eyed me from head to toe, and nodded. "Let's train." Pivoting, she set off for the open area we used as our makeshift practice arena.

"What's got you in such a funk this morning?" I asked, jogging to catch up to her.

"Faelings." She pulled a knife from its sheath and sent it end over end into a tree trunk near where we trained.

"Faelings?" This was not a term I'd heard any of them use before.

"You know, baby Fae." From how she spat out the words, I got the impression she wasn't a fan.

"Aww. Cute!" I'd never have one of my own, but I definitely wanted to know where they were hiding these babies, and when I'd get to see one.

She shook her head. "Not cute. Terrors." Stalking over to the tree, she pulled her knife free and re-sheathed it.

"Are you training them or something?" I tried to imagine Arabella like Yoda teaching young Padawans and failed. If her training of me was any indication, she was more like Han than Yoda, anyway. I definitely couldn't see her with kids, or Faelings.

"Training them?" She glanced at me with a look of shock. Then she shrugged. "Eventually, I suppose. But first, I'm required to birth them. At least according to Fi."

"Oh." The joy drained out of me. I seemed that no matter where I turned, I could not escape Fiona's decree. "I guess she told you about the repopulation decree."

Arabella scoffed. "She didn't need to tell me about it. We've been planning this since before Flida faded, may her force strengthen us all." She paused to remove her cape and toss it onto a nearby boulder. "First, banish Edric. Then, Faelings for all." She crouched into a ready position. "En garde."

"Aren't we going to warm up first?" I asked.

She didn't respond. Instead, she rushed at me, forcing me to twist and dodge or end up tackled to the ground.

"I guess not." I pivoted to face her with my arms up, ready to block whatever she came at me with next.

"Do you think those who mean you harm are going to wait for you to warm up, human?" She feinted, then followed with a leg sweep and nearly caught me, but I jumped away.

That ended the conversation portion of the morning. For the next hour, we alternated between her barking at me while I drilled and attacking me until I landed flat on my ass. Maybe it was the years of track and cross-country training, but I didn't mind the tired ache of my muscles burning or the repetition one bit. It invigorated me. I loved the strength, endurance, and speed I was gaining under her watchful eye. My daily runs had taken on new significance as I considered how Arabella was shaping me into a fighter. After all, how many of the Fae got to have personal training sessions with the commander of the Queen's Guard?

What I did mind was that this personal training marked me as an outsider. I needed her assistance because I couldn't protect myself. Immortality with no magic. Life among dangerous creatures. No longer hunted by a scorned and vengeful spirit, but knowing I may still be attacked by demons for reasons the Fae didn't fully understand, yet.

The next time I landed on my ass, I stayed there, panting. "Liam says you have spies everywhere."

"Liam should mind his own business and keep his mouth shut."

"I'm Sworn, Arabella."

She shrugged. "You're still human."

"More than human." I glared at her. She respected confidence, and I'd learned she respected me more when I stood my ground.

She motioned for me to get up. "Let's go again. You nearly had it that time."

Her words had me hustling to my feet, thrilled to receive even that small bit of praise, but I caught myself. "Have you found Lilium? Do you know why the demons partnered with Edric?"

She crouched into a ready position. "How about you worry about nailing your forms and leave protection of the Fae to me?"

Her words stung. I hated feeling like one moment I belonged and the next I was merely being tolerated because Liam had chosen me as his mate. I crouched but didn't wait for her attack. Instead, I took the fight to her, running through the series of jabs and kicks and holds she'd had me repeat again and again for weeks now. I let my frustration fuel me and feed my aggression. The next thing I knew, I had Arabella's arms locked behind her, and I forced her to her knees.

"Nice work," she said.

I released her and stepped back, shocked that I'd managed to win one round.

"Don't get cocky, now." She stood, brushing herself off and straightening her tunic. "You pinned me in a fair fight, but a fight with a demon won't be fair. Especially not if you're also fighting to maintain control of your mind."

"I know." I hadn't forgotten the feel of Nigel invading my memories. He may have helped us, but he'd also violated my mind. And he would have left Liam there to die. I wasn't sure I could forgive him for either of those things.

"I can't help you keep them out of your head. So, your hope will be to attack faster. Eliminate them before they can control you." She waved a hand in the air between us. "That was good, but if I'd been using my magic, you wouldn't have stood a chance. Keep practicing. It needs to be faster than a thought. It needs to be instinct. A reflex."

"Should we go again?" Liam hadn't interrupted us yet to let me know he had to go and it was time for me to return to Lydbury. So, I hoped I might have time to prove to Arabella that I could do it again. Faster.

She shook her head. "We're done for today. I have work to do." Her eyes darted to the cottage, and she frowned. "Since only a handful of High Fae remain, I need to add motherhood to my duties." She reached for her cape, flipping it around her shoulders as she stood. "Keep practicing," she said, then disappeared.

I didn't realize Fiona had been watching us until I turned and started toward the cottage.

"Well done," she said.

"Thank you, Your Majesty." I bowed, using the pause to take a deep breath and control the equal parts excitement and terror that coursed through me at seeing her standing outside the cottage.

When I straightened, I saw Liam waiting in the doorway behind Fiona. "I have to go," he said.

"Oh. Okay. Let me grab my things. It will only take me a minute," I said, glancing between him and Fiona. It was odd for him to be in such a hurry when it appeared that Fiona had just arrived.

Fiona held up a hand. "It's all right. You go on ahead, Cousin. I'd like to talk with Eve. I'll drop her at Lydbury when we're done."

My heart raced as I racked my brain trying to figure out if I'd done something wrong. Had she changed her mind and decided to erase my memory and banish me, after all? I looked to Liam for a hint, but he didn't seem bothered about this change in plans. "Okay. Thanks." My voice came out softer than usual.

Liam stepped around Fiona and crossed the lawn to meet me. "Don't worry about her," he whispered as he bent to kiss my cheek. "I'll be back soon, and I'll come straight to Lydbury as soon as I'm done." He tucked a strand of sweaty hair behind my ear and grinned.

He didn't bother censoring his goodbye kiss, even though we had a royal audience. I knew my lips were salty with sweat, and I definitely needed a shower. The combined effect of all that, plus the lingering nerves from anticipating whatever Fiona had to say to me, made it hard for me to enjoy his attention.

"See you soon," he whispered. Then he disappeared, leaving me alone with the Faerie Queen.

She wasted no time in getting to the point of her visit. "I've been thinking about your role on the Court."

"Oh." I ran a hand over my sweaty ponytail.

She sat on the bench outside the cottage and waved a hand toward the empty space beside her. "Sit."

I sank down beside her. Before I could ask what she meant, she continued her explanation.

"Every member of my Court has a role, you see. The other positions are established roles that have been in place for millennia. Your addition has presented a bit of a challenge, but I think I can add a role that will help protect this new era of Fae that I am trying to usher in."

"Something that will help you rebuild?" I asked.

"Yes. Similar to the repopulation effort. Liam mentioned that to you already?"

I nodded.

"Good. I'm sure you understand. After the losses we suffered during Edric's raids, it's critical that our kind begin to reproduce. We need Faelings to rebuild, and we need to remain undisturbed by humans. That's where you come in."

"How can I help?"

"Liam's mission at Lydbury gave me an idea. We need a liaison with the humans, and who better to fill that role than a human, and friend of the Fae? It's a wonder that Flida never asked Oscar to join the Court when she met him."

My muscles tensed. "Oscar? My uncle? Met Flida? When?" Back when Fiona had given me the choice to become Sworn or lose all memory of what had happened to me, she'd told me that Uncle Oscar knew the Fae existed. But this was different.

"That's right. You wouldn't know that, would you?" She cocked her head. "He wouldn't have told you. And you wouldn't have said anything to him."

"You made me promise not to." Perhaps Uncle Oscar really did understand more than I'd realized. It definitely helped to explain the books he'd left out for me.

She nodded once. "I did."

"Has he also known about Liam this whole time?" Anger and frustration boiled up at the edge of my question. I'd been so careful to hide my actions from my aunt and uncle, so worried about keeping the secrets of the Fae. If he'd known the whole time, someone should have told me so that I wouldn't have had to bother.

She shook her head. "He didn't know about Liam until after you banished Edric."

So he did know, and I'd wasted all this time trying to keep everything secret. "If he knows, why can't I talk with him about"—I waved a hand in the air to indicate her and everything around us—"all of this?"

Her eyes narrowed as she considered my question. "If you think it will make it easier on you, I see no reason why you should hide your choice from him any longer. You may talk with him openly, but no one else. All right?"

Relief flowed through me. My shoulders relaxed. But it wouldn't do to have a secret shared with Uncle Oscar that I couldn't share with Aunt Vivian. Besides, that Rogue seemed to think Aunt Vivian already knew about the Fae. "What about my aunt? Must we keep all this a secret from her as well?"

Fiona frowned. "I'm not entirely sure what your uncle has told your aunt about us. They were both captured by the Wild Hunt, according to Flida's memories." She paused. Her gaze drifted to the trees nearby as she considered my request. "I suppose she can be trusted. Now that Edric is gone, I'm less concerned about the need for extreme secrecy. Though, I do think it best that we continue to live in hiding from the humans. For now."

"Thank you." Half of me wanted to run over and hug her. The other half was still processing what she'd said about Aunt Vivian and Uncle Oscar and the Wild Hunt.

"If you take on this ambassador role on my Court, do you think you can manage to work on our behalf among the humans without letting them know we exist?" she asked.

"What sorts of things would you have me do?" Keeping their secrets was never going to be easy, but I agreed that the world was not ready to know about the existence of Fae—or demons, for that matter.

"Oh, buy up land when we need more space, protect the land we do occupy from being encroached on by humans, push for more environmental protections, that sort of thing." She waved a hand in the air as though what she asked for wasn't nearly impossible.

"But where will I get the money? I don't know the first thing about land use, or environmental protections, especially not here. I'm an American. Will they even let me do that here?"

"Hmm. I hadn't considered that." She pressed a finger to her lower lip, thought for a moment, then shrugged. "No matter. We'll provide you the funding you need, and I can help you identify others who might be able to help you."

"Others who will take orders from a young American woman?" I hadn't had much work experience, but from what I'd seen, that would prove challenging.

She grinned and reached for my hand, pressing our palms together before interlacing her fingers with mine. At her touch, a jolt surged through me. Instinct made me want to pull away, but she kept our hands linked. The sensation raced up my arm and neck to probe at the base of my skull. It reminded me of Nigel's presence in my mind, but this was different.

"I just need to know what I'm working with. I promise not to probe," she said. "Just relax."

I blinked at her, trying to will the tension from my muscles. "What are you doing?"

"I think I might try crafting you a glamour. It won't change who you are, and we'll still need to get you citizenship papers, but I could tweak others' perception of you, give you a credible accent, that sort of thing, if you'd like."

"Would I be able to control it?"

She studied me, our hands still linked, though I could no longer feel her touch in my mind. "Perhaps. With training. And time." She released my hand. "What do you think? Would you be willing to take up this role on my Court?"

This would be a huge responsibility, but it would allow me to move in both worlds, and give me the opportunity I craved to help protect these creatures I'd come to care for deeply. Still, having to depend on Liam or one of the others to move me about severely limited my independence. If she could craft me a glamour, maybe she could do something to help with that as well. "I'd love to, but I'll need a better way to travel, I think."

She cocked her head. "Of course. How silly of me." Taking my hand in hers once again, she turned it over until my palm faced the sky. Then, she pushed up my sleeve and ran her long nails over the skin on the inside of my wrist. "Yes. I think I can help with that."

6

THE damp air cooled my skin as I followed Cahal deeper into the valley along the stream that trickled out of the lake at the base of the Faerie Falls. My sire's white hair flowed in loose waves down past the lowered hood of his sapphire-blue cloak, in stark contrast to the rich color of the material that covered his shoulders. I trudged along in his wake, exhausted from the series of introductions he'd forced on me.

At first, I'd been encouraged by my meetings with the Elemental Elders. They welcomed me back among them, introducing me to their families and speaking at length and with great enthusiasm about Fiona's decree. I thought I'd be able to quickly determine the power structure and the favored candidate to take Cahal's place as guardian, but the younger Elementals I'd been introduced to turned out to be common Elementals. None were potential contenders in the yet-to-be-announced Conclave.

Instead, the Elders and the younger Elementals I'd met with were specialists, unlike Cahal, who was master of all elements, even though his strongest affinity had always been for water. Anyone who wished to compete to take his place would have to demonstrate that same rare mastery. But at best, the Elementals I'd met had mastery of one or two elements, like me, which meant they weren't candidates for guardian.

The other thing that the Elementals I'd been introduced to had in common took me longer to figure out. They were all unpaired. That explained why the Elders were all so eager to see me back among them, and why they'd been so enthusiastic about Fiona's decree. They thought I'd come to choose a mate. Once I realized their intentions, I made it clear to Cahal that I wanted to meet his apprentices. Immediately. Before we met with anyone else.

Cahal responded by waking me at dawn the next day and leading me out on a hike through the forest. At first, I couldn't tell where he was taking me. Then, we passed a bend in the stream where the water deepened and stilled enough to make a decent swimming hole. I remembered the spot as a sweet escape after long summer days as an apprentice, practicing earth magic on the exposed cliffs not far from here. "Are you taking me to the Cairn Cliffs?"

Cahal grunted in response.

"You're not going to leave me there until I prove that I can still master the forms, are you?" If that was his plan, it might be days before I could get away, let alone return to Lydbury.

"What purpose would that serve? It's not as though you're going to compete in the Conclave. Unless you've discovered some water and air magic while messing about with the humans?" He'd always been disappointed that I'd only shown affinity for earth and fire. But that had paled against his rage at my decision to, as he put it, "learn how to become a festering boil infecting the environment," his interpretation of "studying human history."

I ignored his jab and jumped on the opening he gave me. "So who do you think will be competing, then? You must have a star apprentice hidden around here somewhere."

"Hmph." He picked his way along a deer path that led through the trees and out to the mossy cliffs beyond.

Wind whipped up off the ocean, lifting dust that scraped against my face. I blinked to clear my eyes, then kept them narrowed to slits as I hurried to catch up to my sire, who was already halfway across the clearing and heading toward several figures absorbed in their training. A male in a brown tunic with a high collar turned up against the wind glanced up at our approach and stopped. His thick red-gold hair remained untouched by the gusts. Something about his use of air magic to protect his artfully wild mane and its gravity-defying tousled look made me instantly dislike him.

He called out to the other five Elementals, his words lost on the wind. They must have heard him, because all but one stopped, looked, then turned at the young male's slight chin lift to note Cahal's approach. All except a strawberry-blond young female who looked vaguely familiar.

Cahal ignored the five who had stopped and were now bowing to him. He made his way directly to the female who still concentrated on her task. Sweat beaded on her forehead as she worked, drawing a vine-like plant up from the ground as she guided the gusting wind around it in eddying swirls so that the water she brought down from the overcast skies could condense on the motionless budding leaves. Her control of the three elements didn't waver in the presence of her mentor.

Cahal stopped next to her. His only comment was a quiet, "Hmph."

She stood a little taller, basking in his praise, while I sighed, remembering what it had been like to be in her shoes. The others left their work and wandered over to gather around us as she released her control and bowed to my sire.

"Apprentices," Cahal addressed the three males and three females who stood in a loose group before him. "We have been graced with a visit from Fiona's ambassador."

Six pairs of eyes gazed past Cahal's face to stare at me. All dipped their heads respectfully. But the male with the up-turned collar followed his nod with an arched eyebrow in my direction. I definitely did not like that one. Luckily, he didn't appear to be the favorite. Cahal's star apprentice, the female who glowed with his meager acknowledgment of her work, stood staring at me with wide eyes.

Cahal turned toward me, gesturing to his students. "These, Liam, are the most promising Elementals of their generation."

"It's an honor to meet you," I said, still trying to work out where I'd seen her before. Something about the slightly pan-icked look in her eyes reminded me of a group of Fae females clustered behind Sorcha in the caverns beneath the temple ruins on the night we'd banished Edric. Then I remembered her. She'd been huddled with the others, but she'd been near starved and shivering. And there had been no sign of the fierce determination and confidence she'd just displayed in her mastery of her craft.

Introductions began, starting with one of the other two fe-males and ending with the one I recognized. I'd need to spend time talking with each of them to be certain she was the favor-ite, and to know if there were any hidden rivalries, but I sus-pected that I at least had an answer to one of Fiona's questions.

"Gwawr," Cahal said to the red-haired female whose eyes had followed me the entire time I'd been speaking with the others. "This is Liam." He never introduced me as his child, but it no longer bothered me the way it had when I was younger.

"Unless I am mistaken, I believe I've seen you before," I said.

"Yes, Your Excellence. I believe I have you to thank for my freedom." She bowed deeply.

"I most certainly can't take all the credit for that. After all, Sorcha was the one who led you from those dungeons."

"She was, Your Excellence, but she would not have been at liberty to do so had you not freed her first."

"Enough of this nonsense," Cahal grumbled. "It's enough that Gwawr has returned. Her absence cost her training, and she'll need to make up for the time she lost."

"I will, Honored Guardian." She bowed to Cahal and waited for his command, excusing his apprentices to return to their work.

"Fiona will be pleased to hear of such a strong crop of competitors," I said to Cahal as they left us alone on the cliffs.

"They're not all candidates for the Conclave," Cahal replied. "Not yet, anyway. We shall see what comes to pass."

I glanced at him out of the corner of my eye. With one exception—me—he'd only ever accepted apprentices who demonstrated affinity for all of the elements. And, any Elemental with control of the four basic elements was said to also have control of the fifth element, healing. Blood magic. As far as I knew, there weren't any Elemental kinfolk who could control only the four basic elements. The ability to control all five Elements was rare. I was surprised to see that he'd found six apprentices to train with him.

All Elemental Fae had mastery of at least one element. That's what made them Elementals. Many could command two elements; those were Twintails, like me. Less common even than the ability to control all the elements were those who could work three of the basic elements but lacked control of one.

They were considered unlucky, and usually cast out and forced to live solitary lives.

Before I could ask him what he'd meant, he leveled his guardian stare at me. "Bit of advice? That modesty of yours won't help you win a mate."

He'd been with me through all the introductions to the Elemental Elders and their families. He knew what they'd been up to and hadn't said a word. It made sense that the Elementals were all in violent support of Fiona's decree. The only Fae faction hit harder by Edric's rage than the High Fae were the Elementals. They so closely resembled High Fae that they'd been easily mistaken for Godda's kin and captured during the Hunt's raids. It shouldn't have surprised me that Cahal would approve of their using this as an opportunity to pair me off with a suitable Elemental Fae mate.

"I have a mate, sire," I said, resisting the urge to take my annoyance out on him.

He huffed and waved his hand in dismissal. "A human is not a mate, child. A human is a plaything. You need a proper mate. Any of these females would make a fine selection, if they'd have you." He eyed me with an appraising look.

"Even if you don't accept Evelyn as my mate, Fiona does, and that's all that matters." I crossed my arms, leveraging every ounce of confidence I could muster under the scrutiny of a face that had me quaking every minute of every day I'd spent as his apprentice.

"Fiona's too kind to tell you the truth." He shook his head. "Find a true mate. Honor your duty to your kin."

"Thank you for your advice, and for your hospitality. I wouldn't want to keep you from your students, and I should return to the Court to make my report to Fiona." I dipped my head, out of respect, even though I outranked him. Then, I turned and walked away from the cliff edge and back toward the forest we'd traveled through to get here.

"See that she announces the Conclave soon," he called after me.

"I'll do what I can." Before I'd made it halfway to the tree line, I reached for Mother's cottage and disappeared.

Suffering my sire's views on duty and proper mates after a week visiting with the Elemental Elders had me ready to run away with Eve to someplace largely devoid of Fae relations. At the cottage, I wrote a quick note to Fiona, warning her I'd drop in on her tomorrow to give her my report.

While I waited for the sprite to arrive and pick up my message, I considered where Eve and I might escape to. Perhaps I could convince her to take me home with her to California to meet the rest of her family. From what Cahal had told me of his travels, magic had almost completely left the area around where she'd grown up. It was unlikely I'd run into any Fae there.

The sprite arrived. We exchanged a few words, and I sent him off with my letter. Then I was free to spend the evening with Eve. But, in my rush to see her, I forgot the promise I'd made to show up at the front door like a "normal boyfriend."

7

LIAM had been gone for a week, and I'd had no word from Fiona about my new role on her Court. Their absence should have given me more time to dedicate to my work and family, as well as plan for Angie's visit. But, as it turned out, Uncle Oscar had gone out of town for a few days, and Aunt Vivian had come down with a cold the day after he'd left.

That meant I'd been left to my own devices to train and read the books Uncle Oscar had left out for me. Unfortunately, I had no one to discuss the contents with, and I was getting restless. Without Arabella to train with, I made do with morning runs, then practiced my drills among the chickens in garden, hidden from view by Aunt Vivian's manicured hedges.

Since I'd returned, I'd been rehearsing how to bring up the topic of the Fae with my aunt and uncle, and I'd resolved to put off the conversation until Uncle Oscar returned. But, when I returned from my morning practice session to find Aunt Vivian waiting for me in the kitchen, I decided I couldn't wait any longer.

I slipped off my shoes inside the mudroom door and pushed open the door leading to the kitchen. "Are you feeling better?" I asked, squeezing my aunt's shoulder as I made my way over to the sink to splash water on my face. My heart raced in anticipation of her reaction to the topic I planned to discuss.

"Much," she said, looking up from her magazine. "You were up and out early this morning."

I poured a glass of juice and sank into the chair across from her. "I wanted to get in a run while there was a break in the weather." My arm still throbbed a bit from the magic Fiona had worked. I wanted to push up my sleeve and check that the marks she'd made were still there, but before I could show my aunt Fiona's magic, I wanted to learn what she knew.

"Oh! Did it stop raining, finally?" She twisted to glance out the window at the sky. "I've been cooped up in here too long. I should get out and stretch my legs." She folded her magazine closed and set it on the table.

"You may want to wait until it warms up a bit. It's still pretty chilly outside. Did you already eat breakfast?"

"I made a pot of oatmeal. I left some for you on the stove. Let me fix a bowl for you." She started to push back from the table, but I reached across and placed my hand over hers.

"No. It's all right. I'll do it in a bit. I'm not hungry yet."

"Oh. Okay. I hope I've managed to keep my germs contained. I'd hate it if you ended up catching whatever nasty bug I got."

"I'm sure I'll be fine." I took a sip of juice and prepared myself. "Auntie...I met a faerie the other day that seemed to know you."

Aunt Vivian paled. "Oh?" Her fingers brushed the edges of the placemat in front of her, and she looked down, avoiding my eyes.

"I didn't think it could be possible. But it said it made a deal with you."

She groaned like an animal in pain. "I'm so sorry, dear. It's all my fault." Her hand gripped the edge of the woven mat and twisted it. "I know that it is. But I couldn't tell you. That awful faerie made me promise."

"What do you mean? What's your fault?" I stretched across the table and scooped up her hands, giving them a squeeze.

Her eyes met mine. Tears welled in the corners. "I thought if I just didn't have any children the faerie wouldn't have anyone to lure away. But then you arrived, and the way you stared at that tapestry of Godda... Once you started asking all those questions, I just knew."

"I don't understand, Auntie. What did you know? What does this have to do with me?"

She pulled her hands free and laced her fingers together, squeezing them until her knuckles turned white. "Is it done now? Have you made your choice? I promised not to say anything."

I stared at her. "It's all right. The Faerie Queen told me it's all right. You can tell me what happened."

She hesitated. Then her words came out in a rush. "That night I made a promise that I didn't think I'd ever have to keep. I was scared. I didn't know what to do. The Rogue said it wouldn't let me go unless I gave it someone in exchange. But I bargained and made sure you would have a choice when the time came."

"That faerie captured you?"

She nodded. "Yes. Your uncle tried to save me. I didn't know him then. He was very brave, but there was nothing he could do. I promised. He didn't know I promised. I couldn't tell him.

But I thought it would be okay if we didn't have children." She moaned, covering her face with her hands. Her muffled voice continued. "It wasn't until you came to visit with your parents and your brothers, when you were just a child, that I realized my mistake. The faerie said 'my heirs.'" She dropped her hands and twisted them together. "When you started playing near the tapestry, I got scared. I convinced Brian that if he wasn't careful you might get involved with magic and the occult. He believed me. You know how devout your mother is... Well, he kept you and your brothers safe, and I made sure you had no reason to visit. Until you showed up on our doorstep a few months ago. Oh, Evie. I'm so sorry. It's all my fault. What did it want? What did you decide?"

"I don't understand. I haven't decided anything. It just said it wanted to eat my lies." I shook my head. "What was the promise you made to the Rogue?"

"I promised one of my heirs to the faeries in exchange for my life."

"Oh." I sat back in my chair and blinked at her, trying to remember exactly what the faerie had said. Something about being responsible for me living among the Fae.

"It said it would give you a choice." She stared back at me with wide eyes. She'd been keeping this secret for so long, and she looked terrified that I was going to hate her, or that the faerie was going to come and harm her. "What did you decide?"

"I..." I wanted to tell her that she was mistaken, that it wasn't her fault. But I had made a choice. Only, Fiona had been the one to offer me that choice, not the Rogue. But Fiona couldn't have known. She didn't know. Did she?

The doorbell rang before I could consider it further.

"Who could that be? Are you expecting anyone, dear? It's not Liam, is it? I told him he could just come in through the mudroom." She stood, wiped her eyes, and straightened her blouse and skirt.

I followed her down the hall to the front door, hoping that it was Liam. But, when Aunt Vivian opened the door, an entirely unexpected face stared back at me. Well, expected, but not yet.

"Oh, good! I have the right house!" My best friend's face, framed by straight, chin-length hair with several pink and purple streaks, grinned at me from the front step.

"Angie?" I blinked. She wasn't supposed to be here for three more weeks.

"Evie!" Angie dropped her luggage and threw her arms around me. Then she turned to hug my aunt. "You must be Vivian. I've heard so much about you."

"Likewise, my dear." Aunt Vivian raised her eyebrows at me over Angie's shoulder. "It's lovely to finally meet you." Aunt Vivian stepped aside and ushered Angie into the foyer. "Come in, come in. Can I get you something to eat or drink?"

"Some water, maybe?" Angie extracted her water bottle from her tote bag and held it up.

"Of course!" Aunt Vivian reached for the bottle, but I snagged it before she could.

"It's okay," I said. "I can do it." I wanted to be excited about Angie's arrival, but all I could think about was the discussion I'd been having with my aunt.

"Nonsense." Aunt Vivian appeared relieved by the interruption. Either that, or she had much more practice than I did morphing into hostess mode when required. "Why don't you show your friend up to one of the rooms upstairs, and I'll fill this and bring you two up something to eat." She plucked the bright-pink bottle from my hands and gave my arm a squeeze. The look she gave me let me know we'd finish talking later.

I nodded. "Okay, but you don't need to bring anything up.

We'll come back down after we drop off her luggage."

"All right, dear. If that's what you'd prefer." She started back down the hall to the kitchen.

I lifted Angie's small suitcase and waved to her to follow me up the stairs. "You weren't supposed to be here for weeks! What happened?"

"My business trip got canceled at the last minute, and I decided to hop on an earlier flight. I thought I'd surprise you." She followed me down the hall, gaping at the paintings that dotted the walls upstairs. "This place is like a museum."

"You'll get used to it." I pointed at the door to my room. "This is where I sleep."

"Oooh! I want to see!" She started toward my door.

I paused, setting her bag down to give my arms a rest. My arms were sore from my workout, but whatever Angie had in her bag weighed a ton. "Let's drop off your bags first, then we can come back."

"Okay." She released her grip on the doorknob and followed me to a room just past mine and on the other side of the hallway.

"This one should work." The door swung open to reveal a room similar to mine but smaller. There was only room for a bed, a dresser, and a straight-backed chair shoved into one corner. It was also missing the attached bathroom. I hoisted her suitcase onto the bed and turned to catch her reaction.

"Cozy." She turned in a slow circle just inside the door. "I like it." She tossed her tote bag onto the bed next to her suitcase. It toppled over, and her makeup bag and tablet slid out of the open top and landed on the comforter.

I reached for the bag to set it upright.

"Leave it," she said, waving her hand at me. "Let's go see your room." She tugged on my arm and pulled me back down the hall, stopping outside my door just long enough to let herself inside.

I followed her in and plopped down on my bed. "You know I love you, Ang, and I'm thrilled you're here, but you didn't need to come check on me."

She lifted a framed photo of my family off the mantel to get a closer look. "I had to come see for myself what was keeping you from coming home." She returned the frame to the mantel. "I missed my best friend. So, I decided to come to you." She sank into the armchair next to the fireplace. "Does this thing work?" she asked, pointing to the empty grate.

"Of course." I pushed off the bed and crossed the room to kneel by the fire. "I've missed you, too." I hadn't realized how much until she was sitting in front of me.

She watched while I stacked a few logs up, stuffed some crumpled paper between them, and added a bit of kindling from the bucket before striking a match and sending the whole thing up in flames. "I didn't know that you knew how to build a fire."

I shrugged. "I didn't, but it's been a cold winter, and I decided to figure out how to do it myself so my aunt wouldn't have to keep helping me." I checked the progress of the flames. "I'm still only successful about fifty percent of the time. So, we'll see how this goes."

Angie stretched her legs toward the fire and wiggled her toes. "Feels nice and warm to me."

"So." I scooted back until I was sitting cross-legged on the floor at her feet. "I'm beginning to get the feeling that something's up with you. Wanna tell me what's going on?"

She took a deep breath and let it out. "I flew across the damn country to visit Max, and I'm not over him. Not even a little bit." Her voice cracked a little on the last few words.

"Oh." The fact that she hadn't even told me that she'd gone to see her ex-boyfriend worried me. "What happened?"

"Nothing." Silent tears dripped down her cheeks. "That's just the point. We had sex. It was great. But when it was time for me to go, he didn't ask me to stay."

I reached up and rubbed her knee. "Ang, what did you expect? You broke his heart."

She let out a sob. "I know." Her hand swiped away tears as she attempted to sniff them back inside. "I've broken a lot of hearts, Evie. But he's the only one who haunts my dreams. I just can't seem to get him out of my system."

I pushed myself up onto my knees and shuffled over to her so that I could throw my arms around her and give her a hug. "It's okay, sweetie." I let her cry.

After a few minutes, she let out a sound that was half laugh, half sob. "See. That's what I needed. I shouldn't have to fly halfway around the world to get a hug from my best friend."

I let go and sat back on my heels just in time to see a flash of light out of the corner of my eye. Oh, no. Angie's tear-stained face turned toward the flash. I didn't need to follow her narrowed eyes to know that Liam had ignored Aunt Vivian's suggestion that he enter through the mudroom.

"Um. Evie?" Angie blinked at me, then glanced at Liam before turning back toward me. "Please tell me I'm not hallucinating." She tilted her head, raising her eyebrows as her eyes darted toward Liam.

Liam coughed. "Right."

"This is why we use the door," I said, still not looking over at him. I bit my lip, took a deep breath, and exhaled. "So, Ang, you know how you wanted to meet Liam?" I turned toward Liam. "Liam?" I gestured toward my best friend. "Meet Angela." I gave Angie a sheepish look. "Ang, meet Liam."

Angie scooted to the edge of the armchair, swiping at her face with the heel of her hand. "You have got to be kidding me."

"Guess now's not a great time to drop in?" Liam ran a hand through his hair, revealing the points of his ears. He hadn't even bothered with a glamour.

I plopped onto my butt and wrapped my arms around my knees. Relief that my secret was out overwhelmed me, and I started giggling even though part of me thought I should be worried.

"Nice to meet you, too," Angie replied. Then she turned back toward me. Her eyebrows arched so high on her forehead, they appeared to want to merge with her asymmetrical bangs. "*This* is Liam?"

I nodded as I struggled to get a grip on my laughing fit.

She squeezed the arms of the chair and bounced a little. "I knew I was right to come check on you. I knew something was up. But this..." She stood and walked over to Liam, then stopped in front of him with her hands on her hips. "This is insane. Is this real?"

"Fiona is not going to be pleased about this," Liam muttered.

"Forget Fiona. Arabella is the one who's going to be pissed." I leaned back, pressing my hands against the floor behind me to prop myself up. I stretched my legs out in front of me and crossed my feet at the ankles. Now that the secret was out, I was enjoying watching my best friend and my mate size each other up.

"Excellent point." Liam's face twisted like he was anticipating a punch to the gut from his cousin, even though she wasn't there to supply it.

"But if Arabella thinks she's going to try to kill Ang like she tried to kill me, you better let her know that she's going to have to get through me first." As soon as the words left my mouth, I realized maybe I had a tiny idea why Liam was so protective of me.

Angie twisted toward me. "She tried to what?" She hit me with her fiercest glare. "You did not mention a near-death experience. I am absolutely sure I would remember if you had."

"No one is going to try to hurt anyone," Liam said. "This is my fault. I'll deal with Fiona. And Ari."

"Well, look at you owning your mistakes." Ang gave Liam an appraising nod. Even though she now had her back to me, I could picture her smug grin, and it made me smile. "I like this one, Evie," she called to me over her shoulder. "Now, who exactly are Fiona and Arabella?"

8

BEFORE I could decide how to respond to Eve's friend, her aunt appeared in the doorway to the bedroom.

"Girls, I hope I'm not interrupting—" She sucked in a breath, and the color drained from her face when her eyes landed on me. "You," she said. "You're one of them. I should have known." Her fingers dug into the doorjamb as she stumbled backward.

Eve leapt to her feet and rushed toward her aunt. "It's okay, Auntie." She put her arm around Vivian's shoulders and led her to the chair by the fire. "Have a seat and let me explain."

"So this is how that faerie lured you away." Vivian glared at me. Her fingers dug into the plush upholstered arms of the chair as she leaned toward me. "And to think I let you live here. And Oscar...did Oscar know?"

"Uncle Oscar didn't know," Eve said. She placed a hand on her aunt's shoulder to keep her from lunging at me.

I could only hope that Eve and Vivian never found out what Oscar knew, but the likelihood of that happening was slim, especially because I sensed through the wards surrounding Lydbury that he'd just pulled his car into the carriage house. I mentally kicked myself for not having paused to think before transporting myself to Lydbury. The fact that I'd been careless and appeared before two humans in my Fae form was going to undo all the good I'd done attempting to prove myself to Fiona with my trip to the Elementals. I'd just made another huge mess that she'd have to deal with.

"I should go," I said.

"No." Eve tore her attention away from comforting her aunt. "It's okay. Fiona said I could tell them."

"Angie, too?" I asked, glancing over at Eve's best friend, who had gone silent after her initial excitement but hadn't taken her shocked eyes off me.

Eve grimaced. "No. Only Aunt Vivian and Uncle Oscar."

"Right." I breathed a sigh of relief. It was still a mess, but it was not as bad as I'd originally thought. "Well, now's as good a time as any. Your uncle is on his way inside."

To her credit, Eve didn't bother asking how I knew, and she didn't appear surprised. When the front door opened downstairs, and Oscar's voice called out to the house a moment later, Vivian stood, ready to flee the room and warn her husband that his former secretary was actually a faerie.

"Why don't we all go downstairs and have a chat?" Eve said, hooking her arm through her aunt's and glancing over at me. "Would you mind popping down to the kitchen and making some tea while I get everyone settled in the library downstairs?"

"Right." I nodded. "Solid plan. I'm on it." I disappeared before she could change her mind. When I reappeared in the kitchen, I reached for the teakettle and started to fill it at the sink. The door hinges squeaked as someone entered from the hall behind me. I turned my head and found Oscar staring at me.

"Hello, Liam. Didn't expect to see you here. Where is everyone?" He set his briefcase on the table and shrugged out of his sport coat. "I caught the early train and was hoping I might get home in time for breakfast, but I see I must have missed it."

I lit the burner and set the kettle to boil. "I couldn't say, sir. I only just arrived. Eve asked me to make some tea and bring it to the library."

"Excellent. Would you mind adding a cup for me?" He started toward the door, then paused. "And maybe add some of those biscuits Vivian keeps trying to hide from me?" He unbuttoned his shirt sleeves and rolled up the cuffs. "I'll go say hello and let them know I'm home."

"Sounds good, sir." I extracted the tea tray and began assembling mugs and biscuits, feeling only a bit guilty that I was leaving Eve to deal with the disaster I'd caused.

Perhaps Eve had a point that it wasn't my job to protect her. Ever since her connection to me had managed to get her captured by the Wild Hunt, I'd been focused on keeping her safe and protecting her. But I hadn't been able to do that then or after, when Arabella nearly killed her. Now there was a Rogue who wanted to feed off her for some unknown reason. The demons weren't the only threat to her safety, and I couldn't possibly anticipate everything and serve Fiona as well. These thoughts tumbled through my brain as I poured boiling water over the tea leaves I'd added to Vivian's favorite teapot. Once everything was arranged, I carried the jam-packed tray down the hall and into the library.

"So, your boyfriend is a faerie." Angie stood facing away from me when I entered the room, but hers was the first voice to reach my ears.

"Appears that the cat is out of the bag, so to speak," Oscar said, looking up to meet my eyes. He stood behind the arm-chair where Vivian sat, her face still as pale as a bedsheet.

"You knew and didn't say anything?" A bit of color returned to Vivian's face as she stopped cowering in fear of me and twisted to glare at her husband.

I set the tray down on the table and backed away, unsure of my place in the unfolding drama.

"I didn't know for sure until that new Faerie Queen paid me a visit," Oscar said. "A few months. That's all. And I couldn't tell you. She reminded me of my promise to keep their secrets."

"You made a promise to them as well?" Vivian asked, her voice softer.

"The Rogue was telling the truth," Eve said, her words directed at me. "Aunt Vivian made a deal. Her life in exchange for one of her heirs. Only that heir had to be given a choice..." Eve's voice trailed off, but I knew we were thinking the same thing. What did Fiona know of this?

"That's why you suddenly decided you didn't want children?" Oscar asked. He knelt next to Vivian's chair and scooped up her hand.

"Can we get back to the part where you explain how there are faeries, and they live in England?" Angie asked. "I have so many questions." She stared at me.

"Not only England," I said.

Her eyes widened, and she leaned forward in her chair. "No way. So, are there faeries in California, too?"

I looked at Eve for help. Her friend already knew too much. I should report this to Fiona, apologize, and deal with the repercussions. At this point, I was only making things worse.

Eve met my gaze and shook her head, then turned to her friend. "Listen, Ang, the faeries don't want anyone to know about them. You shouldn't even know they exist in the first place."

"So, you've made your decision. You're going with them." Vivian choked on a sob.

"If all of you would just give me a minute, I can explain." Eve paused and waited for her aunt and best friend to fix their attention on her. "First off, I'm not going anywhere. Fiona..." She paused and turned to Angie. "That's the Queen of the Fae," she explained before turning her attention back to the group. "Fiona asked me to be her ambassador to the humans, and I accepted."

I grinned. So that's what Fiona had in mind for Eve. It was brilliant.

Eve held up her hand to signal that her anxious audience should hold their questions. "But only on the condition that I could tell you what I'm doing and where I'm going. I'm tired of keeping secrets from you." She directed this to her aunt and uncle but finished by turning to Angie. "And you, too."

"What about the Rogue?" Vivian asked.

"I'm not sure," Eve said. Her eyes met mine.

I crossed my arms. "I haven't talked with the Rogues yet. Or Fiona, for that matter."

"It will be all right, Vivian. Liam will protect our Evie. He promised me he would."

Eve looked between her uncle and me. Her lips pressed together and her neck muscles tensed as she glared at me. Before she could say anything, I spoke.

"Right. About that." I coughed to clear my throat. "I shouldn't have promised to protect Eve. I don't want anything to happen to her any more than any of you do, but we can't keep her in a bubble. She chose this life, and she's learning how to protect herself. After all, she's the one who saved me from Lilium when we were captured by the Wild Hunt. And she's the one who figured out how to banish Edric."

Vivian's head swiveled toward her niece. Then she bounced up out of her chair and hugged Eve. "Oh, I wish I could have seen that! I want to hear every detail, dear."

"I'll tell you all about it some other time." She extracted herself from the embrace and squeezed her aunt's hand, then walked toward me. "But first, if it's all right, Liam and I have a few things to discuss. We'll be back soon."

"We'll be right here if you need us, dear," Vivian called after us.

"Who's Edric?" Angie asked.

I didn't hear the response because Eve had pulled me into the hallway and shut the door behind us. Then she flung her arms around my neck and kissed me.

"Thank you," she said.

"Thank you? What for?"

"For what you said in there about me being able to protect myself."

"Oh. Right."

"I'm so glad you're back. I've been dying to tell you about the ambassador thing, and to show you this." Eve pushed up the sleeve of her sweater to expose the inside of her right wrist. "Fiona did it."

Black marks in the shape of a compass rose stood in sharp contrast to her beige skin. Just beyond the tip of one of the four long points was a tiny heart. The effect resembled a tattoo, the kind you might find on the skin of any human these days, only this was no ordinary ink. This creation pulsed with magic. I cradled her wrist in my hand and ran my fingers over the tender skin.

"Watch," she said. When she twisted her arm back and forth, the compass shifted so that the heart always pointed in the same direction. "It points—"

"Home," I finished for her, impressed at Fiona's skill. She had a knack for finding excellent solutions to problems I didn't even know should concern me. I glanced up from the marks on Eve's wrist and caught her eye as I placed a kiss in the palm of her hand. "It's brilliant."

"Fiona thought it would make it easier for me to come and go if I...you know, had my own compass and transportation." She grinned.

I released her hand and slid my arms around her waist. "Does that mean you're moving in with me?"

"Maybe." Eve ran her hands down my arms. "But first I'd like to go with you to talk with Fiona. Aunt Vivian thinks the Rogue lured me here. To England. She said something about making it promise to give me a choice. You don't think the choice Fiona gave me was actually because of the bargain Aunt Vivian made before I was even born, do you?"

I shook my head. "Fiona would have told me if she knew anything about a bargain."

"Maybe she didn't know." Eve tugged on my hand, leading me down the hall and into the kitchen. "We'll have to ask her. Besides, I'm going to convince her to allow me to let Angie in on the secrets of the Fae. I can't believe I didn't think of it before, but Angie would be the perfect person to help me with this whole 'ambassador to the humans' thing."

"If anyone could convince Fiona, it's you." I paused once we were inside the kitchen and waited for her to stop and turn to face me. "Should we try out that magic tattoo of yours and go talk with her?"

"Okay but first, let me make sure Angie will be okay with my aunt and uncle for a bit, and then we can go find Fiona and get this sorted out." She started to turn toward the door, but I held her back.

Stepping close to her, I pressed my palm to her cheek. "We'll figure this out. I promise."

"Together, right?" The corner of her mouth crept up into a grin.

"Together." I sealed our deal with a kiss.

Seren's Secret

1

STUMBLING back across the border, into the Fae forest, I was almost too exhausted to care about the Elders' gossip whispered on the wind. Tracking the demon had taken longer than I'd expected, and my precious winter cloak had been splattered in incubus slime. But the demon was dead, the humans' daughter was safe from corruption, and I had a brace of rabbits to roast as partial payment.

Once my belly was full, I'd tend to my garments and rest. The news was just a distraction. One that shouldn't concern me.

So what if Cahal had resigned as our guardian? What did it matter to me that they were calling a Conclave of the Hands to determine who would take his place and become the next Guardian of the Elementals?

I wasn't an Elemental and Cahal was not my guardian. At least not according to the Elders or any of my kin. According to them, I was cursed. I'd been cast out. Left to survive or fade away, it didn't matter to them so long as I wasn't ever found returning to the Fae forest.

Unfortunately, the forest was the only place where I was safe from the demons. After decades of hunting them for humans willing to trade with me for the service, there were more than a few that wanted me in chains. They didn't care that my magic was cursed. It would still feed them.

I hung the rabbits from a low branch while I collected fallen branches for a fire. After draining the water from them with my magic, I dug out the flint and steel I'd earned banishing a chaos demon who had been tormenting the residents of a nearby estate. Then I focused my frustration on the task of scraping metal against stone like a magicless mortal.

One. Two. Three strikes. Sparks I couldn't create with my bare hands scattered off the tip of the stone.

Four strikes. All because of that elusive fourth element I couldn't control.

Five strikes. If I had fire magic, I would also have blood magic and wouldn't have to suffer the stitches from that human healer.

Six strikes. One for each of the Hands of the Ancients who would compete in the Conclave. The Hands I'd trained with in crèche before being cast out. We were friends once. According to the winds, soon one of them would take Cahal's place as guardian. Would any of them care enough to change the rules that banished cast-outs like me?

The little bundle of tinder refused to ignite under the shower of my angry sparks. I shivered and started again. My knees were aching and my muscles cramped by the time the mound of fuel finally caught a spark.

I nudged the embers closer to the fallen branches and fed the blaze with my air magic. Only when I was certain that the fire would continue to burn did I return my attention to the rabbits. The point of my knife flashed in the firelight as I separated pelt from the muscle, organs from meat.

My future had also once been balanced on the point of a knife. Control of two Elements on one side. *Twintails*. Common among the Elemental Fae. Control of four on the other side. Four that would open the key to the fifth. Blood magic that would have made me a competitor in this upcoming Conclave.

But no. I'd slipped off the edge, into the abyss, with control of only three elements. The fourth that never came. The third that couldn't remain hidden. Cast out. Hunting demons to protect humans who feared me but were desperate enough to trade.

Finished with the dirty work, I called water to cleanse my hands and my knife. Then I stood, roasting my dinner, staring into the flames, and aching. I twisted the wrist of my free hand until the palm faced up. Closing my eyes, I concentrated on the pain and channeled it to my empty hand, imagining heat. Fire. Flames.

When I opened my eyes, there was nothing but bare pink skin to show for the effort. I swore and a branch snapped behind me. I ignored it at first, assuming my exclamation had disturbed a fellow lonely forest creature. If not that, there was always the chance that one of the pixies was messing with me.

They loved to taunt me by imitating the scrape of flint against steel. They didn't need tools to make fire. They could accomplish the same spark with just a snap of their twig-like fingers. Not that they'd ever deign to help me.

After I was cast out of the Elemental faction, none of the other Fae factions would have anything to do with me. There was only one Elemental who ever came to search me out. I'd crossed paths with her before leaving the forest, but I didn't disturb her. From what I'd glimpsed, she was struggling with her own problems.

Turning my head, I expected to see empty forest. But,

standing there at the edge of the flickering firelight, were two female Fae. I nearly dropped my dinner into the flames. Fat hissed in warning as it dripped from the carcass.

One of the pair I identified immediately. The other I recognized, but it took me a heartbeat before I remembered her name. Brianne. She was a Twintail Elemental who'd also been in crèche with me. Her recently shaved head must have been part of her Queen's Guard initiation, which explained why she stood alongside of the second most powerful Fae in our realm.

"Commander." I stood so I could properly dip my head and curtsy while trying to keep the stick with my partially roasted rabbit balanced over the fire. When I straightened, I lifted my chin and locked my knees to keep them from trembling in the presence of the High Fae Commander of the Faerie Queen's Guard. Arabella of Rionach. Beloved cousin of the recently crowned Queen of the Fae.

"You're Seren Cursehand, correct?" she asked.

I winced at the surname. I'd once been Seren Twintail, until my affliction became impossible to hide. "I'd prefer just 'Seren,' if it's all the same to you."

"May I?" She held out her hand for the stick.

I handed it to her and watched as she crouched low and took over roasting my dinner. I wanted to laugh at the absurdity. Instead, I turned to look at Brianne and raised my eyebrows in silent question. She ignored me.

"I apologize for bothering you in the middle of dinner," Arabella said, pulling my attention back to her.

"Did I do something wrong?" I asked. A few moons past, a crop of nearly mature Elemental Faelings ran me out of my campsite in the middle of the night. I crossed the border to escape them and took shelter among the ancient ruins of the temple dedicated to the Lady of the Hunt. Now here was the Lady herself, expertly roasting my rabbit.

"How should I know?" she asked. "If you have, that's not why I'm here, and it's none of my business." She turned her head until her eyes met mine. The fire flashed in their reflection. "My spies tell me that you've been hunting demons."

"Is that a problem?"

She returned her eyes to the flames. "I trust you are a loyal subject of the crown?"

"I am." I had no issue with the Queen, only with my Elemental kin.

"Say it," Brianne prompted.

Arabella shot Brianne a look to quiet her but waited for my response.

"I am a loyal subject of the Faerie Queen, Fiona of Isleen, long may she reign." My words, accompanied by no sign of liar's pains, reassured the Commander.

"May the Ancients make it so." Arabella gestured toward the flat moss-covered stump behind me. "Sit. I have something I'd like to discuss with you."

"I'm perfectly comfortable—"

She silenced me with a gust of wind that forced me back and down. I plopped my arse onto the stump and folded my hands in my lap, gripping them tightly as I waited for her to speak again.

"Are you aware that your guardian has resigned and called a Conclave to select his successor?"

I wasn't sure if I should admit what I knew or remain silent. I couldn't lie, but agreeing would mean admitting that I'd been spying on my Elemental kin. "I believe the Elemental Elders would say that he's not my guardian."

Arabella nodded. "True. They likely would. Fools. But that's Liam's problem, not mine."

I blinked at her. "I'm sorry. I'm not sure I understand—"

"Never mind." She paused to rotate the rabbit, shifting it to a different angle above the flames. "I'm told that the favorite to win is named Gwawr. Gwawr of the Ancients."

A snort escaped before I could contain it. "Apologies, Commander."

"Did I say something amusing?" Her eyes flashed as her fist clenched around the roasting stick.

"No." I shook my head. "It's just that… Gwawr? Really? That's what you've heard? That she's the favorite to win the Conclave?" I wanted to laugh. The Commander clearly didn't know what I did. She hadn't seen what I'd seen. Heard what I'd heard on the wind.

"According to your guardian, she is his star apprentice."

"That is true, but…" I hesitated. Gwawr's secrets were hers and not mine to share. She hadn't even trusted me with them. As far as I knew, she hadn't trusted anyone. I'd never have discovered what she was hiding if I hadn't happened onto her practicing with her fire magic, deep in the forest. She'd been so absorbed that she hadn't even heard me approach. I'd seen more than enough to know that she was struggling to control the same element I lacked, the one that made me a Cursehand while she was, at least according to Arabella, Cahal's favorite to win the Conclave.

"But?" Arabella prompted.

Something about the way she was looking at me made me cautious. "Why are you suddenly so interested in Gwawr?"

Arabella returned her attention to the roasting meat. Then, deciding it was done, she removed it from the fire and jabbed the end of the stick that she'd been holding into the ground. She stood, brushing her hands off on her leather trousers and glared down at me.

"The Conclave is expected to start in two days and will decide the next guardian. The guardian sits on the Queen's Council, representing the Elemental Fae. Since the Queen's safety is my highest priority, I want to be sure of every Fae with a seat at the Council's stone table. If Gwawr is Cahal's favorite, I want to know everything there is to know about her. If there is another who might defeat her, then I'd like you to spy on them for me as well."

"Spy? I'm no spy."

"Really? Are you so sure about that?" Her eyes narrowed in the firelight.

If she thought she'd get me to admit it that easily, she was mistaken. Commander of the Queen's Guard or not, my secrets were what kept me alive. "You're asking me to spy on my own kin."

"By your admission, they don't claim you as kin, do they?" She paused to let that reminder sink in. Then she added, "But we would."

"We?" My breath caught on the word.

"The Queen's Guard."

I laughed. "You're joking."

"Brianne, am I, or am I not the Commander?" She asked her guard without taking her eyes off me.

Brianne replied, "You are, sir."

"And as Commander, I say who is or is not allowed to serve as one of the Queen's Guard. Isn't that right?"

"Yes, sir," she replied. I didn't have to turn to look at her to guess that she was standing at attention.

"So, who is going to stop me from taking you on as one of my guards, little cast-out?" She placed her hands on her hips.

My neck ached from looking up at her, and I didn't much appreciate being called a 'little cast-out,' so I stood to face her.

"The Queen."

Arabella grinned. "Quite right. But I know my cousin, and I know her opinions on the practice of casting out Elementals. She may not be able to voice those opinions directly due to faction politics, but you can trust me when I say she will not mind me claiming you as one of our own."

I swallowed my shock at Arabella's assertions, but she'd lodged an unwanted sliver of hope in my heart, even though I knew that even our Queen would never be able to change the minds of the Elemental Elders. Rather than take Arabella's bait, I focused on the obvious flaw in her logic.

"The other guards might mind." My eyes cut toward Brianne.

Most of the Queen's Guard was composed of Elementals. Their distaste at serving alongside a cast-out would test even the most loyal among them and likely put Arabella's command at risk.

"Let me worry about that," Arabella said. "The guard needs someone with your skills. Spy for me. Bring me useful information on all the candidates, but especially the favorite, whoever that may be. If you serve me well, I will repay you by initiating you into the guard, one way or another."

"Are you making me a deal?" The fact that she'd come to me, that she'd asked this of me, must have meant she was desperate.

"I am."

There was more at stake here than she was telling me. "Why?"

"Let's just say that I'd rather not leave the length and success of Fiona's reign entirely up to the Ancients."

With Edric and his Hunters gone, I'd thought all threats to the Fae had been eliminated. Unless she was referring to an internal threat. "You're worried that the Elemental Faction will push Queen Fiona aside and try to take over?"

There were only three High Fae remaining after centuries of attacks by the Wild Hunt. Four, now that Sorcha of Maeve, who they all thought had been killed, returned very much alive, and with a clutch of prisoners rescued from Edric's dungeons, including Gwawr.

But only one of those High Fae had taken a mate, and his mate was a human. There were no heirs to Queen Fiona's throne. There were whispers among the Elementals that it was only a matter of time before the High Fae were extinct and an Elemental took the iron crown.

Arabella tensed at my question. "Will you accept my offer or not?"

I reached for my knife, thankful that I'd taken the time to clean it after I'd used it to prepare my meal. With just a slight press of the blade tip against the heel of my hand, blood began to drip into my open palm.

Arabella echoed my motion, using her own knife. Then she pressed her hand against mine.

"I accept your offer, Arabella of Rionach."

She wiped her hand on her trousers and paced over to where Brianne waited at the edge of the clearing. "I'll come to you, or send Brianne in my place, for a report after the first round of competition. Until and unless you succeed, no one else will know of our arrangement."

"Yes, Commander." The words had barely left my lips when the pair of them disappeared.

Once they were gone, I allowed my knees to go wobbly, and I plopped back down onto the stump. For several long minutes I stared into the flames, not once thinking about the gap in my power. My mind turned the deal I'd just made over and over, trying to anticipate the pitfalls and worrying that I'd just sold my only friend's secrets to improve my own miserable life.

2

I WASN'T planning to return to the Dragon Fae caverns after Alpha Boro took control of the clan. My position in the village gave me an excuse to stay away. But, when I received my grand-sire's message, I knew I had to go back.

Ivo, my wing-mate, fled after his sire was defeated in the Challenge, but our other wing-mate, Ved, had remained. Ivo and I hadn't been able to convince him to go. And now he was in chains, awaiting his trial.

I knew it would only be a matter of time before something like this happened. With Ivo gone, it was up to me to do something. Only, I couldn't challenge the new Alpha. I had a different, and hopefully less bloody plan, to free Ved. One that Ivo would absolutely hate if he were here.

Good thing for Ved that he wasn't.

The caverns didn't look any different since I'd last visited, but I no longer recognized the faces of the guards. With any luck, that meant that they wouldn't recognize me, either.

There were two of them positioned just outside the cave

where Alpha Boro was keeping Ved chained until his trial. That pair would be replaced by a new pair in less than an hour, which meant I didn't have much time. Still, I waited a bit longer, wanting them to be sufficiently restless and lazy when I approached.

Sensing my moment had arrived, I straightened my back and prepared to argue my case. I needed them to trust me enough to let me inside so I could deliver my message, in person. There was no one else I could trust to do it for me.

This wasn't a jailbreak. Not yet anyway.

It wasn't until I stepped out of the corridor and started walking toward the guards that I realized what a stupid risk I was taking. If the guards recognized me as Ved's wing-mate, or even if they suspected me of sympathizing with him, I would end up chained alongside him, awaiting a trial of my own.

But it was too late to turn around. They'd seen me.

A movement in the shadows to my right caught my eye, but I didn't dare turn my head to look. I suspected that I knew who lingered there, and I didn't want him interfering with my plan, anyway. I kept my eyes fixed on the opening to the cave as I walked, ignoring the guards as though I'd been sent on business by the new Alpha.

My ruse didn't work.

"Halt." The guard on my left dropped his spear so that it blocked my path.

"Just where do you think you're going?" The other asked, lowering his spear until it crossed with the other.

I stopped just shy of the lowered spears and narrowed my eyes, preparing my act. "I've been sent to check on the prisoner."

"You're no medic."

It was true that I wasn't wearing medic robes, but that didn't necessarily mean I wasn't one. Still, I couldn't lie. "I've come directly from the village at the request of Alpha Boro's medic. He should have sent word to expect me." I crossed my arms and waited with feigned confidence, ignoring the bead of sweat dripping down my neck and slipping under the collar of my crisp white button-down.

As it happened, my grandsire was the clan's medic, so what I said wasn't a lie. Grandsire had been the one to send for me when Ved's hotheaded actions landed him in chains. The catch was that his message had been a warning about Ved, not an invitation to examine him.

The guards exchanged a glance, then lifted their spears. I took that as approval and started forward.

"Five minutes," the one on the right said.

"Then we're coming in after you," the other added.

I scoffed. "Examinations can't be rushed."

"Rush this one," said the one on the right.

"Or you're going to have an audience." The one on the left laughed.

I scowled but didn't reply. Five minutes would be plenty of time to say what I needed to say. Or at least I thought it would be, until I got a look at Ved.

Stepping inside the cave, the temperature dropped by several degrees, sending a chill up my spine, but that wasn't the only thing that made me shiver. My once strong and fierce wing-mate lay curled and beaten on the ground, wearing only a loose pair of ash-smeared and singed linen trousers. The steel chains clamped around his wrists and ankles had been shackled to the weeping rock walls.

I hurried to his side, but he didn't even look up or acknowledge my approach. "Ved, it's me. Damir." I stretched out a hand and rested it on his shoulder.

He flinched away from my touch, then shifted so he could

turn his head to look at me. "Bullshit," he said. "Mir knows better than to come to this piss hole. Nice try pixie bugger."

I grinned. "I do know better, but you know there's no way I'm letting you die in here."

Ved groaned. "Then you really are dumber than a rutting troll, aren't you?" His swollen eyes opened a crack and found mine. Once he'd confirmed my identity, he closed them again and turned his face toward the stone floor.

"We don't have much time." I jostled his shoulder in an attempt to keep his focus on me.

"*I* don't have much time, you idiot. *You* would have had plenty of time if you didn't have smoke for brains and knew enough to stay away from this place." He coughed and his body shook with the effort. I could count half his ribs under his skin. They weren't feeding him, or he wasn't eating.

"I have a plan to get you out of here."

"If you think you can do that, then you really are one pixie fart short of a rainbow."

"Would you please shut up and let me talk?" I tried to keep my voice low so that the guards wouldn't come in. His stubborn, ungrateful ass was going to get us both killed.

Ved started coughing again. Then I realized he wasn't coughing at all. He was laughing. "You're too easy to rile. You've always been too easy. Too soft."

"Fine." I ground the word out through clenched teeth. "Just let me say what I came to say before Boro's goons realize I'm not here to patch you up."

"You shouldn't have come."

"I'm not letting you die in here." Before he could respond and argue, I continued. "That's why I'm going to England, to the Fae Forest, to find my mother's kin and get them to help."

"What in the name of dragon kits would make you think

they would lift a finger to help *me*?"

"Velibor and Milomir were your sire's wing-mates."

"And?" Dirt flaked from the creases that formed in his brow when he raised his eyebrows at me.

I glared at him. "They were Niamh and Meara's mates."

"If I were Niamh or Meara's offspring, perhaps they might spare a tear or two, but I'm just the ruddy wing-mate of you and that no good—"

I cut him off before his ranting gathered steam. "Enough. Ivo did what he had to do. You know Boro would have killed him if he stayed, which is exactly what he's going to do to you if I don't get you out. So, don't waste your breath. I'm going. I'll be back, with help, before your trial. My grandsire is going to send word if anything changes. Don't die before I return." I squeezed his shoulder.

The corner of his mouth twisted up in a half grin. "Can't promise anything like that."

I dug my fingers into his bruised flesh. "Yes, you can."

He winced and tried to pull away, but I held him fast. He exhaled, panting to keep from making a noise that might draw the attention of the guards. "All right."

I relaxed my fingers but didn't remove my hand from his arm. "Say it."

"Damir of Niamh is a right pixie bugger."

I squeezed my fingers, and he grit his teeth.

"I promise," he said. "I promise I won't die before you return. All right? Happy now?"

"Very," I said.

"Now get the bloody hell out of here before you're hanging alongside me." His eyes locked with mine.

"Ancients be with you," I whispered.

He scoffed. "They best be with you if you hope to succeed.

Not much for them to do around here when I've already promised you not to die."

"You stink. I'm going to tell those guards you need a bath." I wrinkled my nose as I stood and brushed my hands off on my jeans.

"Love you, too, smoke for brains." Ved started to chuckle, but it turned into another coughing fit.

I hesitated, wondering if I should stay to help him, but he waved me away. I turned and hurried out of his prison cave, slipping back into the haughty air I'd adopted when I entered. I took two steps past the guards, then paused and looked back over my shoulder.

"I'm going to find the clan medic to give him my report. If you two know what's good for you, then you'll consider bathing that prisoner before we return. He'll never last a week in that state."

One of the guards laughed. "A week?"

I turned toward the guard who'd spoken. "Alpha Boro wants him alive for his trial."

"The trial is in three days." The second guard said, narrowing his eyes at me.

I tried to appear as though his statement didn't surprise me and shrugged. "I suppose that's up to the Alpha, though I believe a week has always been customary in these cases." I had less time than I thought to execute my plan. At least I found out before I returned to find the trial done and Ved dead because he'd refused to swear fealty to the new Alpha. I had no time to waste.

Rather than wait for a response, or for one of them to see through my ruse, I hurried away down the cavern toward the nearest exit where I hoped I'd find Grandsire waiting to intercept me with the book I'd asked him to retrieve for me.

As I rounded the final bend, the night black sky, dotted with pinpricks of light, filled the yawning opening at the end of the tunnel. I searched the shadows for a familiar figure.

"Here." Grandsire stepped into the sliver of moonlight and stood silhouetted against the mouth of the cave. A lump on his right shoulder shifted, and a smaller, triangular head appeared alongside his.

Sillag flicked her forked tongue to taste the air, then called out to me with a coo as she shifted her wings, restlessly. She too was ready to be gone from here. I clicked at her to stay at her perch until I reached them. I didn't want her any further inside this place, because if she were captured, I would be unable to protect her.

In the time of the Ancients, faerie dragons frequently associated with the members of our clan. But, as dragons disappeared and humans took over the earth, the sole surviving strain of dragons, the smallest and most easily hidden of their kin, retreated to the hidden Fire Isle. Only those of our clan brave enough to make the journey had a chance to win over one of these magnificent creatures as a familiar, and only after we were deemed worthy enough.

My grandsire had journeyed to the Fire Isle as a Faeling and earned himself the loyalty and companionship of a dazzling blue and gold faerie dragon whose lifespan couldn't quite match that of Grandsire's. Now that Dormog was gone, Sillag would settle on Grand-sire's shoulder to provide him some comfort whenever she sensed his sadness. I was glad she respected him enough to stay with him for a short time, especially because I knew Grandsire would look after her like she was his own.

"Took you long enough." Grandsire let Sillag step onto his hand, then extended that hand toward my shoulder so she could reach me without flying. "I worried that they'd caught you."

Sillag bumped her nose against my ear in greeting.

"You needn't worry. Though, you didn't tell me that he only has three days. Three days! What is Boro thinking?" I scratched Sillag under her chin until her rumbling coos vibrated through my fingertips.

"You know what he's thinking." Grandsire rubbed a hand across his bald head. "He's thinking that your wing-mate is trouble. Ved is the only one who could possibly succeed in challenging for Alpha…unless you've changed your mind?"

Sillag hissed.

I clucked a reprimand before responding. "I haven't."

Grandsire shrugged. "With Ivo gone, the offspring of his sire's Sworn lieutenants are the only ones with enough pull to unite the clan behind them. You have your sire's strength. If I were still your age…"

"Yes. I know what you would do. Let's just focus on saving Ved right now, shall we? He seems to be the one of us most likely to challenge for dominance, but he'll never survive a fight if Boro's only giving him three days to recover from whatever put him in his current sorry state. I need to leave. Now."

Grandsire shifted the strap of a large sack off his shoulder and held it out to me. "Supplies," he said. "And that book you wanted."

I thrust my hand inside the bag to search for the small, leather-bound volume written in my mother's script. My fingers flicked across the soft hide, then clutched it and pulled it from the sack. Angling the book so the moonlight hit the pages, I searched for the passage that told of her home. She'd described the location so that, if she didn't return, I might travel there someday to find her. It had been centuries since she'd left with Aunt Meara to help their kin. Ivo and I were only Faelings, just old enough to join the other young Dragon Fae in the clan crèche.

I'd wanted to go after them, but Ivo had always talked me out of it. But that was before his sire's death. Before Boro took control of the clan. Some part of me knew that, if he were here, he wouldn't approve of what I was about to do. But he'd left, and I was responsible for keeping Ved alive. I had to try.

I memorized my mother's words, then slid the volume back inside the cloth bag.

"Thank you," I said.

"Be safe." Grandsire reached up to wrap a gnarled hand around the base of my skull so he could tilt it down and kiss my forehead. "May the Ancients travel with you and keep you well."

I gripped his forearm with both my hands. "May the Ancients hold you and Ved safe while I'm gone."

"I'll take care of Ved. Don't you worry about him."

"I worry about both of you."

"Go on, now, before one of the guards walks out this way and finds us talking. Best they don't remember who you really are, or you won't be leaving without swearing loyalty to Boro."

"Or killing him."

"Don't tease me." He slapped my upper arm and gave me a shove toward the mouth of the cave. "Watch out for Mir, my little love," he called after us.

Sillag cooed her response, then we disappeared.

3

S PYING for Arabella was going to require that I get a lot closer to my kin than I had ever dared to do. I had a lot of practice sneaking around and sitting still in damp places, but the last time I'd walked among the Elementals, I'd been a Faeling. Decades had passed since then. I wondered if any of my kin would still recognize me.

My worried thoughts had woken me with the sun. Rather than try to go back to sleep, I scattered any sign of my camp with a little earth and air magic and took advantage of the daylight to cleanse the crusty remains of incubus guts from my cloak. Then I set out to observe the flood of Elementals and other curious Fae heading toward the Faerie Falls.

As much as I feared being caught, I had no choice but to follow through on my deal with the commander. If I was lucky, it wouldn't take long to locate a few of Cahal's apprentices. Then I could keep an eye on them from a distance. Even finding one would lead me to the others, eventually.

With my hood pulled up to hide my face, I attempted to

blend in with the crowds. Working my way among them, I listened for any interesting gossip. It wasn't long before I stumbled into a trio wearing the long blue robes of Elemental Elders.

My heart raced as I slipped into step behind them. So far, I'd encountered no wards keeping me from observing the Conclave, but that was probably only because the Elders thought me dead. If any of them discovered me here, among them, they'd surely ban me and ward the forest to prevent me from returning. One misstep, and I'd be forced to live among the humans. I couldn't let that happen. As much as I enjoyed chopping heads off demons, the life I wanted was here in the forest, accepted by my kin.

I took a few deep breaths to calm my pulse and directed the wind to bring their words to me.

"There are so few of them now. I remember Cahal's Conclave. There were over a hundred Hands competing. The moon waxed and waned at least twice before Cahal emerged, victorious." The oldest of the Elders tapped his staff against the earth with each step and tiny golden flowers sprung up in his wake.

"And now there are only six." The female who spoke looked similar to a Faeling I'd known in crèche. The Faeling who'd discovered my secret. But Anwen wasn't old enough to be included in the Council of Elementals. That meant this Elder must be Anwen's dam or grand dam.

"Perhaps there would have been more if it hadn't been for the Hunt." At least that was a theory that didn't put the blame on Cursehands like me. I tried to catch a glimpse of the speaker's face, but the third Elder had their hood pulled up, like me. "Do you know when the Hands will be tested?"

"Today. Cahal is waiting for them under the Falls. He intends to begin the Conclave tomorrow." Of course, the one who looked like Anwen would know, because Anwen would be with the other apprentices.

Once I had that bit of information, I swerved away. As much as I wanted to continue eavesdropping on their conversation, it wasn't worth the risk of being discovered. Arabella wanted information about the competitors, not these stodgy Elders. When I reached the edge of the crowd, I paused to make sure no one was watching me, then slipped in among the trees and took a shortcut that would lead me directly to the mouth of the cave beneath the Falls.

Usually, the entrance to Cahal's lair was hidden, but after a brief exploration around the base of the Falls, I found the entrance he'd made for the Hands. To make it easier for them, he'd opened a wide arch in the side of the hill, near the edge of the pool at the base of the falls, just around the corner from where the water tumbled over the face of the cliff.

It was still early, and I hoped that I was the first to arrive. The morning dew glistened on the mossy rocks clustered around the stone archway, and no footsteps marked the dirt leading up to the entry. I searched for a tree with a good view of the cave opening and climbed up into the branches. Once I'd found a solid perch where I could watch everyone coming and going, I used my earth magic to weave a nest of vines that would keep me comfortable while hiding my body from anyone who might happen to look up.

Concealed, I had only to sit and wait. And wait. And wait.

If Gwawr was going to compete, she'd have to prove she could control all four elements. It had been less than one cycle of the moon since I'd caught her practicing in the forest and watched as the flames sputtered and surged. She had been unable to control them, and eventually broke down, sobbing and pleading with the Ancients for help. I snuck away, not wanting her to know I'd seen her failures and knew her secret.

Part of me almost hoped that she wouldn't appear for the testing. I didn't want her to fail and be cast out, and if she somehow managed to succeed, I didn't want to spy on her for Arabella. Unfortunately, as I searched my memory in an attempt to list the other five potential competitors, I realized that she was the only one I wanted, the only one I could trust, as our next guardian.

The first of the candidates didn't arrive until the sun had nearly peaked in the sky. From my perch, the first thing I glimpsed was the top of a head covered in thick red hair. Gwawr had red hair. I shifted to get a better look, thinking it might be her. My palms began to sweat where they clutched the vines of my perch as I squinted through the mesh to get a better look.

It wasn't Gwawr. The approaching Fae was a male. He'd grown since our time together in crèche, but I still recognized the self-satisfied smirk on his face. Barrfhionn the bully.

He sauntered past my tree without looking up, then paused at the edge of the water where it lapped against the rocks. After admiring his reflection and running a hand through his hair, he ducked to clear the top of the archway and disappeared inside Cahal's cave.

It appeared as though Barr hadn't changed a bit in the time I'd been gone. He would be a terrible guardian, and not just because I doubted that he would ever do anything as unpopular as pushing the Elders to change their mistaken ideas about Cursehands. Still, his magic had always been strong. The others would have to be stronger if they hoped to beat him.

Shortly after Barr disappeared inside the cave, three more candidates arrived nearly the same time. Even though I hadn't seen them since they were Faelings, I recognized them as the other Hands from our crèche group. Ioryn, Eira, and Anwen.

My hand gripped a nearby branch. It would be so easy to

send a surge of magic through the thick limb, causing it to break and fall right on Anwen's pretty little head. But that would cause the others to look up, and I didn't want to give myself away. I was a spy. Spies watched and listened. They didn't interfere, even when the person they were spying on was their least favorite Elemental to walk the earth.

"Anwen. Eira. Blessings of the Ancients to you both." Ioryn bowed to the others in greeting. He always had the best manners. "I will be happy to wait, if you two would like to go in ahead of me."

Eira sat on one of the rocks and pulled off her boots so she could slide her bare feet into the water. "I wouldn't mind a swim, before I go in. Anwen, why don't you go first? You are older than either of us, after all."

I pinched my mouth shut to keep from laughing.

Anwen waved a hand. "We're close enough in age, what do a few cycles of the moon matter?"

"I remember you being rather concerned about those extra cycles when we were back in crèche." Ioryn flicked his wrist and a round pebble flew into his hand. He curled a finger around the edge of the rock and sent it skipping out over the still water.

"Well, I don't." Anwen lifted her chin as she settled down onto the earth at the base of my tree. "And I'd prefer to rest a bit. One of you may go ahead."

Eira sighed and stood. She picked up her boots and stepped across the rocks toward the archway. "Fine. I'll go. I can swim later."

Beneath me, Anwen lifted a stick off the ground and used her earth magic to transform it into a comb. "I didn't think she'd actually go first."

Ioryn shook his head. "Have you seen any of the others?"

Anwen pulled her comb through her long brown hair. "No.

Have you?"

"You two are the first."

A pebble rolled out of the cave and came to rest against Ioryn's boot.

He glanced down, then over to Anwen. "I suppose that means I'm next."

"May the Ancients guide your hand." Anwen's blessing followed Ioryn into the cave. Once he was gone, she huffed out a breath and leaned against the tree. "That went well."

She crossed her arms and waited. I glared down at her until a large, bright beetle scurried out of the cave. It hurried toward her, then stopped and vanished.

Anwen stood and brushed herself off. She held her head high as she passed beneath the archway and disappeared into the darkness.

Four had entered, and none had returned. Only two apprentices remained unaccounted for. Taliesin may have arrived at dawn and beaten me to the cave, but knowing Gwawr's secret, I doubted that she would have been early. I decided to wait until dusk to see if either of them showed up. If Cahal had set a deadline for the testing, it would have been sunset.

I ate one of the apples that the grateful humans had traded me in exchange for the incubus head and waited as the sun sank closer to the horizon. There was still no sign of Gwawr. I was almost about to give up and find a place to camp for the night when she finally strode into view, accompanied by a male Fae I didn't know. He had antlers, which wasn't unusual among Elementals with particularly strong earth magic, but it was unique enough that I should have recognized him.

They stopped and shared a whispered conversation that I couldn't quite decipher, even after I tried to gain control of the wind and direct their words to my ears. Gwawr entered the cave and the strange male sat down at the base of my tree where Anwen had been resting, earlier in the day. He immediately dropped his chin to his chest and appeared to fall asleep.

If Gwawr didn't manage to control her fire magic for the test, I wondered if Cahal would take her before the Elders for trial as a Cursehand. I didn't want to have to spy on her, especially now that she appeared to be traveling with some strange, or possibly foreign Fae. But I didn't want her to fail and be cast out, either.

I waited as the sun went down. Then I waited some more. None of the candidates emerged from the cave, and the strange Fae remained at the base of my tree. I started to think that perhaps the Hands were leaving via some other entrance. Then, a figure stepped out of the cave, cloaked in the darkness of the night. I wasn't sure which of the Hands it might be until the male Fae below me sat up. Then I knew it was Gwawr. It had to be.

She had returned, but I didn't know what that meant. I watched as she ignored the male with the antlers and walked toward the nearby field that had been set up as an arena. Gwawr picked her way through the clusters of Fae who were dancing in the glow of floating balls of light and drinking merrily. Below me, the mysterious male stood and followed her until I could barely make out either of them amongst the revelers.

Near the edge of the tents that had been erected at the far edge of the field, I caught sight of her again. Gwawr stopped and turned. The glow of faerie lights illuminated her face as she appeared to confront the male who had followed her. After a brief exchange, he backed away. She turned and left him, then continued on towards the tents.

Once I was sure no one else was around, I scrambled down from the tree and trudged through the dark forest, over and around to the far side of the falls, until I found a place where I could approach the tents without being seen. Waiting, hidden among the trees until I was sure no one would come close, I watched figures coming and going from the tents that had been set up. It wasn't until I spotted Taliesin that I knew I was in the right place.

He entered one of the smaller tents nearest to me. I counted. There were six identical to the one he occupied. That meant these were probably the ones reserved for the competitors. If Gwawr had passed her test, she would be in one of them. And if I wanted to catch her alone to speak with her, I needed to figure out which was hers.

With so many Fae coming and going through that area, getting into Gwawr's tent without being seen seemed to be too difficult. Rather than take that risk, I pulled up my hood and skirted the edge of the forest, searching the crowd for anyone with antlers. I wanted to try to find Gwawr's friend. If he wasn't an Elemental and he wasn't from the Fae forest, he might not recognize me as a cast out. I could ask him some questions and get more information about why he'd been traveling with Gwawr.

I searched and searched but couldn't find him anywhere. While I was watching, I did see the other Hands return to their tents. I kept track of who went into each of the structures, until I was sure about which one was Gwawr's.

When I reached Gwawr's tent, I whispered her name, hoping to get her attention. She didn't respond. I hesitated, not sure what to do. The tent could be empty. Gwawr could be with the Elders, facing trial. Or she might be inside and already asleep.

I spoke again, louder this time. "Are you in there?"

A rustle from inside the tent confirmed that it was occupied. I decided Gwawr must have gone to sleep. Lifting the edge of the flap, I peeked inside to confirm my suspicion. If she was there, she had probably passed her test and was competing.

A shaft of moonlight illuminated my shadow as it slid across the two bodies entwined on the cot. I caught a glimpse of red hair on one head and antlers on the other. Then dropped the canvas flap and ran. My heart raced as my feet pounded away from the tents, delivering me to the safety of the trees. I didn't stop until I was sure that I wasn't being followed. Then I leaned my back against a tree and panted until I caught my breath.

Gwawr was keeping secrets, and I was going to have to tell Arabella.

4

THE cottage appeared just as my mother had described it in her journal, down to the vine-like carvings on the front door. Unfortunately, there were no lights on inside and no sign that anyone was at home, at least from where I stood in the garden.

I had expected to trigger some sort of ward that might signal my arrival and braced myself for an attack. I waited with my muscles tensed in anticipation. When no one emerged to challenge me, I took a few tentative steps toward the cottage.

If Niamh or Maeve lived, I was certain they would have returned to the Dragon Fae, at least to tell me and Ivo what happened. I expected to find that they had died protecting their sister, the queen. But part of me still hoped I'd find my mother or aunt here, living happily among their kin.

Sillag nipped at my ear, urging me to continue forward. There was just enough light from the moon that I could follow the stone path through the garden toward the house. When I reached the front door, I inhaled deeply and exhaled, hoping it would help me relax the band of tension that had wound around my chest.

Rather than knock and wake anyone who may be sleeping, I pressed my face close to the window glass and peeked inside. The front room was empty, so I continued around the outside, peering into each window, searching for any occupants and wondering when someone would appear to chase me off.

There were teacups on the table in the kitchen and a pair of blue and white trainers lying on the ground inside the cottage door. A bag like I'd seen humans use to carry clothing when they traveled had been left on top of the dresser in the bedroom. The blankets on the bed were rumpled as though someone had been sleeping there recently. If it weren't for the Fae magic and wards I could sense surrounding the cottage, I would have thought this was a human's home.

Confused, I dispatched Sillag to the skies, instructing her to circle and keep watch as I retreated to the edge of the woods surrounding the clearing, just outside the protection of the wards. I found a spot near the base of a large oak and sat down on the cool, slightly damp earth to rest and think.

It was only a few hours until sunrise. I could wait that long to see if anyone returned and plan my next step in case no one did. I closed my eyes and linked my mind with my faerie dragon, high above. Using her sharp vision, we searched the nearby forest for any signs of my mother's kin.

The only creatures roaming in the nearby forest were night grazers and hunters. Sillag begged to swoop down on a particularly fat rabbit but agreed to wait until after we'd located the closest Fae. It only took a few more loops of the sky to find them.

Just a bit further away, near a large pool of water at the base of a waterfall, there seemed to be a large gathering of Fae. A few moved about at the edge of the water. The sound of drums and flutes drifted up on the winds to reach Sillag's keen ears. Nearby, a large platform had been set between two fenced in rings, and a dozen or more tents were clustered off to one side. It appeared to be a festival of some sort. Perhaps that was why no one was home at the cottage.

I decided to set out in that direction at first light if no one returned before then. With that settled, I relaxed my link with Sillag and released her to hunt. Knowing that she would keep watch while I rested, I allowed the sound of the wind in the trees to lull me to sleep.

As the first rays of sun crested the horizon, Sillag settled on my shoulder and nudged my mind awake.

"Anything?" I asked, as I stood to stretch.

She fluttered up to rest on a low branch near my head and cooed her response. No one had returned. The cottage was still empty.

"All right, then. Lead the way to the gathering, and let's see what we find there."

Sillag raised her head and squawked before taking flight. Her blue scales stood out among the browns and greens of the forest, making it easy to follow her progress through the trees.

I estimated that we'd traveled about half the distance to our destination when I came across a fresh trail. Reaching out to Sillag with my mind, I told her to scout ahead while I followed the trail that appeared to lead in the same direction we were heading.

The path emerged in another small clearing, one that looked as though someone had recently been there. Near the center were the remains of a campfire. When I bent to examine the ashes, Sillag cooed a warning. I caught a glimpse of sunlight reflecting off steel and lunged, ducking just in time to miss the blade aimed for my throat.

I spun to face my attacker and found myself facing a female Fae. Her long hair fell loose past her shoulders, and her tunic was rumpled as though she'd slept in it. Her long fingers still gripped the hilt of the knife she'd attacked me with, but she held the weapon down at her side with the tip pointed at the ground.

Aside from my mother and aunt, who left when Ivo and I turned ten, I'd never seen a Fae female before. There were no female-born Dragon Fae. The males of our clan primarily reproduced with females from nearby villages. Female offspring were always human and left to be raised by their mothers. Any male offspring were retrieved after birth and raised by the clan. That had been my job and the reason I was able to live in the village and not in the mountains with the rest of the clan.

This Fae female radiated equal parts beauty and power. Something about her eyes captivated me enough that I couldn't look away. Perhaps it was that they flashed silver, like the point of her knife. A warning, but one that cut me in a way I didn't have time to analyze before she spoke.

"Who are you?" she asked, drawing me out of my thoughts.

"My name is Damir, of the Dragon Fae. Who are you?" Given our proximity to the cottage, I wondered if this Fae female might be one of my cousins. Even though I'd come to locate my kin, I suddenly hoped we were not related.

"Dragon Fae? You're pretty far from home if that's true." She sheathed her knife and took a step back, closer to the trees. The way she kept her weight balanced on her toes made it seem like she might run away at any moment. "What are you doing here? Come to see the Conclave?"

"The what?" I sent a thought to Sillag, warning her to keep to the trees and remain hidden.

"The Conclave." She must have read the confusion on my face because she continued to explain. "It's an Elemental Fae ritual to select a Guardian. That's what we call the leader of the Elemental Faction."

I shook my head. "Never heard of it."

"Right. Not from around here." She paced the edge of the clearing, keeping well away from me. "If you're not here for the Conclave, why are you here?"

"I came to find my mother's kin." I watched her, admiring the way her muscles flexed under her leggings as she prowled gracefully just out of reach.

"Your mother?" she asked. "Who is your mother, then?"

"Niamh of Maeve."

She froze at the name. Stepping back, she pivoted like she was about to take off running into the forest. "You didn't see me. I was never here."

"Wait." I called Sillag to me, hoping the sight of a faerie dragon might pique her interest enough that she might stay. "Please. Don't go."

Sillag glided down from a nearby tree and landed on my shoulder.

"Is that…" The spooked female hesitated, then took one step closer. "Is that a faerie dragon?"

Sillag yawned and flicked her tongue, tasting the air.

"Yes." It wasn't kind of me to use my familiar as a lure, but I desperately needed information and was running out of time to save Ved.

"I've never seen one before." She crept another step closer.

"Why did you start to run when I told you my mother's name?" I dared the question, hoping it wouldn't scare her away again.

She tore her eyes away from Sillag and looked at me. "I'm

sorry, Your Highness." She bowed her head, keeping it down as she spoke. "I mean no disrespect. You're not from here, so you don't know who I am. What I am."

I blinked at her. Attacks and challenges I understood. This unearned sign of respect from a Fae I'd never met confused me. "You needn't bow to me."

She lifted her silver eyes but kept her head low. "You may claim to be Dragon Fae, but here, in this forest, you are Damir of Niamh. High Fae. Cousin to the Queen."

Cousin. So, my aunt no longer wore the crown. I wondered if a cousin would be more or less willing to help me. Still, I didn't understand how being the cousin of their queen and a male made me worthy of respect here. My mother had said the Forest Fae were ruled by a matriarchy.

"Who are you?" I asked.

"Seren." She paused. "Cursehand. Cast out. Factionless."

I squinted at her. "How can you be Factionless? And cast out of what? You are Fae, aren't you?"

She raised her head at that. The hair that framed her face appeared white, but glinted silver in the sunlight, and I realized it was almost the same hue as Sillag's breast feathers. "You really don't know?"

"Did you challenge your queen for leadership and fail?" Failing a challenge of our clan's Alpha got you killed, which was what would happen to Ved if I didn't rescue him. Perhaps here challengers were only cast out.

Seren grinned, revealing a sweet smile that softened her features. "If only that were an option." The sweetness disappeared behind a fierce scowl. "I'm not allowed to challenge anyone for anything because I can't control all four elements. Only three."

"What difference does that make? You appear to be strong.

You pulled a knife on me and might have killed me if I hadn't been expecting an attack. Why does it matter how many elements you can control?"

"It's a sign that I've been cursed by the Ancients, and if the Elementals fail to cast out the cursed, there will be no more Hands." She shrugged. "Ask the Council of Elemental Elders. Ask your mother's kin. She was half Elemental."

"Was?" The word caught in my throat.

"May her Force strengthen us all." She bowed her head.

"She's gone." My chest tightened as the truth of what I'd come to suspect hit home.

She glanced up. "You didn't know? I'm sorry."

When her eyes met mine again, they glistened with emotion.

"Meara, too?" I asked.

She nodded. "There's been a war with the Underworld."

"Yes." I knew that much. "They returned to help their sisters fight."

"Right. Those sisters are all gone now. All except the youngest. Sorcha. And everyone thought she was gone, too. But she was being held captive. Your cousin, Liam, freed her." Seren's lips pressed together as though she wanted to stop herself from saying more.

"Another cousin." It made sense. My mother had six sisters and female Fae could have more than one Faeling, unlike the males. "Will you take me to see them?"

"I'd love to, but—" She motioned to herself, waving her hands alongside her body. "Cast out. Remember? I'm not welcome near any of the Fae."

I saw nothing wrong with her body and would certainly not cast it out if it landed in bed with me. I had no love for the brutal laws of the Dragon Fae, and I'd always thought my mother's kin might be better. Now I began to realize how little I knew of them, especially if their superstitions allowed them to isolate an obviously powerful Fae like Seren.

"Can you just show me where to find her?" I asked. "It's urgent."

Her eyes flicked between me and Sillag. "I shouldn't."

Perhaps she would change her mind if I could convince Sillag to be friendly. "Would you like to greet her?"

Sillag flicked her tongue once, then flapped a wing, turning her head away from Seren. She could sense that I was using her, and she wanted no part in it. I sent her a thought, begging her to behave. In response, she nipped at my ear and burrowed her head between the nape of my neck and her body.

Now don't be jealous. I thought at her.

Sillag cooed once in annoyance.

Seren sucked in a breath at the sound. "Would she let me?" she asked.

At that, Sillag raised her head and made a series of clicking sounds praising Seren's manners.

"That was a 'yes,'" I summarized.

Seren took a few more careful steps toward me, but her eyes never left Sillag. She stretched out her hand, reaching palm down toward Sillag's head. Before I could warn or correct her, Sillag reared up and struck out with her claws.

I reached up to settle my familiar as Seren yanked her hand back, cradling it to her arm.

"What in the blazing demon fire was that?" Seren glared at me.

Sillag clicked and stretched her wings out wide, lifting up off my shoulder into the air before gliding down to rest on my forearm.

"I'm sorry. That was my fault. I thought you knew." Privately, I sent a scolding thought to Sillag for lashing out when she knew Seren meant no harm.

"You said it was okay." Seren flexed her injured hand.

"Yes. I did." I laid my palm on Sillag's head and stroked her down her neck, stopping to scratch at top of her wings. "Faerie dragons are sensitive to nails and claws. Always approach them palm up. Like this." I stopped scratching and moved my hand to the front of Sillag's snout to demonstrate.

"They're sensitive to nails." She repeated the fact like a curious Faeling.

"Yes." My eyes raked over Seren's body. Now that my familiar had settled, I wanted to be sure Seren was also okay.

"*Nails*?" This time, her annoyance and disbelief were clear in her tone.

A drop of blood dripped from Seren's hand where Sillag's claws had broken her skin. I stepped closer to her and reached for it, but she shuffled backward.

"I'm sorry. I suppose I should have warned you. It's just that you recognized her, so I thought perhaps you'd encountered a faerie dragon before."

"I've only seen a picture of one in a book." Her voice took on a dreamy tone, but something about her grimace warned me that the memory wasn't entirely a fond one.

"You're bleeding." I motioned again to her hand. "Let me help you."

She glanced down, then wiped the blood away. "It's fine. I'm fine."

"Are you sure?" I asked, taking a small step toward her.

Seren's eyes shifted to Sillag. "Why does she look brighter now? Like she's shimmering?"

"Your book wasn't terribly informative, was it?"

"It was a primer from crèche. More pictures than words.

Why?" She blinked at Sillag, then tilted her head to one side and blinked again.

"Faerie dragons have a toxin in their claws."

"And this toxin is what's making her look all sparkly?"

Sillag clicked and cooed. I translated, putting a slightly kinder spin on it. "It's meant to make her appear fiercer than she might otherwise be considered."

"The shimmering is supposed to scare away a predator?" Again, Seren sounded like she didn't believe my explanation.

Sillag sat up and preened her silver chest feathers.

Show off, I thought at her. *You've gone and hurt her. You could at least be kind and refrain from blinding her as well.*

Aloud, I said, "I suppose there's a reason why they're nearly extinct."

"This is insane." Seren started to reach for Sillag, this time with her palm up. Then she flinched and pulled her hand back. At first, I thought maybe I'd somehow missed Sillag attempt another swipe at Seren, but then I noticed that Seren was no longer focused on my familiar. Something else had caught her attention, because she had cocked her head to one side as though she were listening.

"What is it?" I asked.

"Shh." She waved a hand at me.

I shifted so my body was between hers and Sillag's to prevent any misinterpretation of her gesture by my familiar.

"Someone's coming." She looked around the clearing, then pointed up at the treetops. "Can you get up there?" she asked.

I nodded.

"Good. Try to keep hidden and don't come out until I say it's okay."

"Is there some sort of threat that I should be concerned about?"

"I'll explain later. Just go."

I gave Sillag the signal to fly up and hide in the trees. Then, I selected a spot nearby and transported myself up to crouch among the branches.

Seren nodded at me from the forest floor, then disappeared, reappearing on a limb next to me wearing a cloak. She pulled the hood up to cover her head, as though that might help her blend in with the branches. She'd barely managed to position herself when a red-haired female emerged from the forest and walked out into the clearing. A second figure followed her.

When I glanced over at Seren to gauge her reaction, she was gone.

5

I'D heard Gwawr's call, but I hadn't been sure it was her, and I didn't want her to see me with the Faerie Queen's long-lost cousin. I had just returned from the first set of matches, hoping to get a bit of rest after a mostly sleepless night, when the missing High Fae princeling stumbled into my hideout. I'd panicked and attacked even though I should have run. He didn't appear to care if he was seen with me, but that wouldn't matter if we were caught together, especially when I was supposed to be banished and far, far away from this particular gathering of my kin.

Materializing near the base of a tree on the opposite side of the clearing, I sent a prayer to the Ancients that Damir would stay hidden in the trees. I didn't want him to mess up my opportunity to speak with Gwawr, especially when she'd brought along her curious friend with the antlers.

As I strode out to meet her, the strange antlered Fae caught sight of me first and rushed at me in some misguided attempt to protect Gwawr. He clipped me with his outstretched arm, then grabbed ahold of me and wouldn't let go.

I squirmed and my hood fell back. My eyes locked with his, and I saw past his fake antlers and realized what he really was.

"You ruined my surprise," I said, trying to maintain my composure and not think about the fact that the male I'd caught sharing a bed with my only friend was a half-demon. And not just any half-demon. This creature was a cambion.

"I thought you were dangerous," he said, releasing me.

I blinked, but the horns were still there, hiding underneath the antlers. I panicked, wondering if he'd recognize me, given the fact that I'd been killing his kind just to keep food in my belly and clothes on my back for decades. The incubus guts I'd scrubbed from my cloak could have belonged to his sire, depending on which half was the demon half of his bloodline.

Gwawr laughed. "Oh, she's dangerous all right."

She spread her arms, and I moved forward to hug her, even though I wanted to scream at her, instead. *What was she thinking, bringing a half-demon here, to the Conclave?* Even if this one didn't appear to be here to take revenge on me, hadn't the demons been helping the Hunt? Weren't they our enemies?

Instead of confronting her, I said, "I'm so glad I found you. Who's this?" I gestured to her companion, knowing Gwawr couldn't lie and hoping she had a really good explanation.

"A stray, like you," she said.

So, I was a stray now? I hadn't wandered off. I'd been banished. She knew that. I didn't like her calling me that, so I gently turned her comment back on her. "You seem to attract them, don't you?"

She ignored my jab and gestured to the cambion. "This is…Nye. He needed some help finding the Conclave, so I traveled with him."

I stared at Nye and wondered if maybe the faerie dragon's toxin was making me hallucinate instead of see the truth. "Right."

"Nye," Gwawr said, "This is my friend Seren."

He had horns. I was staring at his horns, even though someone had managed to cleverly cover them up with something that looked like antlers. Another thought occurred to me. Perhaps she didn't know.

I turned my attention back to Gwawr. "Why did you bring a demon with you to the Conclave?"

Gwawr's eyes darted between me and her companion. "How did you—"

I cut her off. "I'm cursed, remember, not stupid."

I might not have known, if not for that scratch from the faerie dragon. Still, some instinct told me that it might be better to let her think she'd done sloppy work concealing him than to reveal the Dragon Fae hiding above us. I'd thought I could trust her, but now I wasn't so sure, and I didn't want to give her anything that she might be able to use against me. As it was, she wouldn't be able to prove I was here without giving away that she'd come to speak with me.

"Fine." Gwawr pulled at the end of her braid, a habit she'd had since we were Faelings and something she did whenever she was nervous or worried. "He made a bargain with me, and I needed his help. So, I accepted."

I didn't like this at all. "First, you shouldn't even be here, with me. If they catch you, it will ruin you. Second, if anyone finds out that you brought a demon here…" I shook my head.

"I know. I know. I was desperate. Let's not get into it now. Tell me, who won the match between Anwen and Eira?" she asked.

I could guess why Gwawr might have been desperate, but

why would she have gone to a demon for help? And what did she promise him in exchange for his assistance? I could ask her, but what if the demon had her under his thrall?

"Eira," I said, ignoring my questions for the moment.

It was a bit presumptuous of Gwawr to think I'd been watching the matches, but of course I had been. This assignment had gone from bad to worse, and it wasn't even close to being over. Even if I somehow managed to avoid telling Arabella about the cambion Gwawr brought to the Conclave, Arabella's long lost Dragon Fae cousin was up there in the tree, watching and could tell Arabella whatever I didn't.

I decided to worry about that later and expanded on my response. "Anwen took an unlucky hit. She better have improved her healing skills or she might as well concede her next match."

"Good for Eira, but damn, I would have preferred to go against Wenny." Gwawr began to pace.

The fact that she'd used our old nickname for Anwen softened my annoyance with her a bit. "Aw. Wenny. Bloody brat."

Gwawr shrugged. "She's not that bad."

Any warm feelings I had fled at that response. "Easy for you to say. Did you forget that she's the one who got me cast out?"

"Peace, Ser." Gwawr held up her hands. "I've not forgotten. But it was a long time ago, and you'd have been exiled regardless. You wouldn't have been able to hide your nature for much longer."

"'My nature.' Stars, Gwawr, you already sound like one of them." I'd worried how her time in Edric's dungeons might have damaged her, but she appeared to be fine. Perhaps I should have worried more how competing for the title of Guardian might go to her head.

The cambion must have sensed the tension brewing between us and interrupted. "Lovely as it is to meet you…" He nodded to me before turning his attention to Gwawr. "What are we doing here?"

Gwawr looked at me, her eyes pleading. "I need your help."

That was the second time I'd been asked for help in the last hour, and the third time in as many days. I was used to humans asking me for help, but not Fae. This was new and everything about it made me uncomfortable.

"You know I can't go in with you," I said, brushing her earnest plea off as a joke.

"Ha ha. That's not what I'm after." Gwawr twisted the end of her braid around her finger. "I need someone to keep an eye on Barr."

"What about him?" I pointed to the cambion.

"He can't stray that far from me. He'll need to stay near my competition arena."

"And Barr's competing against Ioryn next?" I asked.

Gwawr nodded.

"Poor Ioryn. He's going to get crushed." It was a very unlucky draw.

"Ioryn can hold his own."

"Oh, believe me, if any of you deserve to be on the Court, it's Ioryn. He's the purest of you Hands. No offense." I shouldn't have been speaking my mind so plainly to her.

"None taken." Gwawr shrugged. "If I thought he could win, I wouldn't even bother competing."

"But he won't win." Ioryn was strong, but Barr fought dirty. He always had, since we were Faelings.

"No," Gwawr agreed. At least she appeared sad about it.

"So, why should I bother watching Ioryn's match?" I asked, softening again. If she thought Ioryn deserved to win, perhaps she hadn't gotten as full of herself as I'd feared.

"If it's going to be me and Barr competing for guardian, I need to know everything. His weaknesses, his go-to attacks, all of it. Can you help me?" she asked.

She was asking me to spy for her, just as Arabella had, but with all of the risk and none of the potential reward. "If I can get close enough without being seen."

The cambion interrupted, again. "Out of curiosity. Seren is Fae, is she not? So why isn't she welcome at this Conclave? There appears to be every other sort of Fae in attendance."

I'd already just finished explaining this to the lost princeling and wasn't about to do it again. So, I shook my head and gestured to Gwawr. "He's your demon. Go ahead."

She glared at me. "He's not my demon." But then she turned her attention back to him to explain. "Seren is an Elemental, but she's been exiled."

"I'd gathered that much. But why?" he asked.

"What is it that you find so difficult about minding your own business?" Gwawr addressed her question to the cambion, but she shocked me with her sudden flare of anger.

Since when had she become so temperamental? It wasn't like her. Whatever was going on with her, she needed help. Maybe if I told Arabella…but if Arabella found out about the cambion, she'd think only of the queen's safety. Gwawr could be killed for allowing an enemy to get this close to our queen.

I decided to take over the explaining and give Gwawr a chance to cool off. "According to Elemental lore, I'm cursed. I've been blessed with three, but not four, Elemental gifts. So, instead of controlling fire and taking my place as an apprentice alongside these other striving Hands, I've been sentenced to live alone and fend for myself, so as not to further pollute the pristine Elemental bloodlines."

Gwawr folded her arms across her chest. "If you two are

quite done, can we get back to the matter at hand?"

A horn sounded in the distance.

"You should go. I'll watch the match and find you later to fill you in on the details you missed." I hugged Gwawr and then she took off, running toward the arena, with the cambion close behind.

Her behavior had surprised me enough that I'd almost forgotten about the lost princeling until he appeared in the clearing beside me.

"Is your friend all right?" he asked.

"I don't know." I shook my head. "I hope so."

"It sounds like she needs you." He turned his head toward the spot where they'd disappeared into the forest.

"It does." A sinking sensation had taken root in my stomach, and I couldn't shake the feeling that this wasn't going to end well.

"You appear to be quite in demand for one who claims to be exiled." The corner of Damir's mouth lifted into a grin. He was teasing me.

"Do you know how to summon a sprite?" I asked.

His eyebrows raised. "Why would I want to do that?"

Perhaps sprites didn't deliver messages where he came from. Maybe they scratched your eyes out if they caught you looking at them. That would have explained his surprise. I found a pinecone near my boot and used my earth magic to turn it into a sweet honeycomb. Then I whistled for a sprite.

"Don't be shocked when a small, winged Fae appears any moment now." I grinned at him. "And don't make any sudden moves."

"Are sprites dangerous?"

"That depends. Take this." I held up the honeycomb. "Tell the sprite you have a message for Sorcha. That you want to meet with her. They won't deal with me, but they'll carry a message from you. Oh, and tell your faerie dragon to keep to the trees. I don't know if sprites and faerie dragons get on, and I'd rather not test the matter at the moment."

Just then a bright blue flash proceeded the flutter of tiny wings. The sprite took one look at me and scowled. I gestured toward Damir who waved the honeycomb to attract the sprite's attention, keeping it just out of reach. The greedy little fool licked his lips, then flashed his fangs.

"I need you to deliver a message to Sorcha of Maeve. When you return with her response, you can have this." He paused for a moment. His eyes darted to me, then back to the sprite. "Tell Sorcha that Damir of Niamh would like to meet her and to please respond with preferred meeting time and location."

The sprite bowed his head at Damir, hissed at me, then disappeared.

"Sprites send messages if you feed them?" Damir asked once the sprite was gone.

"They're meant to send messages regardless, but a little something sweet seems to put a bit of spring in their step." As much as I appreciated the company and conversation, I needed to get away from Damir before someone caught us together. It was bad enough that the sprite had seen me. "Listen… Would you mind not telling your aunt, or anyone else, that we met? Say you got help from an Elemental if you want, but just don't tell anyone it was me. Okay?"

"Why not?"

I sighed. "I'm not even supposed to be here. Cast out, re-member?"

"But you came to watch this competition that will deter-mine the leader of your faction." His eyes widened as though something finally clicked in that thick head of his. "Is that red-headed friend of yours going to die?"

"Die? Why would she die?" If I didn't get back to the Conclave soon, I'd have nothing to tell Arabella when she appeared for her report. Nothing aside from the fact that Gwawr brought a cambion along to watch the competition. Gwawr would probably die for that, but I didn't think that was what Damir meant. Just the thought of it made me shudder.

"Is it not a fight to the death?" Damir gestured in the direction Gwawr had run off in.

I shook my head. "Of course not. That would be a waste of some of the most valuable Elementals. They fight in pairs until one concedes. Then they advance in the style of a tournament until one has essentially defeated all the others."

"How civilized." He frowned.

"You sound disappointed. I take it that's not how things work among the Dragon Fae?"

"No. It's not."

The sprite reappeared before I could find out more. I decided not to wait around to see if Sorcha appeared as well. While Damir was distracted, I slipped into the forest.

I'd only made it a few steps from the clearing when Damir's familiar glided down from above. She beat her wings as she hovered in the air, blocking my path. Even though the shimmering halo had diminished, and the creature was only the size of a hawk, she was still intimidating.

I stopped, but before I could change directions and swerve around her, a hand landed on my shoulder. Every muscle in my body tensed, ready to flee.

"Wait. Please?"

6

S EREN turned to face me, as Sillag swooped up, over her head, and settled on my shoulder.

"I need to go before I miss Barr's match entirely. Besides, I thought you were in a hurry." She crossed her arms.

"I am." I didn't have time to waste, but I needed to know how I could find her again.

"Well? What are you waiting for?" She raised both her eyebrows in question.

"I…" What I wanted was irrational, but if I didn't ask, I knew I would regret it. Especially since she'd said I couldn't tell anyone I'd spoken with her. "How can I find you again?"

She stared at me in disbelief. "You shouldn't try to find me again. You should go and pretend you never met me."

I almost laughed at the thought. Forget the first female Fae I'd seen since gaining my maturity? That would not be possible. This fierce woman with the strange silver eyes had captured my attention. If not for Ved's imminent trial, I'd insist on staying, on joining her to watch these Conclave matches, if only to have more time to get to know her better.

"Do you say this because you don't want me to find you, or because of the laws of your Elders?" I would respect her wishes if she didn't want to be found, but I wouldn't let her hide from me for the sake of a Council who did not control me.

"You're wasting time."

"You're avoiding my question." I stepped closer to her.

Her eyes flicked to Sillag, but my familiar ignored her. "Once you talk with your aunt, you'll understand, and you won't return."

"I will return. It may not be until I'm sure my cousin is safe, but if I say I will return, then I will."

She cocked her head to one side. "Why?"

"I want to spend more time with you."

Seren pressed her lips together.

Before she could say anything, I continued. "I've chosen to live alone, away from my clan, for my safety, but also because I don't want to live under the rule of our Alpha, and I don't want to challenge him." I paused, considering my next words. "I know what it's like to live away from your kin, even though for me it's by choice. No one should be isolated in that way if they don't choose it for themselves."

Seren remained silent for long enough that I worried I may have said something wrong. When she tugged her hood up over her head, I was sure she'd decided to have nothing to do with me.

"Your cousin Arabella knows how to find me." Her eyes were hidden by the hood of her cloak, so I focused my attention on her lips. "If you decide to return, ask her, and only her, to send me a message. I'll let her know when and where it will be safe to meet."

"I will return." I pressed my palm to my chest in promise.

She dipped her head, then turned and walked away.

I watched her go, waiting until I could no longer make out her shape among the trees.

Sillag nudged my ear with her snout.

"I know." I was acting like a village maiden who'd encountered her first Dragon Fae. This Fae female had captured my attention in a way I hadn't thought possible.

Dragon Fae didn't take mates. My sire and uncle had been ridiculed by the rest of the clan when they'd claimed my mother and aunt Meara as mates. It just wasn't done, and it had led to my uncle's downfall. Boro had seen him as weak and threatened a challenge over and over until Ved's sire died in a hunting accident, leaving my uncle with only one lieutenant. Boro used that opportunity to follow through on his threats, killing my uncle, my sire, and the young guard they anointed as second lieutenant in place of Ved's sire.

Ved had been furious that they hadn't let him take his sire's place in the challenge, but if they had he would be dead. And if I let this attraction distract me, then Ved would have to face the new Alpha and his lieutenants alone. He would die, and I couldn't let that happen. I also couldn't ignore my desire to see Seren again. But if I could get my aunt and my cousins to agree to help me, I wouldn't have to do either.

I sent a thought to Sillag, warning her that I was about to transport us. Then, I closed my eyes and focused on my destination. When I opened them, I found myself facing another Fae female, this one with long golden hair, braided back from her face. Faint creases at the corners of her eyes and mouth hinted at her age, but she otherwise appeared youthful and glowing. I searched her face for some hint of resemblance to my mother's and found none.

"You must be Damir," she said. "I'm Sorcha of Maeve.

Your mother's youngest sister." She held out her hands to me.

"Call me Mir. And this is Sillag." I gestured to my familiar as I stepped forward, closing the distance between us. Sillag flew up to perch in a nearby tree while I bent to kiss my aunt's bony knuckles before raising my eyes to meet hers. "Thank you for agreeing to meet with me."

"You look so much like your mother." She slid one of her hands free so she could press her palm to my cheek. "I'm glad you've returned home."

"I would like to call this place home, but before I can do that, I need to get help for my cousin."

"Did Meara also have a Faeling? Are there more than just you two?" Her eyes brightened.

"Yes." I remembered that Seren said my aunt had been captured. I wondered if she'd had the chance to speak with my mother or Meara before they were killed. "Meara had a Faeling. His name is Ivo, and he escaped after our sires were killed. It's Ved who needs help."

"Ved is not Meara's?" she asked.

"No, but his sire was a lieutenant to Meara's mate, who was our Alpha. By Dragon Fae tradition, that makes him our wing-mate. Our kin." My throat tightened, and I swallowed the emotions that threatened to spill out.

Sorcha nodded as though she understood. "Where is Ivo of Meara now?"

"Ivo left the clan after his sire was defeated, before he could be killed by the new Alpha. I don't know where he is, but it's better that way. At least for now."

"Why worry about this 'wing-mate' and not your blood kin?" Sorcha frowned.

"Ivo can take care of himself. He knows how to find us, when he's ready to return. It's Ved that's in trouble and needs our help. I can't save him alone. I'll be killed if I try. I came to you hoping you might be able to help me."

She took a step back and rested both palms on her belly. "Unfortunately, I cannot."

My eyes flicked between her hands and her face. I was so used to dealing with the young human women in the village that it took a moment before I guessed what my centuries old Fae aunt was implying. "Are you pregnant?"

She nodded. "I'm just completing the Settling phase and don't have much control over my power. It will be another moon cycle before I can trust my magic again."

I shouldn't have been surprised, but her response hit me like a blow, knocking the hope out of me almost entirely. "Is there anyone who can help me? I was told I have cousins. Do you think they might help? I can't let Ved die."

"You could ask the Queen." Her brow furrowed in thought. "You say he's not a blood relation, but he's Dragon Fae?"

"Yes. He's as much my kin as this Queen."

She squinted at me. "Who is it that you've spoken with before coming here?"

"An Elemental." I couldn't lie to her, so I used Seren's suggested response, instead.

Sorcha nodded. "If you ask the Queen for help, she will likely ask you for something in return."

"I will give whatever is required to rescue Ved." I was so relieved that my aunt hadn't asked for Seren's name that I didn't care what the queen asked.

"Even your seed?" she asked, once again taking me by surprise.

"Of course." I shrugged. "If that's all she requires, I don't have much need for it. She's welcome to it. Only, I don't see what she'd want with her cousin's seed."

"Not for her," Sorcha said. "You'll need to find an appropriate female to give it to. She'll likely have some suggestions. Fiona is in need of an heir."

"There is no heir?" I tried to remember if Seren had mentioned how many High Fae cousins I had. Perhaps none were female.

Sorcha shook her head. "Many Fae were captured and killed by the Wild Hunt. All my sisters are gone. We thought only three of their offspring remained. Flida's son, Isleen's daughter, and Rionach's daughter. With you and Meara's son, that will make five. My offspring will make six. But none of you have yet to produce any offspring of your own."

"Will she allow me to choose?" I asked.

"Do you have someone in mind? Perhaps the Elemental you met who sent you to me?" Sorcha grinned. "What is her name?"

"I'd rather not say."

"Interesting."

"Will you take me to speak with my cousin, the Queen?"

"I will, but you'll need to transport us." She instructed me as to where I would find the queen's cottage, then set her hand on my forearm.

I waited for Sillag to return to my shoulder, then I transported us to a different cottage than the one my mother had described in her journal. This one was newer from the look of the bright white paint coating the outside.

Two guards stood at attention outside the front door. They didn't startle at our sudden appearance, so I guessed that it must have become common for Fae to be popping in and out on business with the queen.

My aunt strode toward the door, head held high, and requested an audience with Fiona. I followed her, staying a few steps behind. Both guards bowed to her as she approached, then one slipped inside to announce us. As soon as she'd gone, Sorcha turned her head to look at me.

"You should leave your familiar outside," she said. "The guards will likely fuss if you try to bring her in."

I glanced past her shoulder to the guard remaining at the door. He was staring at Sillag, who stirred on my shoulder, uncomfortable with all the attention. I sent her a thought, asking if she'd mind waiting.

She cooed and clicked, pleased to be released. Then she took off to circle the skies.

The other guard returned a moment later, gesturing for us to enter. She stepped aside to allow us to proceed her down the hall inside the cottage.

We emerged in a cozy room where a fire burned in the hearth. Two of the walls were covered in shelves weighed down with trinkets and thick leather-bound volumes. Large glass panels closed in the back wall of the room. They opened onto a patio with a garden and stone circle beyond. A tall female with short hair stood before the glass, waiting to greet us.

"My Queen," Sorcha said, bowing her head.

I echoed her gesture as the guard closed the door behind us, leaving the three of us alone to talk.

"Fiona of Isleen, I bring you Damir of Niamh," Sorcha said, moving aside and turning halfway to face me.

"It's true, then. I'd hoped we'd find that there were more of us." Fiona stepped past Sorcha, reaching her hands out to greet me. "I've seen your mother's face in the memory stone. You look just like her. May her force strengthen us all."

"Thank you." For a moment, I stood tongue tied, blaming the heavy crown nestled among her tight curls for the fact that I seemed to have forgotten why I'd come.

"Did you come alone?" Fiona said. "Did Niamh and Meara have any other Faelings?"

"One. Ivo of Meara," I said, finding my voice. "Though, he is currently in hiding. I believe he'll find his way here in his own time. He left the Dragon Fae clan after his sire was defeated in a challenge."

"The Dragon Fae still rule by Challenge?"

"They do."

"Well, then I'm glad he escaped, and I'm glad you've come to live with us, now." She paused, tilting her head ever so slightly and arching one eyebrow. "You have come to stay, have you not?"

"I am considering that, but first I am hoping you might agree to help me with a rescue operation."

"A rescue?" Fiona turned and paced over to one of the chairs clustered in a group at the center of the room. "Perhaps we should sit. Make yourselves comfortable. I've already sent for tea."

"If you would prefer, my Queen, I will leave you to speak with your cousin alone." Sorcha lingered near the door while I moved towards the chairs.

"You're welcome to stay or go as you please, Aunt Sorcha. Perhaps you've already had time to catch up with Damir and already know what brings him to us?"

"I do," she said. "Unfortunately, I am unable to help him. That's why we came to you."

A small Fae, no taller than my knee, with large floppy ears hurried into the room by passing directly through a wall while carrying a large tray laden with a teapot and matching cups and saucers. His burden rattled and threatened to spill, as he slid it onto a low table set between the chairs.

"Thank you, Birch," Fiona said.

Birch bowed low, then turned and marched himself back through the wall.

"Join us, Aunt Sorcha." Fiona gestured to the chair next to mine. "I may require your advice on the matter."

"Yes, my Queen." Sorcha sank into the chair next to mine as Fiona poured the tea.

"Now," she said. "Tell me about this rescue and how you think I might be able to help."

$$7$$

BARR'S match was already underway, and I'd probably missed most of it listening to empty promises from that lost princeling. He wasn't going to return. Not after he talked to Sorcha and the Queen. Besides, I had enough trouble on my hands without that clueless Dragon Fae looking at me like he'd been dying of thirst in a desert and I was a crystal-clear lake in the middle of an oasis.

The crowd of Fae surrounding the ring cheered, and I broke into a run. If I didn't hurry, I was going to miss all of Barr's match and have nothing to tell Gwawr. Or Arabella, for that matter. Unless I mentioned the cambion with fake antlers hanging out in Gwawr's tent. Of course, if I ripped his horned head from the rest of his body, then I wouldn't have to tell the commander that I thought my friend might be in the thrall of a half-demon. Unfortunately, it would be irresponsible to do that before I figured out the terms of their agreement.

Tugging my hood lower and holding it tight around my face, I lurked behind the Fae pressed up against the arena fence.

I kept moving until I'd found a spot with a decent view, but that also allowed me to retreat to the shelter of the forest if anyone got too interested in sneaking a peek at my face.

Inside the ring, Barr had Ioryn surrounded by chest-high walls of fire. The runes painted on the sides of Ioryn's face glowed as water welled up from the earth to pool at his feet.

Barr paired his earth magic with his fire magic and began lobbing balls of flame at Ioryn who attempted to dodge them while keeping inside his fiery prison. A few grazed his upper arms, slicing through his tunic and leaving behind blistered welts. Despite all that, Ioryn managed to raise a wind that whipped the water up to swirl around him in a protective shield.

The whole thing was incredibly thrilling. It was easy to get caught up in the excitement, especially as Barr's flames leapt higher and he took control of the air. Ioryn's water shield fell to the ground with a splash. Then he stumbled and fell to his knees.

No, no, no. Get up. My fists clenched the fabric of my cloak. Around me, most of the Fae were cheering, but a few were shouting encouragement at Ioryn. I didn't dare add my voice to the clamor, but I silently urged him on with every bone in my body.

It wasn't enough. Ioryn's painted runes flickered. Then he signaled his defeat, and it was over. Barr the bully had won. He let the flames die, then reached out a hand to help Ioryn to his feet. Ioryn congratulated Barr. By the time he turned to wave to the crowd, the welts on his arms had disappeared.

I groaned as the celebrations around me increased. Someone on my left hooted and whistled as they jumped up and down, trying to get Barr's attention. When they stopped to catch their breath, their companion grumbled that it wasn't much of a match. He'd expected more and thought they should have been watching Eira and Gwawr, instead.

"He's just a bit showy," the disappointed Fae explained. "And a bit of a one trick pony, to boot. Did he use anything besides fire in that match?"

"Why would he?" his giddy friend asked. "When you're that good at wielding fire, and you know that's your opponent's weakest element, you don't have to worry about your opponent turning your attack against you. Strong offense forces your opponent to defense. That's just smart, if you ask me."

"I suppose." He glanced over at the opposite ring. "If we hurry, maybe we can catch the end of the other match. All right?" He tugged on his friend's sleeve, dragging him away from the still celebrating crowd.

I followed the pair at a safe distance, keeping close to the trees. The two combat rings were on opposite sides of a viewing platform. I could only make out one figure watching from up there. I assumed it was Cahal. At least from this distance, he'd have a hard time picking me out of the crowd.

My eyes skimmed the backs of the Fae watching Gwawr's match, searching for an opening where I might be able to watch without drawing too much attention to myself. That's when I spotted the cambion, leaning against the fence that surrounded the competition ring. I started toward him, then realized another figure was making their way through the crowd, heading in Nye's direction. I paused to watch.

Liam of Flida, cousin to Arabella and the Faerie Queen, had spotted the intruder without my having to say a word. He sliced through the crowd and clamped one hand down on the cambion's shoulder. *Caught.* I almost cheered. Instead, I hid my grin behind the edge of my hood and savored the sense of relief.

The pair disappeared, and I hoped Liam was taking the cambion to question him and then slice his head off somewhere that wouldn't cause a scene. With that problem solved, I turned my attention to the final moments of Gwawr's match. In the ring, Gwawr stood over Eira with hands blazing.

So, it was true. The Ancients had answered Gwawr's prayers and she had regained control of her fire magic. Eira struggled to stand but lost her footing when Gwawr shook the earth beneath her. That was it. Eira dropped back, conceding the match.

Gwawr turned to face the crowd. Unlike Barr, she didn't appear thrilled with her win. She seemed to be in shock. It wasn't until Eira stood and hugged Gwawr that Gwawr finally smiled. Eira may have also whispered something to Gwawr, I couldn't hear her over the chanting. The Fae were cheering for Gwawr. They'd loved her performance almost as much as the other crowd loved Barr.

Perhaps it was the spectacle of the matches, perhaps it was jealousy, but I lost all interest in the competition after seeing how the other Fae were treating this Conclave like a giant party. These weren't just games meant to entertain. This was an important tradition that would determine the strongest of our Hands. The one who would sit on the Queen's Council. Didn't they care about that?

Keeping an eye on the ring, I made my way back to the edge of the forest. Once I was close to the trees and further from the other Fae, I relaxed a bit. Then I paced along the perimeter of the clearing until I once again stood across from the spot where the two competition rings were joined by the platform in between. It seemed as good a place as any to wait and see what happened next.

The spectators had started moving away from the competition rings to gather in clusters and make their way toward the open field to continue their celebrations. If I wanted to speak with Gwawr, I would have to find a way to sneak into the tents positioned at the edge of the competition ring. Eira had slipped into one, and Gwawr entered the other. If I hoped to intercept her while she was alone, this would be my best chance.

No one paid me much mind as I walked closer to the rings. I kept one eye on the tent Gwawr had entered to make sure no one else went in and she didn't leave. The rest of my attention went to avoiding recognition.

If Liam had spotted that half-demon among the spectators, he could just as easily spot me. Not that I was sure he'd recognize me. He'd spent too many years away from his Elemental kin to make note of me, even though I'd been the only one banished during his lifetime.

Even if Liam wouldn't recognize me, all of the Elemental Elders knew my face. So, I watched for them and changed course whenever I spotted Fae wearing long blue robes. My erratic path made the journey twice as long as it might have been if I could have walked among my kin openly.

When I reached my destination, I circled around the back side of the tent and listened. Someone moved inside, but no one spoke. The shuffling of feet and rustle of clothing was my only clue that the tent was still occupied. I ran a hand along the fabric wall, searching for a flap or seam where I might be able to catch a glimpse inside.

My fingers found the edge of one panel and started to curl around to pull it aside when the tent wall lifted inward, revealing Gwawr staring out at me.

"Oh, good, this is yours," I said, stepping inside. "I'd hoped I wasn't poking about the wrong one." I glanced around as though I expected that cambion to be hiding somewhere, even though I knew he'd been captured. "Where'd your demon go?"

Gwawr rolled her eyes. "For the last time, he's not my demon."

"Good." I knew she couldn't lie, and I was pleased that she didn't seem to care that he was gone. Her response increased my confidence that he wouldn't be a problem, after all.

"Barr won his match," Gwawr said, beating me to the report she'd asked me to provide.

"How did you know?" I plopped myself down in the only chair.

"He stopped me outside to tell me he welcomed me in his bed." She dragged a low stool over and sat down on it across from me.

"Lovely." I didn't like how close I'd come to running into him. If he'd found her after her match, that meant he'd been outside her tent only moments before I'd arrived. I was going to have to get better at this sneaking around if I hoped to make a decent spy for Arabella.

"How's Ioryn?" Gwawr asked.

I shrugged. "Bit of wounded pride, I'd say, but nothing he won't recover from. He was healed up before he stood to congratulate Barr on his win."

"The runes." She must have seen them earlier in the day.

I nodded. "Brilliant work, that. But if you're thinking of doing the same, I'd advise against it. I think it sapped some of his power. Certainly, dulled his responses. He should have been more difficult to defeat, unless Barr's improved that much since crèche."

"What attacks did he use?" Gwawr asked.

"Mostly fire. He certainly prefers the flashy stuff. I don't think he used water once in the whole match. But then again, water is Ioryn's best. If he'd risked anything like that, Ioryn could have easily turned it against him. I wouldn't have given Barr credit for being terribly strategic, but I have to admit, he must have at least half a brain in that pretty head of his." Repeating what I'd heard and expanding on it didn't seem like much of a report, but I'd been distracted by that Dragon Fae and his familiar. I wished I could tell Gwawr that I'd just seen a faerie dragon, but if I did, I'd have to tell her about the lost High Fae princeling, too.

Gwawr shifted on the stool. "Right. Well, I suppose I should prepare for my next match."

I was beginning to suspect that she was trying to get rid of me. I hoped it wasn't so that she could run off and try to find that cambion. "You should have a bit of a break now, shouldn't you? At least until after the redemption matches have been decided."

Gwawr nodded. "Ioryn's up against Anwen, right? And Eira competes against Talie?"

"That's right. And if Anwen loses again, she's out for good this time." Much as I tried, I found it difficult to dampen my glee at the thought that Anwen might soon be well and truly defeated.

"Right. Well, I suppose I'll watch that match then. I'd like to see who makes it out of that round."

"My money's on Ioryn, but you never know." I squinted at her. "Worried that Barr will defeat you, and you'll have to fight your way back?"

Gwawr shrugged. "He's good, and it pays to be prepared."

My stomach gurgled, reminding me that spying for Arabella didn't fill my belly as well as hunting demons. I glanced around the tent, searching for the refreshments. "They don't give you any food or anything?"

"They've probably left something for me to eat in my tent. It's just down the row a bit. I'll walk you over there on the way to view the match."

I shook my head. "No. Don't risk being seen with me. I'll find it on my own. You go enjoy the match. Give Wenny my best, and tell her I hope Ioryn wipes the ring with her." I grinned.

"You know I'm not going to do that."

"I know." I stood and peeked outside. "Would be nice if you could, though."

"Leave something for me, yeah?"

I made no promises and slipped out of the tent with a wave and a smile. That smile died when I stepped out into the open and tugged my hood up over my head. Gwawr had won her first match. She'd shown that her fire magic was as strong as ever. As much as I wanted Ioryn to make it out of the redemption matches and win, Gwawr and Barr were the best of the bunch. Of those two, I knew who I wanted as guardian.

But, if Liam or Arabella found out that Gwawr was connected to that cambion, she'd be killed. If Liam questioned Nye, and Nye told the queen's cousin who brought him to the Conclave, that would be the end for Gwawr. And if the cambion told Liam that Gwawr had gone to meet me, and I didn't tell Arabella what I knew when she showed up asking for my report, I would lose my chance at earning a place in the Queen's Guard.

I needed to figure out what Gwawr had promised the cambion, and then I needed to silence him, permanently, before he could get us both in trouble with our kin—or worse, get us killed.

8

AS Sorcha predicted, Fiona agreed to help only after I'd promised away my literal firstborn Faeling. Likely my only Faeling, since most male Fae could only produce one. As a Dragon Fae, there was always the possibility that any males sired by me and born of human mothers would still be Fae. But unlike the rest of my clan, I had no interest in seducing the village women.

Still, I didn't hesitate before agreeing to help Fiona's chances at securing an heir. If my Faerie Queen cousin needed High Fae Faelings, I would do my part. So long as she allowed me the freedom to negotiate my own choice about which Fae female might be willing to carry my Faeling, which she had. She had also explained that, at least among the Elementals, Faelings were traditionally raised in a crèche rather than by their sires and dams.

This was the traditional practice within the Dragon Fae clan, as well. So, it didn't seem so outlandish to me. However, she noted that High Fae females typically chose to raise their own offspring. Sorcha planned to raise hers, and Fiona suggested that, once she'd found the right sire, she also planned to care for her own Faeling. She also intended to have more than one, if she managed to live that long.

With that settled, I did my best to hurry them past the talk of Fae reproduction so that we might return to the topic of saving Ved. When I finally managed to steer the conversation back in that direction, Fiona explained that our cousin Arabella of Rionach, Commander of the Queen's Guard, would be the one to help me rescue Ved.

Part of me seethed as I realized that she'd known that all along and could have sent for Arabella earlier, but she'd wait until she'd secured my pledge to tell me that. The rest of me thrilled that I had an excuse to meet the cousin who could reconnect me with Seren.

Fiona left to ask the guard to send for Arabella. She returned carrying a tray with additional refreshments for us to enjoy while we waited.

"You mentioned Meara's son escaped from the Dragon Fae clan. Do you know where he is?" Fiona asked as she poured more tea into our cups.

"I do not." I hadn't wanted to know. Boro had been furious when he found out that Ivo got away. He'd sent two of his lieutenants to my hut in the village. One held me captive while the other searched the few rooms of my home, looking for any sign that Ivo had been there or sent me any message. Then they'd questioned me for hours and kept a watch on me for weeks after that.

"But you're sure that he got away safely?" she asked.

"His familiar spoke with mine. Sillag, my familiar, may know more than she told me, but my knowing anything about Ivo's whereabouts would only put him in more danger. He's a risk to Boro's leadership so long as he lives. We all are." I sighed into my teacup. Time was running out for Ved as I sat here playing politics.

The front door banged open and a dark-haired female with golden brown skin barged into the room, unannounced. "What's this all about, Fi? I was in the middle of training." She stopped just inside the doorway when she locked eyes with me. "Who's this?" she asked.

I set down my cup and stood.

Fiona made the introduction. "Ari, this is Damir of Niamh, our cousin."

"Where have you been?" Arabella asked, setting her hands on her hips and narrowing her eyes at me.

"Living with my Dragon Fae kin." I pressed my hands against the sides of my trousers.

"Have you come to help us fight the demons?"

Fiona spoke before I could answer. "He's come to ask our help in rescuing his wing-mate from the Dragon Fae Alpha who intends to kill him. I've agreed and offered him your help."

"My help?" Arabella raised both eyebrows and peered around me to look at Fiona.

"I thought that would be more effective than me going along to assist him. Don't you agree?" Fiona sipped her tea, then set the cup down on the table.

"You're joking." Arabella waited for Fiona to respond. She was met with silence, so she continued. "Between preparing my guard for war, bolstering our defenses, and monitoring that Elemental Conclave, I don't have time for rescuing a ruddy Dragon Fae." She turned her attention to me. "Why can't you do it yourself? You appear powerful enough."

Fiona didn't give me a chance to respond. She spoke softly, but firmly. "The Conclave is Liam's responsibility, and I can help reinforce the border defenses. Our cousin needs our help, and I've agreed."

Arabella and Fiona stared at each other for a few moments, caught in some silent negotiation. Then Arabella bowed her head.

"Yes, my queen."

"Good," Fiona said. "It's settled then. I'll let you two leave so you can discuss your plans. I have a few things I'd like to speak with Sorcha about while she's here." Fiona stood, stepping around the table to embrace me. "I do hope you return in time to catch the final matches of the Conclave. I hear there are several very promising Elementals competing. The favorite is a very powerful female. I'd love to introduce you to her."

I grinned. If only she knew that I'd already seen this Gwawr and didn't think much of her. In fact, I much preferred her friend. "If we are successful, I would certainly like to attend, especially if you think I might find a suitable female there." I bowed my head to Fiona, then followed Arabella outside.

"She convinced you to give up your seed, didn't she?" Arabella asked, as soon as we'd passed the guards.

"In exchange for her—your—assistance, yes," I said.

Arabella laughed. "She's a crafty one. I suppose I should feel bad for you."

"It's all right. Sorcha warned me what the cost might be. I don't mind, so long as we get Ved to safety. He doesn't have much time before he'll be sent before the Alpha for his trial."

"What sort of trial?" Arabella asked.

"He refused to pledge his loyalty to our new Alpha. He has until tomorrow to do so, or he'll have to fight a challenge."

"I take it this Alpha isn't deserving of your friend's loyalty?"

"Wing-mate," I corrected. "He's family, and this new Alpha killed our sires.”

“Sounds like the Alpha should be the one on trial.”

“Our sires died for their loyalty to the defeated Alpha, and Ved would just as quickly follow them, if I can’t manage to save him from himself.”

She made a soft noise of acknowledgement in her throat. “Sounds like I’d get on well with this wing-mate of yours. Don’t suppose he fancies a leadership position in the Queen’s Guard?”

“Let’s rescue him, first. Then you can ask him, yourself.” I grinned.

“Right. What’s your plan?”

“He’s currently in a prison cave, guarded by two Dragon Fae. I plan to create a distraction, allowing you enough time to enter the cave while it’s unguarded. Once you’re inside, you’ll need to release him and get him out. The Dragon Fae lair is shielded. There’s no transport in or out, so you’ll need to get him back to the entrance to the caverns before you can transport him away.”

“Do you think it will be easier for me to get inside if I enter in my animal form?”

“That would be ideal, depending on what it is. An animal wandering into the caverns might be overlooked, especially if you manage to keep to the shadows.”

“My form is a wolf. Are wolves common around there?”

“Common enough.”

“What about you? Couldn’t you do the same? Don’t you have an animal form? You are High Fae, after all.”

I scowled. “Yes. But I’m also Dragon Fae.”

She raised her eyebrows in question but didn’t respond.

“I can take the form of a dragon, like all males of our Clan, but once I do, all the other members can sense my presence.

There is no hiding as a dragon among Dragon Fae."

"I see."

"So long as I remain in my Fae form, or even my human disguise, they cannot locate me. Because of that, I haven't shifted form since our Alpha was killed. Boro, the new Alpha, knows where I reside in the village. It won't be long before he puts me to trial as well, but he'll deal with Ved first. It serves him to keep me where I am, so long as I don't cause any trouble. None of his wing-mates want my position."

"And that position is?"

"I steal the male offspring of the Dragon Fae from the village women who birth them and return them to the clan."

"And here I thought we were desperate for Faelings." She shook her head. "All right. Let's get this over with, then. Care to transport us to this lair?"

I sent a quick thought to Sillag, warning her to stay hidden and safe while I was gone. I couldn't risk bringing her with me. Then I returned my attention to Arabella.

"I'll take us directly to the mouth of the caverns. So, perhaps it will be best for you to transform now."

"If I travel that way as a wolf, then I can't bring any weapons," she said.

"You'll have to risk it," I said. "You won't be able to bring them into the caverns with you, anyway. You'll have to rely on your magic and your combat skills once we're inside."

She frowned, then stripped herself of more knives and daggers than I'd realized she'd been carrying. Once they lay in a heap at her feet, along with the short sword that had been strapped to her back, she glanced down with a sigh, and the lot of them disappeared.

"Reassure me that these guards of yours are lazy and un-trained," she said, looking up to meet my eyes.

"Given what I've seen in my short time in your forest, I think your guards are probably better trained, but the Dragon Fae do have the advantage of physical power and size, especially if they shift." As much as I wanted to promise her this would go smoothly, I needed her to be prepared to fight.

"Then I suppose we'll have to keep them from shifting." She didn't wait for a response before transforming into a large grey wolf who stood nearly hip high when she took her place at my side.

I tentatively stretched out my hand to her, palm up, as though I were reaching for Sillag. When Arabella's wolf sniffed my fingers and didn't move away, I set my hand on the thick fur covering her neck and prepared to transport us to the mouth of the caverns.

The sun had just dipped below the tip of the mountain top when we appeared on the ledge near the opening to the Dragon Fae caves. I crouched down until my face was level with Arabella's muzzle.

"Follow me but keep to the shadows and remain hidden. If you lose sight of me, follow my scent. Get him out and get him back to your forest. Don't wait for me."

Arabella lowered her head and growled.

I had enough experience with Sillag to interpret this as displeasure with my command. "Get him to safety. Based on how he looked when I last saw him, he's going to need a healer. If I don't appear shortly after you return, I'm sure Fiona will send reinforcements to bring me back. I can't say the same for Ved. He may be my wing-mate, but he can't provide Fiona with a High Fae heir."

As soon as the words were out of my mouth, I realized that I was wrong. There was a way that Ved could offer Fiona an heir. I wondered if she'd already thought of that, and if that had contributed to her easy agreement. "She wants all three of us, doesn't she?"

Arabella's wolf shook from head to tail, then stretched back to bow down on her front paws. I interpreted this as agreement and marveled at how out-maneuvered I'd been. I sent a prayer to the Ancients that Ivo and Ved would understand and forgive me, then another for our safety and success, before starting toward the opening to the cavern.

Grandsire wouldn't know to prepare the guards to receive me this time. So, the ruse of pretending to be a village medic wasn't going to work. My only option was to enter as myself, even though I had no reasonable excuse for visiting. That meant the guards outside Ved's cave would assume I was either there to stir up trouble, or with the intention to pledge my loyalty to Boro. If they sensed trouble, they'd shift to attack and ask questions later.

Faking an intention to bow to the new Alpha would be difficult given that I couldn't lie. I had to admit, my plan was weak, but there wasn't time to come up with a better one. Things were about to get interesting.

9

S INCE most of the Fae attending the Conclave were there
to watch the matches and celebrate, there was almost no
one in the area around the competitors' tents. I still kept
my hood up and my head down as I made my way to the tent
I remembered had been assigned to Gwawr.

Ducking inside, I found one straight-backed chair with a
woven seat next to a cot covered with a tangled mess of wool
blankets. The furnishings were so sparse that there wasn't even
a pillow or plush cushion for comfort. Yet, opposite the cot, I
found a feast fit for the lost Dragon Fae princeling—the one
that I doubted I would ever see again—laid out on wooden table. The feast was the only hint that anyone of importance was
meant to reside within the canvas walls of this musty enclosure.

Whatever Gwawr had brought with her to the Conclave,
she must still be carrying on her body, because there were no
personal effects in her tent. There wasn't so much as a box to
peek inside of. Which, as much as I wanted answers, was good,
because I was hungry, and the scent of summer fruit was mak-

ing my mouth water.

It had been almost a year since I'd last sunk my teeth into the soft flesh of a peach or plum. But, since fruit was easy to carry, I stashed a few in my pockets for later. Then I reached for a skewer loaded with roasted meat and vegetables, hoping that filling my empty belly might help me think.

Liam had the cambion, but I didn't know where they'd gone. Gwawr didn't seem to know, so he must not have gone far. She had said that Nye needed to stay close to her, according to their arrangement. Unless they'd fulfilled their promises to each other. Then it wouldn't matter.

Or maybe the cambion had enchanted her to think they had a bargain when they never had one at all. What if Liam didn't know Nye was a cambion and thought the antlers were real? I'd been assuming that he took the cambion off to question him, but what if the cambion managed to corrupt Liam as well?

I polished off the last bit of goat meat and licked the juices off my fingers. At least it wasn't rabbit. I was thoroughly sick of rabbit. I bet these Hands didn't even know what rabbit tasted like. Why kill a rabbit and eat it when you could heal it and send it hopping back into the hedges? While they were busy learning how to heal small forest creatures, I was figuring out how to identify demons and decide which part needed stabbing in order to banish them from the earth.

Humans didn't want to pay me to use a bit of simple Elemental magic to clean their drinking water or help their crops grow. No. The local wizard could do that sort of thing. They called on me when they needed someone to rid them of the creatures that preyed on their loved ones' souls.

I scowled at the heavily laden table, letting my eyes skim the mountain of fresh food and realizing that almost none of it was in season. What were seasons to Elementals? A pair of them could have produced this feast without breaking a sweat. There would need to be at least two because they would need to draw on three types of Elemental magic, and any normal Elemental only had control of one or two Elements.

I could have done it on my own. I had control of all the elements needed to create this spread. But using that much magic would draw too much attention. It would be like setting off a beacon to my kin and saying, "Here I am! Come toss me out on my arse because I didn't leave properly back when you thought I did."

That thought reminded me that I still hadn't figured out how Arabella and Brianne had located me so easily. It had been stupid to tell that Dragon Fae that Arabella knew how to find me. Not that he would ever ask her about me.

I lifted a bunch of grapes from the table, plucked off a plump one, and dropped it into my mouth. Closing my eyes, I savored the sweet juice swirling around my tongue. Perhaps I would ask Arabella what clue had tipped them off to my location when she checked in on me for my report.

My eyes popped open. *My report.*

I stuffed as much food as I could into my pockets, then started back toward the competition rings. Gwawr had said that she was going to watch Anwen's match. If I found her there, alone, then I could question her about the cambion. Until I could be sure that he was gone, I would have to assume that he was a threat. That meant that I would have to tell Arabella. But maybe there was a way to do that without saying that I'd seen him with Gwawr.

I could tell Arabella that I'd seen Liam remove a cambion from the crowd of spectators watching Gwawr's match. She knew I hunted demons, so she might not question how I identified him. If she did, I'd have to tell her about my encounter with Gwawr. Or I could tell her that Damir's faerie dragon had scratched me and given me some sort of truth-sight that allowed me to see through the cambion's disguise. Then she would know that I'd spoken with the princeling, but I could honestly say I'd just been helping direct him to Sorcha. If Arabella was willing to offer me a place in her guard, then she probably wouldn't mind me admitting to meeting Damir.

I popped a few more grapes in my mouth and chewed on the idea as I tried to determine which of the rings held the match between Anwen and Ioryn and which held the one between Talie and Eira. The one on my left had more spectators, so I thought I might check the less popular match, first. Then the smaller crowd started chanting Talie's name. I pivoted and started in the opposite direction. No luck for the cursed. I'd have to risk the larger crowd if I wanted to find Gwawr.

At least there was the small bonus that I might get to see Anwen lose. If Ioryn beat her, she'd be eliminated from the Conclave. No chance to be guardian. Defeated. The thought made me grin. She deserved it after what she'd done to me. She could have kept my secret like Gwawr did. But no. She had to go and snitch to her sire and dam.

I wanted so much to find Anwen losing badly, but when I finally caught sight of her, there was barely a scratch on her. My attention was torn between watching the already-in-progress match, where Anwen was deflecting Ioryn's attacks and returning them blow for blow, and searching the Elementals gathered around the ring to see if I could spot Gwawr. I only realized too late that I should have been paying closer attention to my immediate surroundings.

Distracted by the match, I didn't notice the male Fae who had edged closer to me until his shoulder brushed up against mine. The sudden pressure made me flinch, and my hood crept back to reveal my profile. I tugged it back into place, but it was too late.

"Thought that was you," Barr said.

"Going to turn me in?" I tensed. If I ran now, he might try to stop me. Or he might call out for someone else to grab me. There were too many Fae between me and the forest, and the Conclave grounds had been secured with High Fae magic to prevent transport in or out.

"I should," he said.

I waited, keeping my eyes on Ioryn's rune-covered face and silently urging him to do something, anything to defeat Anwen. I didn't dare look at Barr. I just hoped he couldn't sense my growing fear and panic. If I kept my head down, maybe he'd take pity on me.

"Can't blame you for coming to watch." Barr folded his arms across his muscular chest. "Must be rough knowing you're so close but will always be missing that piece of magic that could have put you in the ring."

My hands formed fists at my sides. The fingers clenched so tight my nails dug into my palms. My shoulders shot up toward my ears as a wind rippled against my cloak, threatening to rip it from my shoulders. I couldn't tell if it was caused by my power—an unintended side-effect of my anger—or Barr's magic. It wouldn't surprise me if he was taunting me with a subtle threat. I risked a glance at him out of the corner of my eye, only to find him grinning at the competitors in the ring.

While I'd been distracted, Anwen must have hit Ioryn with a blast of earth magic. Ioryn was struggling to free himself from the vines curling around his legs and pulling him to his knees. He stumbled but managed to direct a jet of water at Anwen, freezing it with a cold wind mid-flight so that, by the time it reached her, it had morphed into shards of ice that sliced at her outstretched arms.

I winced as blood dripped from Anwen's wrists. I also wanted to cheer, but I resisted giving in to my glee and focused my attention on continuing the search for any sign of the other red-haired competitor among the spectators. "What do you want, Barr?"

"I want to be Guardian." He turned his grin on me just as my eyes scanned in his direction.

"And then what?" I shifted my stance, readying to bolt at the first opportunity. Then I forced my fingers to flex and relax. "Convince the queen to take your seed?"

He tapped a finger against his lips. "Not a bad idea, Ren. I'll have to remember that one." He pressed his palms together and rubbed them against each other as he smiled. "Just think… My offspring, heir to the throne. Our Faeling would be a force, don't you agree?"

I glanced around to see if anyone was close enough to hear him say my name. At least he hadn't turned me in yet. That didn't mean he wouldn't. I was risking everything just being here. I didn't have the luxury of arguing with him.

The crowd roared, pulling my attention back to the match just in time to watch Ioryn concede. My heart sank. Anwen would be one of the final four competitors. She raised her bloody arms in triumph and turned in a slow circle to absorb the excitement of the crowd.

Barr reached up to wave as her eyes moved toward where we stood. If she spotted him, she'd see me, too. Rather than stick around so she could snitch on me a second time, I ducked and bolted into the crowd. I had to get out of there, fast.

I swerved and slowed, attaching myself to the back of a group moving away from the ring and toward the celebrations at the edge of the lake. I did my best to blend in, knowing that, if

Barr was searching for me, he'd be looking for a solitary figure. Curling deep into my cloak, I counted my steps until we were close enough to the edge of the forest that I could peel away from the group and disappear into the shadows under the trees.

That had been much too close for my comfort. Arabella wouldn't protect me if I got caught. She wouldn't even admit that she'd made a deal with me unless I provided her with the information she wanted. And now two of the four contenders for guardian were Elementals who had made my life miserable. That was before they had any authority. If either of them became guardian, I might as well go live among the humans. I'd rather be covered in demon blood than see Anwen or Barr on the Queen's Court.

I had more questions than answers, but I was running out of time. Now that the matches were over for the day, Arabella could show up asking for a report at any moment. If I told her what I knew about Gwawr, she would be eliminated from the competition, at best, and killed, at worst. But I would have a position in the Queen's Guard.

If I didn't tell Arabella what I knew, then the beast that Gwawr brought with her might infiltrate the High Fae, starting with Liam, paving the way for his demon kin to destroy us.

The rich goat meat and summer fruit sat heavy in my stomach and soured on my tongue. Perhaps I really was cursed.

10

THE guards stopped talking when they realized I was walking toward them and not passing the cave on my way deeper into the caverns. They straightened and lifted their spears, making a passable attempt to stand at attention in case it turned out I was someone of importance. Once they got a good look at my face, their shoulders slumped a bit and they relaxed.

I sized them up as I approached. The one standing to the right of the cave entrance sported pale arms with thick, veined biceps and metal cuffs around his wrists that matched the armored plate he wore strapped across his broad chest. His partner was shorter with dark brown skin but had much more muscular arms and a thick chest that put the other guard's to shame.

Dragon Fae stature wasn't always a direct indicator of one's strength in dragon form, but it usually wasn't far off. Both of these males would likely have an advantage over me if we shifted. Plus, if it came to that, the rest of the clan would be instantly aware of us and those loyal to the new Alpha would come to the aid of the guards while any who might prefer to see me succeed would cower and wait for the outcome. I needed to keep them from sensing a threat and shifting.

"Greetings." I grinned at the pair, stopping just shy of the reach of their spears, should they choose to point them at me. "I must have spent too many months in the village. I think I've taken a wrong turn."

The taller of the pair leaned his spear against the wall behind him and rubbed his palm against his shaved scalp, but the shorter one didn't budge except to narrow his eyes at me.

"Gathering hall is that way," the taller one said, pointing down a tunnel that branched off to my right.

"Haven't seen you around. What did you say your name was?" the shorter one asked.

I'd hoped it wouldn't come to this, but I had to tell him the truth or dodge the question. "Damir Firewing of Milomir."

"Have you come to pledge your loyalty to Alpha Boro?"

"Actually, I came to visit the nursery. One of the old crones thinks there's been a mix-up and wants me to check the last clutch I brought in." Luckily, this was true. Whenever I liberated one of the Dragon Fae male offspring from the unfortunate village woman who gave birth to him, there was always an old crone who came calling after the lost child. Sometimes she came with the crying mother in tow and sometimes she came alone to bargain with me, but I'd yet to retrieve a Faeling without having at least one old woman appear on my doorstep requesting an exception or claiming there had been a mistake.

The women of the village knew the price of laying with a Dragon Fae, even if most insisted on believing it was only a tale mothers told their daughters to keep them away from men the families didn't approve of. Little did they realize that the old women spoke the truth. Some of them knew from experience, having paid the price of a lost babe in their youth.

Even though they'd tried warning the younger women, the maidens almost never listened, and then the old women came to bargain on their behalf. I served them tea and biscuits, heard them out, then sent them on their way. I'd never bothered to follow up on any potential mistakes. I didn't make mistakes. Yet, here I was, hoping these two young Dragon Fae guards might accept my story.

"Can't get into the nursery without the passcode," the taller one said, shoving his hand under his breastplate to scratch his chest.

I smiled wider. "Yes. I was hoping that one of you might help me with that. You have the passcode, don't you?"

The shorter one looked at the taller guard, then back at me. "We can't take you. We're on duty."

I made a show of glancing around the cavern. "No one here but me, and it will only take a minute. Surely you don't both need to stand here guarding some out of the way cave from our own kin."

The taller one yawned and stretched. "I'll go," he said. "I could use a bit of a walk."

His partner shook his head. "We've been assigned to guard this cave. Don't expect me to cover for you if one of the Alpha's lieutenants show up to check on us, and you're gone. It will be your ass, not mine."

"Aww. Come on, Luka. I'll only be gone a minute." He retrieved his spear and moved a few steps toward me.

One down. "Thank you. I really appreciate the help. I'm hoping to get back to the village before nightfall, so I promise not to dally."

"Oh, don't mind him." The guard I'd drawn away from his post waved toward his companion. "He's a stickler for protocol.

You're right, though. We've been standing guard outside this cave for days, ever since the last pair of guards got thrown into the pit for letting some bloke pretending to be a medic in to see the prisoner. It's a good thing the prisoner didn't escape, otherwise that pair would have been flayed and left for the vultures. At least this way they got to live, even if they did take quite the beating."

"And that bastard talks too much," Luka muttered, just loud enough for me to hear. Then, louder, he added, "If you're going, go. Don't just stand there yapping."

"I'll bring him right back," I said, following the taller guard into the tunnel that branched off to the left.

The guard ahead of me kept up a steady stream of chatter as we made our way further into the tunnel. Once we'd rounded a bend that prevented us from seeing the opening to the cavern we'd left, I caught him in a choke hold and held him until he passed out. Then I hurried back to the cavern to attempt to get the other guard to come and help.

Except, when I returned, I found the shorter guard slumped in a heap near the mouth of the cave. I hurried over to him and checked his pulse. He was still alive. I breathed a sigh of relief, then poked my head into the cave in time to see Arabella, now back in her Fae form, using her magic to break the cuffs that held Ved.

She'd propped him up by slinging one of his arms around her shoulders and wrapping her arm around his waist. When my feet scraped the stone at the mouth of the cave, she glanced up. Once she realized it was just me, she relaxed. "Help me with him."

I wrapped my arms around Ved's too warm body so I could hold him up while Arabella finished breaking his chains with her magic. Then, supporting my unconscious wing-mate between us, we retraced our path through the tunnels and out into the fresh air without being seen by any of the other Dragon Fae.

I stared back down the tunnel once we were outside. "That was too easy,"

"Your clan's guards are fools," Arabella said. "I can't believe they fell for that nonsense." She squatted, transferring more of Ved's weight to me as she adjusted her grip and repositioned the arm she'd draped over her shoulder.

"Honestly? I can hardly believe it myself. We should get out of here. Fast. Before they figure out what happened and come after us."

"Let me transport us this time. There's an infirmary next to the guard barracks."

"Do you have healers?" I thought of my grand-sire and glanced back toward the mouth of the cave.

"Yes." Her hand grasped my wrist, pulling my attention back to her. "So, whatever you're thinking of doing, don't. We're leaving."

I frowned. Grandsire would have to fend for himself for now. He'd understand. He wanted me to get Ved to safety. "All right."

Arabella nodded, then closed her eyes to concentrate.

In a blink the rocky outcropping was replaced by soft, moss covered turf. We stood facing a pair of long, low buildings surrounded by ancient trees.

"Take him inside," Arabella said. "There will be a guard in there who can assist you. I need to go retrieve one of the Hands."

"Aren't they all competing in the Conclave?" I wrapped both arms around Ved and lifted his unconscious body over my shoulder to make him easier to carry without Arabella's assistance.

"The matches should be over for the day. I'm sure at least one has been eliminated by now." She disappeared before I could respond.

I'd made it halfway to the door of the barracks before I realized that, if a Hand had been eliminated from the competition early, it must mean they were worse than the others. I hoped that only extended to their combat skills and not their blood magic.

By the time I had Ved settled in a bed at the far end of the infirmary, a broad-shouldered female with wet hair slicked back from her lean face strode through the door. She checked with the guard, then continued down the aisle to where I waited with Ved.

The Hand that Arabella had sent was only the second Fae female I'd met who wasn't a relation. I couldn't help but compare her to Seren. They were both beautiful, each in their own way, but I didn't feel drawn to this healer in the same way I'd been drawn to Seren from the moment I first looked into her silver eyes.

"You must be the Dragon Fae. Damir, right?" Her question pulled me from my thoughts and reminded me where I was and why.

"Yes. I'm Damir Firewing, or as you lot would say, Damir of Niamh. Thank you for coming." I gestured to the bed beside me. "This is my cousin, Ved."

"I'm Eira of the Ancients, but you can just call me Eira." She slid past me and bent over Ved, scrutinizing him from head to toe. Once she'd completed that exam, she started again at Ved's head, this time exploring my cousin using her hands. She'd reached Ved's shoulders when she paused and glanced back at me. "You don't have to stay. I can call for you if I need anything."

"Are you sure?" I asked. I hated the idea of Ved waking up

in a strange place without any familiar faces. Once he realized he was safe and healing and away from Boro, he would probably want to immediately return and fight.

"I work better without an audience. One of the reasons I'm here instead of still competing." Eira grinned at me.

"All right. I'll go, then. Just… Will you make sure that he doesn't leave? He needs to heal properly."

"Glad you agree. Don't worry. No transport in or out of the infirmary. He'll have to make it past that guard." She jutted her chin toward the figure standing near the door.

I nodded, hoping that Arabella was right about the talent of her guards. Then I backed away from Ved's bed and started back down the aisle.

When I stepped out of the barracks infirmary, I turned my head up to the sky and called for Sillag. My call was returned by a shadowy figure, leaning up against a nearby tree. It wasn't until what I'd mistaken as a high collar shifted and released a second whistling call that I recognized my other wing-mate and his faerie dragon.

Before I could say a word, Sillag swooped down to land on my shoulder and returned Tarmog's greeting. Her talons pierced the woven fabric of my button-down and pinched into my skin. Then she flapped her wings like she wanted to drag me forward, closer to the figures waiting to meet us.

I sent her a thought, reminding her she wasn't big enough to carry me and requesting she settle down. Her response was a low hiss in my ear followed by the bump of her spiked head against my own.

"How did you know to find us here?" I called to the shadowy figure under the tree.

Ivo stepped forward, allowing his face to be lit by a shaft of moonlight. Tarmog arched his long neck and stretched his wings wide, presenting his pale lavender chest to Sillag. The two cooed at each other, and I caught Ivo rolling his eyes.

"Well, go on already," he said to his familiar.

Once the pair took flight, circling above our heads and nipping at each other's tails and wings in playful greeting, I returned my attention to my cousin.

Ivo shook his head at the antics of our familiars. "Tarmog tracked Sillag here." He gestured toward the sky to where the pair had disappeared above the treetops. "When he told me that Firrag had joined you, I decided I'd better come as well."

"Firrag's here?" I asked.

"According to Tarmog." Ivo crossed his arms. "I took that to mean that Ved had escaped with you."

"Have you been here long?" I asked.

"No. Why?"

I shook my head and sighed. "It's more like I escaped, found help, and *then* returned to rescue him. We just got back."

"I see. And I take it Boro planned for Ved's challenge to be less than fair?"

I nodded. "He's in no shape to fight. He was weak as a Faeling when I left and unconscious when I returned. One of their healers is with him now."

Ivo scowled. "I want to see him."

"Come on." I waved for him to follow and started back toward the door to the infirmary.

11

WHEN Arabella finally arrived to collect my report, it was deep into the night. I had just managed to fall asleep and woke to find her standing over me. The moonlight shown bright enough to reveal dark streaks of blood smeared across her tunic, and the breeze carried the sour stink of sweat she hadn't bothered to magic away.

It was a look I was familiar with. I panicked at the sight of her and told her about the cambion, managing to keep my head enough that I left out the bit about Gwawr.

Arabella nodded and said, "Good work." She told me that she'd follow up with Liam, but first she needed to find a Hand to work some blood magic. Her only question was who had been eliminated from the Conclave so far.

I gave her Ioryn's name. She grimaced and asked who else. I admitted that I hadn't watched the end of Eira and Talie's match, so I didn't know which of them was out. She thanked me, and then she was gone. She didn't ask about Gwawr or about how I'd recognized the cambion.

I breathed a sigh of relief and laid back down on my cloak, thinking I'd get a bit of sleep. But I couldn't. I tossed and turned for the rest of the night, worrying about what or who Arabella had been fighting and who needed healing. Had my warning been too late? Had the demons already attacked?

At the first sign of light on the horizon, I gave up on rest and stood to stretch. Then I started the long walk back to the Conclave to find a safe spot to watch the day's matches. Gwawr would be up against Barr, first, while Anwen faced off against whoever won Talie and Eira's match.

The decision of which to watch was an easy one. Arabella cared about the favorites, and I cared about Barr and Anwen getting eliminated as quickly as possible. I also didn't want to get caught. Both of the people who knew I was lurking around the Conclave would be in the ring, so I didn't need to worry about them. But Barr could have warned the Elders to keep an eye out for me. So, I needed to be extra careful.

I made my way toward the lake, hoping to attach myself to a large group heading up to the matches. The shoreline was dotted with Fae, dipping into the cold water for a morning rinse. I longed to join them, but that would mean stripping down to bare skin, and that was something I couldn't do without risk of being recognized.

I started to move on when I spotted antlers out of the corner of my eye. I turned to look, and there he was. The cambion was bent at the waist, splashing water on his face, right there in the midst of a hundred or more Fae. I tensed, unsure what to do. I thought Arabella was going to deal with him.

He straightened and shook the water from his hair before turning to walk away from the lake. I followed his progress, taking care not to lose track of him, even as I maneuvered around the other Fae and tried to keep my head down. I lost sight of him for a moment when a trio of Faelings ran past, blocking my view. When I spotted him again, he was pulling on his shirt, and Brianne was at his side.

I exhaled. *Good.*

I didn't know why he was still at the Conclave, but at least it appeared that Brianne had been assigned to keep track of him. If Gwawr knew what was good for her, she'd keep far away from them. I had a thought to warn her but dismissed it. She wouldn't be that stupid, no matter what bargain she'd made with the beast.

The first horn blew, signaling that the matches were about to start. So, I left the cambion in Brianne's capable hands and hurried to catch up with the nearest group of Fae. Except, once I located a secluded place to watch and looked up to the raised platform positioned between the two rings, there he was again. This time he stood next to Liam. Brianne was still nearby, but neither seemed the least concerned about the cambion who was trying not to stare too long or too obviously at Gwawr.

When the match began, I noticed how his fists clenched every time Barr landed a hit. The tightness in his jaw was obvious even from where I stood. Watching him watch her was such a distraction that I almost missed the moment she conceded. For a breath, the cambion and I appeared to be perfectly aligned in our desire to rip Barr's throat out.

Then it was over, and everyone started moving around. Their attention was no longer on the competitors. Instead, they started searching for familiar faces to discuss and analyze what they'd just witnessed. I needed to relocate before someone spotted and recognized me.

I planned to disappear into the woods until the next match. There would be a break before Gwawr would have to compete against the winner of the redemption bracket. If she won, she would get another chance at beating Barr. I sent a prayer to the Ancients that Anwen hadn't also won her match, but either the Ancients weren't listening, or I truly was cursed. A group walking past in the opposite direction were just coming from the other ring where Anwen had defeated Talie.

I wasted no time retreating into the relative safety of the woods to sulk and think things over. Sure, Arabella had promised to find a position for me in the queen's guard if I spied for her. But if Barr, or worse, Anwen, ended up winning the Conclave, they would become the representative of the Elemental Faction on the Queen's Court. Neither of them would ever approve of Arabella's scheme, and I would be forced to continue trading demon heads for food, clothing, and shelter.

What was it that Damir had said about living alone? It was all right if it was your choice, but not if it was forced upon you. Something like that, anyway. I knew it was true, I just hadn't wanted to admit it to myself. But I couldn't ignore it any longer.

I needed a back-up plan, just in case Barr ended up winning. There wasn't any point in planning for the possibility that Anwen might win. If Gwawr didn't defeat her, then Barr would. Anwen was no match for either of them. The fact that she'd lasted as long as she had in this tournament surprised me. She should never have been able to beat Talie, not after how hard she'd had to work to defeat Ioryn.

It occurred to me that she might have secrets of her own that were worth uncovering. If she did manage to beat Gwawr, then I would focus my attention on exposing them. Until then, I needed to figure out what I could offer Barr to get him on my side.

Bargaining with humans was one thing. Bargaining with another Fae was something else entirely. I needed to be careful about what I said and when. I was going to have to promise something to Barr that might help him win the Conclave, but the only thing I had that might help was information about Gwawr. It would only be worth something if Gwawr beat Anwen. And even then, I only wanted to do it if I was sure that Gwawr couldn't, or shouldn't, win.

I considered my options until the horn blast announced that the competition would be starting soon. Then I took my time returning to the Conclave. Barr wasn't competing in this round, so it was very likely he'd be lurking among the spectators. I couldn't let him see me until I was ready to speak with him, so I hid until after the final horn that signaled the start of the match.

By the time I'd searched the crowd for Barr's unmistakable red hair and positioned myself where I could keep an eye on him while still keeping my distance from any other Fae who might try to speak with me, the match was almost over. I turned my attention to the ring just in time to see a cyclone swirl up around Anwen, trapping her inside. She only lasted a few moments before she signaled defeat.

The whirlwind dispersed as Gwawr moved to Anwen's side. Together they extracted Anwen's leg from the crack in the ground that had swallowed it up to her calf. Clever move, that. I was sad I missed it but seeing Anwen concede made up for it a bit. Once she was free, the crowd cheered. The pair of them smiled and waved until Anwen hobbled off and the spectators began chanting Gwawr's name.

I was about to leave when Gwawr turned her head toward the platform. I followed her gaze. There, alongside Cahal, stood Liam and his human mate. Between them was the cambion. Even though Cahal had begun to address the spectators, the half-demon's eyes were locked on Gwawr. Worse, she stood there staring back at him in front of all her Elemental kin.

Suddenly it was obvious. The cambion hadn't taken control of her mind. It was worse than that. He'd captured her heart. The Elementals would never accept a guardian with a half-demon for a mate. As it was, he had to be glamoured and accompanied by a guard in order to walk among us. What was she thinking?

Barr hopped the fence and took off at a loping jog toward where Gwawr stood. He waited for Cahal to finish his speech about how the pair of them would compete tomorrow for the honor of being named Guardian. Then he grasped Gwawr's hand and raised their joined fists to the sky.

As the crowd cheered him on, he proceeded to twirl and spin Gwawr, dipping her over one arm like a besotted fool. Gwawr grimaced and played along, but as soon as Barr released her, her eyes returned to the podium. To the cambion who'd been watching. Unless she was looking at Liam? That would be better, but foolish in a different way.

Gwawr retreated to her ready tent while Barr continued to hold the attention of the spectators with his antics. I pushed through to the outside edge of the crowd, then made my way around to catch Gwawr before she left the tent. I needed to test my theory about which of the two young males on the podium had claimed my friend's heart.

I crept around to the back of her tent and waited a few breaths, listening to make sure it was quiet inside. Then I used a bit of air magic to direct my whisper through the canvas.

"Gwawr?"

Soft footsteps approached the opposite side of the tent flap. Gwawr lifted the edge of the fabric and waved me inside.

Fixing a smile onto my face, I tugged the hood of my cloak back and flung my arms around my friend, squeezing her tight. "You did it! You really did it! You're one of the champions." I leaned back, holding her at arm's length and grinned. "I'm so proud of you."

Despite everything, it was true. I was proud of her, and I still wanted her to win.

"Thanks." Her cheeks flushed pink.

An idea occurred to me as I noticed her blush. "Do you remember when we were in crèche, and we used to play at being on the Queen's Court?"

She nodded and laughed. "Yes."

I danced away from her, mocking our carefree Faeling selves. "We used to take turns pretending Liam was our mate and our child would be the next Faerie Queen."

Gwawr sighed. "Ugh. Don't remind me."

I stopped and turned to face her so I could catch her reaction. "I saw you look to him after the match." I kept my accusation vague, needing to be truthful.

"What? Who?" If she had been looking at Liam, she might have blushed again. Instead, she looked a bit panicked. Like I'd caught her staring at the cambion.

I set my hands on my hips and decided to apply a bit more pressure, just to be sure. "The High Fae are dying off. Just look at them. He's taken a human as a mate! There are only four of them left, you know. You don't need him. If you become guardian, you can bring power back to the Elementals. We can rule the Fae. Don't you see?"

Gwawr's eyes narrowed, but she didn't jump to Liam's defense. "You sound like you've been talking with Barr."

"So what if I have?" I shrugged, pretending for a moment that I didn't loathe him. "You'd be better off looking to him as a mate. Forget about Liam."

"You think I should take Barr as my mate?" Gwawr wasn't buying it.

"You should at least take his child." I offered a pragmatic

reason as I grabbed her hand. "Just think. Your Faeling with Barr would be a force. If it's female, she could be the next Faerie Queen. Who among the High Fae will produce a Faeling to rival yours?"

"Fiona, for one. Or Arabella. Or even Liam. Just because he's taken a human as a mate doesn't mean he won't let a Fae female take his child."

Maybe she was thinking she might be that Fae female. Maybe she had been looking at him and not the cambion, after all. I decided to push one last time to see if I could get her to admit her feelings. "Forget Liam. He's not even a strong Elemental. He barely has a pair of elements under his control."

"I didn't mean…" Her denial was somewhat less than convincing, making me think maybe she had been thinking about Liam. I hoped that was true, for both our sakes.

I dropped Gwawr's hand and shoved it toward her as I released it. "Think of your kin. If you defeat Barr and become guardian, then what? What will you stand for? Would you even stand up for cast outs like me?" I hoped my questions might remind her of what was at stake.

"Of course I would." She reached for me, but I backed away.

"Just think about what I said, all right?" I pulled my hood up, retreating into it as I ducked out of the tent before she could respond.

My stomach growled. All of this lurking around and spying on spoiled Hands made it nearly impossible to keep myself fed. My hunger was yet another reminder that I was on my own. No one was going to take care of me, so I needed to take care of myself.

I considered my back-up plan. If Barr knew that I had information that could help him win, he might be willing to negotiate and agree to end the practice of banishing Cursehands. I could plant the seed and make up my mind about what to tell him if I thought that Gwawr was going to do anything stupid.

While I hesitated, considering my next move, a figure stepped out onto the path in front of me. As though I'd conjured him with my thoughts, Barr stood, facing me with his hands on his hips.

"Still here, then?" he asked.

I stepped back and flexed my hands, preparing to call on my magic, if needed. "Were you following me?" If he had been, he would have made a better spy than me. I only hoped he hadn't seen me leaving Gwawr's tent.

"Don't flatter yourself, Ren. I thought I warned you about hanging around where you're not wanted."

"You didn't. Worried that I'll mess up your match tomorrow?" I grinned.

Barr sighed, ignoring my taunt. "I suppose I should turn you in, since you don't seem to have enough sense to stay away on your own. Better for everyone if you leave."

"What if I have information that might help you become guardian?"

"What sort of information?" His eyes narrowed.

"I'll only tell you if you agree to my terms."

He glanced around. "What do you say we take this conversation someplace a bit more private?"

"I hear they bring champions a feast in their tent each evening."

"Oh, you've heard that, have you?" He squinted at me in the darkness. "I haven't eaten yet, and I suppose there's enough to share. Care to join me?"

"Only long enough to eat and agree on terms. I'm meeting someone later, and if I don't show up, they'll be looking for me."

"Don't worry, Ren. I wouldn't dream of touching a hair on your faulty Fae body." He gave no sign of liar's pains, so I followed him back to his tent.

12

IVO and I entered the barracks infirmary just as the healer, Eira, was leaving. She said she'd done what she could, for now, and would return after he woke up to see if there was anything else she could do to speed up his recovery. In the meantime, he needed to rest.

I thanked her and led Ivo to Ved's bedside.

"So where have you been?" I sat on the empty bed next to Ved's, suddenly realizing how long it had been since I'd slept.

Ivo took one look at me and shook his head. "You should get some rest, too. We'll talk when you're both awake."

"Are you sure? You're not going to disappear again as soon as I shut my eyes?"

"No. I won't leave. I promise."

"All right." I yawned. The sun would be coming up soon, but it didn't matter. Both of my wing-mates were safe. I could allow myself a short nap.

Stretching out on the cot, I closed my eyes. When I opened them again, the sun was setting and sending beams of golden-orange light through the window. They lit up Ved's profile in the bed across the aisle from me. He appeared to still be asleep, which didn't surprise me, given the extent of his injuries, but I was surprised that Ivo had let me sleep all day.

I propped myself up on one elbow, searching for my cousin. When I didn't see him right away, I sat up. True to his promise, he hadn't left. He had moved to the other end of the infirmary, near the door, where he was engaged in an animated conversation with the guard currently on duty. Ivo glanced over when he felt my eyes on him, excused himself, and made his way back down the long aisle toward me and Ved.

I waited, watching Ved breathe, until Ivo stepped between the two beds.

"He's still asleep?" I dipped my head toward Ved.

In response, Ivo reached out and set his hand on top of Ved's. I thought the gesture sweet until Ved surprised me by flinching away from Ivo's touch and turning over on his side so he faced away from us.

"So you *are* awake." I reached over to shove his shoulder, but Ivo caught my hand and shook his head.

Ved ignored me.

"Enough of this, you fire-brained fool." Ivo plopped down on the edge of Ved's cot. He gripped Ved's shoulder and attempted to roll him back onto his back. "You're not mad at Mir for rescuing you. Are you?"

His question made it sound like they'd discussed this already while I'd been asleep.

Ved opened his eyes to glare at Ivo. "I told him not to, and he didn't listen."

I crossed my arms. "It's a good thing I didn't. If I'd left you there, I'd have been coming to collect what was left of your body for the pyre."

He turned his glare on me. "Or I might have defeated that power hungry usurper."

"Right. After he'd starved you and allowed your wounds to fester until you were nearly delirious with fever. The odds were most certainly in your favor." I'd had just about enough of his single-minded grudge against the new Alpha. I hated Boro as much as he did, but I wasn't about to lose either of my wing-mates over it.

"Would you two give it a rest?" Ivo sighed. "Velibor was my sire, and while I appreciate your loyalty, it's not your fight. It's mine." He folded his hands in his lap and looked down at his feet.

"What?" My attention shifted from Ved to Ivo, shocked at what I'd just heard.

Ved struggled, trying to sit up and get a better look at Ivo's face. "You changed your mind?"

Ivo shook his head but kept his eyes on the floor. "I don't want to defend my sire's claim. I hate these blasted rules we adhere to like we're shackled to tradition. But if I do nothing, Boro will destroy what's left of our clan. He's even more fire-brained than you, Ved. He'll pick fights and call trials with any-one who so much as looks at him cross-eyed until there's no one left."

I didn't say anything because I couldn't disagree. Every-thing he'd said was true.

"You can't fight him," Ved said.

Ivo glanced up and grinned. "That's funny. Last time we talked, I'm certain you were the one trying to convince me to do exactly that."

Ved scooted back against the headboard so he could prop himself up in a seated position. His face paled with the effort. I started to reach out to steady him, but his body curled away from my touch. "I'm fine," he snapped at me.

I shoved my hurt feelings down. He'd get over his wounded pride eventually. "Ved's right," I said. "You'll need at least one lieutenant if you hope to succeed in challenging Boro. Better if you had two."

"Let me do it," Ved said.

"No." Ivo stood and paced to the end of the bed, then pivoted to face us. "It needs to be me. I couldn't live with myself if either of you attempted a challenge in my name and didn't survive."

"Blast your name. I planned to challenge for myself." Ved winced and pressed a hand to his side. If arguing was proving too strenuous for him, I doubted he would be ready to follow through on that challenge anytime soon.

"Not that I would deny you, Ved, but…" I let my voice trail off. Even putting aside his injuries, long ago we'd all agreed that Ved would make a terrible Alpha. Even Ved had shuddered at the thought. But if I dared to say as much while he was in this proud and angry mood, he'd snap my head off.

Ivo saved me from having to finish my awkward statement. "You would hate being Alpha." He sank into a chair at the foot of Ved's bed like the weight of our clan already rested on his shoulders.

"I might have changed my mind and installed one of you as Alpha after I won," Ved grumbled. He twisted his hand in the bed sheet.

Ivo stared straight ahead, back toward the door where we'd entered the infirmary. He ignored us as though he was listening to guidance we couldn't hear. Finally, in a quiet voice he said, "Regardless, I came to tell you both I'm going back. I'm going to challenge to take my sire's place. Boro will be the shortest reigning Alpha in the history of our clan, or he will reign over my dead body."

"If you're going, I'm going with you." Ved shifted his weight, preparing to swing his legs over the side of the bed and stand.

Ivo's reflexes were faster. His hand reached out and clamped down on Ved's ankles, directly above where they'd been shackled. Ved winced but refrained from crying out in pain.

"No." Ivo stared down Ved in a display of confidence and command that reminded me of his sire.

So much so that I responded without thinking. "I'll go with you to serve as your lieutenant." Without Ved, that would put me against both of Boro's lieutenants, forced to eliminate them from the fight on my own, or at least occupy them long enough that they couldn't interfere in Ivo's challenge of their Alpha. If I failed, they'd take out Ivo before he had a chance to defeat Boro.

"You can't let Mir fight them alone." Ved jerked and squirmed, trying to free himself from Ivo's grasp, even though he grimaced and paled with every movement.

I set a hand on his shoulder to keep him still. While I appreciated his insistence and agreed with him, in his current state he'd be more of a liability than an asset against Boro's lieutenants. He'd make for an easy target, and I'd have to work twice as hard to keep him from getting himself killed.

"Stay," I said. My command voice wasn't nearly as good as Ivo's. So, instead of expecting Ved to listen to reason, I gave him some incentive to obey his potential Alpha. "At least this way, if we die, you'll live to avenge us, right?" I tried to keep my voice light and confident, even though inside I trembled at the mere idea of combat.

I'd stopped training when Ivo's sire sent me to the village. I'd never liked it and used my assignment as all the excuse I needed to eliminate the painful and humiliating practice sessions. Still, Velibor sent Ivo and Ved to visit me each week and made them drag me out into the wilderness to transform and spar. I'd always spend the day following their visit slathered in healing balm from the village wizard, recovering with a book and feasting on the largest steak I could find.

After Boro and his lieutenants defeated our sires, I'd made a half-hearted effort to step up my training, anticipating the day when Ivo would decide to challenge the new Alpha. Ved and I kept it up even after Ivo left. But we couldn't risk transforming anymore, lest Boro know what we were up to. I hadn't shifted to my dragon form since before our sires were killed. I was out of practice, and this fight would likely be my last. But Ivo had declared his intention, and my place as his wing-mate was at his side.

"Mir's right." Ivo paused, tilting his head to one side like he was listening. Then he added, "Besides, we need you to look after Sillag and Tarmog. I don't want to take them with."

Boro and his lieutenants didn't have familiars. Bringing ours into the fight would allow them to exploit the familiar bond to weaken us. Any blow they managed to land on our familiars would be like a blow to ourselves, and if they managed to kill them… I shivered at the thought.

That thought reminded me of my promise to Seren, and I wondered if I had time to say goodbye. If I died in the challenge, Fiona would be annoyed at losing my seed, and Ivo's as well. If Seren wasn't interested, and I could hardly blame her if she wasn't, given that we'd had no time to get to know each other, I at least owed Fiona an explanation and an apology for not sticking around to uphold my end of our deal.

"All right," I said. "I owe our cousin, the Faerie Queen, an update, and there's someone I need to find before we can go."

I left before my wing-mates could start asking questions. As soon as I stepped outside, I called for Sillag. She coasted down from the roof of the barracks to land on my shoulder. Once she'd settled, I transported us to the clearing where I'd first encountered Seren.

But she wasn't there. I turned in a circle, not daring to call out to her. I'd hoped this would be easy. I didn't want to waste time trying to find Arabella so that I could ask her to locate Seren for me, but if I had to, I would.

When Sillag sat up and flicked the air with her tongue, it gave me an idea.

It hadn't been that long since Sillag had scratched Seren. If there was any faerie dragon toxin remaining in her system, Sillag would be able to locate her. Confirming my suspicion, Sillag cooed, her head facing a faint drumbeat coming from somewhere in the distance. Following my familiar's lead, I picked my way through the forest, moving toward what began to sound more and more like a celebration, already underway.

Sure enough, as we reached the edge of the trees, bright colors and movement filled the clearing beyond. Sillag nipped at my ear, nudging my head to the right until a figure separated from the tree trunk she'd been leaning against, her silhouette lit by the glowing lights of the party. I whispered her name as I crept closer.

Seren twisted around to face me, her body an arm's length from my own. "What are you doing here?" she whispered.

"I told you I'd come back." My fingers flexed at my side as I resisted the urge to touch her.

She took a step back as though she sensed my intent. "Did you save your cousin?" she asked.

"I did." I took a breath.

"Now what?" She glanced over her shoulder at the Fae

dancing in the clearing at the edge of the lake.

"Now I must repay the Faerie Queen for her assistance." I took half a step toward her. Leave it to me to end up drawn to the prickliest Fae female to walk the forests of England. It was as though she had no idea that I fancied her, that it was possible for anyone to fancy her.

"What does that mean?" she asked.

I jutted my chin in the direction of the celebration. "Care to dance?"

She stared at the hand I'd extended to bridge the gap between us and let my offer linger in the air unanswered for several heartbeats. "I'm not supposed to be here," she said.

I stepped closer. She hadn't refused me. "Then we'll keep to the shadows."

"I'm not dressed for a party." She gripped the edges of her cloak and tugged it tight around her shoulders.

I gazed out at the Fae, mingling and celebrating in the clearing, trying to judge what might be appropriate attire for this sort of affair. Then I returned my attention to Seren. "You're an Elemental. You have earth magic?"

"Yes." She opened her mouth as though preparing another excuse.

"Humor me, please?" I closed the distance between us and rested my hand on top of hers, where her fingers still curled into the fabric of her cloak. "Fancy us up, and let's celebrate. I've rescued my cousin, and I told the Faerie Queen I would attend the Conclave, hoping that would mean I'd get to spend more time with you."

She shook her head but didn't move away. "This is a very bad idea."

I was about to take that as a no and drop my hand when she closed her eyes. As I watched, her cloak shrank to become a velvet cape hugging her shoulders. Beneath it, a dark gown that shimmered in the moonlight and skimmed the forest floor replaced her tunic and leggings. My breath caught in my throat as my gaze traveled down, following the line of silky fabric as it flowed over the curves of her breasts and hips and thighs.

When I dragged my eyes back up to her face, I found her silver eyes framed by a mask that hid her features from the bottom of her nose to the middle of her forehead. A wind whipped at her hair, twisting it up into a swirling twist. As it settled atop her head, the color changed from spun silver to dark brown.

"A clever disguise," I said. "Though it does nothing to hide your beauty."

A frown pulled at the corners of her lips. "All Fae are beautiful," she said. "So, I'll hardly stand out in that regard."

I hooked a finger under her chin and tilted her face up to mine. "Perhaps," I said. "But I find it hard to believe that any are as stunning as you." Her lips parted, and I longed to kiss them.

"You've been here all of two days and already you've decided this?" She shifted her hands underneath mine, wrapping her fingers around my palm before twisting away and setting off toward the clearing. "Let's do this before I change my mind."

I let her pull me along behind her as she wove her way through the mingling Fae, closer and closer to the group of musicians playing jigs for the dancers at the edge of the lake. A few heads turned our way, but no gaze lingered for more than a passing glance.

She'd been right about the beauty surrounding us. Long and lithe Fae with skin in every shade from the palest white to the deepest brown were in attendance. All were dressed in their finest linen and silks with polished boots and gleaming sword and dagger hilts protruding from jeweled sheaths. They moved with the grace and power of predators as they circled and shifted among their kinfolk, grinning and greeting each other.

I'd never seen so many Fae gathered in one place. Fewer than fifty males made up the entire Dragon Fae clan, including the Faelings I'd rescued from the village. There had to be hundreds of Fae attending this celebration, more when you considered the smaller sorts like the Brownies and Pixies who darted about at our feet and the Sprites who flittered and swooped overhead.

Seren paused at the edge of the dancing and turned to face me.

13

DAMIR caught me spying and interrupted me before I'd had a chance to locate Gwawr among the guests. When he suggested we join the party, I agreed in part because I thought it might help me locate Gwawr, but we'd made it this far, and I still hadn't seen any sign of her. I was beginning to question what I'd been thinking allowing him to talk me into this plan.

"You're sure about this?" I asked.

Damir studied my masked face before responding to my question. "I would like nothing more than to dance with you until the sunrise, but if you wish to return to the forest, I'll go with you. We don't need to stay."

Even with my attempt at disguise, my body remained tense, anticipating the moment I would be discovered and punished for disobeying the rules of the Elders. This Dragon Fae offspring of Faerie Queen Godda's sister had no business accompanying me anywhere, especially to this celebration. Yet, he'd kept his promise and returned. And that promise had been freely given.

We'd made no bargain. He owed me nothing.

I dropped his hand, and stepped closer, raising my chin so I could continue to look him in the eyes. "Why are you risking being seen with me?" I asked.

"What your kin have done to you is wrong. You deserve to be here as much as any of these Elementals. I may not have the power to undo what's been done, but I will stand by your side and support your right to take your place within your Faction."

I lifted my hands to rest them on his shoulders. "All right, then." I could survive a few dances, and maybe even enjoy myself a bit. Besides, being able to move around might make it easier to spy on Gwawr and Barr.

Damir's hands slid around my waist. We stood that way for a moment, at the edge of the dancing as the rhythm of the drums and the melody of the flute washed over us. Then he lifted me into the air and turned in a half circle. My heart leap in fear and anticipation.

When my feet touched the earth, Damir took one of my hands in his and guided me into the fray with a hop, step, and twist. And just like that we found ourselves in the midst of the swirling mass of bodies. I followed his lead, trying not to think of all the rules I was breaking. The corners of my mouth twitched up into a grin that grew with every step and turn.

The more we danced, the more the world around us blurred into a kaleidoscope of colors. Despite my intention to keep watch for the two red-haired champions, my focus narrowed to just Damir's face, the steps, my laughter, and the beating of my heart in time with the drums. When the music slowed, he pulled me close and held me pressed against his chest.

"I'm thirsty." My parched tongue managed to produce only a scratchy whisper.

Damir heard and guided us to the outskirts of the dancing.

"Shall I get us some refreshment?"

I interwove my fingers with his, reluctant to let him go. "I'd rather not be left alone, I think." Since he'd very nearly promised to protect me from the wrath of my kin if I were discovered, I wasn't in a rush to leave his side.

"Then we'll go together." He smiled and started to guide us toward the tables of food and drink, but the enormity of what he was doing—siding with me, of all people, in spite of what I was—overtook me.

I pulled him back to me. When he turned, I closed the distance between us in one step, rising up on my toes to press my lips against his. His breath caught in surprise, and a spike of fear rammed through me. I shrank back, inhaling the musky scent of his skin as I sank back onto my heels, worried that I'd made an embarrassing mistake.

"Thank you," I whispered.

Before I managed to break away from him, he slid his hand around the curve of my waist to keep me pressed against him.

"Thank *you*," he replied. "I've been wanting to do that all night. Would it be all right if we tried that again?"

I nodded, staring into his eyes until they fluttered closed and our lips met a second time. First, with a feather light brush. Then again with more force, and a hunger that pressed us closer until my hand tangled in his hair and his fingers dug into my flesh and our mouths parted, allowing our tongues freedom to taste and feast on foreign flesh. My thirst disappeared, replaced by unfamiliar desire that burned low in my belly and radiated out to make my arms tingle and my legs weak.

The musicians paused between songs, and Barr's voice drifted to my ears, ruining the moment. I caught only a few words. *Blood*, *Hands*, and something about the Faerie Queen's decree. I didn't need more than that to fill in the rest. With the taste of Damir still wetting my lips, I tried to ignore Barr, already regretting my plan to give him information on Gwawr and suspecting that, even if it did prove useful to him, he'd find a way to slip out of our bargain.

Damir sensed my tension and broke our kiss to search for the cause.

"I need to go," I said. "You can stay if you like." I let my hands drop to my sides and started walking toward the refreshments. My cheeks burned with the knowledge that I'd let myself get caught up in a moment that didn't belong to me and never could.

Damir hurried to catch up. "I have no interest in staying if you're not with me."

I couldn't look at him, so I kept my eyes on the fruit laden table ahead and kept walking. "That's sweet and all, but you really don't get it, do you?"

His fingers brushed against mine, catching them and wrapping around my palm. I glanced down at our entwined hands, then increased my pace. He didn't let go until I stopped to pour myself a goblet of honeyed wine. So long as I'd risked attending this celebration, I'd at least eat and drink my fill.

Damir stood close to me, keeping one hand on my back as I selected fruit and meat from the overflowing platters.

"Aren't you hungry?" I asked, keeping my eyes fixed on the feast in front of me to avoid facing him.

"I won't be frightened away by your kin." He kept his voice quiet to avoid being overheard, and it came out in a low rumbling growl.

I paused with one hand hovering over a golden-brown leg of perfectly roasted turkey. "So you heard him, then?" Of course Damir had heard Barr spouting his theories. He may have bonded to a familiar like one of those human wizards, but he had Fae ears, like his true kin.

"I heard enough. Who is he?" Damir pressed his hand firmly against the thin fabric covering my skin and guided me away from the pointed ears of the other Fae at the refreshment table, toward the trees at the edge of the clearing.

"One of the Champions," I explained. "His name is Barrfhionn, and if he defeats Gwawr tomorrow, then he'll be the next Guardian of the Elementals."

"Then Gwawr must win." He stopped within a short sprint of the tree line, but far enough away for us to still be considered guests seeking a bit of privacy away from the heart of the festivities.

"She may not be any better." I positioned myself so that we stood shoulder to shoulder, facing the party. Gripping my plate in one hand and my goblet in the other, I searched the crowd for any sign of Gwawr among the mass of giddy, carefree immortals who wouldn't hesitate to attack me if they discovered what I was. "None of them think I belong here."

Damir turned to face me and brushed his fingers down the curve of my neck so they skimmed across my bare shoulder, then traced the edge of my dress across my back. "I do," he said.

His touch warmed me as much as his words. Too bad I couldn't give in to this emotion. "You may be the cousin of the Queen, but your opinion on this won't change anything."

"Even if I claim you as my mate and give you my seed?"

I spun toward him and nearly dropped my plate. He grasped it, steadying the contents before they tumbled to the ground, as I stared at him. "You can't do that."

"Fiona says she wants me to produce a Faeling. With an Elemental. I agreed in exchange for her help in saving Ved."

"She didn't mean *me*." I gaped at him.

"She said I could choose."

"Well, you need to choose someone else." I straightened my shoulders, attempting to adopt an aloof, disinterested composure, even though my heart refused to slow, and my damp palms made it difficult to grasp the stem of the goblet in my hand.

Damir squinted at me. "Is that because you don't want me? Or because you're scared of them?"

"I'm not scared of them."

"Then you don't want me." He frowned.

"I didn't say that." I couldn't say that. Not without suffering from liar's pains.

Damir cocked his head to one side as though he was listening. He scowled. "I need to go."

I sighed with relief that he hadn't pressed the issue. "Finally, you're talking sensibly." I didn't want to lose my only ally, but I refused to let him do something stupid that he would later regret.

"No." His hands slid up my arms and settled on my shoulders. "I meant everything I said. My seed is yours if you want it, even if you don't want me as a mate. But right now, I need to go tend to my cousin. Did you hear Sillag's call?"

I shook my head. I hadn't heard anything over the roar of my panic.

"I'll find you later, all right?" He kissed the backs of my hands, then hurried into the forest.

I longed to follow him. Not to see his cousin, and not because I wanted to take him up on his ridiculous offer. That was out of the question, and the sooner he figured that out, the better. Cast outs weren't allowed to reproduce. Someone should have told him. I should have told him. But I'd held my tongue.

Who was I kidding? I wanted what he offered. All of it. I wanted to dance and celebrate the champions. I wanted to celebrate my friend, even if she was behaving like an idiot. If she lost to that purist prick Barr, I might never have a place among my kin. The best I could hope for would be Barr agreeing to the terms I'd offered in exchange for information. That would at least allow cast outs like me to live our celibate lives among the Elementals, even if we remained tainted by superstition and fear.

More likely, my life would continue as it had been, risking my life killing demons for humans just so I could survive in the forest, alone. No family. No home. No respected position in the Queen's Guard.

And here was this strange Dragon Fae offering me everything I'd always wanted. How could I resist?

The answer came easily. I was cursed. Inevitably, if I accepted Damir's offer without Fiona's blessing, once she learned what he'd done, she would be forced to either confront the Elemental Elders or banish a cast out Faeling with a High Fae sire. A Faeling who would one day sit on the Faerie Queen's Court or be named an heir worthy of wearing the queen's iron crown.

Then again, Fiona wouldn't have to confront the Elders and change the rules about cast outs if she wanted our Faeling. She could just force Damir to claim the Faeling and abandon me.

It wasn't worth it. I had no hope of a future with Damir, regardless of what he offered me. We'd danced, and I'd stolen my kiss. That alone was more than I'd ever dreamed possible. The Ancients had seen fit to grant me control of too many Elements to be a normal Elemental and too few to be a Hand. Kisses from princes only broke curses in human fairy tales, not among the Fae.

14

LEAVING Seren alone was the last thing I wanted to do, but I couldn't ignore Sillag's call. She found me as soon as I stepped into the forest, and I transported us back to the infirmary without asking any questions. When we arrived, Ivo was standing outside, waiting for me.

"What is it? What happened? Is Ved all right?" The questions spilled from my mouth in a worried rush.

Ivo nodded. "Peace, Mir. Everyone's fine. Sillag didn't tell you?"

I turned my head toward where my familiar was curled on my shoulder, and she lifted her head. *Tell me what?*

Her vertical eyelids blinked closed as she settled her head back down on her wing with a gentle coo that told me nothing aside from the fact that she knew exactly what she'd done and didn't mind one bit.

"Apparently not." Ivo chuckled. "The Faerie Queen is here. You said you needed to go meet with her. When she arrived here, I thought I'd send for you so that you didn't spend the rest of the night searching for her."

"Fiona is here?" That did save me the trouble of going to see her, but the discussion I needed to have with her could have waited, and Sillag knew that. I shot her a glance out of the corner of my eye, but she ignored me and pretended to be asleep.

"She's inside with a healer named Talie who's having a look at Ved and hopefully telling him that he's still in no shape to transform."

"Do you really think we can do this without him?"

Ivo shrugged. "I don't know. We could wait until he heals, but the longer we wait, the more time Boro has to turn the clan against us."

I nodded. "Then we better get inside so I can disappoint our cousin."

Sillag raised her head when I said the word "inside" and decided to relocate herself to the trees as I started walking toward the infirmary door.

"Disappoint Fiona?" Ivo hurried to catch up with me.

"I promised her something in exchange for help rescuing Ved, and she's not going to be happy when she hears what we're planning."

Ivo and I walked down the aisle between the rows of mostly empty beds. Two other beds besides Ved's were now occupied. One had been taken by an Elder Brownie, and another by a badly wounded Rogue. Their beds were both closer to the door. Ved remained at the far end of the room. As Ivo had warned me, he wasn't alone.

Talie and Fiona were talking in low voices at the end of Ved's cot while Ved was busy examining a long gash in his side that had previously been hidden under a bandage. From across the room, it appeared that the healer had done an excellent job patching him up.

The wound was closed and no longer weeping blood and pus, which was a definite improvement. The skin would probably be knitted back together by morning. Perhaps Ved was closer to full strength than we thought.

"You're looking much better," I said, drawing everyone's attention to me.

Talie rubbed his palm against the shaved side of his head. "Outside is looking good. Inside is going to need a while, still."

"How much longer?" Ivo asked.

Talie turned to look out through the window where a thin crescent moon lit up the sky. "Should be up and sparing again by the new moon, but I wouldn't recommend transforming until the one after that. Dragons are big, complex creatures. Too much of a risk shifting too soon after injuries like this. Better to be safe."

"You want me to wait nearly two cycles?" Ved's fingers dug into the sheets.

Talie nodded. "Could be sooner. I'll keep checking in on you. We'll have you back in tip top shape in no time. Queen's orders." He bowed to Fiona then dipped his head at me and Ivo. "I'll leave you to your meeting."

Fiona's eyes followed Talie down the aisle. For a moment, I thought I saw something in her look, but before I could be sure, she flashed a smile at Ivo. "Have I mentioned yet how pleased I am to have both my cousins returned home to the forest?"

She motioned for us to sit on the bed next to Ved, but she remained standing. "I hope you know that you are welcome to stay as long as you like. You needn't rush back."

"Ved told you we're leaving, didn't he?" I asked, plopping down at the far end of the empty cot so there was plenty of room for Ivo and Fiona to sit as well.

Fiona glanced at Ved then back at me. "Your wing-mate might have said something to that effect."

"If you'll allow me to explain, Your Highness." Ivo didn't bother sitting down. I got the feeling that he wouldn't unless she did.

"Please. Call me Fiona. We are cousins, after all." Fiona's eyes pinged between the three of us, watching us closely, almost like a hawk. "Ved mentioned something about a challenge?"

Ivo shifted his weight between his feet. "Damir will have told you that Meara's mate, my sire, was the Alpha of our clan until recently. The Dragon Fae who killed him is a dangerous ruler. He will be the ruin of our clan. It is my duty to avenge our sires by challenging this new Alpha and taking his place. If I am worthy."

Fiona clasped her hands together. "If it is a matter of disposing of an unworthy ruler, allow me to dispatch a unit of my guard to assist you. It is in the interest of all Fae that all our Factions remain strong and healthy."

Ivo spread his hands, palms up between them. "If I could accept your generous offer, cousin, I would. Unfortunately, the traditions of our clan require a challenge be between an Alpha and his two lieutenants on one side and the challenger and his two lieutenants on the other."

"Two lieutenants?"

"Yes."

"Then you plan to wait until Ved is healed." Fiona's shoulders relaxed as she exhaled.

"They're not waiting. They're not planning on taking me with them," Ved grumbled.

Fiona looked from Ved to Ivo to me. Whatever she saw on our faces caused her brow to wrinkle. "Correct me if I'm mistaken, but I only count one challenger and one lieutenant among you, in that case."

"You are correct, cousin." Ivo folded his arms across his chest.

"All right." Fiona nodded. "Then, as you are short one lieutenant, allow me to offer one of my finest guards to take Ved's place at your side."

I grinned. Ivo still had no idea why this cousin we'd never met was suddenly so concerned about our safety. I could have jumped in with a suggestion that might help alleviate Fiona's true concern, but I decided to keep my lips pinned shut, at least until Ivo finished explaining why we couldn't take one of her guards with us.

"Your guards are Elementals, are they not?" he asked.

"Their Commander is Arabella of Rionach, and there are some Rogues who serve in my guard, but yes, they are mostly Elementals. Why? Is that a problem?"

"Only in that a Dragon Fae challenge is executed in our Dragon forms. Unless you have any other Dragon Fae hiding in your forest, I think Damir and I are on our own."

A flush colored Fiona's brown cheeks. Her passionate response made it clear that Ivo had pushed her to the limit of her attempts at diplomacy. "What about the rest of your clan? Is there no one who would stand with you? If you can't draw on the loyalty of even one other member, what makes you think they will follow you if you win?"

One corner of Ivo's mouth twisted up in a lopsided grin. "Simple. They hate Boro. We all do. But they also fear him. None will stand against him until after there is no longer breath in his body, and I've covered the floor in his blood."

Fiona swallowed. "I see."

I cleared my throat to draw her attention away from Ivo and the graphic image he'd chosen to present. "I do want you to know that I haven't forgotten the promise I made you in exchange for the help you provided bringing Ved to safety."

"What did you promise, Mir?" Ved whispered the question to me in a tone still loud enough for Fiona and Ivo to hear.

I responded without looking at him. "My seed."

"But she's your cousin!" Ved lurched forward too fast, trying to shove into my field of view, and winced.

I glanced over to make sure he was okay. "Not for her, you fire-brained fool. She needs a High Fae heir. She can produce them herself, but it will take time. Better that all the cousins pitch in to help."

Ved grimaced. "Ivo, too?"

Both our heads turned to look at Ivo, but he was already looking at Fiona.

She raised one eyebrow in question. When Ivo didn't respond to her silent inquiry, she said, "Ideally. Yes. Ivo, too."

"So that's why you're so keen on sending along your guards to keep us from getting ourselves killed in challenge combat? And here I thought you were being generous because we're family."

Fiona opened her mouth, shut it, then opened it again. "How about both?"

"Do you already have females selected, ready, and waiting, as well?"

"I wasn't exactly expecting you."

"Well, then. I suppose this will have to wait until we return."

"And if you don't?"

"Then I suppose you'll have to hope a few more cousins appear on your doorstep looking for assistance."

"Um…" Ved raised a finger. "What if—and I'm not saying I'm huge fan of this option, but we're not related, and this deal you made with Mir was all on account of me in the first place—what if you took my seed instead? Would that help?"

Fiona turned her fierce brown-eyed stare on Ved. "I had already planned to do that, but since you've offered, I accept."

Ved squirmed under Fiona's intense gaze. "Do you, uh… want it now? Or… Should I take you to dinner first? How do you forest dwellers usually do this sort of thing?"

Fiona raised her eyebrows. "Well, I am queen. So, I do need to consult my Court before I impregnate myself. There are the usual diplomatic issues that must be discussed. We wouldn't want to offend any of the other factions by allowing the firstborn of the queen to be sired by a Dragon Fae. Though it does save me having to choose between the Rogues and the Elementals."

Ved's forehead wrinkled in confusion. "So I'll just wait here until you have that all figured out?"

"Given how devoted you Dragon Fae seem to be about putting yourselves in situations that will inevitably get you killed, I rather think I better take it now. But I can't call a meeting of the Council until after we have a new Guardian." Fiona leaned toward Ved. "So long as I have your word that you will not leave this infirmary without my permission, that will be enough, for now."

Ved nodded. "You have my word. I'll be here. About that date, though…"

Fiona straightened and fixed Ved with a look. "No. There will be no dates. This is a purely business arrangement."

I lifted a hand to cover my smirk. Perhaps I had been right about her feelings for that healer. It was certainly interesting that she was turning down my objectively handsome wingmate's attempts at romance. Granted, they were being offered from a sick bed by someone who had only recently regained consciousness after being left to die of infection in a cold, damp cave. He wasn't in top form. I'd seen him do better with the young women in the village.

Fiona returned her attention to Ivo. "Don't die." She turned to look at me. "Either of you." Then, without waiting for a response, she stepped past Ivo and stalked down the aisle, straight out the door.

"That was certainly… interesting." Ivo caught my eye. "You could have said something. Warned me?"

The laughter I'd been holding back bubbled up. Once I started, I couldn't stop. Until Ved joined me and immediately doubled over in pain. Then I sobered and switched to rubbing circles on his back until he could sit up straight again.

Ivo sat down on the end of Ved's cot and shook his head.

I wished I knew what he was thinking. "I'm sorry. I thought I could take care of it without getting you involved. That's why I left."

"Speaking of leaving…" Ivo tilted his head to one side and stared out at the room. He was quiet for a moment. Then he said, "It will be best to go now while our faerie dragons are distracted."

"You want to leave now?" If I left without speaking with Sillag, she'd be cross for weeks. Then again, if I did try to say goodbye, she'd insist on coming with. At least this way, if I didn't survive, she would live.

Ivo nodded. "I'm not sure where Firrag is, but I have a good idea what Sillag and Tarmog are up to. If I'm right, they won't be back until morning."

Ivo patted Ved's leg, then started toward the door.

Ved grimaced. "I hate this."

I squeezed his shoulder. "I know. I'm sorry we're leaving you behind. But, before I go, there's something else I need to ask of you."

Ved waved a hand in my direction. "Of course I'll look after Sillag. And I'll look after Tarmog, too."

I snorted. "Thanks, but that wasn't what I was going to ask."

"What is it, then?" Ved crossed his arms and leaned back against the wall at the head of the bed.

I hesitated. "There's someone else I'd like you to look out for if I don't return."

"Someone else?" Ved smirked. "I've been chained to a wall awaiting trial, allowed to waste away until I was nearly dead, and somewhere in between all that rescuing you were supposed to be doing, you had time to find yourself a female? Well played, Mir. Is it the wolf Fae you brought with you?"

"No, you fool. Arabella is my cousin. The female I need to you to look after is named Seren. Sillag knows how to find her. Tell her… tell her to fight for what she wants, and that I'm sorry I can't be there to fight at her side."

"Fascinating… Is she my type? Since it doesn't look like I have much of a chance with the queen, maybe this Seren might be interested…? If you're out of the picture, of course."

I punched his shoulder. "Find your own mate."

"Only if you come back and claim yours." Ved grinned. "Now go defeat that smoke for brains furnace arse already. And return. Queen's orders, remember?"

I nodded, then hurried to join Ivo outside.

15

DAMIR never returned, and I spent the rest of the evening hiding in the trees, watching my kin celebrate and gaining no new information in the process. I stayed up, expecting either Arabella or Brianne to appear, asking for a report, but even they seemed to have forgotten about me. In the morning, there was nothing left to do but return to the Conclave to see if my friend or my foe would emerge victorious.

Crouched among the trees, I watched the Fae gather for the match. Even though most had already found their places around the outside of the ring when the first horn sounded, calling the champions to their ready tents, I remained in my hiding place. I waited until after the second horn, the one that called the Champions to the ring and officially started the match, before I crept out and made my way toward the arena.

Between bodies, I caught a glimpse of short red hair and a burst of fire, then the spectators sucked in a breath, almost as one, held it for a moment, and released it in a roar of approval.

I had no idea what was going on, so I kept moving. The crowd thinned as I neared the ready tents. I wasn't sure which was whose, but it didn't matter. At least not yet. It would only matter after the match, and only then if Gwawr won.

I caught my first glimpse of her as she sent a gale force wind whipping him back toward an enormous crevice in the earth. Barr fought her for control of the air, but even I could tell that Gwawr was the better Hand. She attacked aggressively. She moved like she wanted to win as badly as Barr said he did. Every attack used multiple elements. I found myself caught up in the action, my heart racing, cheering with the rest of my kin who had traveled from the farthest reaches of the forest to attend this event.

The last Conclave had been held centuries before I was born. I wondered if my sire and dam had stood around a ring like this watching Cahal defeat some other Hand to be anointed Guardian of the Elementals. Cahal stood on the platform now, watching the match with his offspring, Liam of Flida. They were the only two on the platform. At least the cambion was no longer at Liam's side.

The information I had wouldn't be helpful to Barr with the cambion gone. But that didn't matter. If Barr won this match, I would shrink back into the forest and remain isolated and alone.

Barr tumbled into a gap Gwawr opened in the earth. Then she sent a blast of water up from the depths of the crevice that spat him back out and washed him to her feet. She pressed her advantage by pinning him to the earth with vines. Barr struggled briefly, then conceded. It was over.

Gwawr reached down to help him to his feet, but Barr leapt up and grasped her hand only long enough to bend and kiss her knuckles. Then he waved to the crowd and walked toward the tent closest to where I stood. His eyes found mine and his grin faltered. He glanced toward the side of his tent, then back at me before disappearing inside. I took that as my cue to join him there.

Pulling my hood tight around my face, I hurried to the far side of his tent. He wanted the information I had offered. If he agreed to my bargain, then I would follow through with my back-up plan. Now that the cambion was gone, maybe it wouldn't matter that Gwawr had been the one to bring him here. If Gwawr was removed from the competition, at least I would have a chance at living a normal life when Barr was anointed guardian. I inhaled deeply and exhaled before reaching for the edge of the tent flap and sliding inside.

"Tell me everything you know. Now," Barr commanded, not bothering with any greeting or pleasantries. The grin he'd worn for the Fae gathered outside was gone. Alone, protected by the canvas walls of the tent, he fumed and paced. The air around him shimmered with heat.

"First you have to promise me—"

He cut me off. "Yes. I promise. The Cursehands will be allowed to remain among the Elementals. I'll spin it so that our caring for those who are cursed is a way of doing penance to honor the Ancients or some nonsense like that. But…" He held up one finger and glared at me. "The cursed will still be barred from breeding. I might even make your lot take a vow of silence."

I met his glare with one of my own. "You will do no such thing."

"Tell me."

I decided his promise was good enough. "Gwawr came to me in the forest before the Conclave and she had a demon with her."

Barr's eyes widened to show the whites, and his mouth

dropped open. It took him a moment to recover. "You must have been mistaken. She would never have brought a demon to the Conclave."

"She did. I confronted her about it, and she admitted it. She tried to pass him off for Fae. I may be cursed, but even I can see through a glamour." I'd had the help of faerie dragon toxin, but he didn't need to know that bit.

He crossed his arms. "Even if this is true—"

"It is true." I held my arms out from my sides, allowing my cape to drape down my back and giving him full view of my body.

He waved a hand at me and rolled his eyes. "I can see that. You're obviously not suffering from the pains. But still. What does it matter now? I haven't seen a demon hanging around."

"He might still be here. I saw him yesterday during Gwawr's match against Anwen."

"You're sure?"

"I'm positive."

A rustling movement in the tent canvas caught my attention. Barr and I both turned our heads to look, just in time to watch Anwen step into the tent. She tossed her hair over one shoulder and squared her shoulders.

"I heard my name," she said.

"How long have you been listening," I asked.

Her eyes narrowed at me. "Long enough to know that, one, you shouldn't even be here, and two, Gwawr doesn't deserve to be guardian."

I sighed. "This was supposed to be between you and me, Barr. Tell Wenny to keep quiet."

Barr began pacing. Anwen and I glared at each other as we waited for him to speak.

"No." He stopped moving and turned his back to me so

he could face Anwen. "Wen, I think your sire and dam should know about this breach in security right away. If Seren is right, then there could be a demon walking among us."

Anwen's eyes softened as Barr spoke. "Of course," she said. "I'll go and tell them right away."

Barr caught Anwen's hand in his, then bent at the waist as he brought it to his lips so he could kiss the back. She nearly swooned. I nearly gagged. Her free hand fluttered over her breast as she curtsied. Then she scurried out of the tent.

"You can't be serious," I said.

"What difference is it to you?" he asked. "If this information succeeds in removing Gwawr from the Conclave and anointing me guardian, you get everything you asked for. I'll even take back that bit about making you take a vow of silence." He grinned.

"You're impossible."

"You have to admit, it's better for everyone if this comes from Anwen. If it came from me, it would appear to be petty. Retaliation for losing a match."

I had to admit, he had a point.

"You should go," he said. "I don't want anyone finding you in my tent."

"Whatever else she may be, Gwawr is still a better champion than you." I pulled my cape tight around my shoulders and prepared to leave.

"We are well matched. I agree." He tapped a finger against his chin. "Perhaps I'll take Gwawr as my mate instead of convincing Fiona to take my seed. Together we could take the throne from that trio of High Fae weaklings."

"You're dreaming. Gwawr will never agree to be your mate."

"Shall we make it part of our bargain?"

I shook my head. "No. We've already spoken more words to each other than I'd intended. If I stay, you'll only find ways to use mine against me. I'm leaving. Just remember your promise."

I lingered outside his tent, waiting and listening to see what he'd do. He remained inside only a few moments longer, then emerged through the flap on the far side. My view was blocked by the tent, so I started to edge around the outside to try to get a glimpse of which way he'd gone.

The scrape of a boot on gravel followed by a yelp and an apology rooted me to the ground.

"Watch where you're going." Barr's scolding sent the other party into a fit of awkward blather. Barr interrupted the groveling in a smooth, low tone with a more inviting edge to it. "Where are you off to in such a hurry anyway?"

I could almost hear the grin in his voice, and it made me want to roll my eyes back into my skull. Instead, I mentally kicked myself for being idiot enough to think I could bargain with him. No good would come of it, no matter how well thought out my words had been. He'd find a way to slip free of our agreement.

The response from the poor soul he'd run into caught my attention. "Master Cahal wants to see Gwawr in his tent right away, Champion."

"I see." Barr's voice practically purred with satisfaction. "Well, I mustn't keep you, then."

"I *am* sorry, Champion. I hope I didn't injure you in any way."

Barr chuckled. "Not to worry. I'm quite well. Quite well, indeed."

I waited until the sound of boots on gravel diminished enough that I judged it safe to take a peek. By the time I reached the edge of the tent, both Barr and the messenger sent for Gwawr had disappeared. With my hood up, I started towards the woods, keeping my eyes straight ahead and adjusting my path to avoid any encounters with any passing Fae.

I'm sorry, Gwawr. I had to do it. The thoughts tumbled through my head on repeat as I fled to safety among the trees. Pain pinched at my sides, nothing strong enough to indicate lying, but then again, I hadn't actually spoken the words aloud.

I didn't have time to consider my motives further. As soon as I stepped into the forest, a fluttering in the branches above caught my attention. When I looked up, a blue scaled head with twin silver horns stared down at me. Vertical eyelids blinked across orange eyes, once, twice, before I recognized Sillag. She arched her neck, showing off the silver feathers that covered her belly, then stretched her wings. When she took flight, it was only to glide to another tree, just ahead.

She folded her wings once she settled on the branch and twisted her long neck to look back at me. Her forked tongue flicked in and out, tasting the air. I turned in a slow circle, searching between the trees, looking for some sign of Damir, but he wasn't there.

When I lifted my head to the treetops, the faerie dragon spread her wings and glided on to the next tree. Catching on, I began walking, following her through the woods. Once I realized that she was leading me back to the clearing where I'd first encountered Damir, a nameless fear took root in my belly. I hurried, worried that I would emerge from the trees to find the prince bloodied and broken, lying on the forest floor. Sillag's eerie call did nothing to ease my worry.

I reached the clearing to find not one, but two faerie dragons circling overhead, and still no sign of Damir. I stared up at the pair, letting my hood fall back, unsure what this meant.

Damir wouldn't have left without his familiar, and now his familiar had a friend. He'd said he needed to leave to see to his wing-mate. Perhaps this other faerie dragon was his wing-mate's familiar?

The pair of them glided down until I could nearly reach up and touch them. Then, the green faerie dragon swooped up to perch on a high branch as Sillag drifted lower to land on a lower branch that hung out into the clearing. She settled facing me, folding her wings neatly against her sides, and stared at me.

I took one step toward her, and she cocked her head to the side. Remembering Damir's instructions, I extended my hand, palm up, and spoke to her in a low, calm voice.

"What is it? Where's Damir?" I crept closer, keeping my hand out, feeling like an idiot for speaking to a creature who clearly wasn't going to respond.

Sillag opened her jaw and let out a melodic squeak, then flicked her tongue and cocked her head to the other side. I stopped, unsure what to make of her behavior. Before I could decide what to do next, she stretched her wings, flapped once, and glided over to land on my outstretched arm. Her talons cut into the sleeve of my tunic, piercing through it to press into the skin of my forearm, as her tail curled in my palm.

An image of the queen's guard barracks flashed in my mind. I didn't have time to consider how, or what it meant, because a flash of light signaled the arrival of a sprite, one bearing a request from Arabella. She wanted a report.

16

IVO led the way down the long, winding cavern that took us deep inside the mountain. We walked in silence, directly to the largest cave, where the clan gathered to honor everything from feast days to challenge trials. My fingers curled and flexed at my sides as the tension in my body filled and released. This fight might be the end of me. I might die inside this mountain, just like my sire. I didn't want this, but I had no choice. This was the way of our clan. Senseless and stupid and brutal traditions that spanned millennia and kept the blood of the Dragon Fae fierce and strong. Or so we believed. I wasn't convinced.

Lights and laughter lit up the inside of the gathering cave. Boro lounged in the center of the room, surrounded by his three lieutenants. There had been only two when he'd defeated our sires. I glared at the new pledge, trying to remember his name and lineage, as I followed Ivo onto the balcony carved into the rock walls above the main floor of the cave.

There was a steep drop off at the edge with no railing. The

sheer face descended to form the top of a ring of tiered seating that circled the bare center floor. To descend from this height, we'd need to transform into our dragon skins.

The new pledge must have felt my eyes on him, because he turned his face up to where we stalked the balcony above. When his eyes met mine, he recoiled but quickly recovered. His hand went to the curved short sword that hung from a belt at his waist, and he whistled an alert to get the attention of the others.

Ivo stopped walking and turned to face the pit. I stayed just behind his left shoulder, struggling to keep my face steely as I sized up our opponents and calculated the odds we'd succeed in a two to one fight.

"Come looking for your wing-mate?" Boro called up to us. "Hate to disappoint you, but he's no longer here." His eyes narrowed, lasering past Ivo's shoulder to lock with mine. "Though I suspect Damir probably already knows something about that. Don't you?"

"That's not why we're here." Ivo folded his arms across his chest.

"Came to pledge your loyalty to your Alpha, then?" Neno, the lieutenant who'd gouged my sire's eyes out stepped forward, blocking Boro's view of us.

The other two lieutenants chuckled, but Boro shouldered Neno out of the way, so he could take his place at the front of his pack. The three lieutenants scrambled into wing positions, revealing their ranks and revealing that Toma's lethal foreclaws had earned first lieutenant.

"Come down and feast with us." Boro gestured to the roasted goat laid out on the table set for four on a platform at the opposite end of the cave. "There's more than enough to share. I have some ideas on how you might prove your loyalty. There doesn't have to be more bloodshed."

Ivo's shoulders tensed. Then he exhaled. For a moment I thought that maybe he might not say… "I challenge you for Alpha."

The words I'd dreaded hung in the air. Toma and Neno smiled toothy grins as the new pledge paled and shuffled back a few steps. Probably hadn't thought he'd be seeing much action so early in Boro's reign. His panic marked him as the weak link. He wouldn't be dangerous until he got desperate. Toma and Neno would be my first priorities, but I'd need to keep an eye on the new pledge, just in case.

I hated everything about this, but I especially dreaded what came next.

"Challenge accepted." Boro tapped his chest twice then pointed at Ivo. "I name my lieutenants as Toma Broadwing, Neno Spikewing, and Aco Cavewing."

"Can he do that?" I whispered the question to Ivo, hoping he might point out that clan tradition allowed two lieutenants in a challenge, not three.

Ivo ignored me and called down to Boro to announce me as his lieutenant, as though it weren't obvious already. Then he asked, "Who will act as arbiter?"

The three males behind Boro were busy stripping themselves of their weapons. They'd shoved aside the place settings on the table so they had room for their stockpile.

Boro motioned to Aco, the new pledge, and bent toward him to give him instructions. Aco jogged off through the lower entrance as Neno and Toma bounced on their toes and rotated their thick necks, waiting for the moment Boro would give the signal to shift form.

Ivo turned to me while we waited for Aco to fetch an arbiter. "I'm sorry about dragging you into this, especially without Ved." He let his arms drop to his sides, but the veins in his neck bulged with tension. "If I don't make it through—"

"If you don't make it, neither of us will, so I don't think there's any need for a speech." I set my hand on his shoulder and squeezed. "We've trained for this, right?"

Ivo nodded and swallowed. The color had started to drain from his face. Over his shoulder I caught the return of Aco. He brought with him the short burly guard who I'd failed to lure away from Ved's cave. The one Arabella had knocked out.

I edged closer to Ivo so that he stood between me and the view of the guard below. If I could shift form before the guard recognized me, I might be able to avoid a scene. If Boro found some reason to detain me, Ivo would have to fight without any lieutenants. I couldn't let that happen.

I lifted my other hand so that they both rested on Ivo's shoulders and locked eyes with him. "Your sire was Alpha Velibor. He reigned for hundreds of years. He took a Fae princess as his mate. He trained us and taught us how to survive in this clan. How to fight. His power is within you. You're Ivo Lightwing of Velibor. We will fight them, and we will win. For your sire. For my sire. For Ved's sire. And for Ved."

Ivo grinned. "Don't forget about Firrag, Sillag, and Tarmog."

"And because our cousin the queen commanded us to." I dug my fingers into the muscles of his shoulders. "We will win."

He nodded. "We will win."

"Fire. Ash. Light. Wing-mates for life."

He set his hands on my shoulders and pressed his forehead to mine. "Wing-mates for life."

"If you two are ready," Boro called up from below. "We have an arbiter and are ready to shift."

Ivo nodded to me. I stepped backwards and bowed my head, pulling my thoughts in and down to wake the beast that lived within me. *It's time.*

The rush of heat that pulsed from my core out to my finger-tips and down to my toes brought with it a rippling sensation on my skin as my human-made shirt tore and fell to the stone floor in tatters. Scales layered across my forearms and chest, down my back, covering every inch of my now exposed and expanding skin as muscles morphed underneath, reshaping me into a bigger, fiercer version of myself. The transition completed with my head. When I blinked and opened my eyes to dragon sight, I clawed my way to the edge of the balcony and stretched my wings wide.

Ivo swiveled his spiked head to look at me, then roared his command. My senses attuned to the shifted forms of Boro and his lieutenants, below us. To avoid confusion, the rules of a challenge forbid anyone else from shifting. The arbiter scrambled to the top tier of balconies, trying to keep away from the ripping and clawing and bloodshed that was about to unfold. Other Fae-shaped specks of heat filled in the mid-tier balconies, hurrying to find seats, but I paid them no mind.

Reaching out with my dragon sense, I located my targets. Neno and Toma flanked Boro. I needed to draw them away and keep them occupied so Ivo could attack. I roared a response to Ivo, then stepped off the edge of the balcony and spread my great orange-flecked black wings. Circling once, I angled for my attack and dove toward Neno's raised head.

Fire spewed from the bellows of Neno's lungs, but I anticipated his counterattack and swerved around, coming at Toma from the side with my talons extended and caught him off guard. Toma believed my feint and thought I was going for Neno. Instead, I ripped into the delicate flesh where his wings sprouted from his thick back muscles, and I shredded the paper-thin tissue, grounding him for the fight.

Above me, Ivo circled, avoiding Neno's flames. He dove for Aco, even though dispatching the lieutenants was my task. His maneuver distracted me, but I recovered and took to my wings before Toma or Neno could reach me. Rising up, I curled my fore and hind legs tight against my body to keep out of range of Boro's lieutenants. Then I glided to the far side of the makeshift arena, attempting to draw the three of them away from Boro.

Only short, gliding flights, used to move quickly from one part of the arena to another, were allowed during a challenge. I held my wings out from my body in a textbook glide so I wouldn't give the arbiter any reason to bar me from the fight.

When I reached the edge of the arena, I dug my talons into the dirt and skidded to a stop, turning in time to catch Ivo taking one threatening swipe at Boro's newest pledge, before facing off with Boro. His feint was just enough to herd Aco back toward the other lieutenants who already stood wingtip to wingtip, ready to attack me. Dark red blood oozed from the tears in Toma's wings. He crouched low on his thick hind legs and roared his rage at me. The world narrowed to the hulking bodies of my opponents, as I prepared for my next attack.

Neno breathed fire in my direction, but he was still too far away to do more than warm the air directly in front of me. The shimmering heat made it difficult to judge the distance between me and Toma, who continued to advance, keeping low to avoid Neno's flames. I waited for Neno to take a breath, then pounced onto Toma's back, using his crouched position to my advantage.

I landed so that the thick claws that extended from my hind legs pinned Toma's already damaged wings to his sides. Wrapping my fore claws around his neck, I grabbed and scratched, seeking a weakness in his scales that might allow me to puncture his hide.

Beneath me, he thrashed and roared, slamming his body sideways in an attempt to throw me off, but I held firm. Neno didn't dare breath his fire at me and risk roasting Toma in the process. Instead, he paced around us, searching for an opportunity to come to his wing-mate's aid.

I kept my eye on Neno as I squeezed and scratched, trying to take Toma out of the fight. We didn't have to kill Boro's lieutenants. Only the Alpha had to die for the challenge to be successful. But any lieutenant worthy of the title would fight to the death defending their Alpha. With three of them, it would be nearly impossible for me to succeed in keeping them off Ivo and Boro without taking them all out.

Toma reared up on his hind legs, but I held on, even as I sensed the approach of another dragon behind me. I couldn't turn my head to look without taking my eyes off Neno, and I refused to do that. I hoped that what I sensed behind me was only Ivo or Boro, but I hadn't seen any sign of Aco since Ivo had sent him scurrying after the other lieutenants.

I couldn't leave my back exposed. Ved wasn't there to guard it. I was on my own to fight off three of the largest male dragons in our clan. And every moment I spent wrestling with these three was one that left Ivo with no back-up. I couldn't waste time trying to scrape through Toma's scales to slice open his hide.

The presence behind me loomed closer. Neno's head arched up, then bobbed down, like he was signaling something. If I left my perch on Toma's back, I'd have to face all three of them, and they'd quickly surround me. I had to find a way to keep my mount or take him out of the equation.

Training with Ivo and Ved meant we'd practiced countless maneuvers where two opponents collaborated to take down a third. But I struggled to anticipate what Neno might be attempting, and I couldn't see what Aco was up to behind me, in case that might give me a clue. I needed to be sure and swift or, I'd lose any chance of gaining the advantage.

17

WHEN the sprite disappeared, I returned my attention to Damir's familiar. Sillag stared back at me, waiting for something, but I still didn't know what.

"Look," I said, "I don't know where Damir is, but I need to report to Arabella, so whatever it is that you want is going to have to wait, all right?"

The image of the barracks flashed in my mind, again. Then Sillag flexed her wings and glided up onto my shoulder. She butted the side of my head with her horns, then made another one of those eerie piercing cries.

I winced away from the sound, and she butted against my head a second time.

"Fine." I glanced up, looking for her friend, but the other faerie dragon was no longer perched on the branch, or circling in the sky above. "I am beginning to get the feeling that you want me to take you to the barracks. I have no idea why, when you can just as easily fly there yourself, but if that's what you want, I suppose I can take you and maybe find Arabella while

I'm there and save her the trouble of coming to find me."

Sillag flicked her tongue against my cheek, and I flinched.

"Eww." I wiped my cheek with the back of my hand, even though it wasn't wet. "None of that, thank you. You've already scratched me full of toxins. Who knows what's in your saliva? I said I'd take you. Now settle down so I can concentrate."

To her credit, Sillag listened. She crouched down, tucked her horned head against my neck, and curled her tail around the back of my shoulder. I took a deep breath, focusing on our destination, and transported us to the barracks.

When I opened my eyes, I found myself facing the long, low building next to the guards' barracks. Glancing between the buildings, I realized that the image that had flashed in my head, the one I'd used to calibrate our transport, was actually the infirmary and not the barracks, after all. Dread and fear of what I'd find inside pulled at my gut.

"Is Damir in there?" I asked the faerie dragon, even though I knew she couldn't answer.

Sillag stretched her wings and flew ahead, toward the building, then circled back. It was clear she wanted me to go inside. She couldn't go inside. She didn't know that I couldn't go inside. The Queen's Guard was full of Elementals. They'd recognize me in an instant.

The longer I hesitated, the louder Sillag squawked. She circled twice, then landed on my shoulder and nipped at my ear. I flinched away, sending her up into the sky. She settled on a nearby branch and fixed me with her orange-eyed stare while I checked to make sure she hadn't drawn blood with her tiny fangs.

"That hurt." I scowled at her.

She responded with a plaintive coo that broke my heart.

"Fine." I sighed and grumbled. "Fine. Fine. Fine. I'll go."

I glared at her. "But you better know what you're on about be-cause there's a very high likelihood that I'm going to march in there and get promptly booted out on my arse because I don't belong here."

Sillag just cocked her head to one side and continued to stare.

"Ugh. I see you have no sympathy for my plight and only care about your master."

She made a clicking sound, then took off flying in the di-rection of the infirmary. I started walking, dreading whatever was about to come next. If Damir was in there, he'd witness whatever confrontation I had with the guard on duty, more than likely an Elemental, and be forced to choose whether or not to intervene on my behalf. And, if he wasn't in there, I was about to risk everything for no reason.

I shook my head at Sillag, who'd found a perch on the roof above the entrance to the infirmary. "This is such a bad idea."

I paused in front of the door and took a deep breath before reaching out to push it open. A figure inside the door shifted to his feet, swiftly blocking me from entering.

"Who are you and what is your business here?" he asked.

My eyes met a pair of black orbs set in a hairless head framed by pointed ears. I sent a silent prayer of thanks to the Ancestors that the guard on duty happened to be a Rogue and not an Elemental. "I'm looking for someone. A visitor. His name's Damir."

A voice from the shadows on the far side of the building shouted up to the guard. "Let her in, please." It didn't sound like Damir, but the guard stepped aside all the same.

I whispered my thanks and hurried down the aisle between the beds to find the source of that voice. A lump in the last bed in the row on the right side of the building moved, pressing himself up into a seated position.

"You must be Seren," he said, as I approached.

I paused at the end of his bed. A dark-haired male that wasn't Damir stared back at me.

"Who are you?"

"Ved Ashwing of Nenad."

"You must be Damir's wing-mate. The one he rescued."

"Thanks for the reminder." Ved smirked.

"No problem." I crossed my arms. "Where's Damir and how did you know my name?"

"How did you know to come here?"

My eyes narrowed. "You didn't send for me?" I paused, waiting for a response, but he just raised his eyebrows and shook his head. So I told him what happened. "Sillag dragged me here. I don't know why. I don't speak faerie dragon."

"Neither do I." He shrugged. "And the two who do are off getting themselves killed."

My body stilled, unsure if I'd heard what I thought I'd heard, or if I'd possibly misunderstood. "What do you mean?"

"Mir and our wing-mate, Ivo. They went back to challenge Boro. Left me here to rot like an invalid." He shifted on the bed, twisting the sheet around one hand.

I poked at his arm, and his hand relaxed, releasing the sheet. His face scrunched as he winced from the lingering pain of his injuries.

"I'm no Hand, but it looks to me like that was the right decision. You're still healing." I plopped down on the bed next to his and let my legs dangle off the side so I could face him. "They sent someone to tend to your injuries?"

"Yeah. First Eira, then someone named Talie. Friends of yours?"

I shook my head. Both Eira and Talie were quiet and kind.

I didn't know Talie as well, though. He'd been older than the batch of us in crèche, already studying with Cahal while we were still pulling each other's hair and learning not to destroy the nursery whenever our tempers flared.

Talie used to come give special lessons to the batch of Fa-elings who had already demonstrated some affinity for all four elements. He also tested the rest of us, regularly. He'd been the one to console me when I first tried using fire magic and failed. Anwen had teased me, but he'd stopped her and said my magic would come in time. He'd been wrong, but I'd always appreciated that kindness.

"Who is this Boro and why is Damir challenging him?" I asked, hoping he'd been exaggerating the bit about them getting themselves killed. Surely Dragon Fae didn't fight to the death. That would be irresponsible given the dwindling numbers of Fae walking the earth.

"Boro is the current Alpha of our clan. He killed Ivo's sire, the previous Alpha, as well as Mir's sire, and probably my sire as well, even though I was told he died in a hunting accident." He cocked his head to one side. "Rather dangerous, going hunt-ing with friends you thought were allies but who turn out to be lieutenants of your Alpha's rival, especially when that rival is secretly planning a coup. Didn't end well for him, or any of us, for that matter." He turned his head away to stare out the win-dow above his cot.

"So, they're fighting Boro for vengeance? For your sires?"

"In a way." He shrugged, turning his head so he could look me in the eyes. "Ivo is challenging to become Alpha in his sire's place." He sighed and shook his head. "But in order to do that, they're going to have to kill three much older and much stron-ger Dragon Fae. In other words, they're going to get themselves killed, and I'm stuck here, helpless as a Fledgling, unable to lift a wing to help because your Hand won't allow me to transform until I'm fully healed." He grimaced. "By the time that happens, it will be too late."

"When did they leave?" I asked, my voice barely above a whisper. Damir had said nothing of this plan when he'd come to find me at the feast for the champions. He'd offered me his seed, like he'd been planning to stick around and take a mate. This development made no sense.

"Late last night. Or maybe early this morning. Hard to say, exactly." He looked past me toward the guard at the door. "Before this guard arrived. That much I know."

"Well, thank you for telling me." I stood and walked toward the aisle at the foot of the beds.

"He wanted me to find you."

I paused with one hand on the foot of the bed I'd been sitting on, but I didn't turn around.

"You asked how I knew your name," he said. "It's because I was meant to go find you if Mir didn't return. He wanted you to know—"

I held up my hand, cutting him off. "If he doesn't return, you can find me and give me his message. If he's not dead, I don't want to hear it." I knew better than to dare to believe that love might be possible for me. That I, a cast out, a cursed Elemental, might have found someone who saw me for me, who didn't care how many elements I could control, and who might be able to give me a family. A home. So long as there was some hope that he might return, my foolish heart didn't want to ruin it by hearing the rest of what Ved had to say. Not yet. Perhaps not ever, if the Ancients were kind.

Who was I kidding? The Ancients were never kind. Fair, maybe, given how they'd allowed me to live despite my cursed existence, but they'd never shown me mercy before. If I wanted something, I had to go and take it for myself. I couldn't pray to the Ancients like Gwawr and hope to be rewarded.

"There's someone I need to go see," I said. "If you need to find me, don't ask the Elementals. Find Arabella. She can get a message to me."

"I suppose I could always send Sillag. She seems to know how to find you."

His reminder of the faerie dragon was the thing that made me turn. "What will happen to her if Damir doesn't return? They share a connection, do they not?"

He smirked. "I thought you didn't want to hear Mir's message for you."

I scowled at him. "I don't. That doesn't mean you can't tell me how the bond works between a Dragon Fae and their familiar."

"Fair enough." He shifted his position so he could rest his head and shoulder against the wall. His eyes closed briefly, reminding me that he was still recovering, and I shouldn't be bothering him.

"I should go," I said. "It's none of my business, and I'm keeping you from healing."

"You're keeping me from going crazy with worry." His eyes flicked open and caught mine staring. "The bond dies with the Dragon. Faerie or Fae. I'm told it's a devastating loss, Mir's Grandsire suffered enormously when Dormog, his familiar, died during a challenge. I'm sure the memory of that loss is why Mir and Ivo decided to leave Sillag and Firrag here with me. We can mourn them together if they don't return."

I shook my head. "You are a barrel of sunshine, aren't you?"

The corners of Ved's mouth slowly crept up into a grin. "I'm beginning to appreciate what Mir sees in you. I was skeptical when he left that message with me, but—"

"Enough." I cut him off before he could say more. "I told you. I don't want to hear it unless Mir truly doesn't return. Until then, I have something I need to do."

"Shame you can't stay and keep me company." The smile disappeared from Ved's face as his eyes fluttered closed again.

"You're going to be all right?"

He nodded. "I just need some sleep." He curled down onto the mattress and pulled the blanket up across his broad shoulders.

On the way out, I nodded to the guard, then glanced back over my shoulder to the lump of resting Dragon Fae on the cot under the far window. I knew better than to hope that he was wrong about the chance of Damir returning, but the warmth that had crept in around my heart when he'd refused to leave my side at the Champions' Festival refused all logic.

Damir needed to survive. Even if we could never be together because the Ancients had seen fit to curse me, the Ancients would certainly reward his kindness and generosity.

<h1 style="text-align:center">18</h1>

SWALLOWING my squeamishness, I released my grip on Toma's neck. When he tossed his head back, I reached forward and raked my claws across the top of his head from snout to horns. There wasn't time to make sure I'd gouged his eyes thoroughly. I had to hope that I'd done enough damage to blind him. I barely had time to snap my tail against the ground and lever myself up and away, flexing my wings to help twist my body so the wall of the arena was at my back.

I landed facing the flailing Toma, flanked by Neno and Aco, whose hesitation had been the only thing to save me. Neno butted his head into Toma's side, shoving him out of the way so that he could breathe a wall of flames to corner me at the edge of the arena. It might have worked, but Aco missed his cue again, blocked by the stumbling Toma.

In the confusion, I charged at Aco, sending both of us tumbling tail over snout into the center of the challenge pit. Heat from Boro's flames warmed the air around us like the blast from a furnace. The bright white flames temporarily blinded me when

I glanced in that direction. Even after blinking, I couldn't make out Ivo beyond the wall of fire spewing from deep in Boro's lungs.

Aco stumbled onto his hind legs in the moments I'd wasted checking on Ivo. He reared up until his forearms were level with my head, then lunged at me, putting all his weight into his attempt to tackle me to the ground. If he had been as big as Ved and as determined to put me in my place as that older and more impulsive wing-mate of mine, he may have had a chance. But he wasn't bold enough or broad enough to pull it off.

I side-stepped him, and he came crashing to the ground without me beneath him to cushion his fall. The air whooshed from his lungs and with it I sent a prayer to the Ancients to take his soul. Then, before I could reconsider, I sliced a claw across Aco's exposed throat, helping send him on his way. Once I could see, but no longer sense, Aco's body at my feet, I knew he was gone. Amber light spilled from gaps between his scales as his body burned from the furnace within. Soon it would be nothing more than ash and bones. But this wasn't the time to dwell on what I'd done.

Neno lunged at me, sending a blast of fire that would have blistered my hide if I hadn't scurried backward. I flapped my wings once to rise above the heat, then surged forward, aiming my hind claws at Neno's snout. He batted me away with the tip of his wing, but I'd expected him to defend himself and twisted in the air, tucking my wings in and dropping to the ground behind him.

Too close for him to turn and face me, he whipped his tail at my hind legs, hoping to swipe me off my feet. I threw my weight against his back, slamming him into the ground. He thrashed beneath me, trying to break free. Somewhere behind us, the blinded Toma roared. I needed to hurry before Toma's dragon sense compensated for his lack of sight and located me.

I wrapped my fore claws around Neno's neck and yanked his head back, hoping it would be enough to create a gap between the scales that protected his vulnerable throat. He reached back and found my right hind leg, then stabbed at it relentlessly. I winced and tried to ignore the pain. I had him, and I needed to end this. Now.

Slipping a claw up under Neno's scales, I pressed into his hide. "This is for Milomir."

He jerked and spasmed as I ripped through flesh. Warm blood poured over my forepaw, but I waited until he released my hind leg and stilled before I released him. My senses scanned for the other dragons, even as I backed away from Neno's body in a daze.

There would be time to process what I'd done, later. Assuming I survived. I inhaled and exhaled, trying to focus, forcing the deaths out of my head.

My dragon sense pointed me toward the pair locked in combat, ignoring the single remaining lieutenant who had finally located me and was barreling toward me across the arena. Boro had Ivo pinned against the wall. Ivo's hind claws scrapped and scratched the dirt floor, searching for purchase. If I didn't hurry, it would be over. Aco and Neno's deaths would be for northing.

Toma's body slammed into mine, but I twisted away and leapt into the air. Wrapping my hind legs around his neck, I pushed him back as I allowed myself to fall, bringing Toma down beneath me. The furnace in his broad chest warmed underneath my body. Before he could expel those flames, I slammed his jaw shut and pinned his head to the ground. With my fore and hind legs busy holding Toma down, I had no choice but to use my fangs to pierce the scales covering his exposed throat.

The metallic tang of blood filled my mouth as I bit into his hide. The taste combined with the adrenaline from the fight to send my senses into a killing rage. I lifted my head and roared to regain some control.

Wings spread wide, I tucked my legs under me as I pushed away from Toma's body and turned to face the two remaining dragons. Boro was still alive. Ivo needed to end this. I couldn't interfere except to assist my wing-mate.

Ivo must have sensed Toma's death. He risked taking his eyes off Boro long enough to glance at me over Boro's outstretched wings. He nodded and then rushed forward. I guessed what he intended from the hours we'd spent sparring together, and I hurried to get into position.

Before I could reach him, Boro reached back and jabbed his claws up, under Ivo's scales. I froze. Again, my eyes locked with Ivo's over Boro's shoulder. Then I watched as Ivo slumped. His head dropped down and his eyes flicked shut.

I rushed at Boro's spiked back as he released Ivo and tipped his head back to roar his victory to the crowd. He didn't see me, and I didn't hesitate. My wings flapped once, lifting me up to glide over his long tail so I could pounce on him.

Wrapping one foreleg under his chin, I slammed his snout closed and yanked his head back further while the claws of my other foreleg jabbed up, under the scales and into the thin hide that covered his throat. I ripped and tore at him without thinking. Rage drove me until, blood spattered and breathless, I allowed his limp body to drop to the ground.

19

ARABELLA'S new instructions were deceivingly simple. She said she no longer cared about the winner of Conclave. Instead, she wanted me to keep an eye out for the cambion and let her know if he returned without a guard. She said I wasn't allowed to kill him, though. She wanted me to lay low until she had a chance to speak with Fiona about giving me an official position in the queen's guard.

I still wasn't convinced that she could protect me from the Elemental Elders, but I intended to do as she asked. I didn't want to mess up this opportunity. Especially after everything I'd done to make sure that both of the final contenders were sympathetic to my plight. Even if Gwawr ended up getting kicked out of the competition because of the information I'd bartered, Barr had promised to end banishment of Cursehands. If Gwawr did somehow manage to beat him, and I hoped she would, she would never know what I'd done.

Either way, though, I would get to live among my kin again. All I had to do was keep to the forest and keep a look out for that cambion. The later part was easy. It was the first part that proved to be more and more difficult, the longer I had to wait.

After reporting to Arabella, I found that I couldn't sleep. Staring up at the treetops, all I could think about was Sillag, which led to thoughts about Damir and that kiss I'd stolen. And how he'd gone to fight the clan Alpha.

I had no way of knowing if he was safe, or if he'd been injured. Or worse. I didn't know how to call Sillag to me. And I didn't think Arabella would agree that going back to the infirmary for another visit to Damir's wing-mate was in line with her instruction to "lay low."

Eventually, I dozed off, only to be woken again, moments later, by the Conclave horn. The sun had barely crested the horizon. Cahal must have decided to go ahead with the final match, which meant that Gwawr still had a chance to win. I bounced up from the ground and threw on my cape, only to remember Arabella's command.

Attending the match would be too much of a risk. Any of the Fae who could be there, would. It would be almost impossible to watch without rubbing up against countless Elementals, and close proximity would make it more likely that one might get a sense of my magic or a glimpse of my face. Or both. The second horn sounded as I paced among the trees, frustrated that I had to miss this monumental event.

My Elemental kin would be talking about this match for centuries. Millenia. And even though I would hopefully be living among them, whenever they reminisced about the match that gave us our new guardian, I would be compelled to stand there, listening to their stories, unable to participate, and forced to remember why.

I burned with anger, but when I flicked my wrist and called for fire to test my magic, nothing came. Still only three elements, not four. Forever cursed by the Ancients. Destined to be an outsider, even if Arabella succeeded in finding me a place in the guard and the new guardian convinced the Elders to rule in favor of changing our laws.

I stared up at the sky with a prayer on my lips, only to find a large winged creature circling above me. For a moment, I thought it was Sillag. But it was only a hawk. I sighed and buried my head in my hands.

Damir's face floated behind my closed eyelids. Then it was gone, wiped away by the echoing wail of the Conclave horn. My eyes snapped open.

The Conclave was over. We had a new guardian. And I'd missed it.

I shook off my frustration and straightened my tunic, then adjusted my cloak. I'd spent enough time feeling sorry for myself. I could do this. I'd survived on my own for decades. I could manage it a little longer. I just needed a distraction. Something to keep my mind busy while I got a handle on my curiosity. I would find out who won soon enough.

I decided everything would seem better after a bit of food. Hunting would keep my mind occupied and help fill my belly. As I called on my earth magic to form and set my traps, I was forced to focus on the task and forget my worries. Only to have them all come rushing back the moment I was done.

So, I fashioned a bow and arrows, using a bit more magic to keep my thoughts from drifting back to the Conclave or off in the direction of one particular Dragon Fae. Then, when that was done, I set off into the forest, purposely walking in the opposite direction from the barracks and the falls. Still, a hint of sweet flute melodies taunted me on the wind, calling me back to where I knew my kin was gathering to witness the queen anointing the new guardian.

Would it be Gwawr wearing Cahal's robes? Or had she been defeated? I longed to know, and I hated that I couldn't join in the celebration.

By the time the sun sank below the horizon, my stomach was full and I'd been alone with my worries about Damir and my curiosity about the Conclave for too long. I decided I could risk a peek at the party. The Fae would be too busy celebrating to notice one lone figure lurking at the edge of the forest.

I followed the drum beats and dancing melodies toward the falls. My feet bounced a bit with each step, wanting to skip and prance like I had with Damir. I spun myself around a thin tree trunk like it was a partner. The closer I got to the festivities, the more careless I became, until I stumbled into a clearing and froze in the face of a robed Fae. *The* robed Fae I had hoped to catch a glimpse of. But she wasn't with the others. She was alone, like me.

"Why aren't you at the party?" I asked, once I'd recovered enough to free my tongue.

Unfortunately, Gwawr didn't appear as happy to see me as I was to see her.

"Why did you betray me?" she asked. Her fists clenched at her sides, but she didn't advance on me.

I tensed, then forced myself to relax. She would understand. This didn't have to be the end of our friendship. I could make her understand.

"So you know, then." I shrugged. "You would have done the same if you'd been in my position."

"I would not have. I trusted you. I just want to know why." She glared at me. "Why did you tell Barr that you'd seen me with Nigel?"

She'd called the cambion Nye when she'd introduced him to me. A clever deception that didn't require lying since Nye could be short for Nigel or be a name that was common among Elemental Fae. But when did Gwawr become so crafty, and why? Perhaps she was trying to hide the fact that she'd fallen for him.

"I'll answer you after you answer me. Why aren't you at the party?" Suspicion prickled the skin between my shoulder blades as I circled her, trying not to take my eyes off her, even as I shot glances into the forest around us, searching for the cambion.

Gwawr crossed her arms. "I just needed a moment alone."

I paused, watching her closely for any sign of liar's pains. "You're not meeting that demon again, are you?"

"That's no business of yours." She glanced away and up, at something behind me. "Anyway, I have to go."

For a moment I stood there, unsure what to do and convinced that there was someone in the trees, behind me. But I didn't dare turn and take my eyes off Gwawr. While I hesitated, she grasped her chance to get away and disappeared.

I reached for my knife as I turned, ready to fight, but no one was there. So, I crept toward the party and searched for any sign of Gwawr. Keeping myself hidden in the shadows, underneath the trees, I moved around the edge of the festivities.

Barr and Anwen were speaking with a group of Elders nearby. Frightened, I retreated until they'd moved on. Then I continued my search.

Gwawr had to be there, somewhere. In the guardian's robes, she shouldn't have been hard to find. Once I was sure she wasn't near the refreshments, I made my way along the edge of the forest, edging closer to the music and the dancing.

She wasn't there either. I started back toward the feast, thinking I'd check one last time before giving up and finding some quiet place to spend the night. Out of the corner of my eye, the shimmer of bright fabric caught my eye. Gwawr was moving away from the party, toward the trees. I hurried to catch her.

This time, I planned to remain hidden. I was curious to see what would happen, and if she was truly waiting for the cambion to appear. But, as soon as she was hidden from the party, she started to close her eyes.

I sprang out of my hiding place and latched my arms around her. We disappeared together and tumbled to the ground in the clearing next to the altar in the Grove of the Ancients.

"What are you doing?" Gwawr pushed me away so that she could scramble to her feet.

"Following you." I stood and brushed my hands over my cloak and leggings to free them of the dirt and debris they'd picked up while I was rolling about on the forest floor.

"Why?"

"To make sure you don't do anything stupid." I put my hands on my hips and puffed out my chest in an attempt to exhibit a confidence I didn't quite feel.

"And what makes you think I'm going to do something stupid?" she asked.

As if that wasn't obvious with all the sneaking around and casting lustful looks in the direction of a particular dark haired half-demon. "Don't try that with me. I saw the way that demon looked at you and the way you looked at him. I watched that whole exchange."

"What are you talking about?" She leaned against the boulder, all casual like she hadn't been up to anything at all.

That's when I realized where we were. The Grove of the Ancients. The place where I'd caught her trying and failing to call her fire magic. "I know you care for him. I dare you to deny it."

She bit her lip, and I watched her face as her mind attempted to find a way to counter my challenge without lying. But she'd never been as sly as Barr or Anwen. It didn't take her long to give in. "It's true. I do. But it doesn't matter. That's not why I'm meeting him."

"Then tell me. Why? And here of all places?"

She growled in frustration. "His blood holds a secret that threatens all our lives."

"What makes his blood so special?"

"I can't tell you."

"If that demon sets one foot in this clearing without his guard, I'm going straight to Arabella this time." I warned her as I stepped closer. "I kept her out of it last time because I didn't want her to hurt you, but the demon must have you in his thrall. You have no business being guardian if you're under the control of a demon."

"This is why you told Barr about Nigel? You think Nigel has some sort of control over me?" Gwawr pushed off the boulder and paced toward me. "And since when do you report things to the commander of the Queen's Guard?"

I sidestepped, avoiding her, but didn't back away. I'd fight her if I had to, but I hoped it wouldn't come to that. She'd always been the only Elemental to treat me with any kindness and respect. "Since before the start of the Conclave. Since you were clearly Cahal's favorite, and the Court knew nothing about you. Since you spent time in Edric's dungeons doing who knows what and apparently falling in love with demon scum. She needed a spy. I needed the resources."

"That's not what happened." The cambion's voice cut through our argument, causing us both to turn our heads toward him. "I didn't know Gwawr was in the dungeons. Not until after."

Gwawr looked back, over her shoulder, at me, but it was too late. He was here, as I suspected he would be, and he had no guard with him. I raised an eyebrow, as though to say, *I told you so*. Then I shook my head and transported myself to the barracks so I could warn Arabella or get one of the Queen's Guard to send a message to her.

When I arrived, the place was almost deserted. I realized too late that any of the guards who weren't assigned to other duties, were probably at the Conclave feast. I remembered there was at least one guard outside the infirmary. So, I hurried in that direction.

I'd only taken a few steps when Sillag swooped down to block my path. She gripped a torn bit of bloody shirt in her talons. I paused when I spotted the buttons. That was Damir's shirt. It had to be. He'd been wearing one of those odd human shirts with the buttons down the front.

For a moment, I forgot my mission. "Where's Damir?"

"Hey!" A guard came running toward me from the barracks. "Who are you? What is your business here?"

I held up my hands, palms facing the approaching guard. Sillag dropped the bit of Damir's shirt and settled on my shoulder. "I need to get an urgent message to Arabella. The cambion named Nigel has been spotted in the Grove of the Ancients without a guard."

The guard stopped running, paused, then lifted a palm toward the sky. I was so busy staring at the guard, I almost didn't notice the Hand who was with him.

"Seren? Is that you?" Talie squinted at me. "What are you doing with a faerie dragon?"

Before I could respond, a series of images appeared in my mind. The mouth of a cave. Blood. A large obsidian dragon, streaked with red. A bundle of torn clothes in the dirt.

Somehow, I knew that Sillag was trying to tell me that Damir needed help. Talie had blood magic. He'd helped heal Damir's wing-mate. If we weren't too late, maybe he could help Damir, too.

"There isn't time to explain. Talie, do you know where to find the Dragon Fae?"

The guard dropped his hand and looked at me. "I can show you."

20

THERE hadn't been time to think or sleep since the challenge. My first command as Alpha, after shifting back to my Fae form, was for Grand-sire and the other clan healers to see what could be done for Ivo. They'd managed to get an elixir down his throat that shifted him back to his Fae form. After that, they lifted him onto a liter and shuttled him away to somewhere quieter where they could work undisturbed.

I couldn't follow. I had to stay and take formal control of the clan. Then I could assign some Fledglings to clean-up. Since Alpha Boro and his lieutenants died in their dragon forms, their bodies had already been consumed by the internal heat of their flames. That meant there were mounds of ash and bones scattered around the blood covered dirt floor of the makeshift arena.

At some point in the post-challenge chaos, Sillag and Tarmog appeared. I only saw the blur of their forms as they circled near the ceiling, calling to me and searching for Ivo. I sent Sillag a thought, letting her know that Ivo had been injured. Then the pair were gone, and I was alone again. Forced to face my fate.

Alpha of the Dragon Fae.

This was not the future I'd wanted. If Ivo didn't recover, it would be my responsibility to lead our clan. The thought made my stomach turn. I had no idea how bad his injuries were. My mind just kept replaying those final moments of the fight. When Boro released him and Ivo slid to the floor, I didn't think there was life left in his body.

At least there was a chance. I would have to hold on to that hope and do what I could to lead as Ivo would until he healed and I could relinquish the responsibility to him.

Releasing a roar that nearly shook the stone walls, I prepared to address the clan. They all stopped what they were doing and fell silent. Then they fell to one knee before me with heads bowed.

I swallowed. Despite my fears, when I spoke, my voice didn't waver. "I, Damir Firewing of Milomir, claim challenge victory and name myself Alpha of this clan."

"Let it be so." The heads of my assembled clan lifted as they each raised a clenched fist to their chest.

The short, muscular guard who had been named arbiter of the challenge grinned as he stepped forward to present me with the metal torc worn by the clan alpha. He must have retrieved it while I was busy overseeing the healers. The ends of the thick crescent band were shaped into twin dragon heads. The pointed fangs in their open mouths glinted with rubies.

"May your flight be long and your soul burn bright." He dipped his head and bowed, as I slipped the still-warm metal around my neck.

I wondered if he recognized me. He must remember the role I played in freeing Ved. I couldn't be sure, but he seemed pleased that I'd beaten Boro, which came as a relief. I only hoped I wouldn't have to fight him, or any other challengers, anytime soon. I'd tasted enough blood for one lifetime.

A movement on the upper balcony caught my eye. Two new figures had appeared there. I recognized them immediately, and my heart slammed against my ribs.

Seren was here. Her silver eyes stared down at me with Sillag curled on her shoulder and one of the Forest Fae healers at her side—the one Fiona favored.

The rest of the clan followed my gaze. I wondered if they saw what I did—a Fae female fit to be queen. Or at least the mate of a Dragon Fae Alpha.

Sillag stretched her wings and glided down to perch on my outstretched arm. She bowed her head as she landed, then butted my chin with the spikes on the top of her head.

Thank you, I thought, scratching the silver feathers covering her chest.

She cooed in response, then glanced up at Seren before climbing my arm to settle on my shoulder.

I longed to go to Seren, but first I had to deal with my new responsibilities. Returning my attention to the arbiter whose name I had finally remembered; I cleared my throat to get his attention. "Luka, have the remains collected and laid to rest in the catacombs. Then prepare this space for a feast. I must welcome our visitors. One of them is a healer, and I will need someone to lead him to my lieutenant."

The title soured on my tongue. It was I who should be the lieutenant, and Ivo who should be the Alpha. Not to mention that he hadn't yet officially sworn his oath to me, and for all I knew he could be dying while I stood around commanding our clan and wishing I could return to the forest with the Fae female who had come here. To see me.

Sensing my growing frustration, Sillag raised her head to nip at my ear.

I scratched the scales under her chin as Luka bowed and hurried off to do my bidding. It wasn't until he was gone and I was halfway up the stone steps on my way to meet Seren and Talie that I realized I didn't know the names belonging to many of the faces around me. I'd been away from the clan, living in the village for so long. They were as much strangers to me, as I was to them. Except now I was their Alpha. How was I ever going to convince them to obey me?

Seren's eyes scanned my body as I stepped onto the balcony. Her scrutiny reminded me that I was no longer wearing a shirt. My trousers had been of Fae construction, spelled to disappear when I shifted and return when I resumed my Fae form. But my shirt had been human made, worn to fit in among the villagers. It would have been torn to shreds when I shifted before removing it.

"You're all right." Seren sighed and her shoulders relaxed.

I had suffered my share of injuries, and I was certain my body was smeared in dirt and blood, but I hadn't been as badly wounded as Ivo. My body had already started healing. As painful as that was, I supposed I must not look as bad as I felt.

"How did you know to come here?" I asked.

"Sillag found me. She was carrying this." Seren held up a torn and bloody piece of my shirt.

I glanced at Talie before returning my attention to Seren. "So, you revealed yourself to your kin, for me?"

Talie shifted back a half step, breaking eye contact with me to look at Seren.

"I thought you needed help. Sillag—" She motioned to my familiar. "I couldn't understand what she was trying to tell me. I…I panicked."

A Fledgling came running up the stairs, skidded to a stop, and bowed to me. "Alpha Mir, I've come for the healer."

I waved him toward Talie. "Ivo needs your help, if you don't mind. Our clan healers are with him now, but I would appreciate it if you would see if there is anything you can do to assist in his recovery. I don't—" My voice caught.

Talie dipped his head. "I will do everything in my power to help."

The Fledgling stared at the tall male with the dark brown skin. Then he held out a hand. "I will take you to him."

Talie's large hand closed around the smaller one and the pair disappeared, leaving me alone with Seren.

I took a step closer to her. "Thank you."

"Alpha?" She cocked her head to one side. "Did that Faeling call you Alpha?"

"We call them Fledglings, but yes. I'm afraid so." I plucked the scrap of shirt from her fingers and stuffed it into my pocket.

Her eyes narrowed. "You say that like it's a curse."

I cringed. "I supposed I do think of it that way. A bit."

She tugged at the edges of her cloak, pulling it tighter around her shoulders. "I should go. I'm glad you're all right. I hope Talie can help your wing-mate. I better leave while he's busy."

I frowned. "I can't return with you."

Seren laughed. "I didn't expect you to."

I reached for her hands. "But I want to. I'd planned to. I'd hoped to convince you to take me as your mate."

She shrugged but didn't pull away from my touch. "I told you that it would never work, and that's before they made you Alpha of your clan. You can't be Alpha with a cursed mate."

"You aren't cursed."

"How do you know?"

I searched my mind for something that might convince her. "Sillag trusts you. Faerie dragons are very particular. She wouldn't trust my life, or Ivo's, to someone she didn't deem worthy."

Sillag bumped her head against my chin, then glided down, off my shoulder. She may have grown to like Seren, but she let me know she would rather find Tarmog and check on Ivo than stick around while I courted this Fae female.

Seren watched Sillag fly away. "Doesn't seem like it."

I grinned. "She's just jealous."

"Jealous of what?"

"Not what. Who. She's always been my favorite female. Since I met you, she has had a bit of competition." I lifted my fingers to brush against Seren's jaw. "Would it be all right if I kissed you once more before you go?"

"Like a goodbye kiss?"

"Unless you would like to stay?" I paused, but she didn't respond. So, I told her what I was thinking. "I don't want you to go, Seren. I want more time with you."

"Stay *here*?" She lifted her eyes toward the stone ceiling.

"I know it's not the same as being surrounded by trees, but it's home. It could be your home, too. If you'd like."

"Arabella said she was going to give me a position in the queen's guard."

"Is that what you want?"

"I don't know."

"What do you want?"

Seren leaned forward until her lips met mine. Her palms pressed against my bare chest, then slid up, over my shoulders, to meet at the back of my neck. Trails of fiery sensation followed her touch, sending shivers up my spine. When she finally pulled away, she smiled. "This. I want this."

"Then stay. Please?"

She shrugged. "I suppose this is as good a place as any to lay low. I'll just have to let Arabella know where to find me."

I pulled her close and pressed my lips against hers, resuming our kiss before she could change her mind.

Epilogue

DAMIR and I were lounging on the rocks at the mouth of the cave watching Sillag and Tarmog circle and swoop against the backdrop of the blue skies when a sprite appeared with a letter from Fiona for her cousin.

Once the sprite delivered the message, she bowed to each of us in turn, then disappeared.

"That was odd." I squinted at Damir.

He didn't seem to notice that the sprite delivering his mail hadn't hissed at me or made a face or even so much as a rude gesture. She'd bowed. I wondered if the cream paper with the Crown's seal that he had already begun reading held an explanation for that oddness.

"What does the queen have to say?" I scooted closer so I could look over his shoulder.

"She says Arabella just returned, but she doesn't say from where." He read a few more lines, then continued. "Arabella would like you to return. She wants you to help train her guards to kill demons. Apparently, they are expecting an attack."

"When?"

Damir frowned. "Summer Solstice, according to a half-demon spy who is working with the new guardian and the rest of Fiona's Court."

I squinted at Damir. It couldn't be the same half-demon I'd seen with Gwawr. "His name isn't Nigel is it?"

Damir glanced at me. "Is that the one with the antlers? From the forest?"

I nodded. "Except he doesn't have antlers. He has horns. That was a glamour."

"Right. Well, that's the one. Turns out he shares a sire with Arabella." Damir pointed to a line written in looping script that I had already tried and failed to read because I couldn't make sense of the writing from where I was sitting.

I remembered what Gwawr had said in the forest about the cambion's blood being important, but she couldn't tell me why. "And Gwawr is still the new guardian?"

"Yes."

I sighed with relief and shifted closer to him, nudging his arm until he wrapped it around me and pulled me flush against his side. In that position, I could read the writing, but I laid my head against his shoulder and closed my eyes, instead. "What else does it say?"

He kissed the top of my head. "She wants to know when I'm going to honor our agreement."

I tilted my head up to search his face. "Have you told her about us?"

The corners of his mouth twitched up. "I have."

"And what did she say?"

"Nothing."

"Nothing?"

He let the letter drop into his lap and twisted to face me.

"She has no objection to our pairing she only cares that I honor our agreement."

"Even if your Faeling's mother is a cast out?"

"Even then."

"It says that in the letter?" I craned my neck to peek at the writing.

Damir caught my chin with his fingers and tilted my face up to align with his. "It does."

"Oh."

My eyes fluttered closed as his lips drifted closer. For a moment the world fell away around us.

He lifted his mouth from mine much too soon. "Seren, my love?"

"Yes?" I blinked my eyes open.

"Can I tell my cousin our news?" He let his hand drift down to rest on my belly.

I scowled. "I suppose you're going to have to, since you'll need to explain why they are going to need to send someone to fetch me if they expect me to travel anytime soon."

A low growl escaped his throat. "Oh no. Absolutely not."

I shrugged. "Fine then. Don't tell her. It doesn't matter to me if she knows."

"No, I'll tell her. But I'm not allowing anyone else to transport you. If you must go, I'll take you." Damir pocketed the letter so both hands were free to wrap around me.

"But what about the clan?" I nestled against the warmth of him.

"I think Ivo has recovered enough that he can handle things until we return." He glanced up as Tarmog swooped down to distract us with a bit of acrobatics. "And we should probably bring Ved home before he gets into too much trouble and overstays his welcome."

I shifted in his arms. *Home.*

Arabella wanted me to return, but the forest was no longer my home. My home was here, in the caves of the Dragon Fae. I'd found a place where my magic was valued and wasn't considered a curse, and no one was going to take this new family away from me.

Thank you for reading!

If you want to be the first to know about what's coming
next in this world, be sure to sign up for my newsletter at
http://www.tinyletter.com/emenozzi.

ALSO BY E. MENOZZI

Eve of the Fae
Dawn of the Fae
Will of the Fae
Hunter of the Fae
Ash of the Fae

ABOUT THE AUTHOR

Elizabeth Menozzi is an award-winning writer of science fiction and fantasy with romance. A former Midwestern girl, she currently resides on Orcas Island with her husband. In her spare time she is a competitive swimmer, reluctant runner, and devourer of books.

You can follow her on Twitter (@emenozzi) and Instagram (emmenozzi), or contact her via her website at `http://www.elizabethmenozzi.com/`.